ANTICHRIST

BOOKS BY

Cecelia Holland

Antichrist (*1970*)
Until the Sun Falls (*1969*)
The Kings in Winter (*1968*)
Rakóssy (*1967*)
The Firedrake (*1966*)

ANTICHRIST

Cecelia Holland

A novel of the Emperor Frederick II

Atheneum   New York

1970

FOR JON AND DICK

I am the Lizard King;
I can do anything.

Note

Even before his birth at Iesi in the March of Ancona, on December 26, 1194, legends surrounded the only child of the Emperor Henry VI and the Empress-Queen Constance, of the royal Norman house of Sicily. Joachim de Flora pronounced him Antichrist; other prophets saw in him the long-expected child who would usher in the Golden Age. Such high expectations are rarely even halfway met. In the case of Frederick II, the prophecies were only the start.

From a glorious infancy, election as King of the Romans in his cradle and coronation as King of Sicily at three, he passed into a childhood full of kidnappings, near assassinations, intrigue and obscurity. His mother, dying, had made Sicily a papal fief and put her child into the care of the Pope, who promptly made the Hohenstaufens' worst enemy the Emperor. The people of Palermo sometimes had to feed their boy King to keep him from starving, and the long Regency reduced his kingdom to anarchy. When Frederick declared himself of age at fourteen, he was a power-less minor prince. Suddenly the Pope declared the Emperor Otto deposed, and Frederick was elected Emperor in his place. After a fairy-tale journey through hostile armies and pirate fleets, the seventeen-year-old "Apulian Boy" reached Germany to immediate acclamation. He never fought a battle against Otto; King Philip Augustus of France took care of that for him at Bouvines, in 1214, and Frederick was crowned Emperor. After a long stay in Germany, where he won the enduring support of the nobility and the people, he returned to Sicily.

The great kingdom of the south was in chaos. Always a jurist, Frederick established his control by resurrecting two old Norman laws and giving them new applications, and he destroyed the power of the baronage by playing off the nobles against each other. He wasn't satisfied with making himself a feudal king: what Frederick had in mind—what he, in fact, established—was the kind of state that, when we find it two centuries later, we call absolutist. Nobody had an army except the King. Nobody made laws except the King. Nobody minted money except the King. In short, nobody had any power except the King, who was limited only by his imagination and ability and ambition.

Frederick had all three in abundance. He founded a university to train jurists for his bureaucracy, headed by Piero della Vigne. He dabbled in state monopolies of staple commodities. He built a Sicilian fleet and made a former pirate, Henry of Malta, High Admiral. He minted the finest gold coins in Europe. He forced all the barons out of their drafty castles and made them live in palaces. He fostered philosophy and wrote poetry that Dante praised as the first good verse in the Italian vernacular. He exhibited a strange tendency to move entire populations back and forth over the countryside—switching all the people of the town of Celano from the mainland to the island, transporting thousands of Sicilian Saracens from the island to the mainland (where they built the walled city Lucera and provided Frederick with bodyguards and servants). He kept an exotic menagerie. He built fortresses according to one uniform plan and garrisoned them only in time of war. He spoke six languages, corresponded with learned men on philosophy and mathematics, and wrote a book on falconry that is still a pleasure to read; in it he proved himself an excellent naturalist. Admiring contemporaries called him *stupor mundi*, the wonder of the world.

Others of his contemporaries called him a heretic and a tyrant and a libertine. The Popes spent a good deal of their time and energy trying to destroy or at least contain his ambition, just as he spent a good part of his life trying to woo, conquer, or cow Lombardy and thus contain the Papacy and unite his kingdom and his empire. A passionate astrologist, he was charged with calling Christ, Moses and Mohammed frauds, and once, while riding past a wheat field, he asked how many gods grew there. Raised in the liberal, skeptical atmosphere of polyglot Sicily, he was always tolerant toward non-Christians, but heretics he persecuted as harshly as any Pope. His sensuality and licentious appetites were legendary: according to rumor, he kept a harem, and his mistresses were legion. He loved falcons more than he loved most of his women.

Frederick makes the most objective historians partisan, and what one makes of the evidence depends almost entirely on what one thinks of Frederick. I have been under his spell for years.

Most of the book is based on fact, but the facts are flexible. Frederick's reasons for going on crusade after his third excommunication and the events on shipboard during the voyage to Cyprus are my surmise. The quarrel with John of Ibelin on Cyprus has never been explained to my satisfaction; yet even Sir Steven Runciman, a fan of the Ibelins, admits that there is no record of John's having been appointed bailli of Cyprus; and given Frederick's experience during his own minority, he might well have reacted harshly to what he would have considered a usurping of power during a regency. There is no evidence that the Templars tried to kill the Emperor in Acre, but they did suggest to the Sultan that he have Frederick murdered during his side trip to the Jordan River.

The Templars may not have been Satanist in Acre; they were beyond doubt Satanist in France, as the records of their trial under Philip the Fair show very clearly. The rebuilding of Jaffa was probably not as extensive as I have made it. How Frederick managed to talk al-Kamil into handing over Jerusalem is obscure, and he might have done this as I've indicated. The coronation in Saint Sepulcher did happen. If Frederick crowned himself King of Jerusalem, it seems odd that his son Conrad should wear the crown and use the title while Frederick was still robust and ruling; but Frederick was an odd man.

Finally, Theophano may well be the Syrian girl who is buried in Sicily next to one of Frederick's Empresses. And she may have been the mother of the bastard Frederick of Antioch. On the other hand, she may not. But she, like nearly everyone else in this book, is based on a real person.

As for Frederick himself, the liberties I have taken with the way a man born in 1194 might think and act are justified, I hope, by this: Frederick was an outrage and an amazement to his own century, but is only an anachronism to ours. "The wildest dreams of Kew," as the man said, "are the facts of Khatmandu." To recreate his impact on his world, and at the same time to make him understandable, I would stoop to every liberty on earth.

ANTICHRIST

Frederick. I, Frederick. I, Frederick.

Black shadow drowned the gallery with its wide archways; the sunlight laid its bright edge along the nearest rail. In the courtyard below, a hammer rang on metal, a soft beat, a sharp one, even and monotonous. The wisteria growing up the wall to the gallery archways was blooming, its scent like a fruit in the air. For three days he had been at Barletta, waiting for the news from Rome.

He rose and went into the sunlight by the railing, leaned on the wall, and looked out. From this distance he couldn't see what the man in the courtyard was hammering on. He thought of calling down to Hasan to find out, but Hasan, leaning up against the side of the door directly below him, was too obviously dozing. Over the slanting tile roofs of the town he could just see the glitter of the sun on water.

He drew a deep breath of the perfumed air. His strength delighted him. Even at Gaeta, fourteen days before, he'd spent the mornings weak, so that he'd had to pay attention to keep his hands from trembling. Like an old man. Behind him the wind rustled the charters on the table, and he thought of going back to put a weight on them but did not. If they blew away, Michele would simply have to recopy them.

Charters. His throat tensed to spit. For six months he'd forced himself mild. Being sick had helped. Now his rage darkened the sunlight before his eyes and his hands wound violently into fists. He noticed that and carefully spread his fingers.

There was nothing to do but wait. Everything necessary and possible he'd already done, for six months working steadily and patiently to make what he knew was coming profit him, not his enemy. The letters—"Royal cousin, in the name of God I beg that you give me impartial hearing"—all the letters carefully composed, carefully sent to all the princes of Europe. He had shown no one his rage, not even Piero. He wondered if Piero guessed. When it comes I will let myself be angry for exactly long enough to upset Piero.

But already the corked-up fury was draining away. He began to wonder why his temper was so short. He'd been courting this for years: it was his own fault, after all. Putting off the Crusade from season to season—Not now, Papa, I have other things to do. He thought, Maybe I'm afraid of the ban. He tested that—his reactions to the idea—and decided he was. But in September, when Gregory had stood on the balcony at Rieti and first declared him excommunicate, he'd been more afraid.

He was angry mostly because, after all the flagrant excuses he'd given three Popes, Gregory had picked on the fact he'd had no control over: getting sick. After some thought and rereading of the charges pouring like a stinking flux from Rome, he was satisfied that, even to Gregory, his failure to go piously off to Jerusalem, shaking with chill and parched with fever, was only an excuse. A matter of polity.

Good. He watched two pages saunter across the courtyard, their heads bent together in conversation. One saw him and jerked to a halt and bowed, and the other wheeled, blushing to the hairline, swept off his cap, and bent double. He lifted one hand and they raced off.

Excommunicated. Yet it could serve him. It divided them up, the Pope on one side and the Emperor on the other, which was only proper, after all. I am the Emperor. The world belongs to me. Let him take heaven. Do I involve myself in the judgment of souls?

His eyes narrowed; he stared over Barletta's red roofs to the sea. It was unkind of Gregory to use the weapons of religion in a purely terrene conflict. He spread his hands out so that the sun could warm them. All winter he had pointed out to the princes of Europe how unnatural and impious were the Pope's uses of his office. Now again he felt what he hoped the kings and dukes would feel: ruffled indignation. It isn't fair. How dare he. This time he did spit, and he grinned.

"Sire."

"Yes."

Piero came out onto the gallery and started toward him. In his hand he held a letter covered with seals. Frederick swung toward him, and his back muscles clenched. It had come. All the uncertainty and the last faint hope balled up like ice in his stomach.

"Read it."

Piero opened the letter, turned it right way around, and began to read, with his fingers smoothing out the ribbons stuck to the page. After the first few phrases, when he knew what the letter said, Frederick leaned up against the wall and let his muscles slacken. He drew one of the long brushes of the wisteria into his hands and pulled off the lavender trumpets. Pollen clung to the ball of his thumb and the creases in his fingers. He did not listen to Piero, which made it easy to keep his face untroubled.

The third time. He was cast out, damned and doomed, and nobody could consort with him without earning the grave disfavor of Holy Church. They'd made up a new bundle of charges: he had robbed the Sicilian clergy, mocked the Templars and the Hospital, plundered his own kingdom. Piero stopped reading and folded the letter in his long Greek hands.

"Oh, Gregory," Frederick said. He smiled at Piero; his hands were full of wisteria blossoms.

"He is most intransigent," Piero said.

"That's a word for it. And I've been so penitent, so accommodating, so very Christian. Call a council here for the end of April."

"Shall I tell them what it's for, Sire?"

"That I'm going on crusade, of course."

Piero turned his face away slightly, but his stare remained on Frederick. "I thought we'd discussed that and decided it was unwise."

"I've changed my mind. Why, don't you think the idea attractive? This unseemly Pope has placed me under the ban, and in penitence and true devotion to our Lord Jesus Christ I make pilgrimage to . . ." He eyed Piero. "No?"

"You're excommunicated. I've never heard of—"

"Neither have I. When the Archbishop comes back from Cairo I'll make up my mind. When you send the summonses tell them I'm just considering it. After all, we've got the ships and the men—what a pity to waste all that money. Find out what they think."

"It's incautious."

"Where did he announce it? I didn't hear."

Piero looked down at the letter. "The Lateran."

"Good. He's afraid to go into Saint Peter's. The crowds, the noise. You'd better send for the Grand Master."

"As you wish, Sire."

"Here, give me that."

Piero handed him the letter and went to the table for the charters Frederick had signed in the morning. "You don't think another letter is necessary."

"I've sent too many letters."

He read through the bull, and suddenly his black fury swept over him again. His fingers tightened around the heavy vellum. He thought of tearing it to shreds, of balling it up in his fist. He said, "This man is arrogant beyond all telling." His voice shook.

Piero said, "He's frightened. He expected them all to turn against you at the first breath of it, and they did not."

"Take it." Frederick thrust the letter at him. "Keep it somewhere. In the small chest." His eye caught the formula: *Gregory, servant of the servants of God.* "Whose servant? If Jesus appeared before him this Pope would offer him his shoe to kiss."

"Perhaps another letter." Piero was arranging the charters in his hands. He laid the bull on top.

"No. They must all see now that he—how Christian he is. He steals money from the Crusade to raise an army against me, he bribes my subjects—" He kept his voice low, so that no one would overhear, but the words jarred in his ears as if he were shouting. "Is he a priest? He's a baron, he fights me like a baron, with all his fiefs and money. Am I to fight him like a priest?"

"Sire, no man of sense could support him."

"The world's full of senseless men." He drove his fist against the stone of the gallery arch. His skin split, and the sharp pain widened his eyes. He looked thoughtfully at his bleeding knuckles. Piero was immobile, watching him, heavy-lidded. Frederick grinned.

"Maybe I'll let him kiss my shoe, hah?"

"Your Majesty, let me advise—"

"I won't attack him. I'm not that stupid. Go away."

He turned his back on Piero, and after a moment footsteps marched away. The door opened and closed. His breath whistled through his teeth. If he attacked he'd lose everything, all the winter's careful work, all the work of his whole life. He ground his lacerated knuckles against the stone. The gritty pain shot up his forearm to his elbow, and he spread out his hands on the rail. O God, isn't it mine? Isn't it mine alone? He watched his blood dribble slowly down over the uneven stone.

The earliest thing he could remember clearly was his coronation in the great cathedral in Palermo. He remembered the weight of the vestments, the slippery cold of the golden throne, and the height of the nave. All those heads, bobbing, and the voices, and the peppery smell of incense mixed with the stench of sweat and dirt. In all that crowd he had recognized not one face. Finally, after a torrent of words he hadn't understood, the Archbishop dropped the crown on his head, the people shouted, "Christus vincit, Christus regnat, Christus imperat."

"And I burst into tears."

"Kings don't cry."

"I was only three." Frederick cut up a peach and gave half of it to the child beside him. "Can't you make allowances for kings of extreme youth?"

Enzio devoured the peach and threw the pit out the window. "Wasn't your mother there?"

"She must have been. I don't remember."

Enzio smoothed the embroidered silk of the bedcover. "So there was one person there you knew."

"I doubt it. I'd only seen her once or twice before that." The first time he'd seen her, he'd cried; the Duchess of Foligno had told him so. His mother he recalled best from the wild days in Castellamare, where the sick old woman had roamed the corridors at night—the swish of her gowns, the terrible shuffling of her feet, like a ghost past his nursery door, women with lamps lighting her way. Adelaide came in, throwing back her long yellow hair.

"Mama is naked," Enzio said. He was leaning around Frederick to see her.

"Far better than Mama clothed."

Enzio giggled and pressed his face against Frederick's back. "She's not your mother, she's mine."

"Just a manner of speaking." He pinned Enzio down with one arm, still watching Adelaide, who was walking around the room. She paused in front of a gold mirror and admired herself. Two of her maids peeked in the door from the alcove, and Frederick waved them away. "My mother was old and wrinkled, and her breath smelled bad."

Enzio squirmed, and Frederick let him go. Red-faced, the boy sat up, his shirt bunched under his armpits. "Was she a queen?"

"She was the Empress." He tugged Enzio's clothes straight. Adelaide's breath was sweet, and her skin always yearning, soft. She stopped, across the room, and looked at him through the corners of her eyes. One narrow foot reached out to stroke the carpet.

"Enzio, maybe—"

"Tell me another story."

"Two knights met in a forest, rushed together, and died on the spot, one of heart failure, the other of the heat. Kiss your mother and go outside and play."

"That wasn't a—"

"By imperial decree I declare that a full and valid story. Go out and play, and you can ride on the elephant when it comes."

"An elephant?" Enzio's eyes rounded and his mouth opened. "An elephant?"

"The Archbishop's bringing one back from Egypt, it's a present from the Sultan. Go on." Frederick shoved him. Enzio disappeared over the side of the bed; there was a soft thump. "Kiss your mother before you go."

The boy rose and ran over to Adelaide. She bent down —Frederick grinned—and Enzio pecked her on the chin. "An elephant." He dashed out, and Frederick leaned back on his elbows.

"Is there an imperial decree for me as well?" Adelaide pulled a lock of her hair over her shoulder and veiled her lower face with it. Her eyes narrowed and grew dark.

"I'll consider it."

She came slowly toward him, her hands at her sides. The cream skin of her breasts, the coarse dark pelt between her thighs made him tremble. She knelt on the bed and slowly bent and kissed him, and he dragged her down into the silks. She pulled open the front of his shirt and wrapped her arms tightly around his waist.

"You talked to Bianca," she said, kissing him. "I saw you."

"I saw you watching." He dragged a cushion from behind her head and slid it under her hips.

"Do you like her better than me?"

"Don't talk to me when my attention is elsewhere." He slipped his arms around her and rolled onto her. She whimpered and pressed her lips to his shoulder. He ducked his head down. Her soft moans and the rasp of her breath sounded far away. His head spun and his toes tingled. His whole body flowed massively out through his loins. He collapsed, drained away, and shut his eyes.

"Please don't talk to Bianca."

"Be quiet." He opened one eye and looked at the hour-candles in the corner. At Vespers he had to sit and listen to an ambassador from the French King. It was only nones, but the candle was guttering, and he rolled over onto his back and said, "Go light another candle."

She got out of bed, and he sprawled out; the breeze dried the sweat from his chest and face. His back stung where she'd clawed him. That irritated him, and he pursued the little nudge of feeling back to its source: he didn't like being reminded she'd been involved. Interesting.

"You don't love me," she said, sitting on the edge of the bed. With a long ivory comb she smoothed her hair.

He stared at the mosaic on the far wall. From there, she could see the details, but he couldn't. "I never said I did." If he concentrated, maybe he could force his eyes to see.

"I love you so much, though."

"I love Enzio. Isn't that enough?"

"No."

"That's too bad." He stretched; the pleasant lassitude ebbed, and he began to think of getting up.

"Do you care for me at all?"

"If I didn't, I wouldn't lug you around everywhere I go."

Too late to stop, he saw what he'd gotten into. She said, "Then when you go to Syria you'll take—"

II

"I'm not sure I'm going to Syria." He tried to force his eyes to see the little Greek horsemen on the far wall. She touched him, stroking his chest where the red hair grew thick over the breastbone. He cupped his hand over her buttock. Adelaide, dear, I'm afraid . . . Bianca Lancia's heart-shaped face crept into his mind, her blue-black hair, her clear blue eyes. It's all over. Her heavy head pressed against his chest.

"Let me up."

"Where are you going?" She raised her head to look at him.

"To my room."

"Oh, that's right. The audience."

He stood up and took off his wrinkled shirt. "Don't let the candles go out."

She snorted. He knew that she ignored the candles; when she thought he'd be there she sent pages all the way to the chancery to find out what time their candles showed. He'd proved it once by setting the chancery candles back three hours. His shirt was incredibly dirty, and the thought of putting on his hose and coat just to go six rooms over made his skin creep. He tossed the shirt onto a chair. "Have somebody wash that."

"Take it with you."

He spun around. "God damn you, Adelaide, if I tell you to wash one of my shirts, you can do it yourself. Don't you ever talk to me like that again. Do you hear me?"

Her mouth dropped open. She shrank back, her arms raised against her breasts.

"Do you hear me?"

She whispered, "Yes."

"Good." He went to the door into the antechamber, glanced at her again, and pulled the door open. "Corso?"

"Sire." The page dashed up, all his gold lace flashing.

"Send somebody down to my room for clean clothes."

"Yes, Sire." Corso spun and snapped an order to one

of the other pages. "May I do anything else?"

"Do you have any sherbet?"

"Yes, Sire. Shall I—"

"Yes." He turned and went back into Adelaide's room. She was still huddled in the covers, but her eyes had narrowed. He said, "Cover yourself up."

Her hands pulled obediently at the bright silks. Frederick walked to the window and looked into the pear orchard just beyond the wall, where Enzio sometimes played. He heard the pages come in and turned, delighted at the thought of sherbet. Corso carried the cups, a younger boy, Giancarlo, the tray. Giancarlo succeeded in keeping his eyes away from Adelaide, managed to put the tray down, saw Frederick, and turned gray. Corso lifted the ewer out of its bed of snow.

"What's wrong, Giancarlo?" Frederick said. "Haven't you ever seen a naked emperor before?"

The page opened his mouth, but nothing came out. Corso turned to watch him. Anything the boy said would be ridiculous, and suddenly Frederick regretted what he had said. "Go on," he said. "Leave me, Corso."

Giancarlo whirled and ran. Corso brought the cups to Frederick, bowed, and backed calmly around the bed toward the door.

"That was cruel," Adelaide said.

He handed her one cup. "I know." He would have to bathe before the audience. "What do you think would happen if I walked naked down the hall?"

She was relieved that his mood had changed, and her smile glowed with it. "A lot of people would talk."

"Do they think I end at the neckline?" He'd never dare do it. He might see Bianca Lancia and get an erection, and the flap would bring Barletta down around his ears. He laughed and finished the cup of sherbet. She was stroking his upper arm.

"You're beautiful," she said. "You could do it. But think of the others, the fat ones and the old ones. They need clothes to cover themselves up. Think of the Archbishop."

Into his mind leaped an image of the Archbishop, stringy hams and protruding round belly. He made a face. "I'm not beautiful. You're beautiful." He took her by the chin and kissed her, and she clutched his shoulders.

Corso said, "Sire."

"Come in." He stood up, and Adelaide dove under the covers. Followed by the third page, Corso strode in, his arms full of clothes.

"Is the Frenchman here yet?"

"Yes, Sire." Corso got him into his underwear and hose. "De la May, or something like that." He stood on his toes to slip the undertunic over Frederick's head. "The Grand Master is waiting in your antechamber. And a messenger from the Frangipani."

"From the—!" He straightened up and pulled on the tunic himself. "When did he get here?"

"Just at nones, Sire." Corso held up the coat. "Do you—"

"No. Bring it." He strode toward the door, only half dressed. The other page tore around to open the door for him, and he walked straight through to the curtained archway into the next room. Corso was close behind him. The sentries outside the archway straightened so swiftly their half-armor clashed. Corso raced around in front of him and settled into a jog—he couldn't keep up with Frederick's stride at a walk.

"You should have told me before," Frederick said.

"Paolo found out when he went for your clothes, Sire. That's why I didn't knock."

"Corso, I command you not to grow up—you're too good a page." He wanted to run. It cost him to walk, even as fast as this. They passed through a big, empty room and into the next, and the tide of people there all swept around and bowed, glittering like waves in the sunlight streaming through the windows. A pair of Cistercians came out of the office to the right, saw him, and paused, their heads bent. One of them was Klaus, from the Abrussi estates. Frederick stopped—so abruptly the page behind caromed off him and fell—and looked up and down the room, trying to see who had left and who had come to Barletta since the excommunication. All these people were waiting to see Piero and Marino. Half the courtiers behind him had risen again after he'd passed, and seeing him turn, they dipped down.

"Klaus," he said, and the monk smiled. Frederick went on. He was a lay brother of the Cistercians. Remembering that comforted him. The Cistercians wouldn't desert him, and surely . . . They passed a staircase flooded with girls, and the sentries on either side of the next archway jerked themselves upright; they were all Saracens.

"Corso," Frederick said. "Go get Manfredo Lancia." He stepped through the archway into a smaller room, turned left, and waited for the page Paolo to open the door for him.

The Grand Master, Rinaldo of Spoleto, and a tall Italian Frederick didn't know stood and bowed when he entered. The Italian sank down on one knee. "Your Majesty."

"Rise. Hermann, your pardon a moment."

The Grand Master bowed. "Sire."

The Italian said, "Your Majesty, Piero Frangipani sent me. The Romans have chased the Pope out of the city for setting the ban on you."

Frederick threw his head back and crowed. The Italian twitched, and Rinaldo emitted a burst of harsh laughter. Corso was back, Bianca's elder brother in tow. The messenger from the Frangipani knelt, twisting his velvet cap in his hands.

"My deepest respects and love are reserved for the people of Rome." Frederick pulled the gold ring off his little finger. "Here. Manfredo, take charge of this man, he's to be fed and given a full suit of good clothes, and he'll be at the audience."

Manfredo nodded. His forehead wrinkled up. "Yes, Sire."

Frederick couldn't keep from grinning. He bent and hauled the messenger to his feet. Clutching his ring, the man suddenly started to babble thanks—his eyes staring over Frederick's head. Manfredo took him by the arm.

"Wait," Frederick said. "Where is he?"

"Rieti, Sire." The messenger sank down on his knees again.

"Good. Go." His chest swelled with triumph. They'd run the Pope out of Rome. Out of his own city. He didn't want to look at the Grand Master and see the misery that would be drooping the old man's mouth. Rinaldo was still grinning. Frederick chewed his lip. "Corso, send somebody for Michael Scot. Hermann, come inside. Corso, I want a bath. Get the water hot. Hot, damn you, not tepid." He headed for the inside door, and a page yanked it open. The Grand Master followed him.

The sunlight in this room nearly blinded him; unimpeded by balconies, it shone through all the windows, reflected off the gold and the mosaics. He walked into the center of the room and started to take off the undertunic, but before he had his hands to his throat a page was there, lifting it over his head.

"Hermann," he said. "Is he out of his mind?"

The Grand Master stood bent-legged beside the door. "They think so in Rome, obviously."

"Speak German, I need the practice." He switched languages. "I shall order prayers for his guidance. Sit."

"Thank you, Sire." The Grand Master lowered himself into a chair and sighed. The pages brought Frederick a gown. He stood still so that they could belt it and sat down. One of them got a chair under his rump just before he would have fallen flat.

"I hoped and prayed that His Holiness would realize how treacherous is his course. How strewn with temptations into grievous error. As I pray for you, Sire."

Two servants came through, lugging wood for the fire in the bathing room. Frederick said, "Hermann, the world is my arena. I know how to deal with it. My blood prepares me. What can he act on but experience? Is there no way to vindicate myself?"

"I know that you've tried," the Grand Master said. "But I know as well how the Holy Father feels about your transgressions."

"They are not transgressions."

"My Lord—"

Wrong approach. Michael Scot came in, smiling, and bowed. Frederick waved at him impatiently. "Hermann, I've sinned, but I've also begged him to allow me to expiate my sins." He curled his bare toes into the carpet. "He's accusing me of things I've never even considered doing. Did you see the bull?"

"Della Vigne sent me a copy."

"I love the Church, Hermann. Since my childhood I've had neither father nor mother, and Holy Church fostered me." In Latin he said to Scot, "Did you cast that horoscope?"

"Yes, Sire." Scot sank down on a white fur robe thrown across a low chest. His eyes rolled toward the Grand Master.

"Since the founding of the Christian world," the old man said, "the Popes have judged the Emperors. Which is only right—because if the Pope does not, who will?"

Frederick slapped his palms down on his thighs. "I have no objection to being judged by the Church, Hermann. By the Church, not by a man who sits inside the robes of his office and will not uphold his own law."

The Grand Master frowned, puzzled. Corso had come in, his arms full of soft linen. Exasperated, Frederick stood up; the old German there didn't understand the essential difference between Gregory and his office. "Come along with me."

He walked across the mottled carpet to the side door, let a servant hold the curtain, and went through into the vast tiled bathing room. In its center the shallow pool steamed, half full of water. He threw off his gown and stepped into it, gasping at the heat, and waded out until the water came to his waist. Sweat popped out on his chest. He splashed himself, sank down on his heels, and scrubbed his hair with his hands. Swiftly his body accustomed itself to the heat of the water, so that when he stood the air seemed cold. Corso was standing on the edge of the pool. Frederick held up one hand, and Corso tossed him a cloth. The others had ranged themselves around the tiled edge.

"No news from Constantinople," he said, "is there?"

Rinaldo sat on his heels, "No, Sire. I'm sure they'll elect him, though."

Frederick wrinkled his nose. The little boy they called the Emperor of the East wasn't old enough yet to rule, and the Pope had been engineering the election as Regent of John of Brienne, the ex-King of Jerusalem. Frederick was now King of Jerusalem, having married John's daughter, the heiress. John was old but energetic, and he hated Frederick. Scrubbing himself with the cloth, Frederick decided that he hated John back. Arrogant old bastard. John was in Rome, along with all the bishops and nobles Frederick had booted out of Sicily in the past eight years, and he suspected they spent their time together plotting revenge.

"Hermann. The Popes never excommunicated Diepold or Walter or Markwald or any of the others for robbing Sicily when I was gone."

The Grand Master frowned. "No."

Frederick combed his long hair through his fingers. The idea of going on crusade returned to him; there was something charming about the whole idea. The door from the next room opened, and the Admiral, with six of his friends, walked in, bowed, and sent a page running for chairs for him and the Grand Master. Frederick walked around in the pool, frowning and shaking his hair dry.

"Hermann, go to Syria as soon as you can find a ship."

"Sire?" The Grand Master twitched. The others around him muttered, their eyes on Frederick. Michael Scot, smiling and cynical, perched on a window sill and watched them.

"Go to Syria. Ricardo Filangieri and the Duke of Limburg have been rattling around there with nobody to supervise except Tommaso, and he's too busy elsewhere. They may need some getting into shape."

"Sire—for what?"

"And, anyhow, you have a perfectly good reason for being there—to govern your order." He beat his hands on the water and grinned. "Enrico. Get a ship for him, hah?"

The Admiral bowed. "Sire."

Enrico da Malta had been a Genoese pirate before Frederick made him Grand Admiral of Sicily. Frederick studied him covertly. Sometimes, when he could do it without seeming too eager, he got Enrico to tell him pirate stories. Piracy sounded like fun, like an adventure. He lowered his eyes, almost embarrassed. What do you want to be when you grow up? They were all watching him, the way they always did. They watched me being born, they'll watch me die. He put one hand on his chest, feeling the bones under the heavy skin and the curling little hairs. Why don't the hairs on my chest grow as long as the hair on my head and my beard?

"They're going to canonize Francesco," Michael Scot said comfortably, and Frederick looked over at him and laughed. "I thought that would amuse you."

"They make him a saint, they excommunicate me." He scrubbed himself vigorously. The Grand Master was talking quietly to Enrico. Rinaldo glanced at them and leaned forward.

"Why shouldn't they make him a saint? Didn't he receive the very wounds of our blessed Lord? Francesco was very holy. Everybody said so."

"I never met him," Frederick said. "I just mean that it's odd. They're inconsistent, the Curia. We're both heretics, Francesco and I."

"You're no heretic," the Grand Master said. "Don't let them talk you into believing that."

"How is Francesco a heretic?" Enrico said.

"For Christ's sake," Frederick said. "He received the wounds of Christ without the intercession of the priest, didn't he? He made a Sacrament of his own body, didn't he?"

"That's rather a new interpretation." The Grand Master smiled. "You've got a lively mind, Sire."

"Thank you for the compliment." He walked back to the shallow end of the pool and sat down to wash his legs.

Enrico laughed his high, braying laugh. "Francesco and Federigo. Saint Emperor."

Frederick whirled and splashed him. "Watch yourself. I'll string you up on a yardarm."

Everybody laughed, Enrico the loudest, but the Grand Master only smiled. Frederick walked over to the side of the pool and splashed water on the Grand Master's feet. The old man flinched, startled, and looked down; Frederick looked up, and grinned, and winked.

"Sire." The Grand Master looked from side to side, his face tightening. "Do you wish to come up?" He reached down one hand to pull Frederick out of the pool.

Frederick shook his head. "No. I'm sorry. I can get out by myself." He turned his back and walked to the far side of the pool. Pages and servants with his gown, his slippers, oils and towels fled around to meet him. No matter what he did, he hurt the old man. He thought, Is

that why I like him so much? Putting both hands on the
tile rim of the pool, he heaved himself out and stood up.
On the far side all the men watched him, immobile. If I
were not Emperor, would I stand and stare at the man
who was? He could not conceive of not being Emperor.
Piero della Vigne came in, papers in his hands, while the
pages dried and oiled Frederick's body.

"Sire, do you want to read this before the audience?"

"Yes." He reached out one hand. The breeze from the
windows cooled him. He stood so that they could put
the gown around his shoulders and started forward, and
like dogs on leashes or birds with thin strings around
their necks, they followed him into the next room.

Peacocks and fanciful trees covered the walls of the
audience chamber, small gilt flowers and majolica leaves
and stems. Against the elegant forgeries the real flowers
seemed to tingle with life. De la Moile, the French envoy, sat straddle-legged between two gigantic clumps of
yellow lilies, glaring at Frederick; he'd been playing
rough, honest warrior ever since the audience began.

Piero read the opening statement. On either side of the
room the officers of the court and the courtiers stood silent, bored. Frederick had been staring at the wall above
De la Moile's head for so long that the elaborate birds
and trees were changing color and blurring. He shut his
eyes, counted to five, and opened them again.

"Honest and loyal, these virtuous men—"

Four more sentences and the prepared note would end.
He concentrated on keeping still. Serene, he thought.
The majesty of the Emperor is beyond mortal details,
like tired eyes and sweat under this robe. The robe
pressed like chain across his shoulders, and under the rim
of the crown his forehead itched. He wanted to look like
a statue, an envelope of flesh for the mind of the Emperor. With his ears he listened to the speeches, but the

words never reached his brain; he was thinking of the miracle.

Every once in a while the memory overcame him, like a renewal of it. He remembered running barefoot through the courtyard to look at the sundial, dressed in nothing but an old shirt, and he remembered, a few years later, stealing peaches in the bazaar at Palermo. He remembered his first marriage and his elder son's birth and the fear, the shame when the false Emperor Otto the Welf invaded Sicily and he had to make a ship ready to carry him off to Africa in case . . . When he was only Henry VI's son, who wasn't old enough, who had been forgotten, even by the Pope who had sworn to protect him. And the day they brought him the news that he had been elected Emperor—that Otto was deposed and he, Frederick, was Emperor if he would only come to Germany.

Transfigured, as if a lightning bolt had drilled into his body and turned him to pure fire. Constanza, his first wife, hadn't believed it. She'd pleaded with him not to go: it was a trap, it was too dangerous. He had known it was true. When the messenger told him, he felt in it the rightness, the ineluctable simplicity of truth. I am Emperor. Fourteen years I labored for Rachel. But Constanza had wept and begged; she had been ten years older than he and just out of childbed.

I am seventeen. For three years I've been of age and done nothing, no, nothing; jumped around like a hare, sniffing up conspiracies and blocking them just before they would have . . . Seventeen and a father, and my dumb wife won't let me go to Germany to be crowned Emperor.

Piero was answering De la Moile's prepared note, full of the hopes and fears of the French Queen, ruling for her young son. They'd worked it out the day before, anticipating every possible question the Frenchman might ask and writing up answers. Piero's Latin was bet-

ter than Frederick's, smoother, the phrases more balanced. My Latin is Italian translated. De la Moile had
praised the mild and humble tone with which the Emperor had addressed the Pope. Yes, and if you only
knew, child, how—

The miracle. That whole journey, that wonderful
spring, had been nothing but miraculous. Sailing to
Rome on a Genoese ship, dodging the Pisan pirate fleet,
and the acclaim of the people of Rome. He'd never seen
any of them before, but they had cheered him—he remembered the vigor of their voices. They were still his
friends. To Cremona, and from Cremona the race to the
Lambro River, with the Milanese closing in from two
sides. Milan he would destroy someday, raze her to the
ground, city of vipers and poisonous lizards—they've always hated Hohenstaufens. My father . . . whom I
never met, but still . . .

"Finally, Her Grace the Queen Regent of France
wishes to express her firm devotion to His Majesty the
Emperor and her fervent prayers for His Majesty's soul
throughout these perilous, grievous days."

How touching of Blanche. He'd met her with her King
at Vaucouleurs, during his years in Germany—fortu-
nately, living in Germany had prepared him for the style
of the French court. The drafts, the chilly stone, the narrow little windows, and no sunlight, no flowers, no
music, all the brooding about sin and heresy; he remembered his shock when he found out they pitied him because he was poor. But I am Sicilian, I know what your
lives could be like. It had amazed him that those people
could laugh.

De la Moile was asking about the possibilities of a Crusade, and Piero answered at some length, expressing
Frederick's earnest and passionate wish to follow the
Cross, his intentions to do so as soon as practical, and the
careful, flexible clause they'd worked out: "Provided, of
course, that the situation in Italy does not require His

Majesty's continual vigilance for his kingdom. His Majesty dare not leave without assurances of the safety and peace of Sicily."

And so forth. He listened to enough of De la Moile's next question to know that Piero could answer it. His neck burned where the brocade had rubbed it raw and the sweat had gotten in. He hated clothes. In Sicily it was warm enough to go without. Especially the ridiculous long coats that tangled themselves around his legs and tripped him up. The new ones were slightly better—they came just to the middle of his thighs—except that the sleeves, full as a woman's and slit from cuff to elbow, tended to get into the food and slap people if they knelt too near him.

When he'd ridden up to the city of Constance, seventeen years before, he'd worn a green velvet coat with a big gold buckle on the belt and patches on both elbows. I am here, I am the Emperor. . . . The city had prepared a banquet for the imperial visitor, for Otto IV, not Frederick II, and the people were amazed to see him there. With only three hundred men and the Welf's huge army just across the lake—knock on the gate, let me in: the Emperor. So at last he came in from the dark and sat down at the feast cooked for his enemy, and when Otto finally arrived, after the dishes were taken away to be washed, they barred the gates and would not let him through.

That was when I beat him. De la Moile was asking a question he'd have to answer, and he drew himself back into the imperial body.

". . . most urgently desires to know how the information that the Holy Father had misused the fund for the Crusade reached the notice of His Imperial Majesty."

Frederick said, "Whatever abuses and misuses occur within our realm we will surely learn of, even though they be committed by those once believed beyond accusation. His Holiness paid the Lombard cities more than one hundred thousand ducats over the past years, much of it in the gold augustales that we ourself provided him for the Crusade. Milan received four hundred new augustales alone, still in the sacks bearing the imperial seal. This His Grace our cousin may verify, since the Milanese did not bother to smelt the coins down; they have transferred some two hundred of them through the bankers of Florence to certain hands in Paris who have in their turn paid out fifty of them to agents of our cousin His Grace."

De la Moile stared, open-mouthed. Frederick fought the urge to smile, to shift his gaze, to yawn or spit or pare his nails—anything now would ruin it. He'd spoken Latin, purely because De la Moile had spoken Latin, and in his inner ear he heard the harsh contrast between his style and Piero's. De la Moile was stammering out another question. Piero could handle this. He retired to contemplate the wall again.

Much more of this and I'll die. I'll die, right here, let Heinrich be Emperor and to hell with them all. His eyes were fighting him, trying to look elsewhere, and his skin under the robe shuddered with each breath he drew.

Otto, gigantic, brave as a bear, had died under the whips of priests, thrown flat on the floor to confess his sins before a German bishop. His raw skin quivered away from that. Heretic-hunters. Ludwig, the Landgrave of Thuringia, had spoken of his wife, back last summer in Otranto, where Ludwig lay dying of the malaria that had wrecked the Crusade. Elizabeth the saint. Northern saints are different from our southern species. Caught himself in the fever, whimpering sometimes, he'd found out how German he was. Hell frightened him. I don't mind dying, but to go to hell afterward. Goat-footed demons, the lank hide of their shanks and thighs— he'd dreamed of them. Francesco never spoke of hell; he'd loved birds and flowers, and the stigmata had come from love, not fear. Not terror. To burn forever the way

I burned in the fever—I would go mad. Maybe that was the worst thing about hell; you weren't allowed to go mad.

Still, there might be something in that, to endure hell without submitting. If they're right, I'm going, so I may as well talk myself into a proper attitude. Piero was walking forward to knock his staff on the floor.

"This audience is ended. Go and bear the word of the glory of the Emperor."

Frederick bit down his sigh of relief. His court charged the door; there was a fierce but muted struggle to see who would get out first, the courtiers on the left or the officers on the right. The courtiers won, whooped, and streamed out into the great hall beyond. De la Moile followed, surrounded by pages and notaries and his personal attendants. Piero joined him at the door, spoke quietly to him, gave him two copies of the prepared note, and bowed him out. The Saracens guarding the door from the outside slammed it shut at De la Moile's heels, and Frederick collapsed.

"Oh, God. I'm sweating to death." He pulled off the crown and shook his hair. "I want a facsimile of that made of something light. Tin. Paper. Paste. Feathers. Piero, do you see what I mean? They were impressed, weren't they?"

"Very." Piero opened a side door and let in the pages and servants. "When you spoke that time, it shocked them. Us." He smiled. "You'd been quiet so long."

"I'm thirsty." He still held the crown in his hands, but the two guards were walking toward him, and he held it out to them. The state robe was already half off his shoulders; he shrugged, and it fell off completely. The pages and his gentlemen brought him a cup of chilled wine with rose petals floating in it.

"De la Moile was just startled that you knew about the augustales, I think," Piero said.

Frederick shrugged. "They all think they're so subtle

and secretive, it shows on their faces as soon as they try anything sneaky." He ducked so that Corso could slip a tunic over his head. "If they were either smarter or stupider than they are, I'd be helpless. Not that coat, Giancarlo. The black one."

The side door opened again, and Hasan walked in, strode around to face Frederick, and saluted. Above the spotless white of his robes his dark face split into a flashing smile, and Frederick grinned back. "What did you find?" he said in Arabic.

Hasan raised one fist, worked his fingers deftly, and held up the first two, an Augustus between them. Frederick roared. He thrust one arm into the coat Giancarlo held for him and raised the other. Hasan threw the coin underhand to him.

"Who had it? De la Moile himself?"

Hasan nodded. He backed off, still smiling. Piero had seen the Augustus and made a face.

"I don't remember what the bet was," Frederick said to him, in Italian.

Piero clasped his hands before him. "Sixty ducats."

"I'll take it out of your salary."

The pages bustled around him, brushing off his shoes and the gold hem of his coat. He looked around for his jewel case, and Marco advanced, holding it out to Corso. Frederick squinted. "The garnet, the big ruby, all three signets and the diamond chain."

Piero said, "Perhaps just the Jerusalem signet, Sire."

"Don't be short-sighted." He held out his hands so that Corso could put on the rings. Immediately another page grabbed his wrist and buffed them. He bent so that they could put on the chain and medallion, stood while they buckled his belt, and took his cap from Marco. The horde of pages and servants backed away, their eyes critically on him. Piero and Hasan opened the main door, and he started out toward the roar and dance of his court under the immense vault of the great hall.

The stir of brocade and gold cloth struck him like flashes of lightning. They all saw him at once and the clatter of voices died. They bowed, tier on tier of satin and silk and fine cotton, all sewn with pearls and rubies. He heard the herald bawling out his titles, but he didn't walk forward; he stood, sweeping his gaze from one end of the room to the other, delighted. They were all so beautiful, so rich—the light shone on the sleek hair of the women, brighter and finer than gold.

"King of Sicily, Duke of Apulia, Duke of Calabria—"

He waved impatiently at the herald and stepped forward. Suddenly they were surrounding him, all their voices murmuring, "Your Majesty." He flung his head back and laughed. Pages in scarlet and black held up trays full of sweetmeats, cups of wine and sherbet and milk. "Your Majesty—" He saw Fulk of Ancerra, small and dark and neat; he saw David the Jew and Adelaide and Piero, Michael Scot, Enrico da Malta, the Archbishop Jacopo of Capua, and the Cistercians—all the faces floating around him, all their eyes on him. "Your Majesty."

"Papa," Enzio called. He was tugging at his sleeve. "I'm here, Papa."

Frederick bent and picked him up. "Isn't it late for you to be up?"

"Mama said—"

He lifted Enzio onto his shoulders and grabbed a handful of plum tarts off a tray passing by. "Enrico, have you found a ship for Hermann yet?"

"He sails from Brindisi in ten days, Sire."

Fulk of Ancerra shoved past the Admiral. "Are we going on crusade, Sire?"

"I haven't decided yet." He ate a tart. "Ezzo. When did you get here?" He handed another of the tarts up to Enzio.

"This morning," Ezzo d'Iste called. "I brought you six new merlins."

"You're trying to buy my favor," Frederick said. He started across the hall toward the banquet tables. "And you're succeeding."

"I live but for your favor, Sire." Ezzo bowed himself out of sight behind Fulk.

"Well, as long as you don't ask for anything else . . . Klaus, are these your plums?"

The monk smiled. "Unfortunately not, brother. They are from the north, I believe."

"You should raise plums."

Adelaide was beside him, and he turned and beamed at her, to prove he hadn't really been ignoring her. She smiled back. All in silk, her waiting women fluttered around her, keeping her enormous sleeves from tangling and making sure nobody trod on her skirt. De la Moile was standing to one side, bowing and smiling, his eyes everywhere. Somewhere behind the crowd, musicians tuned up.

"Papa, let me down, let me down."

Frederick swung him by the hands to the floor. "Don't eat too much." He started toward De la Moile. Adelaide followed him, and he glanced over his shoulder at her to keep her away. Her face fell. Damned woman.

"My dear Count." He hadn't spoken French for months. "How do you like Sicily?"

"Very well, Sire. Very well." De la Moile flexed rapidly from the waist. His bright eyes kept following the men and women swooping and circling around him. "This is my first visit here, as Your Majesty knows. I can't—I'm overwhelmed."

"My cousin the Queen Regent keeps a charming court." Frederick snatched a goblet from a passing tray. "So . . . austere, so very French."

De la Moile stared down the front of the dress of the girl nearest him; she turned and smiled. De la Moile licked his lips. "Your Majesty, I—" He hemmed. Rustic soldier. His eyes flew from the breast to Frederick, and he smiled nervously. The girl turned away, chattering to a knight. "We in France are used to a more simple life."

"Naturally, with a regent." He looked around, bored. Somebody had brought in half a dozen Egyptian hounds on leashes, and the women were flocking around them, cooing, while the dogs snarled and yapped and tucked their tails between their legs. De la Moile was talking to him, but Frederick ignored him. One of the hounds reared up against its leash, and the courtiers swayed back away from it; wild, excited laughter rang out.

"Is it always like this?" De la Moile asked.

"What?" Frederick frowned at him.

"Are those dogs Sicilian, Sire?"

De la Moile's eyes were bulging, and he couldn't see enough to satisfy him. Frederick shook his head. "They're a gift from the Sultan al-Kamil of Egypt. I sent him a white bear from the north. He liked it, but it died, it hated the heat." He shrugged. "I wanted a zebra, but he tells me they're impossible to tame."

"A zebra." The Frenchman's voice quivered.

"Kind of a mule with black and white stripes. Enzio wanted one. My son." He'd been going to get something to eat. Turning away from De la Moile, he started off through the mob.

Bianca Lancia suddenly appeared before him—the girls around her and the young men had stepped back at his approach. They all bowed, but the rest were only the petals of a flower around her, the fertile center. He realized he was staring, and his mouth moved in a slow smile. She rose and met his gaze, blushing, looked down, and raised her eyes to his again.

"Lady," he said. "Attend me." He held out his hand. She opened her mouth to say something, but nothing came out, and finally she put her fingertips on his arm and followed him away. Her cheek paled, and he saw her take a deep breath.

"What's wrong today?" He steered her into an alcove

under the indoor balcony and stood, his shoulders blocking the way out.

She turned to face him, her hands lost in the heavy folds of her skirt. "Your Majesty, I—Nothing's wrong." She blushed again. He leaned one shoulder against the column.

"You're so shy." The night before, they'd spoken for over an hour, and he'd begun to think she'd grown less wary.

"I'm afraid of you," she said firmly.

"Why?"

She shrugged. She wore no jewels, only a pearl hairnet over the heavy coils of her black hair. He wanted to find a jewel the color of her eyes and have it made into a necklace for her; he stared at her eyes. Her surcoat slipped off one shoulder and she snatched at it and arranged it again.

"Why are you scared of me?"

"I don't know. I'm silly. You know how girls are."

He grinned, and she blushed again, vividly. She didn't look away even for an instant. She said, "Has there—has there been any news of the Empress?"

He blinked. By the look on her face this was something bold; for a long moment he thought she meant his mother, and he frowned, bewildered. "Oh. My wife. She's in Andria, the baby isn't due for a month. If you think that will curdle me with shame, I'm beyond it. I'm not even touching you, see?" He raised his hands. "I'm harmless."

"No," she said defiantly, and shook her head.

"Are you afraid of me, or just of men?"

Abruptly she smiled. "Of you, Sire. Have I your leave to go?"

"Look over my shoulder. Is anyone watching us?"

"Naturally," she said. "The whole court." Her smile deepened, and in a quick movement she dashed by him, out into the hall. He whirled to watch her go. She was wild, this one. Ezzo, who was married to her sister, had said he'd kissed her once, but she'd refused him ever after. She looked back over her shoulder, and he caught a glimpse of her white face, the intense blue of her eyes, before she spun and lost herself in the crowd. The people watching them turned their avid faces quickly away. After sundown all the unmarried girls waited under the trees in the garden for the boys to come along, but Bianca dreamed up crazy plots, escaped over the wall at night with her friends and held midnight picnics by the sea, ambushed the overeager squires and young knights and tied them up with their belts and left them helpless in the dark. His throat tightened, thinking with longing of how the young ones played. He moved out slowly into the midst of the court.

Ezzo, Fulk, Rinaldo and two other knights stood in a knot directly in his path, talking, and didn't notice him; Ezzo threw his head up and roared with laughter.

"Sweet Christ, it's like screwing a bucket. She's had every man from here to Etna."

Frederick glared at him, and Rinaldo noticed it and jarred Ezzo's elbow. Ezzo's face glowed from the wine he was drinking. He saw Frederick, flung out one arm to point at him, and bellowed, "Including you."

The men around him bowed, and Frederick laughed, wondering whom Ezzo meant. He shook his head. When he started forward he saw Adelaide, standing beside the banquet tables. Her cheeks were flushed, her eyes flat, like a hawk's—all iris.

"I hope you sent Enzio to bed," he said. "Such excitement."

"You were talking to Bianca again."

"She asked after Yolande." He took a handful of almonds from a cloisonné bowl. "I have to act married on some occasions."

She reared back her head, snorting. Michael Scot rushed up, bubbling. "They're all talking about Boethius again. Come help me destroy them." Frederick gobbled half the almonds, tossed the rest down the front of Adelaide's dress, and laughing, flew off with Scot to the argument.

"A large number that, unfortunately, means nothing," Brother Emil said in his slurred Latin. He pointed to the bottom figure of the column. "Most of the gross revenues are swallowed up by expenses."

"Brother Frederick knows that well enough," Klaus said. "The revenues of San Germano are at any rate unimportant. Brother Frederick—"

Frederick had been writing down names on a scrap of light paper; he looked over at the numbers and nodded. "It doesn't justify, Klaus. Check it." The names on the parchment had already reached above fifty. He'd have to cut them down—it was a list of his personal suite for the Crusade. He'd sent five hundred knights to Outremer in March with Filangieri; since he didn't mean to fight a war—

"An error of a few pence out of thousands of ducats," Klaus said.

"Justify it."

"The revenues are his, after all," Brother Emil said. He took a quill from the case and totted up one column. While the two monks bent and clucked over the addition, Frederick crossed out the names of ten of his gentlemen. Corso could take care of everything, anyway. He looked off down the gallery toward the far end, where Enzio sat with his tutors. One of Piero's men came out with a handful of papers, bowed, and laid them on the edge of the desk. Frederick nodded toward a list of accountings and the page took them away.

"Brother Frederick—"

Frederick took the sheet. "Good. My God, we've made money. It will ruin the name Hohenstaufen. You think we can adjust the milling rate?"

"Yes, Sire. You'll note they've finally brought their production up above the minimum we set, so the special rate is no longer necessary."

"Yes." He leaned back, staring at the sheet. If he ordered the milling rate for the district raised all at once, few of the farmers would have prepared for it; they wouldn't adjust, they'd all go into debt. If he raised it half this year and the rest the next, they'd bellow. Let them—at least they'd be able to cope with it. Limited peasant minds. He scribbled across the top of the sheet and handed it to Klaus. "Take care of it."

While Brother Emil read off the revenues of another of the Cistercian fiefs, he skimmed through a note from Piero on special taxes and approved a tentative schedule. Doing revenues was fun sometimes, when the algebra got complicated, but most of the time it was a crying bore. He initialed the report Emil had read and sent the monks away, drew a pile of letters over the desk to him, and studied them. Except for the superscriptions, they were identical; he signed them and hit the gong beside him for a page. Leaning back, he stared over the gallery wall into the bright sunshine.

The Archbishop would enter Barletta tomorrow, and with him a cavalcade of messengers and presents from al-Kamil and Tommaso d'Aquino, Frederick's agent in Syria and Cyprus. Cockatoos, the advance reports said, and hounds and hawks and, God above, that elephant. The first elephant in Italy since Hannibal's fleet landed a herd at Reggio, unless the story was true that Harun al-Rashid had sent one to Carolus Magnus. Enzio was wild to ride on it. Gold and silver, diamonds from the African mines, sugar, pepper, myrrh, and a letter saying . . .

What? Before the death of al-Kamil's brother, al-Mu'azzam of Damascus, al-Kamil had been hot as a bride-groom to woo Frederick over, but now al-Mu'azzam was dead, his son too young to rule, and al-Kamil was unafraid and needed no infidel to help him.

On the other hand, with al-Mu'azzam dead, al-Ashraf, al-Kamil's other brother, would make a try at taking over Damascus, and al-Kamil would be wrapped up in that. And there was the inevitable pressure from Khwaresm, from the strange people east of Khwaresm, whom al-Kamil was afraid of in a way that impressed Frederick deeply. In a quarrel with his own brother, al-Kamil would not be madly willing to play friends with a Christian; it would cause too much dissension among the devout of Islam.

Frederick chewed his thumbnail. If he played friends with al-Kamil, the devout of his own religion would scream like pigs. They'd never seen the immediate benefits of cooperation, much less the long-range effects. Stupid, bull-headed—everything in the East was delicately balanced and weighted, counterweighted, poised—the problem was to disturb the balance just enough to gain him what he wanted but not enough to throw the whole area into a state of flux too rapid to control.

Crusade. He wrinkled up his nose. My grandfather went on crusade and all it got him was drowned.

The Pope wanted him on crusade to get him out of Italy, so that all Frederick's craven enemies could come out of their holes, band together, and tear down his kingdom; they were always there, waiting just below the sight, like some species of glum water monster, for his mistakes and overrisky ventures that would let them bite him one more time.

But if I can deliver Jerusalem, now, if I can rescue Jerusalem—

Barbarossa couldn't save the Holy City, the magic Emperor, his grandfather, the greatest of the heroes. I am no hero. He fisted one hand against his chest. Jerusalem—

Amazing. As soon as he started thinking of Jerusalem he got caught up in the words. Deliver, save, rescue, hero, magic—It was just a city, like—like Palermo. And if he could seize it back from the Moslims, he'd raise a bulwark against the Popes no new Innocent could scale. Al-Kamil had offered twice to give it to him, which was generous of al-Kamil, since he didn't own it.

He wondered how long he could afford to be away from Sicily. One year, maybe fourteen months; more than that and he'd come home to find nuns in La Favara and people singing Masses in the apricot-scented hall of Troia. He pulled a clean sheet of paper toward him, dipped a pen into ink, and wrote across the top in big letters UNDER SEAL. Two swallows streaked through the gallery, dove out an archway, and flashed in again through another. Enzio shouted at them, his voice echoing dimly against the stone. Frederick drew a swallow at the top of his page.

I must be crowned in Jerusalem.

The thought came into his mind like a swallow. If he were crowned in Jerusalem, his kingship would have a sanctity no mere man could debate. He drew a little crown above the swallow's head. The difficulty was that he was King of Jerusalem only because he was Yolande's husband, and if the child she was carrying turned out to be a boy, he would be King no more. If it were a boy, he meant to call it Conrad, but he hadn't made up his mind about a name for a girl. He didn't like having girl children. Maria, perhaps, after Yolande's mother. Or Constantia, after his. Girl children made difficulties in the inheritance and were a waste of time. He wrote beneath the swallow and the tall letters: Cyprus.

Cyprus was the ideal base for any attack on Syria; it would be the ideal base as well from any attack on a Christian pilgrim seeking only to worship at the shrines of the faith and to perform his Christian responsibilities in the Holy Land. Therefore he had to control Cyprus. Gervais de What's-his-name had arrived sometime before from Cyprus, the agent of Amalric Barlais, who had once tried to get himself elected bailli there; Frederick had ignored him because Gervais was a bore and a liar. Besides, he had his own agents in Cyprus; the first King of Cyprus had gotten his title and paraphernalia from the Emperor Henry VI. Papa. Frederick grinned, staring at the vellum. Between you and me, Dad, we have them sewn into a sack. I must get my sunny disposition from his side of the family.

"Sire."

Ezzo and Fulk of Ancerra came out onto the gallery and bowed. He looked up, surprised; he hadn't realized it was already noon. "Oh, good." He socked the gong again, rose, and went to the gallery railing. "I need military advice."

Ezzo moved up alongside him, spat over the railing, and said, "Then you don't need Fulk. He can't—"

"Shut up. Command me, Sire."

"Yes, well, it's delicate." Frederick stared out toward the cherry orchard, trying not to grin. "A certain fortress, which I don't wish damaged, holds out against me. Another fortress, in the vicinity and already mine, will rebel if its lord discovers I'm besieging the first."

"Why?" Ezzo said.

"People are strange." Frederick pinned his lips tight to hide laughter.

"I thought we were going to go mess around with the hawks."

"Threaten to destroy it all," Fulk said.

"I can't—the fort would defy me out of principle. I think it believes I'll value it more if I have to work to win it."

"Better you destroy it than anybody else have it against your will," Ezzo said.

"Maybe. But there are certain interesting art works in it that I want to add to my collection."

Fulk said, "I didn't know you had such a collection." He leaned his back against the railing, on the opposite side of Frederick from Ezzo, and frowned.

"I'm starting one. A sustained siege, without using heavy offensive weapons, would certainly win me the fort, but in doing so I run the risk of the other finding out and causing trouble."

"Let's go mess with the hawks," Ezzo said.

"Gull the other fort in some way. A diversion." Fulk shook his head slightly, amazed.

"Do you know what he's talking about?" Ezzo said.

"I . . . might." Fulk's long brown face settled into an impassive stare. "Sire, command me more specifically."

"I accept your advice, Fulk. I want a diversion conducted against the fort already in my favor while I lay siege to the one I want."

Ezzo grumbled something. "What are you talking about?"

"Bianca Lancia," Fulk murmured.

Frederick laughed.

"Oho." Ezzo slapped his hands on the railing. "Art works, hunh? Collection? You already have one. Why don't you just order her?"

Frederick looked up at the swallows' nest in the arch. "Ezzo, it's more complex than that."

"Adelaide," Fulk said. "Didn't I hear that Adelaide is taking Bianca around with her, to keep the child from the paths of wickedness?"

"Yes." Frederick's eyes remained on the swallows' nest.

Ezzo guffawed. "Look. Bianca is my ward. Let me talk to her."

"Jesus," Fulk said. "You'd turn it into a parley of arms. This is a question of love, Ezzo, you ass."

Frederick said, "Fulk, you're a widower, why don't—"

"Oh, no," Fulk said. "Not either. If I married Bianca, I'd insist on rights, and Adelaide's too bitchy."

"Fulk. After all I've done for you."

"No, Sire."

"Let's go mess with the hawks," Ezzo said.

"Not until we settle this."

Fulk said, "Let Ezzo woo Adelaide. Not obviously, but enough to keep her diverted while you sweet-talk Bianca."

Frederick glanced doubtfully at Ezzo. "Well?"

"Fine with me. Ippolita has been after me to get another mistress anyway, ever since Elena left. She says when I'm home so much I'm a nuisance."

"Be circumspect. If she thinks I know about it she'll figure everything out."

Ezzo laughed.

"Is His Majesty planning to return to Barletta today?" Simone asked Hasan. Looking across the mews to the door, Frederick saw Hasan shrug, glance out the window, and make a mild face. Frederick laughed, looking back at the hawk on the high perch, and pulled his glove tight.

"She's going to be beautiful. Dark-brown peregrines are better than gerfalcons. See to the jesses." He held out his fist to the young hawk. "Come along, pretty baby, come to your old man."

Behind him Hasan muffled a laugh.

The young hawk stepped onto his fist, her talons hooked like scimitars; her dark plumage shone even in the uncertain light of the mews. Reddish bars marked her tail. Frederick took a scrap of meat from the Saracen falconer standing beside him and rubbed it quickly and lightly over the hawk's feet, breast, and beak, and she snapped the meat out of his fingers.

"You're not supposed to feed them in the afternoon," the Saracen muttered.

"I want her to love me."

The peregrine filled him with pleasure—even with her eyes seeled she was alert and fierce on his fist, but calm.

Grave, he thought, and right away knew that was wrong, but he couldn't find the right word and gave up immediately. "What am I going to call you, pretty baby?"

"Lord," Hasan said, "it's going to rain, probably. If you want to return to the palace—"

Frederick turned and glared at him and went back to talking to the peregrine, getting her used to his voice. Her head turned toward his face, and he murmured, "You're going to be a beauty, and a good hunter too."

"Do you want to try for cranes before the season's over?" Simone said.

"No." Frederick put the peregrine back on her perch, and the Saracen hooked up her jesses again. "The season's too short; if one of the hawks got hurt we'd have to mew her again and she'd stay out of action too long. Hasan, let's go."

Hasan sighed and pushed himself away from the wall he'd been leaning on—his arms came unfolded. "We're going to get caught in the wet."

"Maybe." Frederick went ahead of him out of the mews and ran down the circling staircase; the falconers thundered after him like a small avalanche. The guard on the door yanked it open, and he walked out into the courtyard. The raw wind struck his face. Over the far keep the clouds shoved up across the sky, dark gray and mountainous. Hasan was right: they were going to get rained on. A groom trotted out, leading Dragon by the bridle.

"Someday—whoa, you—" He grabbed the reins and stepped up into his saddle. "Someday I'm going to build a hunting lodge that—whoa, Dragon." The black horse half reared and wheeled to the right, snorting. Clattering on the wide stones of the courtyard, the Saracens' white mares surrounded him in a loose circle. Frederick looked up at the walls around him. He'd been sketching plans for a hunting lodge for nearly a year—octagonal, with an enclosed courtyard. Beyond the dark red stone of the walls around him the clouds looked nearly blue. The gate rose with a long squeal of the winch.

"We can stop in Crane Bay if the rain bothers you," he said to Hasan, and walked his horse out the gate; the Saracens drew back to let him through the narrow archway. The road wound off across the macchia toward the marshes near the sea. The wind made furrows in the tall, sere grass, and the air smelled of rain to come. Hasan jogged up to take his place on Frederick's right.

"Build a hunting lodge like the one at Lucera," Hasan said.

"No. This one's different." Twisting, he looked back at the lodge behind them—too small, too ugly, with its low walls and squat red keeps; wild hawks nested on the wide ledges of some windows, ignoring the men who lived and worked there, the dozens of trained falcons in the mews, the doves and pigeons kept for the falcons' food in the lower rooms. "I'll show you the plan sometime."

"When are you going to build it?"

"When I have the money and the leisure. Never. Come on." He kicked Dragon into a lope.

The first huge drops of rain splattered the horses' necks, and the wind roared. Steadily the even rhythm of the horses' hoofs increased. Dragon ducked his head—he hated being ridden into the rain. Reaching behind him, Frederick pulled his hood up and got it over his head, all that fur snug around his ears. They were coming up to the bridge, and the Saracens rearranged themselves into a file with him in the middle. Frederick reined his horse down a little. The thud of hoofs changed abruptly into a booming when Masuf rode onto the bridge, and Dragon nearly shied off.

Over the low rail Frederick saw the clear stream beneath the bridge bubble with the rain, the pebbles on the bottom obscured by a thousand ripples. He looked up at the sky and the rain got into his eyes and pelted on his cheeks. The rain was coming down harder, the drops smaller, stinging and cold. He shouted to Hasan and pointed across the marsh toward Crane Bay.

Hasan nodded. They let the horses stretch out into a fast canter, keeping to the high side of the road. The macchia grass turned to the rougher, darker foliage of the marsh. Ahead, the road forked, the main branch keeping to the drier ground that headed for Barletta, and the small trail off half buried in marsh grass and weeds. Hasan yelled to Masuf to take the little trail. All the horses strained stubbornly toward the Barletta road; Frederick heard a whip hiss behind him, and he had to snap his rein to keep Dragon straight. The big horse settled sulkily into a cross-canter in retaliation. They raced beneath a row of cypresses and around the edge of a salt pond, while the wind lashed the rain against them like a veil, and burst into the meadow behind Crane Bay. Frederick headed straight for the lean-to—he had no intention of walking through the heavy grass and getting his feet wet—and Hasan followed to hold his horse when he dismounted.

"Hurry, it's cold out here." Frederick ducked under the eaves of the lean-to and into the dark beyond.

He'd ordered this place built in his first year back from Germany, before he'd made the lodge out on the plain, and although this one stank and the floor was rotting, he still preferred coming here during a hunt to going all the way back to the other. In the dim light he stumbled over a stool, barked his shin, and nearly fell. Limping, he found a chair and sat down in it.

"Fah," Hasan said, stamping in. "It's solid mud out there. Shall I light lamps?"

"Yes." Frederick was rubbing his shin. "And get me something to drink."

The others came in—Ayub and Yusuf were teasing Masuf again; he'd forgotten something. Masuf was new and hadn't learned all the rules and tricks yet, and he

teased well. The others could drive him into fits in a matter of moments. Frederick stretched out in the chair, and
without letting up his running chatter to Masuf, Ayub
kicked a stool accurately over so that Frederick could
put his feet on it.

"The whole younger generation has no sense of the
rightness of rules. Masuf, someday you'll come to appre-
ciate—"

"Yes. Yes. Yes." Masuf flung off his cloak. "But not
now, Ayub my uncle. No, I—" He took a splinter from
Hasan and lit a small lamp. Simultaneously Hasan
trimmed the bigger one in the back, and warm yellow
light spread through the lean-to. Outside everything was
gray and misty, and water ran in sheets off the eaves into
the puddles in the mud below.

"Masuf," Hasan yelled. "Will you please pay attention
and find the cups?" He sank down on his heels next to
Frederick. "These boys refuse training, Lord. You must
excuse Masuf his—"

"Hasan," Masuf said. "You are the kindest and most
noble of instructors, the father of my devotion to the
Emperor, and I would never consider saying anything
against you. But."

Hasan had a wine cask and was working up the bung.
"Yes, my child?"

"Forget it." Masuf opened the cabinet with the cups
inside.

Fredrick laughed. The lamplight made shadows along
the far wall, past the rows of wine casks and the chests of
clean clothes. "That peregrine is lovely, isn't she?"

"She's huge." Yusuf and Ayub sat down on the other
side of him. Yusuf looked over his shoulder at Masuf,
who had brought only one cup. "What are you doing,
boy? Are we to drink out of our hands?"

Masuf went back to the cabinet. "How many of you
are breaking the law of God?"

"Zeal," Yusuf said. "Zeal as well. What a mix."

"All of us," Ayub called. He sniffed the wine. "Ah. It's the San Pietro again."

Dumping three of the wooden cups on the floor, Masuf handed the other to Hasan. "Listen to it rain."

"Don't you drink, Masuf?" Frederick said.

"Lord," Hasan said, "he does nothing that fits a man, and all the things that fit a boy, whereby you can immediately tell that he is still a child. Deduction." He raised one forefinger in the fabled gesture of the sage and dipped out a cupful of the wine, sipped it, and held it up to Frederick.

"I do all the things that fit a true believer," Masuf said. "None of those that fit a damned soul. Deduction."

"Ridiculous. Ridiculous." Hasan filled a cup, dunked the tip of his little finger into the wine, and shook off a drop. "Boy, God said no man should touch a drop of wine. That drop."

Frederick said, "Am I a damned soul, Masuf?"

"Of course." Masuf looked mildly surprised. "You are an unbeliever, however wise and noble and kind and—"

"Lovable," Frederick murmured.

Hasan shoved Masuf roughly. "Boy, you learned all your faith from books."

Ayub and Yusuf were drinking, their heads thrown back. Frederick listened a moment to the drumming of the rain on the roof and grinned. There was nothing better than this, to sit like this and talk and drink. Masuf said, "How else am I to learn faith except from wise men who write books?"

Hasan laughed and clapped his hands. "That only shows your youth, boy, for hasn't it been said that faith makes equal wisdom and folly?"

"Just consider, Masuf," Frederick said. "If the men who made books were all wise, none would try to make a law against drinking wine, because people will only break it, which weakens respect for the law."

Masuf frowned. "That law wasn't written in a book

but given to Mohammed by God Himself as revealed truth."

"Mohammed wasn't hearing well that day," Ayub said. "Here, Masuf, how can you condemn what you haven't even tried?"

"The drinking of wine leads to further wickedness," Masuf said.

"So does being born," Hasan said. "Lord, are you—"

"More." Frederick handed him the cup. "What if everybody in Sicily grew nothing but oranges?"

Ayub yelped. "Excellent."

Hasan gave Frederick his second cup of wine and dipped out another for himself. "Besides, Masuf, wine"— he flicked out a drop—"wine soothes the mind and induces it to deep thoughts, to self-discovery and meditation on many subjects."

"I'm sorry, Hasan, I was still contemplating oranges." Masuf stretched out on the floor, grinning.

Frederick said, "Well, Masuf, just think of it this way. A rule against drinking is a small matter compared to a law against murder, isn't it?"

"All our transgressions are equally vile in the sight of God."

Hasan snorted. "By the Compassionate and Infinitely Loving God. What a tedious life you must live."

Ayub muttered, "I don't notice us sneaking out at night into harems and dicing our days away."

"The point is," Frederick said, "that if you break a small law and break it often, you won't be tempted into one tremendous crime. Besides, just think, Masuf, what amazement we will cause, when, having sampled every conceivable vice and authored every conceivable sin, we return to righteousness. Think what models we will be to youth when we choose of our own will the path of right and good after exposing ourselves to all possible corruption." He gulped wine, and his head began to spin, and the flickering lamplight threw strange moving shapes before his eyes. "Hasan. This wine is strong."

"Well," Masuf said, "when are you going to—"

"Wait," Hasan said. "Wait. We haven't as yet investigated all the possibilities of sin."

Ayub laughed. "Don't argue with them, Masuf, believe me. They transcend logic."

"God never really intended to outlaw wine," Hasan said dreamily. "He just did it to keep up His credit in certain circles, but we know what He meant."

"That's what I mean," Ayub said.

"Well, damn it," Frederick said, "everything that's amusing and worth doing is a sin, according to people like him." He stabbed his chin at Masuf. "Everything that's good for you on earth is bad for you in heaven, which is ridiculous—they can't be that far apart."

Masuf said mildly, "Nothing is possible save by the will of God, Lord. Isn't that so?"

"Definitely," Hasan said. "And if God didn't will it, grapes wouldn't ferment into wine. And God does not will the wasting of the earth, so clearly He meant it to be drunk." He flung his arms out. "We are truly selfless. We drunks are the only altruists. For behold, Masuf, don't we fill you with the warmth of satisfaction and the glow of righteousness?"

"You fill me with pity and horror," Masuf said, "—when I can keep up with your thinking."

"You pompous ass," Frederick murmured.

"Not toward you, Lord," Masuf said hastily. "Toward Hasan, because he could yet be returned to the truth and light of submission to God."

"I could always be converted," Frederick said. He began to feel injured; the warmth and confusion of being drunk flooded him.

"Never," Masuf said positively. "Lord, I mean no offense, but even in my short experience in your bodyguard I have come to the conclusion that the loudmouths in the churches of the north are absolutely right, and you are willfully incorrigible." He grinned. "But I don't hold that against you, Lord."

"I'm honored."

Hasan filled his and Frederick's cups for the third time. "Consider, then, Masuf. I am the servant of the Lord Frederick, and what sort of servant would I be to make of myself a paragon of virtue and faith when he is in such a sad and irredeemable state of sin? God urges compassion on us all, Masuf."

"You shall be forgiven as you forgive others," Frederick said. "Here we are, providing you with the most marvelous opportunity to store up treasure in heaven, and you keep trying to make us your rivals instead of your allies. God, Jesus, Hasan, think of what good we're doing! I never thought of that, I never did."

Hasan laughed; his arms hung limp over his knees, and his voice was unsteady. Yusuf went quietly off into the darkness and came back with a guitarra, and sitting down, began to play softly.

"I forgive you all every day at least sixty times," Masuf said.

"Thank you," Hasan said, and shut his eyes. His shoulder touched Frederick's knee. "I might even mean it—I'm not sure."

The complex, ringing chords of Yusuf's song mingled with the rustle of the rain and the heavier splashes of the water running off the eaves. Frederick put his head back. "Is it stopping?"

"No," Ayub said. "It's just getting harder, and it's very steady."

"I think we're going to have to get wet."

Hasan shook himself. "There's a big cloak in the chest, Lord."

"Get it, then."

The Saracens drew themselves quietly to their feet and went off in different directions; Masuf carried the cups out and washed them, and Yusuf and Ayub put the wine back and straightened up the lean-to. Carrying the big cloak in his arms, Hasan came over to Frederick and stood waiting. Frederick lay still a moment, hating the idea of action. Opening one eye, he looked up and grinned at Hasan, who laughed. When he'd smothered a yawn, Frederick stood up and let Hasan drape the cloak over him; he fastened it with a clip the size of his hand. Ayub and Yusuf had already gone to get the horses.

While Hasan teased Masuf and put out the lamps, Frederick drifted up to the front of the lean-to. Stooping a little, he could see past the eaves and the wall to the fringe of tall salt grass and cattails, bending in the wind, at the edge of Crane Bay. On the tiny strip of beach the surf beat into foam, and the silver rain hung down over everything. It was a miserable day. Ayub brought up Dragon, and Hasan went to hold him; wrapping the cloak around himself, Frederick stepped out into the rain.

The Archbishop said, "Sire, the time is now."

"Al-Mu'azzam is dead." He sat curled up on the cushions and let Corso and Marco scrub his skin with warmed towels until it tingled. "The whole situation is changed."

"Even so." The Archbishop strode energetically around the room. "The Moslim world is riven and in trouble. Not for years have they been so amenable to conversation with Christians. If they ever mend their differences, or if, as seems more likely, al-Kamil defeats his nephew en-Nasr and his brother al-Ashraf, both—"

"Al-Kamil is my friend. He says so." Frederick struggled one arm out of the towels and tapped the pile of letters in front of him on the stool. "Sit, if you wish." He flipped through the sheaf of paper, looking for the scratch sheets on the problem in algebra he'd sent al-Kamil's mathematicians. They hadn't solved it either. "Did you see Dawud?"

The Archbishop smiled. "Fakhr-ad-Din."

"Yes."

"He asked me to give you his best and friendliest regards and once again thanks you for entertaining him so well when he was in Sicily."

Frederick smiled, his eyes on al-Kamil's letter. "He entertained me." Fakhr-ad-Din Dawud ibn es-Shaikh was an emir and a scholar and endlessly fun to talk to. Corso draped a towel around his head over his wet hair and left.

"Al-Kamil was most . . . charming. And now he does hold Jerusalem," the Archbishop said. "He dislikes war, although he's a pretty good general."

"I'm not." Frederick pulled a packet of folded vellum out of the mass of papers. "What's this?"

"A private letter." The Archbishop sank down on a stool. "You'll note that it's in Arabic and the seals are unbroken."

Frederick reached for a knife. "Dear me, Berardo, if the seals are unbroken, how do you know it's in Arabic?"

"I asked."

"You looked. Pardon me a moment."

"Of course."

The Archbishop spoke some Arabic but read none. Frederick slit the seals and unfolded the heavy parchment. On the top, taking up one fourth the first page, was al-Kamil's ideograph in gilt and red ink, and all down one margin ran a verse from the Qur'an.

"In the name of Allah the Most Compassionate, the all-Merciful, the all-Just, the all-Conquering, the Lord Who is One, Who is All, to the Unbeliever Frederick al-Malik Hohenstaufen Sultan ibn Sultan—"

That summed it up neatly enough. Reading through the rest of the superscription, he reached out and got a towel and dried his hair. Al-Kamil addressed him by all his titles except that of King of Jerusalem. Roumi Sultan. Interesting; few Moslims quibbled over the legality of the Iron Crown, but al-Kamil more than most cared about detail and the subtle weight of phrasing. The next two blocks of writing covered the vital areas of his and al-Kamil's health.

"Coming to that which in friendship we have much discussed—"

"Hunh!"

"Sire?"

"He must have pat phrases, like mine, but do they have to sound like a schoolboy's?"

"Of course not, Sire." The Archbishop was a born diplomat.

The letter went on, "Let us not pose as our forefathers, whose devotion led them in ways more stern and frightful than those avenues now by the benevolence of Allah open to us. The world changes, drawing near the Final Reckoning, and with it change the ways by which wise men meet their problems."

Oh, really? Pages came in with fresh clothes for him; Corso filled a brazier with coals and stirred them up. The Archbishop glanced at Frederick for permission, smiling, and sent a page after wine.

"What is conquest but Allah's curse on the insatiable, who must trudge from battlefield to battlefield, without respite, without even the glory of final victory, but only the infernal pangs of endless desire endlessly unfulfilled? To discipline what is our own is the highest earthly task."

Rhetoric. But it was conciliatory rhetoric. Gently the pages removed some of the towels that covered him and slipped him into clothes.

"Jerusalem the Holy need be a bane to neither of us. Yet I refrain from positive overtures, fearing as I do the rash and narrow spirits among the Christians. Know that for the love I bear you, Sultan, I would indulge whatever suggestions you might extend on this issue, but that I mistrust those who, like wolves against the tender doe, would raven at such rational and proper measures as we might agree upon."

Give with one hand, take back with the other, and of course the implication that Frederick couldn't control his own people would delight a Kurd. He smelled cooked meat and glanced up to see the pages offering the Archbishop a tray of tiny meat pies.

Corso yelped at the pages and they whirled and thrust the tray at Frederick. He grabbed a handful of the little pastries. They were hot, and he dropped them onto a towel and ate one, standing up so that they could get him dressed.

"Concerning that which we discussed before—"

He glanced around at the first sheet, frowned, and went on. "You recall how strenuously I warned you, Sultan, against certain beasts from the desert east of Khwaresm. My information is that the terror has died, stuffed full of foul victories. Yet am I reluctant to think the peril is over. It pleases me you recognize that against this thing we are as one, the Drawn Swords of the cultured world."

The silver-tongues of the West, rather. That was the Tartar King in Greater Asia. Prester John. The more threats pressuring the Muslims, the more liable al-Kamil would be to give up advantages in return for pledges of support and peace. This Tartar, Ghenghis Khan, a French scholastic had called King David, master of the legions of the Lord returning. Except that, if al-Kamil's description of the Tartars were at all true, the Lord was working His wonders in mysterious ways again. The Archbishop had finished his pastries and was shaking crumbs off his lap. Frederick dropped the letter and put on his coat and a page handed him the letter again.

"Much do I welcome your embassies, Sultan, not even so much for their immediate news as for the assurance that between you and me some conversation can continue, even while the wild dogs howl against us both and the swine pollute the holy ground of Islam. Content and humble in your friendship, let me offer the modest advantages of my own."

"Well."

"What did he say?" the Archbishop asked.

"Nothing, but he said it so pleasantly." Corso brought over a chair and he sat down. The boy was still flushed from the mix-up with the pies. Frederick handed him the letter. "Take this yourself to Judah ben Daud and tell him to copy out the relevant passages about the Tartars and stick them in with the other information."

"Sire."

"Tell me about Khwaresm," Frederick said to the Archbishop.

"Well. Since the Tartar invasion and the death of Mohammed Shah, Jelal-ad-Din, Mohammed's son, has been consolidating power among the younger nobility. He's in firm control. They're still, naturally, suffering the aftereffects of the war. They're disorganized, and a number of the hill tribes have refused to acknowledge the sovereignty of the royal house. Jelal-ad-Din is busy bringing them back into line. All their major cities and fortresses in the north were destroyed, but the area to the southwest remains intact. Their control of Baghdad and the Caliph is unopposed. My information is that they're starting to put pressure on al-Ashraf and en-Nasr to accept their suzerainty and acknowledge the Caliph and all that. Jelal-ad-Din will not be free to move west for another year at the least, and al-Ashraf is a tricky fighter, but en-Nasr is weak, and of course with al-Kamil and al-Ashraf both trying to take Damascus from him, God knows what he'll do."

Frederick put his feet up on a stool. It seemed impossible that Khwaresm had recovered so quickly from the Tartar war. "How liable are the Tartars to come back and finish the job?"

"Very liable, in time. But . . . I have the impression

that they're busy elsewhere." The Archbishop frowned and put his fingers to his chin. "There's more east of Khwaresm than anybody thought. Other peoples, other kingdoms—the Tartars are busy conquering their eastern flank, I'm told. Their King was in the east when he died." He straightened up, smiling. "It may be hard to grasp, but the impression I have is that to the Tartars Khwaresm and Syria may be so far west that they can forget about them very easily. Khwaresm is the periphery of their world. I might add that this is not the impression of some of my colleagues, notably the embassies of the Greeks of Nicaea in Cairo and the envoys from Constantinople and Paris, all of whom firmly believe that from Khwaresm to the edge of the world is only a day's easy ride and the Tartars are waiting impatiently for an alliance with us before they attack again."

Frederick laughed. "Naturally, the center of the world is always their little kingdom, and they can't believe that the rest of the world doesn't have their concerns deeply to heart. I agree with you, from what I've heard. Is al-Kamil convinced?"

"Al-Kamil is sure he can beat Khwaresm, provided he doesn't have to contend with a Crusade at the same time."

"The Greeks at Nicaea. What are they doing?"

"Fuming a lot. Waiting. They've mended their friendships with everybody north of Lebanon and they're just waiting for Constantinople to make a mistake and let them back in again. Incidentally, they're madly fond of you. They're hoping that if John of Brienne is elected the guardian of the young Emperor, you'll fight him."

"He's a vicious old man, but it's not in my interests. How is al-Kamil doing against Damascus?"

"En-Nasr is cleverer than anybody thought. Al-Kamil won't take Damascus this year. Everything but, though. Al-Ashraf is a fool and can't stand to be one minute with al-Kamil. There's a letter from Tommaso d'Aquino, who knows more about that than I do."

"Good. Let me catch up on my reading and I'll see you tomorrow. When's the entry?"

"Tomorrow afternoon." The Archbishop stood and bowed. "I hope this rain stops—that elephant is more trouble than he's worth anyway."

Frederick threw his cloak off and sat on his heels under the pear tree. Down the walk on the far side of the hedge two young men came, talking, headed for the fountain. One of them said, "Well, it would be easy enough until you got caught, but I'd hate to have Marco refer me to Big Red." Their feet crunched on the pebbles and the sound diminished. Frederick grinned.

From the fountain came muffled cries and an occasional splash. Most of the young men and girls from the palace were taking advantage of the masque Ezzo was putting on in Adelaide's apartments, which would keep all the elders involved in their own rituals of sin, and the whole park teemed with midnight dinners, mad embraces and hunting games. He could hear them all the way to the pleasure house on the far side of the garden.

"Sire?" Bianca crawled under the branches of the pear tree, weighted down with blossoms.

Frederick said, "I'm right here. Did you give them a good excuse?"

She sank down beside him, her legs drawn up under her skirts, and pulled at her surcoat. "I told you, Sire, I cannot stay long. I said I was unwell and had to go to bed, and I must be there when my sisters go to our chambers."

"But you came." Frederick picked up her hand—she tried to pull it out of his grasp, but he held on, and she gave up right away.

"Well," she said, "it was a dull masque." She grinned.

"I think they're all dull, I hate routine." He held her hand between both of his, stroking her wrist and the backs of her fingers. "Why don't we go over to the pleasure house? We'd be much more comfortable." He hadn't kissed her yet. All this while he'd been so patient, plotting like a squire just to kiss her. He thought of yanking her into his lap.

"I told you, Sire, that I refuse to meet you under a roof alone. I do have to protect myself somehow." She lay down on her side in the short grass. "Don't I?"

"Not from me—why, I must be twice your age. My interests are entirely paternal."

He flopped down beside her and pulled gently at the ribbons on her surcoat, and she took them out of his hand.

"Just the same, Sire, a girl of my innocence must"—she giggled—"avoid inciting you."

Frederick hitched himself forward on his elbows and kissed her on the mouth. She made no attempt to elude him; after all the scheming it seemed ridiculously easy. Somebody else had been kissing her, and he began to get jealous. Lifting his head a little he said, "But I like being incited."

She shrugged awkwardly, her shoulders against the ground. "I'm sure you do. I'm just afraid I wouldn't be able to stop you, that's all." Her soft voice made it sound as if she wasn't sure she'd want to, and he wondered how much was flirtatiousness. Probably all of it. He kissed her again and tugged the ribbons gently loose.

"It's beautiful out here under a full moon," she said. "See?" Her eyes looked up into the pear blossoms, lit by moonlight.

"It's beautiful out here when you're here, and no other time."

She giggled again and pretended she didn't know her surcoat was open. Frederick ran the back of his hand over her cheek.

"You're so beautiful—you're going to be a beautiful woman, Biancetta, you're going to have every man in Italy hanging by his heels." He kissed her and slid his arm around her waist, and of course she stiffened up. Her hand rose to his shoulder and gave a little shove.

"What's wrong?"

She squirmed around and sat up, bracing herself on one arm. "You frighten me a little, that's all. Why don't you just want to kiss for a while?"

He rolled over on his back and stretched. "Because I want you. Not to kiss—I want you to sleep with me." He looked from the depths of the pear blossoms over his head to the white, heart-shaped blossom of her face. "That's a compliment, by the way."

"I know. But it does make me a little frightened, it's like . . ." She grinned. "You don't miss, do you?"

"Never." He laughed and stretched his hand up and took hold of her long, heavy hair. "I can make you very happy, Bianca."

That was the wrong approach. She frowned, and she tried to pull her head back out of reach. "Like Adelaide?"

"Let's not talk about Adelaide."

"She isn't happy now. Maybe at the beginning."

"I said—" He rolled over onto his stomach. "Let's not talk about Adelaide, who isn't you." He caught her by the shoulders. She began to struggle, at first mildly, but suddenly she was twisting in his arms, panicked. He let her go, and she sat still, staring at him.

"I don't want to hurt you. I don't want to frighten you. Biancetta—" He kissed her quickly. When he drew back and looked at her again she smiled and her eyes fell.

"I'm not a woman yet; you said so. I should go."

"In a little while. I'll walk you back."

She touched his hand. "Please, just—let me think it out. Let me decide."

"As long as you decide what I wish." He put his arms

around her and kissed her hard, and her head lay back in his arms, her mouth turned soft under his. "And soon."

The young ones around the fountain screamed and laughed, with splashes interspersed, and along the path beyond the hedges couples walked. Frederick laid Bianca back on the grass and kissed her thoroughly, his fingers curled in her hair. He shut his eyes; the earth beneath him seemed to tilt. Her arms were around his waist. Shifting his weight, he pressed himself full length against her, and she tensed again, resisting him again. It reminded him somehow of Anais, on his and Yolande's wedding night, only that time he'd been the one resisting; she'd surprised him, popping up in his bed like that. Kissing Bianca while thinking of Anais made him guilty. He licked his tongue over Bianca's lips and pressed his face against her hair.

"I could love you so well, Bianca."

Even before he'd said the word, he knew that it was the key. Beneath him her body relaxed, and when he went to kiss her again, she lifted her head to find his mouth. She probably didn't know yet, not with her mind. He moved his hand softly up her side. Her body said yes, but in her mind she probably wasn't sure yet. And he did have to get her back before her sisters came in from the masque. He rolled onto his side and pulled her surcoat away from her body. She caught his hand.

"I won't hurt you. I just want to kiss you." He thought of saying "love" to her again, but that would be overdoing it. "Just let me kiss you." He started to open her bodice, and her fingers tugged uncertainly at his hand. Bending down, he kissed her mouth while he undid the laces and pulled her gown off her shoulder. The pressure in his body mounted, driving him; he forced himself to go slowly, to be gentle, as if this were only casual, but when his hand touched her bare breast he couldn't help stabbing his tongue deep into her mouth. Her hands clutched his shoulders, but her body kept on saying yes. He kissed her throat and her collarbone and pressed his mouth against her breast. Against his tongue her nipple stood up hard, and one of her hands brushed his hair and held him against her. O God, he thought, I could have her now, right now, under this pear tree in the park. I want to, I want to, yes, now. He sat up, throwing his hair back.

"What's—"

"I'm proving my self-control tonight. No, don't." He caught her hand before she could herself. "Let me look —I like to look." Her small breast with its erect nipple made him tremble, and her gown was open low enough so that he could see the delicate skin of her belly, soft to lie on. She sat up, her eyes on his, her face strange and her mouth quivering, and with a quick movement stripped herself to the waist and held out her arms.

"You'll be angry in the morning." He thrust her down into the grass again and pressed his face against her breasts, lipping her skin.

"Maybe," she said. "Maybe I'll change my mind tonight."

He knelt and pulled off his shirt. "Let me know if you do." The branches hung down all around them like strange walls; anyone passing by would have to stoop to see under. The blossoms glowed in the moonlight. He thought quickly that she would never have been willing in the pleasure house. Against his bare skin her skin was warm and soft, and the texture of it changed beneath his fingers, turning silken. "What about your sisters?"

"I'll tell them"—her voice faltered—"I went for a walk."

In the morning they would all know, the entire court would know, but he didn't tell her that. Let her find out in the morning. Naked in the spring grass, with the pear blossoms perfuming the air, she couldn't meet his eyes, and a blush colored her throat and cheeks. When he stripped off his clothes she shut her eyes and turned her head away. She was shy, she was frightened, and he made himself go slowly. Quietly. In his arms she shivered; her mouth brushed timidly over his skin. Beyond the hedges a girl murmured, and a boy whispered cajolingly. Do it in the hedgerows, children. He kissed her thighs, and her flesh quivered. Do you still want to? Pressing against her, like a lance, and her body trembling, calling him, but her mind hesitating. Like limbo, swaying on the verge of . . . I can make you want to. She had pear blossoms tangled in her hair. Her hands moved lightly over his hips, and she whispered. "Yes, do it. Do it." With all his muscles aching with a sweet, dizzy agony he did it, as gently as he could. She was a virgin, but it came out all wrong—she only gasped, and he cried out.

The Grand Master had left Brindisi for Acre; the Archbishop had gone to Rieti to plead Frederick's case before the Pope and to find out all he could about the Pope's plans for Frederick's absence. Enrico had gathered up a little fleet and they were due to leave Brindisi a few days after the solstice, on a day Michael Scot had said would be the most propitious. Frederick took off his coat and unlaced the front of his shirt. It was hot and there was no wind.

Rinaldo of Spoleto had been running around frantically asking everybody for advice on how to defend Sicily, and Frederick hadn't even left yet. Somehow this whole Crusade thing had gotten out of control. He couldn't remember when he'd finally made up his mind, because as recently as two or three weeks before he'd still been saying, "If I go on crusade . . ." Gradually it had turned into "when."

"Papa," Enzio said, "come down and see the elephant with me."

Frederick looked down, startled—he hadn't seen the child come up. "Not now, Enzio. I'm thinking."

"But, Papa, you're going to be gone for so long."

Frederick turned and hugged him. "I know, sonny, and I'm going to miss you." He kissed the boy's neck just above his filthy collar. "But I've got a lot of things to do."

Enzio's arms wound tightly around his neck. "You can't even come down and look at the elephant?"

"No. I'm sorry. I'll see you tonight, before bedtime, and tell you a story."

"Oh. All right." Enzio kissed him. "Don't forget."

Frederick stood up. "I won't."

Enzio trotted down the gallery toward the stairs, past a couple of notaries returning to Piero's office from the chancery; at the head of the stairs Enzio turned and waved to Frederick. He waved back, grinning. Michael Scot came up the stairs past Enzio and turned to watch him run across the courtyard. The heat was enervating, and Frederick hoped Michael wasn't in the mood for conversation—it was so pleasant just to stand here, leaning against the wall, doing nothing.

"Sire," Scot said. "You ought to do something about Rinaldo. Nobody trusts him anymore."

"He'll be all right." Frederick kicked a chair around and sat down in it. "He just wants to make sure everybody knows he's important. Did you do Bianca's horoscope?"

"Yes." Scot perched on the railing next to the wisteria. "She's a wonderfully talented girl, very deep. Marvelous young person. It's wise of you to get a few fire signs into your circle—so many of your friends are earthy. And you're a Capricorn, of course."

"Unh-hunh."

"And I checked up on the time you'll be at sea. It ought to be good weather the whole time. A fair voyage."

"Damn. I was hoping for storms. I've never been in a storm at sea. Is Enrico back from Brindisi yet?"

"Not yet." Scot's eyebrows bounced gleefully. "He's

probably combing the harbor taverns for new pirate stories—that's his stock-in-trade. Between him and the
Grand Master we certainly do have a surfeit of
war stories."

"Don't make fun of them or I'll make fun of you. You
know Hermann isn't fair game. Did you check on—"

He looked toward the railing. Somebody had ridden
in, and down in the courtyard people were starting to
shout and laugh. "What's that?"

Suddenly a cheer went up; Scot pretended to be
knocked off the rail by the force of it. He looked down.
"It's a courier in the livery of the Empress." He spun
around. "Sire—"

Frederick lunged up and leaned over the railing. The
courtyard was filling up with people—servants, pages—
milling and waving their arms. The courier rode his
horse through the mob to just below Frederick. His face
was coated with dust, but he was beaming. In the town a
bell began to ring.

"Sire," the messenger called. "Your Majesty, the
Empress has been delivered of a fine boy."

Frederick threw his head back and whooped. "A
boy!" He grabbed Scot and whirled him around into the
crowd of courtiers, all bursting with congratulations.
The other bells of Barletta began to toll, and in the
courtyard the cheering had doubled. Pages appeared on
the gallery with ewers of wine. Ezzo plunged up, flung
both arms around Frederick, and kissed him on both
cheeks.

"Conrad," Frederick said, "I'll call him Conrad." He
took a deep breath—his chest strained to hold in his deep
pleasure. Another son. Abruptly he flung his arms wide
and started laughing, and all the faces watching him began
to laugh too. Fulk of Ancerra thrust a wine cup at him.

"To Conrad."

"To the King of Jerusalem," Frederick said. "Long
may he reign." He gulped wine. Adelaide and Bianca ap-

peared at exactly the same moment, but on opposite sides, and he straightened. Which to go to first? The wine pitcher came by again and he reached for it. Everybody was screaming Conrad's name and drinking toasts.

Piero suddenly showed up, weaving his way through the mob, his face set and tight. Frederick paused, his cup halfway to his mouth. Something—Piero came up, took him by the sleeve, and turned him slightly away from the others.

"Sire, the child is healthy, but the Empress is not. The courier says she may be dying."

Frederick stared at him. Dying. The bells and the cheers rang out like tin. His eyes left Piero for the joyous faces of the courtiers around him; he shivered and looked back to Piero. That noncommital brown face—He turned and pushed his way through the mob toward the door, shoving blindly at the people in his path. They moved, and he stepped into the cool dark of an empty room.

"Are you going to Andria?" Piero said, behind him.

Frederick nodded. "Get me a riding coat and order out the Saracens and my horse. Dragon."

"I've done so, Sire. They're at the South Gate."

"Oh." The walls muffled the noise outside, that barbaric cheering. She was only seventeen, she couldn't be dying. Pages appeared, and numbly he let them change his clothes. I don't like people to die. That's stupid. Everybody dies. Half into his coat, he turned and plunged across the room toward the door.

Ayub was waiting for him at the foot of the stairs, dressed for riding; he fell in behind him without a word. Immediately Yusuf appeared and walked along in front of Frederick. The hall was empty, and even the sentries were gone from the door. Out reveling. The Saracens went up to hold the door for him, and he walked out into an empty courtyard. Dimly he heard the continuing jubilee—of course, a new heir, a son, a King, everything.

. . . Hasan led up the horses and he vaulted into his saddle.

"Lord," Hasan said, "we of Lucera—" He studied Frederick's face and shrugged. "Later." Turning his mare, he headed for the gate, and Dragon followed without Frederick's urging.

She never asked to be . . . He shut his eyes. Ridiculous to be this upset about the dying of one small girl who had never been anything at all to him—no comfort, no pleasure, only a girl always too thin and too pale who complained all the time. They rode swiftly through the edge of the town, past squares full of rejoicing people, and out onto the high road to Andria. None of the people seemed to notice them. Why am I—How can something like this even reach me? But his chest constricted and his heart beat painfully, out of rhythm with the strides of the horse.

Piero knew I would be going to see her. It must be predictable somehow. Even by Piero. Amazing; I never thought he had any imagination at all. He'd thought that he knew Piero well enough to anticipate everything he did, but this . . . I don't know him at all. He knew I didn't like her. She is so young.

The Saracens ranged themselves around him. At a steady canter they headed west, across the macchia already burning to brown under the April sun. Merchants' carts and riders appeared ahead of them and pulled hastily out of their way. Sometimes the horses' hoofs all beat together, separating gradually out into disorder again. I killed her; I made her pregnant. The triple beat of the horses' hoofs lulled him.

They topped a little rise. Ahead of them the broad plain stretched monotonously, a haze of cloud on the far horizon. Behind them he could still hear the bells of Barletta. Conrad, Conrad. He licked his lips and tasted the acrid dust of the plain.

She'd always preferred Andria; she said she liked the

people there. Never asked her which people. I wonder
if . . . But she never liked me either.

The sun went down before them. He thought that the
unrelenting beat of the hoofs and the glaring light in his
eyes would drive him out of his mind, but each time the
pressure built up through his body he took a deep breath
and bit his lips and it subsided. They raced a party of
peasant boys and girls to a narrow stone bridge, and the
clatter of the stones mingled with the screams and excited chatter of the peasants. Their voices faded away
into the dust. Moving this fast nothing is real, everything
goes by too quickly, it's all somewhere else, not here—I
don't know what that means. He tightened his grip on
the reins and let Dragon carry him on into the dark.

I don't want to die. Maybe that's all it is, this feeling.

A little while later Hasan made him stop and change
horses, walk around, drink some watered wine and eat.
He felt encased in himself, in layers of insensitive flesh;
they couldn't touch him or he them, and everything
sounded distant. Uninteresting. But I have another son,
isn't that enough? He looked up at the sky, more stars
than darkness, clear and bright. The new horse appeared
before him, and he dropped the cup and stepped into his
saddle.

They found that rhythm again. Poor little girl. Poor
little girl. Hasan was carrying a torch, bright yellow
light in front of him. There's something wrong with me
if I can't . . . The pressure surged up in him again,
something he had to outride, but could not because it was
trapped in his body. My soul. Bianca is young too; if I
get her pregnant, will she die? They cantered through a
tiny village, all shut down for the night. Anais will be
there too. The moon rose, aged to a sliver. He smelled
the dust and the odor of sweating horses.

They all die—my mother, Franciscus, everybody. My
dog Kadar. Diepold poisoned him because he barked.
Constanza died. And go to Heaven and there sit. Yes,

well, it's not so bad. But it is. He shut his eyes, and the world spun around him, swooping in great sickening loops around him.

Still later Hasan stopped again, and they all stretched their legs. Frederick put up his hood and bundled his cloak around him. Let no one see me. Fugitive or something. Am I really or just . . . I must be guilty, that's all, it's not anything more than that. But he thought of Yolande and bit his lip. Turning, he reached for his reins and climbed onto the horse's back and started off again, so that the Saracens had to jump to catch up.

Ahead of them, on the level plain, a light showed: the lantern in the bell tower of San Andria. He straightened up and discovered that his back hurt. He'd been crouched over in his saddle, bent in on himself. The palace stood just this side of the little town—looking hard, he could see the square outlines of its towers. No lights there; they'd all be in bed or praying in the chapel for her recovery or happy death. Happy death. Or they could be watching over her. No bells ringing, no sounds of celebration. I am too late, naturally. No time for deathbed forgiveness or long speeches, that's only in the songs. He slowed his horse to a trot to cross the little wooden bridge before the gate.

Hasan shouted; sentries on the wall shouted back. In the midst of the noise Frederick drew his cloak tighter around him. Let no one see me. Why not, why not? His horse started forward, and he followed Hasan into the courtyard. Feet clattered along the ramparts over their heads. In the central building lights burned dimly behind shutters. She always closed the windows at night, she said the night air . . . Easy to remember everything she ever said, we were never together that long. Always with somebody else there. Your Majesty, Your Majesty, yes, Sire, my Lady. Grooms came to take the horses, and he dismounted. Old Tancred, the chatelain, walked across the paving stones toward him. Frederick threw his hood off, and Hasan moved closer with the torch.

"Your Majesty." Tancred knelt and rose again. "You have my congratulations on the birth of your son and my condolences on the death of the Empress."

His stomach contracted hard against his spine. She was dead, she had died. Always a chance that maybe—He took a blind step forward. Tancred's face, expressionless, moved before him. "She lies in the chapel, Sire."

"Thank you." He could barely hear his own voice. He turned left, and Hasan nudged him lightly. Oh, yes, it was straight ahead. He signed to the Saracens to stay behind and walked alone across the courtyard to the chapel door.

Through the cracks he saw light flickering, and he heard voices, the dry old voices of women. They brought you into the world and they saw you out of it, the women. He heaved open the door and went inside.

Down there, before the high gilt altar, shapes rustled and stirred and faced him, all gathered around the block of marble. He made his legs move, carrying him down there. Lying there, Yolande looked much younger, much thinner, her arms like wax candles, her hair dull.

"We wondered if you would come," Anais said in French, and the women murmured and shifted. He glanced at her, amazed she would even speak, and went on toward the slab.

"Did you come to see the child or her?"

He jerked his head around. Leaning forward, her lips drawn back from her teeth, she stared at him: "Did you come—"

"Leave me."

For a moment she met his eyes. His low voice echoed in his ears. Suddenly she turned and walked out, holding up her skirts in both hands, and the other women murmured in something like applause and made faces at her back. He swung his gaze across them and back to the woman on the—the child on the slab. Excommunicate, will it make a difference if I pray or not? His joints ached with weariness and his hands shook, and exhausted, he sank down on his knees and laid his cheek against the stone at her feet.

The baby's face worked; a line of milk lay at the corner of his mouth. He moved his arms and legs strongly inside the monogrammed silk. Frederick looked around for a nurse to take him, and the girl from the village came forward, her arms out.

"He's a pretty baby," she said.

"They all are," the Duchess of Chiara said. "Especially the redheads."

Frederick looked doubtfully at the baby. It looked too big to have come so recently from the body he'd just seen carried into the mausoleum under the chapel. All the women around made him nervous. He turned to the Duchess, who was waiting eagerly for instructions.

"He'll have to be christened while I'm gone. Piero della Vigne will arrange for that, he'll be in touch with you. The city of Cremona will be his godmother. Don't worry about having him crowned—that won't be necessary for a while. He'll need a court and a personal staff—" For an infant? For a King of Jerusalem. "I'll send the Archbishop of Capua here to discuss that with you."

He looked around at the baby. The serving women were cooing over it, their heads bent. Sunshine poured through the wide windows of the nursery—he'd made them open the shutters.

"Is he to remain here, Your Majesty?"

"For the love of Christ. You don't cart a new-born baby all over the countryside. Yes. Andria belonged to the Empress anyhow." Impatience rose up in him. He wanted to go back to Barletta, now, without any more of this—He started toward the door, and Ayub moved to open it.

"Your Majesty."

The door opposite this one had opened and a flock of women entered. He stopped and stared. Clinging to the skirts of the tall woman in the middle of the herd was a small girl in a yellow dress, her long hair tortured into a French style, her eyes swollen and red.

"Your Majesty," the tall woman said and bowed. The little girl hid her face in the woman's skirts. Frederick licked his lips.

"Yolande," the tall nurse said, "go greet His Majesty your father."

Frederick tensed all over. The little girl peeked out, saw him, and hid her face. He said, "That's unnecessary, I'm—"

"Yolande?" the nurse said, ignoring him completely. "Come greet His Majesty."

The child turned, white as ash, and started stiff-legged toward him. Frederick drew a deep breath. The little girl didn't look at him, her eyes were aimed somewhere around his knees, and she moved like a puppet, ungainly. Halfway between him and the women she stopped, jerked out a curtsey, and said, "Good morning, Your Majesty," in stilted Italian. Naturally; her mother had spoken only French.

"Good morning, Yolande," he said in French.

The child looked up, startled, and he made himself grin and nod. She curtseyed again and whirled and raced for the shelter of the nurse's skirts. Over in the corner her little brother let out a howl.

"Unh—keep her here too," Frederick said to the Duchess and spun on his heel and strode out of the room.

Hasan was waiting for him in the porch, and the horses were ready. Frederick paused, looking out at the dusty courtyard, the parade of mourners still entering the chapel to pray. "Is there anything else?"

"No, Lord."

"Then let's get out of here."

* * *

From the dais beside the throne he could see how the court moved in currents and whorls, in clumps surrounding the people known to be his favorites. He paused a moment, juggling the new augustales lightly in his fingers, and watched the people hovering around Adelaide, up close to the dais, packed in by her maids. Used to it, she sent them on errands, to fetch her cups of wine and trays of sweetmeats, but she didn't smile; her haggard eyes kept looking for him. He smiled at her and lifted his hand and pretended to look at the plans spread over the table.

"To add a wing here, Your Majesty, we would have to knock out this wall. There is plenty of stone available, of course. , . ."

Yes, yes. He glanced down the far end of the hall, toward the giant columns supporting that end of the balcony, around which all the young courtiers swarmed. The music of a lute and guitarras played among them. Bianca, less than expert, kept them all in no order, and the bright colors of their clothes churned in a constant jostling. She will learn. She'd been shaken to find herself suddenly the center of attention.

"Manfredo, knock out that wall so we can add on a wing there."

Her brother looked up and nodded, all somber in mourning black for the Empress. That was how they knew, when he gave small honors to her brother, her sisters, two of whom were now attending the King of Jerusalem. He glanced toward Bianca again. He hadn't slept with her since the first time—the memory of Yolande dead dragged at him and made him nervous. Stepping back, he looked all around, at the mob around Adelaide, the people encircling Ezzo and Fulk. Corso was coming toward him, all solemn.

"Sire—" The page trotted up the steps of the dais and

cut in neatly between Frederick and the architects. "The Grand Admiral has arrived, Sire, if you please."

"Where?" Frederick put down the coins.

"In the Peacock Room."

Frederick nodded and turned to Manfredo. "Deal with this for me." He gestured toward the plans and the architects and went down the steps, Corso just behind him. When they were out of listening range of the court, he said, "Send Bianca Lancia to the Peacock Room."

"Sire." Corso went off, swerving around courtiers, who looked keenly after him. At the door into the Peacock Room Ayub straightened and reached for the handle.

Enrico da Malta was standing at the far end, near the windows, sniffing a white lily. He spun around. "Your Majesty."

"Good afternoon, Rico." Frederick turned to make sure the door was shut. Ayub had come inside with him and was leaning up against the wall beside the door, against the painted peacocks with their gilt-trimmed tails.

"We can sail at any time, Sire," Enrico said. "All I need is a few days' notice."

"I'm moving down to Brindisi tomorrow. We'll sail in eight days." Enrico was wearing a black band around his arm, mourning like everybody else as inconspicuously as possible, because Frederick would not wear black. The gnawing guilt and worry pulled at the edge of his mind. "Can we put my suite all on one ship?"

Enrico shook his head. "I'd advise you to take only your pages and chamber servants and ship out the rest on other galleys. Otherwise it would be too crowded for any comfort at all."

The private door behind the throne opened and shut, and Bianca with her page Astorre came around the edge of the throne platform and stopped. Her eyes went from Frederick to Enrico and back again, and she blushed.

"Ayub," Frederick said, "tell Hasan to come meet me

here to get his instructions for this sailing. Rico, we'll be in Brindisi by tomorrow night and we can settle everything then. Thank you."

"Sire." Enrico bowed and went around him toward the door. "I'll send Hasan, Ayub—you needn't leave your post."

Frederick went over to Bianca, who stood beside the throne. Astorre stepped back into the obscurity of a corner.

"I've been negligent." He touched her hand. "Are you angry?"

She shook her head. "No. No. It's better, I need to get used to this." She began to blush again, but her huge eyes looked directly into his, and her fingers moved in his grip. He picked up her hand and kissed it.

"Don't promise anybody anything, that's all." Her hand smelled of rose water. Suddenly he put his arms around her and hugged her. "Bianca, Biancetta—" He kissed her; her arms tightened around his neck, and she pressed her body against his, their thighs brushing through the layers of cloth and embroidered jewels. He shut his eyes.

"I'm going to Brindisi tomorrow. Come with me. The court stays here—they'll all go to Troia in a few days. I'll tell your brother to bring you to Brindisi."

"I shouldn't—they'll—"

Her head rested against his shoulder, and he looked down at her, surprised. "Know? They already know." The door from the hall opened, letting in a gust of noise, and shut again: Hasan had come in. "In Brindisi we can work out some things between us." He slid his hands under her surcoat. "I want you to have some things before I go, too—more attendants, and a palace and a bodyguard." He straightened up, and they separated— she looked quickly over at her page and the two Saracens. Frederick watched her lashes veil her eyes. "They aren't looking."

"No," she said. "They're too well trained."

"I want you to have things," he said. He pulled her surcoat straight over her shoulders; the edge was embroidered with daisies. "I don't want you alone while I'm gone."

"I don't want you gone." She bit her lip. All the people near them made her jittery, and she stole looks at them from beneath her lashes. He grinned.

"You'll get used to it."

"It makes me ashamed," she said, in a tiny voice.

He kissed her forehead. "Astorre, attend her. I'll tell your brother to bring you to Brindisi. Don't worry. I love you, Bianca, don't worry."

That made it all better, of course. She smiled up at him and went out the door behind the throne, Astorre trailing her. He shrugged and turned to Hasan.

"Women. How can they all be so alike, and yet one enchants me and another only bores me?"

Hasan shrugged one shoulder. "Perhaps when you know them better you'll find out the differences, Lord."

"I know them well enough to know I'll never know them." He hunched his shoulders, looking around the bright room. "Bring me a chair, will you?"

Tomorrow.

He rode along the beach, his Saracens all around him, studying the ships in the harbor. Heads bobbed in the water around them—the local children begging from the crews on board. The slaves were loaded, all the baggage —by tomorrow the galleys would stink like floating coffins. Osiris' coffin, that the cypress saved. The falcon screeched on his wrist.

"Hasan."

Hasan galloped up to his side, and Frederick pointed to the flagship. "Keep a watch on her tonight, from the shore. In case."

"Yes, Lord."

He turned his horse and let it walk slowly over the wet sand, just below the ridge of broken shells and seaweed that marked the high-tide line. This time he couldn't turn back, this time he had to go through with it. This time I have to take it all. The memory of Yolande dead came back to him. He'd thought he'd buried her out of sight in Bianca, but now he was sailing to her homeland, and she rose up like a ghost after him.

The sun was setting, and the water gleamed dull gold and orange. Lights appeared on the ships. This will prove something, once and for all. Yes. Suddenly he felt better; he reined in and stared out to sea. If I can win this one, then . . . Like a child: if I see a white horse in the market I'll have good luck. But everybody else will believe it, even if I don't. Grant it, grant it, O Lord.

Over the running sea the darkness flowed like oil. Stars burned in the eastern sky. He kept his back to the sunset, and deep in his heart a fierce pleasure and anticipation stirred.

Frederick pulled back the curtain into his servants' cabin, caught a whiff of vomit, and backed hastily away. The quick glance had shown him Corso, Giancarlo, Marco and Felix all one throbbing knot of green faces and glazed eyes. Sea voyages affected some people that way. He took his own stomach under consideration and appreciated its stability. The only trouble was that now he'd have to dress himself.

He poked around the cabin, ignoring the groans and prayers seeping through the curtain. The galley lurched wildly along a wave and he had to grab for a beam to keep from falling. In the cubicle one of the boys emitted a choked scream. For an instant, until the ship righted itself, he understood. Fresh air and something to eat— that was what he needed. He threw back the lid of a chest full of clothes and pulled out underwear, hose and a linen shirt.

Not in nearly thirty years had he dressed himself completely. It gave him a feeling of freedom, like climbing out the palace window on a rope made of bell pulls and curtains and escaping through the back gate into the city. He put on the underwear and stood up, holding out the hose, trying to figure out how to get in, and laughed.

"Sire."

"What do you want?" He found the empty hose vastly entertaining; he jiggled them to make them dance. Corso whimpered again.

"I'm dying. Please help me."

"You're not dying, you're seasick. You'll get over it." Sitting down, he pulled on the hose. Corso crept into the cabin and curled up at his feet, sobbing.

"I'm dying. I'm dying."

"Don't be a crybaby." He put on the shirt, threw a belt around his waist, and picked Corso up like a puppy under one arm. "Come up on deck. You'll feel much better."

Corso wept bitterly. Frederick shifted his weight onto one hip, carried him out the low doorway, and climbed the ladder to the deck.

Before him the great gilt-railed poop deck rose like a castle keep; the Captain and Enrico and the helmsman stood there, watching him. Overhead the striped sail curved out, driving the ship through the water. He took a breath so deep of the air rushing past him it cracked his ribs. He hadn't realized how musty the cabin was. The free crew shouted back and forth from the poop deck to the foredeck, and the rigging groaned. He dumped Corso on the deck and trotted toward the rail. Halfway there, he saw Corso lurch to his feet and stagger toward the windward side, and he went back to steer him over to the lee rail.

"Over here. Always throw up with the wind." He left the boy doubled over the rail, moved down a little, and climbed into the rigging to look at the other ships.

The little fleet spread toward the coast—he could just barely see blue land in the distance. All the sails were spread, red and green, yellow stripes on black. He thought, I could land on that coast and seize towns, rob all the people there. The wind streaming through his hair delighted him. He jumped down to the deck and ran up toward the poop, took the steps three at a time, and bounced to a stop in front of Enrico da Malta.

The Captain and another officer there went to their knees; the helmsman had to strain to keep hold of the tiller. Behind them Enrico bowed, his back to the carved rail.

"Sail the ship," Frederick said to the Captain. "Forget I'm here." He looked over his shoulder toward the bow, admiring the way his legs adjusted to the roll of the ship. "Enrico, I should take sea voyages more often."

"Naturally you're thriving," the Admiral said. "I spent half the morning flat on my gut with my head over a bucket, and every other member of your staff is similarly indisposed."

"They'll get over it." Frederick leaned over the rail to look at the water boiling away in their wake. "Do you suppose we could fish from here?"

"Probably, Sire."

"Enrico, were you really sick? You're the Admiral."

"That's what I keep telling myself. I see your attendants are all down." He eyed Frederick's shirt, still unlaced.

Frederick lunged grinning against the rail and scratched his chest through the gap in his shirt. "Do I look like a sailor?"

"You look like a street tough, Sire."

Frederick laughed. The galley corkscrewed down a trough, took a wave out of rhythm, and jerked. Enrico paled. Avoiding Frederick's eyes, he clenched his teeth and grabbed for the railing.

"I'm disappointed in you, Enrico. Truly disappointed."

"I haven't been to sea in—" The ship pitched violently across another wave and slithered diagonally into the trough, and Enrico groaned and vomited over the stern. Frederick made a face.

Corso was standing up, one hand still on the rail, looking into the rigging above his head. Frederick started toward the forward rail of the poop deck, nearly lost his footing, and stood still a moment, trying to get the rhythm of the ship's roll into his stride. The sailors all around the deck were grinning behind their hands. He walked with his feet apart, which helped, and leaned over the rail to call down to Corso.

"Are you hungry?"

Corso looked up, and one hand rose to his stomach. "N-no." He bit his lip.

"You'd better eat something." He turned to the Captain. "Have some bread and meat brought up here. And a light wine."

The Captain bellowed unintelligibly into the waist. Corso was mouthing something. Frederick gestured to

him to come up on the poop deck, and after a moment
the boy staggered gamely to the ladder and climbed it.

"I'm sorry, Sire," he said, with a little bow. "I didn't
mean to—"

"Ssssh. Keep busy. Stop thinking about how wretched
you are. Enrico, will you eat with me?"

Enrico turned and nodded, biting his lips. Corso began
to look queasy again, and Frederick backed away from
him to give him running room.

The free crew was pulling back the great hatch covers
that roofed the slave deck. Frederick watched them, enjoying the crisp, deft way they worked. The stench of
the slaves reached his nose, and he started breathing
through his mouth. All those men down there, living in
their own sweat and filth. I wouldn't like it. But they're
criminals, most of them. And Moors. He studied the
faces of the slaves near enough to be seen; they lolled
around on their benches, moving their arms and legs as
much as the chains would allow. Their shoulders and
backs and arms were misshapen with muscle, and above
their wild beards their eyes reminded him of the eyes of
plow horses. He looked quickly away, embarrassed. He
wondered what he'd expected—anger, ferocity, resent-
ment. The food had been brought up and he shooed
away the men awkwardly trying to set out the plates,
took a loaf of bread and a huge chunk of salt beef, and
went to the taffrail to eat.

The gulls no longer followed them, but schools of fish
rippled the water off to the south. Dolphins, he thought.
He loved dolphins. Once someone had sent him a small
antique statue of a dolphin. But no smooth finned back
broke the ruffled water, and when he saw the pelicans
diving he knew these were little fish.

"Wine, Sire?"

"Oh. Yes." He chewed a mouthful of bread, took the
bottle from the Admiral, and gulped. The man on the
tiller caught his eye—the easy way he slackened his
weight against the long bar. "Is that hard?"

The Admiral shrugged. "It's a knack. The wind varies more than you'd think."

"Can I try it?"

"Sure." Enrico swung to the Captain, who was also Genoese, and said, "The Emperor desires to steer."

"Whatever he wants," the Captain said. Frederick grinned at him and went to the tiller.

"Show me how."

The helmsman turned white under his tan. His eyes flew to Enrico, who said, "Show him. Don't worry, nothing will happen."

"Aye, aye." The sailor refused to meet Frederick's eyes. "Just hold it and when the wind shifts you have to keep her so the sail draws."

"Wonderful," Frederick said. He put his hand on the tiller. "If you'd told me I'd have to learn a new language, Enrico—"

The sailor let go of the bar, and it almost swung out of Frederick's hands. He whistled, grabbed a tight hold, and used his weight against it. From the way the sailor had handled it he'd thought it passive, but it moved like a stiff snake, jumping in his fists. He glanced up at the sail and over the bow, trying to find something to aim at. Enrico came up behind him.

"Watch the sail. When it starts to luff—when it starts to snap, you're losing the wind. Bring her up. Toward you. Good, hold her—meet her, you're falling off. That's it."

Frederick laughed. The ship felt alive, surging. Enrico said, "Can you feel the wind? It's hard—when you have more experience you steer by the feel of the wind on your cheek. See the yarn on the rigging there? Try to keep it in the same position all the time, it shows where the wind is."

"No wonder you like to sail." He was getting used to the way the stick moved in his hands; it was a question of balance.

"It's more fun in a small boat," Enrico said. "Maybe

on Cyprus—"

Damn him. "Don't talk to me about Cyprus." He glanced from the yarn on the rigging to the sail and back to the yarn. "How am I doing?"

"Well. Very well, in fact."

"I'm part Norman. Pirates, all of them." The sail didn't look taut, and he drew the stick in toward his body until the striped canvas started to snap and let it off a little. Enrico was staring at him.

"What's wrong?"

"Nothing. That's the way you're supposed to do it. Do you want more wine?"

"Yes. Please."

The sailor started forward to take the tiller back, but Frederick waved him away. The Captain drifted over.

"Look at the wake, Rico."

Enrico, a bottle in one hand, glanced over the taffrail. "Why do you think he's Emperor, because he's anything like the rest of us?"

Frederick looked back over the stern. The wake of the ship stretched off straight to the horizon. His chest swelled with pride. The stick leaped in his hands and he had to adjust quickly; he overcompensated and had to push the tiller away from him. Frowning, he took the bottle, braced the tiller against his hip and drank.

"Enrico. I want to learn how to rig the sail and—" He could think of nothing else. "Everything."

Enrico smiled. "Pull an oar."

Frederick chewed his lip. He glanced toward the open hold, thought of the stink and the sullen brutal faces of the slaves, and nodded. "Yes. Good idea."

"Sire, you—"

"I gave you an order. Where's my page? Corso?"

Corso jogged up, looking livelier than before.

"I want fish for dinner. Fish over the side. This beef is rotten."

"Sailors' meat," Enrico said. "Sailors won't eat fish."

"Hunh."

Up on the masthead his personal banner flew, the Hohenstaufen eagles; from the mastheads of all the other galleys flew the pennant of the Sicilian fleet. But each of the others had its own captain and its own crew, independent of this. He tossed his hair back out of his eyes. I can pretend I'm . . . The glistening blue sea, the pale blue sky and the bright sun brought all his pleasure to the surface again; he drew a deep breath, and with the tiller wedged against his thigh peeled off his shirt. If any of the other galleys got close enough to see a red-headed man at the tiller, no one would guess who it was. The slaves at the oars wore only loincloths. Probably it was easier to row without sleeves to bind their arms. He wondered if he'd be able to pull an oar—if the slaves would resent it. Corso was trailing a line over the stern, talking happily to a sailor splicing a line. The sun beat on Frederick's chest and shoulders; his skin under his long hair grew sweaty. He was going to turn red as a poppy. He wondered what Bianca would think, if she could see him, half naked, steering a galley through the sea to Cyprus.

"Enrico—"

"No. I refuse. Absolutely."

Frederick took two steps around the tiny cabin, bent to keep from knocking his head on the beams. "Enrico, do you remember when—"

"You just might as well give up, because I'm not going to—"

"—they brought you in to me, oh, years ago, all tied up and bloody—"

"Never. Never, absolutely."

"—and I said I could either hang you or make you the Admiral, and you said you'd much rather be the Admiral?"

"This was your idea. You go through with it. Don't—"

"Enrico, how would you like to hang?"

The Admiral put his big fists on the table and glared. "If you hung me, Genoa would go to war with you, you'd lose Malta, and half your fleet would rebel."

"I could always get the Pisans. And you'd be dead, Enrico."

Enrico leaned back. "You're bluffing."

Frederick grinned.

"What do you want to do this for at all, anyhow? Go down there in that filthy hold and tug on an oar—I've done that, it's no fun."

Frederick leaned forward. "But it will be fun, Enrico, you'll see—it'll be exciting and lots of fun. Now, come on. Please?"

"Jesus." Enrico stared at him. His shoulders hunched. "You and me and who else?"

"Angelo. I talked him into it this morning, while he was taking his trick at the tiller."

"Angelo? He's nothing but a common seaman. The least we ought to—This is ridiculous." Enrico looked away and scrubbed his chin with his fingers. "How long?"

"Just until we get tired. I just want to see what it's like."

"How am I going to command respect if I'm down there—"

"You'll be down there with me, Enrico. Please?"

"Oh, God. All right. But as soon as we get bored or tired, that's it."

"Fine. Let's go."

Enrico yelped. "Now?"

"Naturally. It's flat calm and they've been rowing all day. Come on."

Frederick bounded out the door onto the deck. The sunlight blinded him a moment—it was blistering hot and windless, and his sunburn began to ache again. His nose was peeling. Enrico came out, grumbling, and Frederick turned and grinned at him and went on down to the Captain, who was shouting to the man in the lookout on top of the mast.

"Captain," Frederick said, "we're going down there to row."

The Captain wheeled, bowed, and licked his lips. "Now?"

"That's what I said," Enrico said. He turned and bellowed for Angelo, who came down from the poop deck. From the hold came the monotonous groan and rasp of the oars. Frederick could smell the slaves from here.

"This is stupid," the Captain mumbled. "Oh, all right. Let me tell Durante." He went around to the side of the hold and yelled down to the slaves' quartermaster.

Angelo said, "Everybody's betting we don't stay down there more than ten strokes." He grinned.

Frederick glanced around and saw Corso staring at him from the foredeck. "First one to quit buys the other two wine when we reach port." He took off his shirt and trousers. After a moment, the others stripped as well. The Captain came back.

"Well, go on down. They're as ready as they'll ever be." He shook his head and stared out to sea.

Frederick went around to the ladder into the hold, the others trailing him. Straining at their oars, chained and bolted down, the slaves turned their heads to stare up. Durante ran over, his whip coiled around his shoulders, and stood bowing while Frederick descended into the moist heat and stench of the hold. He caught his breath, amazed. It was impossible to breathe. The heat wrapped itself around his chest and belly and sweat poured down his back. Another sailor was unlocking the chains from three men at one bench; the slaves gasped, and a few of them stopped rowing and yelled to be let loose. Durante whirled with his whip and they subsided.

"Well?" Enrico said.

"Don't make me use breath." His stomach heaved. The sound of the oars working thundered in his ears, drowning the beat of the time-keeper's hammer. On the backs of the slaves nearest him he saw tremendous sun-sores, whip marks like ruts, half healed, and brand-new and years old. Under the slats of the false decking, filth sloshed back and forth. The three slaves who had been freed stepped back and sank down on their hams, leaning against each other, their beards and wild hair crawling with lice.

"Sometimes," Frederick said, sliding into the bench, "I'm glad I was born properly." He sat down, stretched his legs out, and laid his arms on the oar. They'd stopped the rowing, and the slaves were all craning around to see. He tossed his hair back.

Enrico yelled, "Durante, one wrong move with that snake of yours and I'll flay you."

"Eh, Rico," Durante said, and grinned. Their voices echoed in the hold; the beams of the ship looked like ribs, as if they were inside the belly of a huge animal. Frederick wrapped his fingers around the oar and grinned at Angelo.

"Remember, first one to quit—"

"Ready?" Durante yelled. "One, two, three—"

The hammer picked up the beat, and suddenly all the backs around them were bending in time. Frederick hung onto the oar, thrusting it out—it was balanced so that moving it took less effort than he'd thought. He braced his feet on the boards of the false deck and swung the oar out, brought it back, swung it out, in time—between each thrust there was a tiny lull, a time to rest. He felt Angelo's hands on the oar, helping, and Enrico's, slightly off-time for a few strokes. The whip cracked. Wood on wood, the oar grated against the rowlock, shrieking in his ears. At the end of each outward thrust, the breath exploded from the lungs of a hundred slaves with a thud like the hammer.

Enrico shouted, "Happy, Sire?"

"It's interesting. I'd hate"—thrust—"to spend my life

at it." His palms and the flats of his fingers started to burn. Blisters. Don't be too energetic, don't waste strength. Sweat popped out of his skin. The whip flew out over the backs of the slaves two rows ahead of him, and he heard a gasp and saw red blood splat onto the oar next forward. His back hurt down to the bone.

"How many strokes have we gone?" Enrico yelled.

"Eight," Durante shouted.

Frederick's hair was in his eyes. He flung it back with a twist of his head and grinned at Enrico. "Ready to quit?"

Enrico's face was twisted into a grimace. He tugged at the oar, sighed, and yelled, "Yes."

"One more. Just one. Come on."

"Sire—" They flung themselves forward. Now Frederick could hear the tiny gurgle of the water past the keel, just the other side of the wood beneath his feet.

"And one more," he yelled. "This one's the last." His hands were bleeding; he saw the trickle of blood along the oar. They heaved the oar back, and he flung up his hands. "Enough."

Durante screamed for a halt, and the slaves sank down, bent over the oars, panting. Frederick turned his hands over and looked at the palms. Half a dozen huge blisters had opened up on each hand, pulpy raw flesh, leaking blood. He stood up and nudged Angelo, and Enrico got off the bench and sank down, his eyes closed. Frederick slid out into the middle of the hold.

"Durante."

The quartermaster jogged up, grinning, and bowed. "We're very pleased to have your company, Sire—"

"Good. The next time we have wind, clean this place out. You can use the slaves to do it."

Durante's mouth fell open. "But—"

Frederick turned and went toward the ladder. The slaves stared at him, dull and bovine, astonished. When he took hold of the rungs of the ladder, his hands hurt so badly he cried out. Scrambling up onto the deck, he stood and breathed the clean, fresh air; his head swam. Angelo and Enrico came up beside him, breathing hard.

"Why clean it out?" Angelo said. "It'll just get dirty again."

"Keep cleaning it out. I'll grant they're slaves, but they'll live longer if they get fresh air every once in a while." He looked at his hands again. Corso ran up with clean cloths and a bucket of water.

"Is that salt?" Enrico said.

Corso nodded. "It's supposed to be good for—"

"Right." Enrico plunged his hands into the bucket. "It's been a long time since I did that."

Frederick thrust his hands into the water, clenching his jaws at the sting of the salt. "It's good practice, I think. For what I don't know, but it's good." He held out his hands, and Corso dried them carefully, murmuring over the blisters. The furious, monotonous action down there stayed with him—the sound of the oars and the whip and the hammer. Corso wrapped linen around his hands and helped him back into his clothes, and he went to the rail and leaned on it and looked out, wondering.

"Land," Corso said. He trotted down to the afterdeck, skirting two men fixing the lead. "Sire, there's land."

"Cephalonia," Frederick said. "Saw it this morning. Pico, roll."

Corso made a small, exasperated noise, and Frederick bent his head to hide a grin. Pico, the first mate, cupped the dice in his hands and blew on them for luck. Bracing himself on the railing, Corso bounced up and down, murmuring, his eyes on the faint gray outline of the land to the north. In the hold a slave shouted hoarsely, and Frederick lifted his head.

"Hah!" Pico flung the dice down. "Oh, Jesus." His face collapsed, and the rest of the sailors laughed. Angelo slapped down a brass coin and snatched up the dice and shook them.

"Any bets on the side?"

Frederick leaned back on his elbows. Pico had rolled a two, and nobody would put up a wager on it. The fresh, salt air brushed his face; when he shut his eyes he saw bright orange-red from the sun. He felt immensely strong, like an animal. The sailors around him cheered absently—Angelo had made his cast and beaten Pico. Frederick opened his eyes and stared into the blazing sky.

"Your turn, Emperor."

That was Miklos, the wicked-minded little Greek. Frederick shut his eyes. Pretty soon he'd have to impress the hell out of Miklos, who alone of all the sailors treated him with less than respect, but this wasn't the moment; the touch of the wind on his cheek was too intriguing. "I'll pass."

"Awww."

Frederick stood up. They all got to their feet, Miklos last, and he glared at Miklos and saw him start to grin and turned his back, walking over to the rail near Corso. Behind him, Angelo's voice grated, just low enough that he couldn't hear the words.

"Wind's changing," Frederick said. "We'll have to make sail soon."

Corso shot him a glance of unmitigated awe, and Frederick struggled to keep his face noncommittal. O the sailor's life. Such simple pleasures: stunning pages with new knowledge. The oars screamed in the rowlocks, swayed across the choppy waves, dipped, and heaved the galley forward. The chop broke some of the waves into curls of foam, and far down the sea Cephalonia showed like a thickness of the air.

"How long now, Sire?" Corso said.

"I don't know. Ask Enrico."

The rest of the fleet bobbed around them, bright, painted ships on a bright, driving sea. A trickle of sweat ran down between his shoulder blades, and he reached one hand up behind his back to scratch his spine. Corso's eyes watched him, shy.

"When we get there, what will it be like?"

"Hunh." Frederick slacked his weight against the railing. "The same as in Sicily. Don't remind me."

Corso wrinkled up his nose, and Frederick laughed. The boy's hair was shades lighter than when they'd left Sicily, and his skin tanned dark and rich—unlike Frederick he'd never burned. But he was darker than Corso, because he never wore a shirt. *Corso is more respectable than I am.* He glanced down at his body, dressed in the short leather trousers the sailors wore, the red hairs bleached pale gold and gleaming on his dark skin.

"Sire?" Angelo yelled, and held up the dice.

"Wait." He lifted one hand. "Corso, go down and get me something to eat. And some wine, ah?"

Corso bowed and ran off, and Frederick went back to the clump of sailors and hunkered. "What's the bet?"

"You're first throw," Pico said.

"Unless you want to pass again," Miklos said softly, and snickered.

Frederick took the dice in the palm of his hand. "You must admit that the stakes aren't too exciting, Miklos." Looking up, he smiled.

Pico shifted his feet. "We'll have to go aloft pretty soon, now, don't—"

Miklos was staring at Frederick, his eyes narrowed. "Oh?"

"The game pales," Frederick murmured. "Distinctly."

"I didn't know we were hired on to entertain you."

"If you were they'd never sign up shaggy little Greeks."

Miklos' jaw tightened. Angelo inched closer to him, his eyes darting from his face to Frederick's. Miklos said, "What will you play for, Emperor?"

Frederick clenched his fist. "Something closer than

money, maybe?"

Corso trotted up with a little basket of bread and a jug of wine and a cup. While he laid out a napkin and poured the wine, Miklos' eyes followed his hands, and Frederick's skin prickled up with excitement: there were rumors about Miklos, interesting and exotic rumors. Frederick picked up the filled wine cup and drank half of it, rolling the wine around his mouth.

"Do you like wine, Miklos? Good wine?"

"Hunh?"

Miklos' eyes narrowed. The others frowned, looking around, bewildered; Frederick held out the cup. "This wine, for example."

The little man's dark hand shot out and snatched away the cup. "Hunh." He threw the wine down his throat in a quick motion, his eyes never leaving Frederick's face. For a moment he said nothing and only looked fierce, but suddenly he grinned.

"That's good wine, Emperor, yes. How much?"

"Full cask. You can stay drunk from here to Acre."

Miklos' face split ear to ear in a white, mirthless grin. "Except the Captain would pitch me overboard."

"I'll tell him to leave you alone," Frederick said. He tore a chunk of bread from the white, soft loaf and ate it.

Pico's feet shifted on the deck. "Jeeee-sus."

Miklos still wore the wide grin. "Against it, I put up—what?"

"How much hashish do you have?"

Angelo roared. Pico whispered, "My sweet Jesus Christ."

"Enough," Miklos said. The grin vanished; two hard red spots appeared on his cheekbones, under his tan. "Enough to keep you dreaming from here to Acre, Emperor."

Frederick threw the dice. They rattled across the deck and bounced off Pico's foot; up on the afterdeck Enrico shouted. The word came down the galley—"Make sail—"

"Ten," Pico said, and Miklos swore.

Frederick stood up. "Make sail." He nudged the dice with his bare toes and ran up the deck toward the mast. Angelo jogged along with him; they parted in the middle, just past the hatch into the slaves' hold, and Frederick went to the lubboard rigging. A ten would be hard to beat. If Miklos didn't have enough hashish to make the bet worth while he'd take it in skin. The fine, clear tingle rippled through his body again. Hand over hand, he climbed the rigging, upside down. Pico and Miklos would man the braces. Maybe he'd take something else out of Miklos' skin. *I love being a sailor but being Emperor is fun too.* He scurried the last few feet to the yardarm and climbed awkwardly onto it. Angelo already stood casually on the swaying round of wood, pulling the lashings free.

This was the hard part. Frederick got to his knees, tested his balance, and reached for the lines strung over his head. True sailors never used them. He stood up and giddiness filled his head and stomach. The yard swung under his feet as if it meant to buck him off. He held his breath. *Don't look down.* The glistening sea looked flat from here, hard as the deck. He bent and pulled the lashings loose from this end of the sail and slid his feet along the yard, still hanging onto the line. Angelo was finished, leaning up against the mast, grinning. Frederick stared at him, took a deep breath, and let go of the line. He hunkered, swayed, lost his balance, caught it again, and unlashed another ten feet of the sail.

"Don't look down," Angelo hissed. "How did you know he has that gunk?"

Frederick straightened, his spine rigid, and walked to the mast. With each step his confidence swelled, and abruptly the breath exploded from his lungs and he sighed. He bent down and jerked the last of the line free.

"That would be telling." He was close enough to Angelo to hear his low laugh; he kicked the sail off the yard.

"Heave," the Captain roared, down on the afterdeck, and on the braces Pico and Miklos hauled away. The sail slid away from the yard and cracked out flat on the wind. Frederick stood up straight, his blood hammering in his ears. He was standing up on the yard, holding onto nothing. Glancing over at Angelo, he saw the sailor's wide grin and grinned back.

"Good going," Angelo said. "I still want to know—"

"Oh, shut up, I won't tell you."

They'd braced the sail taut and trimmed it, down there, and there was no reason to stay up here anymore, even though the wind raking his hair and cooling his body tasted sweet. Angelo turned and walked down the yard to the shrouds and slid lightly down the line to the deck. I would like to be the lookout. He lifted his head and felt his body adjust automatically to the new problem in balance; up there, in the well at the top of the mast, Aste was dozing. I want to be the lookout. But he couldn't tell on Aste either. He sauntered down the yard to the line, hooked one arm and one leg around it, and stepped out into space. The long, controlled swoop to the deck finished it off, like a decrescendo. Just above the deck he let go, landed with a bounce, and walked almost strutting toward the dice game.

Before he reached it, he glanced toward Enrico on the afterdeck, expecting him to be laughing. Enrico was standing rigid, his head back, looking somewhere else. Frederick paused, surprised. He hadn't considered before —Enrico probably watched in terror every move he made. If the Emperor playing sailor fell from the mast . . . With a jerk like a marionette Enrico pulled himself around to put his back to Frederick. Frederick sank down on his heels, his eyes on Pico's face, curious. But Pico didn't look upset.

"Bets still holding?" Angelo said.

"Give me those dice." Miklos reached out his hand. "By God, I'll . . ." He cuddled the dice in his hands and whispered to them.

Angelo said, "This wind will hold until dawn. Bet on it."

"Naw."

Angelo said things like that all the time, and he was invariably right. He'd sailed this part of the Mediterranean all his life. Knowledge hidden in his eyes, his ears, his skin. Miklos was still crooning to the dice, but with a swing of his arm he flung them down so hard they bounced up and hit Angelo in the chest.

Pico slapped his big hand down over the dice; he shouted, "Do you want it or not?" At the crash of his voice, Frederick jumped a little, startled.

"Yes," Miklos shouted. "Show them—I want my wine."

His hand still hiding the dice, Pico looked at Frederick. "Do you want it?"

Frederick nodded. He thought, Cheat—loaded dice? Pico lifted his hand slowly from the deck. Miklos bent, his mouth half open, peering. Frederick's mouth had gone dry with excitement; he refused to stare, even to look—let them tell him.

"Shit," Miklos said, and Frederick sighed. He looked at Pico, who grinned.

"Seven. Fair win."

"No fair," Miklos said. "He put up a cask of wine when he has dozens, and I put up all the hash I have in the whole world. I say—"

Angelo shoved him. "Bring it up. But watch the Captain."

Miklos said, "I won't. If he wants it, let him go find it."

Frederick stood up; Miklos immediately scrabbled like a crab across the deck away from him, his eyes shiny. Murmuring, the others backed out of the way. In the striped shadow of the railing, Miklos curled his legs under him, and his hand slid toward the knife in his belt.

"Sire," Enrico said. "May I be of service?" He walked straight in between Frederick and Miklos. His voice, even and dull, fell like a mallet, but the look he gave Frederick burned with rage.

"Not at all," Frederick said. "Leave me."

"Sire—"

Frederick smiled. "Leave me."

Enrico turned on his heel and marched off, glowering. Behind Frederick someone sighed, and Miklos under the railing licked his lips and watched Enrico go. Frederick hooked his thumbs inside the waistband of his trousers.

"Go get me the stuff, Miklos."

The little Greek's fingers tapped on his knife hilt.

"Now."

A foot scraped on the deck. Miklos looked beyond Frederick, back into his face, and shut his eyes. In a burst of energy he dove out from under the railing and charged for the afterdeck hatch.

"Jesus," Pico said.

"I don't mind telling you that I have hated every day of this voyage," Enrico said, "and I fully expect to hate every day of it yet to come."

"Enrico, how could you? The pleasures of a sea journey, the fresh salt air, the sky—" Frederick looked up at the stars, radiating subtle colors, peppering the sky. "I love it."

"Sire. Forgive me if I'm offensive. Why can't you act like an emperor?"

"Oh? How am I not acting like an emperor?" He leaned his weight against the tiller bar and felt the ship answer. Steering was better than anything else.

"You're . . ." Enrico made an exasperated sound. He moved the lantern closer, between them. "You know what I mean."

"I am Emperor. Therefore everything I do is what an emperor does." Frederick shrugged. "I don't see your point." It was hard to pay attention to what Enrico said.

"What if Miklos had pulled his knife after you ordered me off?"

The hashish was soft enough to spread with a knife, like butter, and Miklos had been right that there was enough to keep anybody in a stupor for weeks. Frederick tried to keep from laughing, but it was hard. Enrico didn't know that he was floating. "He wouldn't have."

"What if he had?" Enrico leaned his arms on the railing and stared out to sea.

"I'd have killed him. Or you would have."

"For the love of God. He's a sailor, he knows how to fight."

"So do I."

"You're diminishing yourself."

"Am I?"

Under his hand the tiller worked and by habit he compensated. Enrico moved his shoulders. In the lantern light his face was full of lines.

"No. But you're defeating your purpose. You know that, don't you?"

"Why?"

"Because we—" Enrico lifted his hands. "We love you. But not because you are Emperor. Because you are Frederick."

"Oh." That was a good point. The hashish fog receded slightly; the thought pierced it like a cold wet draft in a warm room. "Enrico, I didn't know you indulged in the philosophy of statecraft."

"I'm smarter than you think I am. All right. Everything you do is imperial. Fine. I'll stop worrying about it. But will you please not get yourself killed?"

"Promise."

"And if you're going to eat hashish, stay out of bright

lights. Your eyes are the size of saucers."

Frederick jerked, startled. Enrico twitched the lantern a little closer, looked, and smiled. "I told you. I'm smarter than you think I am."

Frederick laughed.

"Cyprus, Your Majesty," the Captain said, nodding.

Frederick smiled glumly, "I see," and went below to change his clothes.

They were all waiting for him in Limassol, on Cyprus—the Grand Master, the Archbishop, Tommaso d'Aquino, Ricardo Filangieri, a dozen barons disenchanted with the current regency, envoys from the Templars and the Hospitallers, envoys from Antioch and Acre and Tyre, and it was like stepping out of the clean air of the sea into a miasma. They were all around him, their voices babbling, from the quay to the castle of Limassol; everybody wanted something or had a report to give him. The King and the bailli of the Kingdom of Cyprus—John d'Ibelin—weren't there. At the castle itself Frederick had to sit through a long and grueling ceremony of greeting, with speeches by nearly every citizen of Limassol, including the chatelain of the castle who twice burst into stuttering fits that turned his face bright red and made everybody else nervous. There was nothing to do for it. While the old man stood there fighting his own tongue everyone had to stand and watch, pretending it actually wasn't happening. Finally everything was over and done with and they got to eat, but the food was cold and so lightly seasoned Frederick couldn't tell the difference in the meats. He snarled at Corso for filling his cup with the wrong wine, and Corso nearly fell over backward in surprise.

The Grand Master, on his left, took one look at him and was silent, but the chatelain on his right maintained a hysterical babble about the affairs of the island, stuttering every other word. Frederick made up a list of comments—"Oh, really," "Quite so," "Fascinating," and "Well, of course"—and used them, in the same order, whenever the situation seemed to call for something from him. The chatelain apparently didn't notice. The envoy from the Templars, a gaunt man in lavish silks, watched him gloomily all through the meal.

Amalric Barlais, the Cypriot who had once had preten-

sions to the place of bailli that John d'Ibelin now held—
Amalric Barlais was not in sight, and as soon as the banquet was over and the entertainment begun, Frederick
asked the Grand Master about him.

"He's here," the Grand Master said. He hitched his
chair closer so that he could talk without the dozens of
people around them hearing. "He's not at the table because he's an outlaw on Cyprus. Why, did you want to
talk to him especially soon?"

"It's not necessary." Frederick twitched one hand.
"I'll see him later." The jugglers were juggling madly
right in front of him, their girl attendants turning somersaults and doing handstands under his eyes.

"Aside from the fact you're in a terrible humor, you're
looking very well, Sire. The voyage must have been
good for you."

"It was fun." He glanced at the Grand Master and
grinned. "Is it obvious I'm in a bad mood?"

"To those who know you, Sire. Tommaso and Berardo
and I all came to the conclusion separately."

Frederick leaned out to look at the Archbishop, who
was chatting with his neighbor. The neighbor caught
sight of Frederick and nudged the Archbishop, who
looked up, cocking his eyebrows. Frederick inclined his
head slightly and sat back. The jugglers' pretty assistants
were dressed in translucent trousers and short tight bod-
ices, and he was considering scandal.

"Sire," the Grand Master said. "I'm very sorry about
the Empress."

Frederick's stomach caved in. "I'd almost forgotten."

"Then I'm sorry I reminded you. Berardo—"

The Archbishop pulled up a stool and sat down on
Frederick's right, opposite the Grand Master—the chate-
lain had gone long before, nearly ill with nerves. "Sire.
My congratulations."

Frederick was still thinking about Yolande; he jerked
up his head.

"You didn't yawn once through the entire ceremony."
Frederick whooped. "I came close." He looked back at
the girls. This was no time to indulge in guilt. Quickly
he narrowed the possibilities down to two, a redhead and
a girl with long, long black hair and olive skin. "Suppose
you tell me about Cyprus, Berardo, it's so tedious being
ignorant."

"Barlais can tell you better than either of us. Or Tommaso can. It's my opinion, Sire, that you—"

The spectators all around them let out a roar that
drowned his voice. The jugglers were tossing lighted
torches back and forth, fluttering cartwheels of fire,
while the girls turned somersaults in the air between
them. The redhead wasn't as nimble as the dark girl, and
Frederick grinned. He stuck one hand out behind him
for Corso.

"—that you call all the major barons of Outremer to
Cyprus and consult with them before you go to Acre."

Frederick nodded; he'd considered that already. "Of
course, if anybody said, 'Thank you kindly, no,' I'd be in
a bit of difficulty, wouldn't I? What about John d'Ibelin?"

In the little pause he watched his girl turn a particularly athletic somersault. Corso had come up behind the
Grand Master.

"He's not here," Hermann said, lamely.

"Obviously. His suzerain comes to Cyprus, and the
bailli of the kingdom isn't here to welcome him. Nor is
the King, who is in the bailli's care."

"The Ibelins don't behave like ordinary men," the
Archbishop said. "As I'm sure Barlais has told you."

"He sent a man to Sicily to make sure I heard of it.
Gavin of somewhere or other. The blond one over there
drinking."

"Sire," the Grand Master said. "Barlais is heavily
biased."

"I know." So am I; Ibelin should be here. "Excuse me
a moment, Hermann." He nodded to Corso, who ducked

in between him and the Grand Master. Frederick drew the boy's head down by the collar of his coat and whispered, "Tell Ricardo I'll take the dark one and he can have the redhead for once."

Corso straightened, bowed, and went smiling off toward Filangieri, who had been staring as hard as Frederick at the girls. The Grand Master said, "In any case, Sire, if you meet with the important men here, you'll have a chance to find out what's going on in Outremer before you go there in person."

Frederick said, "It's infinitely more important that I get some kind of confirmation of my rights as Regent for my son. Whom should we summon?"

"Guy Embriaco of Jebail," the Archbishop said.

"Why?"

"Because he's rich."

"Good, I need money. Guy Embriaco. Bohemund of Antioch, obviously. Who else?"

"Two or three people from Tripoli, and some of the smaller barons from the south. And Balian of Sidon. He's more inclined to you than anybody else, big or little, and he's influential. He's related to very nearly everybody west of the Jordan. Probably east of it too."

"I thought Bohemund held Tripoli."

"He does, but there are valuable men there not in his party."

"Bohemund isn't a vassal of the King of Jerusalem, is he? A pity. He should be."

"The baby's strong, I hear," the Grand Master said.

"He looks like every other baby I've ever seen." The juggling was over, and now they had animals in doing tricks. Frederick drank another cup of wine; he was getting drunk, and suddenly he was sick to death of the whole thing, Crusade and all. "Hell, I'm sleepy. Can't I go now?"

"Soon," the Archbishop said. "Here comes Tommaso."

Tommaso d'Aquino and Enrico were walking quickly

toward them; they bowed and Frederick waved irritably
to them to stop. "Where's Ricardo?"

"Gone to make sure of your girls." Enrico settled himself comfortably on his heels in the packed space around
Frederick. "Your taste is exquisite. You should see her up
close."

The Archbishop frowned. "Sire, perhaps you shouldn't
add to the rumors—"

"Ssssh." The Grand Master knocked him on the arm.
"Sire, when you speak to Barlais, remember: he hates the
Ibelins."

"Oh, God. I'll remember."

"And Tommaso has some—"

Tommaso bristled. "I'm perfectly capable myself of
saying what I have to, Sir Hermann, thank you. Sire, I've
got detailed reports I'd like you to hear as soon as you
can. Before anybody else gets here to cloud the issue."

"Naturally. Look, do you suppose I can leave now?"

"You're the Emperor, Sire, you aren't supposed to—"

"Well, I am." He stood, and the whole huge hall
heaved itself violently to its feet. The trained dogs and
monkeys shambled around on the floor while their master snapped orders, and suddenly even the dogs and monkeys were bowing. Frederick laughed.

"Give him some money. Give the jugglers some
money. Is it hot in here or am I running a fever?" He
plunged for the door behind the high table. The crowds
packed around him suddenly surged toward him, murmuring, but the men around him fended them off and
the mob of courtiers couldn't get near. While pages and
sentries got the door open, Frederick glanced around; he
saw the shine and glow of their eyes and realized that this
was one of the biggest events of their lives. The arrival
of an emperor on crusade—he went through the door
and across a smaller hall to stairs.

"Provincials," Enrico said, lightly. "Why don't you
tell everybody how you got so tanned, Sire?"

"Shut up. And don't you tell them, either." At the top of the wide stone stairs he looked both ways, bewildered. "Where do I go?"

"Down here." Corso appeared from an alcove. "They're beautiful rooms, you'll be amazed, Sire."

"What's in them?"

Corso laughed. "I don't think she speaks Italian." His eyes shifted to the men with him, and he led off, strutting a little. Frederick started unlacing the front of his coat, walking behind Corso and between the Archbishop and Tommaso.

"The envoy from the Templars. Who's he?"

"Treasurer of the Order—Jean de Neuville." Tommaso trotted a few steps to reach the door ahead of Frederick and hold it for him, yanking it from the hands of a page to do so. "One of my reports concerns the Templars."

"Fascinating."

They went into the anteroom and through it into a dressing chamber; Frederick shed clothes with each step. "Start reciting. Ricardo—is he—hey, Rico."

"Sire." Filangieri knelt briefly. "I'm sorry I didn't have a chance to greet you personally earlier—"

"I know. How many men do you have now?"

"Four hundred and ninety-four—two died in passage and four since in Acre. And the Duke of Limburg still has a few thousand men, but they're leaving every day to go home. I'd love to."

Frederick socked him in the chest. "Later. You're doing a good job, I can't afford not to have you here. Think of Tommaso, he hasn't been home in years." He went across the room to a table with a pitcher of water on it and splashed some on his face, trying to get rid of the muzziness of having drunk too much.

"Shall I summon those barons, Sire?" the Archbishop said.

"Yes." Frederick turned, and Corso handed him a

towel. "Be polite. Where's Barlais?"

"Coming," Tommaso said. He was marking something down on a sheaf of notes; he didn't look up.

"Good. Report."

While Tommaso gave him a broad summary of the supplies in Acre, the defenses of the Kingdom of Outremer, the relations of the barons, the proceedings of the High Court, the high and low and middle diplomacy inside the kingdom and with the Arab courts, Frederick changed into light silk and sat and listened. Barlais came in during one of Tommaso's dispassionate speeches; he bowed, advanced a little, and paused, unsure. Gavin of Chenichy was with him. Frederick thought of the girl waiting in the next room and drifted to a window to look at the moon. It was past midnight. He stood in the window listening to Tommaso and watching the lights move around in the next keep—pages lighting other guests to their beds.

"Sire," Tommaso said, "what follows concerns matters probably best kept confidential."

"Oh?" Frederick turned. "All right. Everybody has my leave except Tommaso."

Barlais stepped forward. "Sire?"

"You too. I'll see you in the morning. I'm tired. Hermann, see to anything I've overlooked." He sat down on a stool, took a comb from Corso, and sent him out as well. The others were all swiftly gone, all probably dead tired. Frederick combed his hair.

"First of all," Tommaso said, "there's this business with John d'Ibelin. I assume Barlais and his friends told you he seems to have dispensed with the usual procedure for becoming bailli."

"Yes. They say he's stealing revenues."

"Well, technically he has. Now, this man is the most loved and respected noble in the entire Frankish East. It would do you absolutely no good to accuse him of wrongdoing. You'd never get a judgment against him out of the High Court. His brother was bailli—Philip, that was—and when he died John simply took over. He was never appointed and never confirmed. But he's been working to the satisfaction of the High Court of Cyprus and the nobles, and they'll never stand for your replacing him with a Sicilian, for instance."

"You?"

Tommaso shrugged. "They dislike me. I've made them do things they don't like. I've been effective, and they don't like that."

"Unh-hunh."

"But I would advise very strongly that you do something about him. He seems to have assumed the post of bailli because he was his brother's next of kin."

"That's dangerous. Besides, the King is a child, and during a regency . . ." He frowned. "I know what happens during long regencies."

"Indeed, Sire."

Tommaso was silent a moment, staring toward the window. Frederick turned and studied him; Tommaso was the most efficient man he knew, including himself. He looked tired and a little harassed, but he usually did.

"You asked me, remember, to investigate discreetly the affairs of the Military Orders in Acre."

"Yes. Sit down." The comb caught on a snarl and he had to work the hair loose with his fingers.

"I did, naturally. Not through the High Court, which as you've gathered isn't amenable to control from anywhere, least of all an imperial agent. My sources are not unimpeachable, but they're good enough, and I was careful to verify everything from as many different sources as possible."

"I know how you work."

"First of all, both the Templars and the Hospitallers are much, much richer than the Teutonic knights."

"I know that."

"Well, there's more. Their original purpose seems to

have died. They still conduct occasional campaigns but they seem to be merely for show. The Hospitallers . . . seem merely gluttonous and ambitious. The Templars are somewhat different. They are in close touch—in some cases extraordinarily close touch—with all three important Arab courts, and with Khwaresm."

Frederick looked up, surprised.

"Their interests and investments are closely enough linked to the situation in Outremer that they're willing to manipulate for their own gains—increased pressure on a certain area by the Arabs, for example, will force the region to rely more heavily on the Templars. Considering that the kingdom is nothing more than a scrap now, it's rather selfish and shortsighted of them. The Arabs can wipe them out easily enough. They seem to pay a tribute to al-Kamil. I'm sure they paid a tribute to al-Mu'azzam before he died but en-Nasr isn't worth their trouble."

Tommaso stopped; he looked worn and frail. Frederick squinted slightly. "Go on."

"They cannot be trusted. Either of the orders. They are both far too concerned with their own interests. Plus, they hate you, the Templars especially. And about the Templars—"

He paused again. This time Frederick waited, his fists on his knees, until he was ready to go on.

"This rumor is so curious—I didn't credit it at all when I heard it first. But I kept hearing it, and finally someone brought me proof. Of a sort. Not the sort one takes before the High Court. The charge isn't one I think the High Court should handle. It's said that the Templars are heretical."

Frederick shivered. In the stillness Tommaso turned to look at him, his long, bearded face somber.

"I'm heretical," Frederick said softly. "Be specific."

Tommaso licked his lips. "They brought me a thing in a little box that they'd stolen from one of the houses of the order. It was a kind of . . . anyhow, it was a wooden cross with a bat nailed to it."

"Christ in heaven. What did you do with it?"

"I burned it."

Frederick took a deep breath. His heart thundered under his ribs. "So."

"What does it mean?"

"You should know, you're Sicilian. The hill people still use that kind of talisman in some of their rituals. Either the Templars have gone pagan . . . or they're worshipping Satan."

Tommaso nodded. "That's what I thought."

"How naughty of them."

Tommaso looked down at his hands.

"I wish you hadn't burned the bat."

"I had to. I couldn't keep it. It frightened me."

Frederick nodded. The Templars Satanist—it was explosive, it was shocking even to him. But after the first race of excitement he could think of no use for it. If he charged them with it no one would believe him—too many people said the same thing about him. But it would be an interesting thing to know, to produce at an odd moment. He remembered how the Templar at the banquet had stared at him, and abruptly the skin crawled over the nape of his neck.

"Good. I'll see you in the morning, Tommaso. Leave your full reports here and I'll read them."

"Sire."

Tommaso stood up, bowed, and started out. When he was nearly out the door Frederick called his name, and Tommaso wheeled. Frederick smiled. "Thank you."

Tommaso bowed again, grinning, and went out. The silence after he had gone surprised Frederick; there was something odd about it. Finally he decided it was because he was alone for the first time in months. He stood up and went to look at the moon again.

The Templars. No wonder Tommaso had been reluctant to speak of it. There was something frightening in it, elementally disturbing, and because he was Sicilian, like Frederick, he knew more about it than most people. All the lights were out in the next keep, but beyond the wall a dog was barking insistently. Cypriot dog.

It's all rotten, from the top to the root, all of it.

"Sire?"

"I'm coming."

"This way."

With a candle in his hand, Corso led him through a small dark room into a bigger one, half lit with oil lamps. On the edge of the bed the dark girl sat, her legs curled beneath her. For a moment, while Corso trimmed out all the lamps but one, Frederick composed reassurances in case she was frightened, but when Corso went to the door, she lifted her head and looked at him, and he saw the bold interest in her face. Corso went out and drew the door shut.

The girl slid off the bed and started toward him, taking off her thin gown. Her dark hair swung over her shoulders and lay against her small breasts and her back. Reaching him, she lifted her hands to open his robe, but he grabbed her before her hands touched him. His whole body tingled; the sight and scent and feel of a girl, after so long, made his head reel. He kissed her hard, and her lips parted and her tongue caressed his. Her hands slid under his clothes, stroking his back and hips. He gasped.

"Don't do that to an aging man."

In Greek she said, "I don't speak Italian."

"That's all right. We needn't talk." He kissed her again, maneuvering her backward toward the bed. She clung to him moving against him. Halfway to the bed he finally bent, picked her up, and carried her.

"What did you say before?"

He dumped her onto the bed. "That I'm too old for all this thrilling action." The delicious ache spread in waves through his body. Her mouth brushed his skin, her hands drew him down against her, and she twisted to meet him.

A kind of wild frenzy took hold of him; locked together with her, he rode and rode and rode, blind and deaf, until with a rush that made him cry out thickly he came and thrust one last time and lay still.

After a long while he said, "Unh."

Her husky laugh sounded muffled from beneath him. "Are you content, Your Majesty?"

"Hell. I think I'm dying. And take it easy, I haven't spoken Greek in years." He turned his head and kissed her. "You're supposed to tell me I'm not old."

"That would be silly." Her hands moved over his back. "Actually, we all expected gray hair and a lofty look."

He shut his eyes. "Um-hmm. And you may also tell me that while you were dancing you looked up and saw me and fell instantly in love."

She laughed again. He liked the sound of her laugh. He liked her voice, the way she touched him, her soft dark skin—he was falling asleep.

"Shall I stay?"

With difficulty he pushed his eyelids open. "Naturally. Where would you go?"

"Back with the others." She put her arms around him. "Sometimes men don't like us to spend the night with them."

"Don't be ridiculous." He tangled his hands in her hair. "Stay here. I get lonely when I sleep alone."

Gradually she relaxed; he moved over and she lay beside him, her head on his arm. He fooled with her hair and waited to doze off again. Half asleep, he started awake again and said, "What's your name?"

"Theophano."

"You know what mine is." He yawned and settled himself into the pillows. "My court in Sicily calls me 'Big Red' behind my back."

For a moment she was silent, but suddenly her laughter burst out, half choked back, and she reached out and hugged him. With her arms around him and his hand in her hair he shut his eyes and slept.

Barlais said, "I'm sure Ibelin has been stealing revenues."

"I've summoned him here, and he'll answer for it if he has. Tell me about Queen Alice."

"She's of little importance, really. Since she married Bohemund's son everybody thinks she's too involved in the affairs of Antioch and Tripoli."

Frederick leaned back and half shut his eyes. In a country where boy children died off more quickly than girls a queen was always important, especially if she managed to combine in her person several different kinships. "What's she like?"

"She's a bitch." Barlais paced in a small circle; his body cutting through a shaft of dusty sunlight made the gold on the far wall flash. "And she's part Ibelin."

"She isn't. She's related to them through her grandmother, who married Balian d'Ibelin after the Queen's grandfather died. Don't exaggerate. How strong is John d'Ibelin on Cyprus?"

Barlais shrugged. "Strong enough to make trouble for you, Your Majesty."

And he didn't come to greet me; does he think I'll go looking for him? He brushed his hair back over his shoulders and stared at Barlais, who fidgeted. The door behind them opened, and Marino, the chamberlain, stuck his head in.

"Just a moment, Marino."

Barlais glanced around and turned forward again. "Your Majesty—"

"Yes. I have no real army with me—only two hundred men. Can you raise more?"

With a grin that changed his whole face, Barlais nodded. "As many as you'll need on Cyprus."

"Well, I doubt we'll require that many. Some of the Syrian barons are coming here shortly. Thank you for your information and support. On your way out tell Marino to arrange it so that you can stay openly here. This sneaking around makes me nervous."

Glowing, Barlais bent double and stalked out. Frederick made a face at his back, got up, and walked around the room, stretching. He could hear the sudden babble of voices in the anteroom. Behind a lattice screen in one corner Hasan and Ayub sat cross-legged, and he waved to them. A side door opened, and Corso with two other pages rushed in.

"Sire," Corso said, and sent the other pages on into the next room. "That Ferrante, the one who runs the troupe of jugglers—"

"I thought he'd been paid." Frederick unlaced his coat and reached through to undo the front of his shirt.

"He was, but he wants to know when he can have the girl back, he needs her, he says." Corso glanced toward the front door. "And she won't put on some clothes so we can go in and clean up that room."

"What do you mean, she won't—Oh. Tell Ferrante I haven't made my mind up yet." He started toward the door into the bedchamber, but Marino was already ushering in someone else. Frederick paused a moment, unsure, and finally waved Marino out again and went into the bedchamber.

Theophano was sitting naked in the sun before the window, combing her hair; either she didn't hear him come in or she was ignoring him. He stood still, admiring the sheen of her skin and her supple waist.

"Do you have any clothes?"

She spun around, dropping the comb. "Oh. You startled me. What did you say?" Her black eyes were huge, her low voice unsteady.

"Do you have any clothes?"

"No. Not really." She stood up. Her hands moved uncertainly to shield herself from his eyes and finally dropped to her sides. "Do you want me to go now?"

The way she stood, her slender athletic body poised to run or leap, fascinated him. She's beautiful, he thought, and he nearly said so. "No," he said. "Don't go. But they have to come in and clean up this room, and they can't while you're undressed. I'll take care of that."

She smiled, and her eyes fell. "Thank you." She looked up at him again, and his stomach clenched. For a moment they stared at each other. Finally he turned and went out again, found Corso waiting outside the door, and sent him down to find two women who spoke Greek to attend her and bring her a temporary selection of clothes. Marino stuck his head in again, and Frederick nodded and sat down.

Marino pronounced names, but Frederick wasn't listening. All girls did that, it was a trick they learned in their cradles—to look down, smile, and look up again through their lashes. Adelaide had done it, Bianca did it, even Yolande had done it sometimes. Everybody knew it was a trick. He couldn't understand why Theophano could do it and jolt him to the heels when he was so used to it.

Theophano, he thought. I even like the name.

Holding the state gown at arm's length, Corso stepped awkwardly onto the stool; Frederick maneuvered himself under the gown and settled it onto his shoulders. "God, this thing is heavy."

"They are all here," the Grand Master said. "So, you see, you've still got some currency in Syria—they came as quickly as they could."

"Who is all?" Weighted with gold thread and embroidered with the Hohenstaufen eagles and Frederick's monogram, the state gown hissed when he moved. He walked back and forth through the mob of courtiers, getting used to the burden and settling it more comfortably. "All right. Where's that God-damned crown?"

"John d'Ibelin," Tommaso said, "The King of Cyprus. Very charming boy—no brains, but all the poise in the world. His mother, Queen Alice. Bohemund of Antioch and Tripoli and his wife, Melisande. Balian of Sidon. Incidentally, Melisande is of the Royal House of Jerusalem and must be a cousin of yours. Guy Embriaco and about thirty of his relatives. The Patriarch of Jerusalem, the Grand Master of the Templars, the Grand Master of the Hospitallers."

"Marvelous." Frederick bowed his head so that Corso could put the chain around his neck. Hasan and Ayub had appeared with the crown. "The whole traveling menagerie."

Through the tail of his eye he caught their reaction to that: the twenty-odd men in the room all jerked, upset. Yes, here comes the Emperor in one of his satirical moods. Let them worry, it was good for them. He stopped in front of the golden mirror and looked at himself and clapped his hands together. "Good. Let's go impress the local notables." He swung around, so that the sleeves and skirts of the heavy gown cleaved the air like blades, and winked at the Grand Master. In the corner, Ezzo clapped his hand over his mouth to hold back a laugh; Fulk grinned.

Hasan and Ayub preceded him out the door, while the others jostled each other for position in the train behind him. Moving inside a gown that probably weighed as much as Theophano was a nice problem in mechanics— around corners, he had to lean slightly, and momentum carried him sweeping downstairs, his feet striving to keep up. I should have myself carted around on the backs of Nubian slaves and finish them off entirely. The Archbishop and a local prince of the Church were waiting on either side of the brass doors into the hall, and when he approached they turned, ringed by attendants, and commanded the door to open. Frederick stopped still. Pages sailed around him, brushing his gown, buffing his rings and medallions, and finally plopping the crown on his head. He reached up with both hands and moved it back a little. The heavy, cool edge of the gold forced his head down slightly. Inside the hall, horns and flutes began to play, and when the doors opened he heard the murmur of voices and the rustle of clothes. He advanced—walking was too common a word—into the glaring torchlight and a world of eyes.

For a moment all he saw was motion—the swoop of gowns and heads and hands, a jumble of bodies flexing in bows, the flash of jewels and bullion-trimmed clothes through the slanting light. Thousands of them. He walked straight up to the throne, a prelate on either hand. Dazzling—the gigantic carved marble throne, cushioned in tissue of gold, plastered with jewels—near it, at the foot of a smaller throne, stood the child King of Cyprus, just as burdened down with state regalia, flanked by older men. With his foot on the bottom step of the throne, Frederick met the boy's eyes and smiled.

"Hello, Henri."

The child's eyes widened, but he grinned immediately. Tommaso was right about his poise. Frederick hauled himself up the steps, turned, and faced a hall crammed with people. For the first time he saw individuals instead of a mass of color and light. The heralds were still proclaiming him; horns blasted. With each title the swarm of glittering bodies bobbed and dipped. The little King moved up to stand before his throne. One of the older men around him was John d'Ibelin, probably the graybearded man in the red satin coat. Another stood just behind him, dressed all in black. And nearby a woman watched, not bowing, her hands clasped before her, a middle-aged woman with a long jaw and fierce eyes, who had to be Queen Alice.

He looked around the hall, not moving his head; in the

draft dozens of banners fluttered, worked with the arms of Jerusalem, of Cyprus and Antioch and Tripoli and Acre and Sidon and Beirut—John of Ibelin was Lord of Beirut—the staffs capped with eagles, crosses, gryphons and unicorns. Above them all his imperial banner rippled. The harsh gray stone of the walls, visible between tapestries and paintings on wood, clashed with the pulsating richness of the people, their clothes, their furniture, their attendants. The floor was uncarpeted, covered with rushes through which he knew the vermin swarmed. No matter how rich they were, Cyprus was still only a provincial court. He wished he'd eaten some hashish; this was going to be tedious.

The Patriarch of Jerusalem advanced with his censers. This was ridiculous—because Frederick was excommunicate, the requisite religious ceremony had to be performed before the court but not before him. He stood listening to the old man's mediocre Latin. Piero would have gone into fits: the Patriarch insisted on using ablatives where datives would have been more subtle. At the end everybody crossed himself except Frederick. Time for the speech.

"We are made most welcome in our vassal-kingdom of Cyprus and our pleasure and gratification in the honor thus shown us . . ." Blah blah blah. It was one of Piero's standard speeches for entries into courts not entirely friendly to him, full of praise for the vigor and elegance. The crown hurt his forehead and the gown was making him sweat. At the end of it everybody bowed again and he sat down.

The young King delivered a short speech welcoming Frederick to Cyprus and offering him the resources of the Kingdom for his Crusade. Un-hunh. Nobody was making a fuss about the excommunication; naturally, there was no precedent. Courts transplanted into alien surroundings tended to be conservative. After his speech, Henri dismounted his throne, circled around in front of

Frederick's, and made his obeisance, which meant Frederick had to stand up again. Henri took Frederick's hand and pressed it to his forehead, and Frederick lifted him up. "We are most pleased to accept our cousin and royal vassal." And so forth. He sat down again, and the nobles charged around getting in line to be presented. Frederick's retinue lined up in a semicircle around him; Fulk, on the far end of the left of the crescent, caught Frederick's eye in passing and shook his head slightly.

"Your Majesty," the young King said. "I beg to present Lord John d'Ibelin of Beirut, bailli and Regent of Cyprus."

Frederick's back tensed. He met the old man's blazing dark eyes. "Cousin, why do you come before us in mourning?" He'd been wrong; John was the man in black, not the elegant, elderly other.

"Your Majesty, I am still in mourning for my brother."

A mellow, powerful voice, and arrogance in the way the old man carried himself, a kind of subtle challenge. Frederick said, "The arrival of your suzerain can allow you an exception." He turned to his right. "Tommaso, see that Lord John is dressed as befits his rank." Turning back to John, he smiled. "We wish you honored, cousin. With you, we are honored."

The black eyes narrowed, and the old man's lips twitched. "I am at the service of the Emperor."

Damn right you are. First skirmish mine. Ibelin's two sons were presented, uncomfortable in their mourning clothes and probably furious at Frederick's remarks to their father. The Ibelins left, and Queen Alice took their place, escorted by her new husband, Bohemund's son. She didn't look any too happy about John d'Ibelin's taking precedence over her. Frederick concentrated on being gracious, smiling and commenting softly on the pleasure it was to meet her, and she unbent slightly.

The parade continued—Bohemund, thin and nervous,

and his beautiful, pale wife; Balian of Sidon, all at ease, smiling and vivid. God, this is silly, I'll never remem— Suddenly he saw Theophano, standing in the back, dressed in silk. She lifted her head and smiled. Everybody was staring at her, and he saw the women bend to whisper to their neighbors. Some of the tension eased in his shoulders and back, and he turned to meet the next of the endless line of barons.

Gradually he was able to sort out people by the way they acted before him. Most of them were uncomfortable and would not meet his eyes, and those were enemies or potential enemies. A few, like Balian of Sidon, seemed glad to be presented to him: allies or people who thought they could get something. The pressure of the gown, of the crown, of thinking of the proper things to say, all made him jittery, but when he got the urge to jump up and leave he looked over at Theophano and the feeling left him. I'll understand that later. The end of the line drew perceptibly nearer. In Henri's voice, quavering now with fatigue, he detected relief. Behind him, soft-voiced, Tommaso was murmuring to the Grand Master and the Archbishop, identifying by fief and bloodline the men being presented.

All this gets me nowhere. They've already made up their minds, most of them—Tommaso had suggested that if he borrowed money from Guy of Jebail, it would tie him into the imperial party, but of them all only two or three could be swayed from one position to the other, or even made neutral. The Templars' Grand Master stood in front of him openly hostile. Frederick's nostrils flared; he stared over the man's shoulder and mouthed phrases without emphasis. The bat nailed to the cross: he felt, suddenly, the web of hatred and fear around him, the working of forces against him. I can't leave Cyprus at my back, not this way, we have to . . . Finally the end of the line reached him. The rest of the mob wasn't noble enough to be presented.

For a moment there was silence while everybody waited for someone else to do something. The boy on the next throne looked exhausted. Frederick pushed himself onto his feet. They stirred out there, muttering—the ritual had broken and they weren't sure what to do. He stretched out his arms and snapped his fingers, and from the doors just behind the thrones pages ran, and his Saracens. The crowd before him rippled, astonished and uncertain. I know this doesn't usually happen, people, but —He sat down so that they could remove the crown, stood again, and let them peel off the state gown and replace it with a coat. King Henri was on his feet, staring; he looked envious. Frederick tossed his hair back, descended the steps of the throne, and turned and grinned. In a rush the child came down from his throne, suddenly realizing he'd been standing higher than his suzerain.

"May I—" He came up to Frederick, realized he should ask someone else, and looked around, but John d'Ibelin was gone, getting his clothes changed. He looked back to Frederick. "May I go put on something else?"

"You're the King," Frederick said. "Do what you like." He put his hand on the boy's shoulder a moment and went off through the crowd. His retinue moved around him, Tommaso, the Archbishop, Fulk and Ezzo, the Grand Master, keeping him separate from the mob of Easterners.

The upset murmur of voices died and the court eased itself into the new mood. They were bringing out the food and wine. Gradually the rumble of voices in conversation grew. Frederick looked around for Theophano and saw her near a door, leaving. She met his eyes and smiled and went out, followed by a page in his livery— Giancarlo. He thought, She knows I can't go around in here with her. But she had come—to see all the gaudy show, or just to see him, whatever—

Queen Alice suddenly thrust herself into the midst of his little perambulating court-within-a-court, smiling, her hands armored with jewels. "Your Majesty."

He smiled; be gracious to potential friends. "Your Grace. You have a charming son." Offering her his arm, he headed slowly toward the far end of the room—two of her pages mingled with his men. "And a lovely court." She laughed. "Still, it can't be like Sicily's. You've quite dazzled us, Sire."

"Surely not." Her French was broadly accented, and he had to work to understand it. "Granted, Cyprus seems to be in the hands of the austere, but Antioch and Tripoli are not."

"Oh. John. He has no sense of elegance." Her hand rested lightly on his arm. "Watch him, Sire, he's a difficult man."

"Thank you." That irritated him, and he looked around for her husband to give her back. He was coming through the loose mass of courtiers, a cup in his hand.

"My Lady," he said, mildly, and bowed to Frederick. "Sire, has no one served you? Permit me." He snapped an order to a page. Considerably younger than Alice, he moved with a nearly feminine grace; his green eyes never seemed fully open. Alice transferred her hand to his arm. He said, "Let me precede my lord father this once, Sire, and express to you the devotion of Antioch to the cause which you so admirably pursue."

A page rushed up with wine and a tray full of pastries and glazed fruit, and Frederick looked down at them. He took a cup. "Thank you." Meeting the young man's eyes again, he grinned, and unexpectedly the young man threw his head back and laughed. "Well. At least, my devotion. Your leave, Sire." With Alice reluctantly in tow, he bowed himself out of Frederick's range.

Fulk drifted up. "The feel of treachery in the air, huh?" He took the cup from Frederick and tasted it.

"For the love of Christ," Frederick said, startled. "I really doubt that's necessary."

Tommaso said sourly, "Don't get him upset, Fulk.

Sire, there's Guy Embriaco."

"Damn it. You ask him for the loan." He'd reached the end of the room, and turning, he walked along the wall to the corner, paused to drink wine, and started up the room again. Flocks of minor barons and their women bowed and stared. Bohemund of Antioch fidgeted his way over to him.

"Your Majesty." Bohemund jerked his head in a bow. "Unh—very pleased to—unh—" He pulled himself together with a massive effort. "I'm at your service at any time during the Crusade."

"I'm sure," Frederick said, mildly. "Princess." He smiled at Melisande.

She dipped a tiny curtsey. "You are welcome here, Your Majesty." With a tug on Bohemund's arm, she steered him out of the press.

"God," the Archbishop said. "Definitely frosty, that." Ezzo murmured, "She's damned pretty, though."

Frederick paused to hand his cup to a page. Abruptly, at the far end of the hall, a horn blared, and everybody whirled around. There was a concerted rush among the Syrians and Cypriots toward the far door. John d'Ibelin was coming in. Frederick turned his back just in time and stared in the opposite direction. He knew with a rising uneasiness that almost everybody else in the hall had flown down there to greet John, that very few of the local people stayed here, near him. Well, get it all out in the open. He stared at his banner, rippling slowly in the draft beneath the ungainly vault of the ceiling. If he went over to John, if he made some kind of fuss, they'd all have to pay attention— That was stupid, a salve for his pride. He clenched his fist. There was something else to do, more useful.

Turning, he caught the Grand Master of the Templars staring at him, his eyes glittering, his lips drawn back against his teeth in the ugliest smile Frederick had ever seen. Observe, the man's face said, how you are over-shown by a minor prince. Frederick met his eyes, keeping his face sober and calm. Carefully, behind his back, he folded the index and ring fingers of his left hand in against his palm and thrust the little finger and forefinger straight out; he brought the hand out from behind his back with a flourish that drew the Templar's eyes to it.

The Templar's face went white and his mouth dropped open. Frederick saw him swallow hard. His gaze snapped up to Frederick's face, and Frederick hawked, spat into the rushes on the floor, and with the heel of his slipper ground the spittle into the stone. The Templar took a deep breath, still pale as chalk.

Frederick turned and walked out the nearest door.

"I'm afraid we can't provide you with entertainment like that you have in Sicily, Sire," John d'Ibelin said. "We in Cyprus live quiet lives, dedicated to God and the law."

"My, how noble of you." Frederick played with his fork, drawing furrows across the gross slab of meat rapidly cooling on the plate before him. John's sons were serving as cupbearers at the high table; throughout the rest of the hall people chomped and gurgled their way through what Frederick had decided must be typical Cypriot food, totally unappetizing. He reached for his wine cup. "What do you do for sport?"

John shifted in his chair, almost smiling. "I find prayer and meditation more edifying than racing about after hawks and hounds, myself." He looked around until he found one of Frederick's Saracens, Yusuf, half-concealed behind a buttress. "Of course, the Arabs provide us with some interesting hunting too."

The young King kept stretching his neck to listen. Frederick glanced at him. "It must be unsettling when the prey decides its point of view is as valid as the hunter's, though. But in a game like that such distinctions are obviously arbitrary."

"Yes," John said. "I understand your sympathies lie rather more with the enemies of Christendom."

Frederick leaned back and laid his hands flat on the table, his eyes on the maze of tables before them. "My sympathies as a man, I assure you, are not engaged in this. My only aim is the security and prosperity of my son's kingdom and that of my cousin and vassal, King Henri." They had announced him Regent of the Kingdom of Jerusalem before dinner, which made that legal until the High Court of the Kingdom met to name him officially. Tommaso had said they would not resist.

"How boring it must be for you," John said, "to have to exercise your superb talents among mere provincials. I only hope we can amuse you in some way."

The doors all along the walls had opened earlier and men were moving in behind the people at dinner; nobody, apparently, had noticed. At the far end of the hall Filangieri stood up and lifted one hand to Frederick.

"You may," Frederick said. He glanced at the King again and swept his eyes over the diners. Chewing, drinking, talking to their neighbors, none of them looked disturbed, and yet all around the hall, men stood casually leaning on their swords. Beside him, John abruptly stood up. Frederick thrust his chair back. The scrape of the legs over the rush-covered dais cut through the blur of conversation, and everybody looked up toward him.

"For instance," he said, "you might try accounting to me for the revenues of the Crown of Cyprus, which you seized."

All talk ended; in the silence the growling of the dogs under the tables sounded abruptly loud and harsh. John stared down at Frederick and jerked to look all around the room. The men against the wall, at a signal from Filangieri, stepped forward, throwing off their cloaks— they all wore mail. The men and women at the tables froze, their eyes on the dais, their mouths working.

"This is the basest treachery," John said, loudly. "I was warned to ignore your kind invitation. I was told of the ignoble ways of an irreligious emperor." He flung one hand out. "Before all these witnesses, do you dare display this—unseemly treatment of one who wishes only to serve?"

"Then serve." Frederick realized he was clutching his knife; he made himself put it carefully down. "What happened to the revenues of Cyprus? And for that matter, you'd better account for your dealings in Beirut as well."

"You have no right to require that of me," John said. His voice reached into the farthest corners of the hall. Frederick glanced out toward the rest of the room—Bohemund had stood up, but his son took hold of his sleeve and drew him down. The silence grew heavier and more tense.

"I have every right," Frederick said. He kept his voice low. "As suzerain of Cyprus and—"

Blaring like horns, two dogs started to bark, fighting over a bone. Frederick leaped up, his hand flying toward the dagger in his belt, and a woman screamed, men swore, high-voiced. Two of the soldiers against the wall leaped forward, grabbed the snarling dogs, and threw them bodily out the nearest door. Queen Alice stood up, looking toward her son. The silence crashed down again. Frederick realized that his hands were shaking and he was crouched as if to fight. He stood up, trying to loosen his muscles.

"I am suzerain of Cyprus and Regent of Jerusalem and I have every right to require you to account for your actions."

"Your Majesty," John said, still talking to the whole room, "as bailli of Cyprus I answer only to the High Court, and unless the High Court appeals to you directly, by law you may not intervene. In the case of Beirut, you may demand an account of me only if you are requested to do so by one of my tenants. You cannot legally call me to account on your own initiative."

Frederick thought, I've lost it. The crowd, listening, broke into an excited hum of talk. He glanced toward Tommaso, who was frowning—he hadn't been told of this. Seeing Frederick's eyes on him, he shook his head from side to side.

John said quietly, "If you push this, you know, you're going to undermine the legality of any action you might take in Syria."

Frederick shut his eyes. He hadn't made a mistake this gigantic in years—he'd forgotten about French law, and Cyprus and Syria both were under French customary law. Waves of heat rolled over him. I have to do something, save face, anything—no. That's a sure sign you've —He opened his eyes and looked at John and smiled, and the other man's brows rose in surprise.

" 'Dedicated to God and the law . . .' with reason, I see. And to good account." He was still trembling, but now he saw a way out of this, not a good way, but at least something. "Lord John, the field is yours." He took two steps backward. "At least you can't say I'm a poor loser." He bowed, and in astonishment John bowed as well. The little King was staring at them, his teeth sunk in his lower lip. Frederick turned and went out the door.

In the little room behind the thrones he stood a moment, alone, and with his eyes shut swore under his breath. They'd be laughing at him—John would be so humbly triumphant. Damned old—He clenched his fists before his face; tears stung his eyes.

"Well," Tommaso said. "That was a disaster. Why the hell didn't you talk to me first? Whose idea was that?"

Frederick let his breath out. "Mine."

"Barlais," the Grand Master said. The rest of them— the Archbishop, Filangieri, Fulk, Ezzo, all of them— moved in around him, staring at him, amazed.

"No," Frederick said. "It was all mine. Tommaso; get

me a room, not in my part of the castle, where I can talk. Now. Berardo, you and Hermann—" He paused, wondering how to word it. "You and Hermann go back in there and tell Lord John that I desire to talk with him privately—"

"He'll never agree," the Archbishop said.

"Shut up and listen to me. That I want to talk to him, and that I will place you and Hermann into the hands of his trusted companions as a pledge of my good intentions."

The Grand Master snorted, but the Archbishop only nodded. "Good. I hope you have the sense to say the right thing."

Frederick started for him, but the Grand Master got in the way. "Come on, relax. You deserved that. In my life I've never seen you do anything so completely incompetent as that farce out there. Pull yourself together." He spoke so softly Frederick doubted anyone else heard; he took Frederick by the shoulder and shook him gently. "Calm down."

Frederick shut his eyes again. "I will. I'm sorry." He turned; he could not loosen his muscles, and he ached with tension. He chewed the inside of his cheek, trying to organize himself—his mind felt bruised.

"Sire," Tommaso said. "We can use a room on the second floor of the north wing. I have men there now arranging the furnishings."

"Very good." Frederick looked at the Grand Master. "Will you ask him, Hermann?"

"We will," the Archbishop said lightly, and with the Grand Master left the room for the great hall. When the door opened, Frederick heard a blast of voices; he knew what they were talking about, and his face grew hot with shame. Spinning around, he headed for the far door, and the rest of his staff fell in behind him, like armor against the enemies out there.

* * *

"I want to . . . apologize," Frederick said. He leaned his head back against the chair and stared at the ceiling. "I had some information and I acted hastily upon it."

John said nothing for a long moment. Through the corner of his eye Frederick saw him frowning. At last he said, "Obviously that's an apology I must accept. I do advise Your Majesty to curb your rashness henceforth. Already you've made enemies here. Without the support of the local nobility, you cannot hope to succeed at anything in Syria."

We'll see about that. "I'm in an uncomfortable position. I am the suzerain of Cyprus, after all, and I should, in the normal course of events, investigate the affairs of the kingdom. Especially with the King a minor. Were you ever officially appointed bailli?"

There was a distinct pause. "Of course I was. The law of Cyprus is almost sacred to me, and I would not break it."

"In that case you will have no objections to allowing my agents to see the accounts of the revenues of your tenure in office."

"As I told Your Majesty, such accountings can only be requested through the High Court."

Frederick nodded. He concentrated on keeping his voice soft, almost wheedling. "I intend to go through the regular procedure. The difficulty is that I won't be able to go to Nicosia, where I believe the High Court meets and the accounts are kept, until at least a few weeks from now. May I request you to summon the Court and arrange the accounts for inspection?"

Through the lashes of his half-closed eyes he saw John's face sharpen. They were alone in the bleak little room; the furnishings, hastily assembled, looked out of place and the bare walls cold and damp. John said, "I am at Your Majesty's service, as I said earlier. Anything I can do to hasten your passage to Syria I shall do."

Get me out of here, you mean. "Thank you. I must ask you to leave me some token of your good faith."

"Hostages." John frowned. "Certainly, if Your Majesty believes—"

"I do. Cyprus is already hostile to me; I can't hope to bring her to my side, but with a little time I can neutralize her. To gain time I need peace, and those people adherent to your cause who haven't your honor and sagacity might be put off attacking me if I had in my train the young King, for instance, and your two sons."

The old man made a face. "Your Majesty, I can assure you that no one would consider attacking you."

"As you said, I've already made enemies." Frederick made his voice plead. "I am a timid man, Lord John."

Head bowed, John paced back and forth. "Of course, if Your Majesty requests it of me, I can do no less for the suzerain of Cyprus."

"I am pleased you understand my position. I shall meet you, therefore, at Nicosia?"

"As you will, Sire." John bowed his head. Frederick stared at the gryphon carved over the doorway. After a moment John realized he'd been dismissed and he fussed a little, his hands rising. "Your Majesty." His voice quavered, peeved. "Good evening."

"Good night, my Lord."

He couldn't help biting off the end of the last word, and John, who had turned toward the door, glanced back. Frederick's anger must have shown in his face; the old man lifted his head and nearly said something, but instead he bowed again and went out. The door shut gently behind him.

Arrogant, usurping. "Of course." He was never appointed, he simply took the office, used the minority of the King and the squabble over the Regency of Queen Alice to embezzle power, if not money. To steal power. Frederick bounded out of his chair and charged out the door, headed for his own part of the castle. His Saracens were waiting outside.

He nearly ran down the steps, ignoring them. There was no chance of trying him for it; if he couldn't alter the records he might very well destroy them. He charged through a series of empty rooms and banged into his own antechamber—into the middle of his staff, who were standing around talking. They jumped, startled.

"Well?" Tommaso said.

"It's mended," Frederick said. "Damned clumsy job, but it's mended. He'll be gone by morning, but his sons and the King are staying as hostages. I haven't told him yet that he's no longer bailli, but we'll get to that." He pulled off his coat and threw it to Corso.

"Did you fight with him?" the Archbishop said. "You look furious, Sire."

"I'm livid."

"Then they didn't fight," the Grand Master said. "He's never angry after a fight." He turned away, talking to Filangieri.

Tommaso said quietly, "What about the revenues?"

"We'll check the accounts in Nicosia. They'll be in order. And I don't feel like finding any irregularities anyway." I don't dare. I—don't—dare. He spread his arms wide, threw his head back, and shouted wordlessly.

"I think," Tommaso said, "we'd better leave. Sire, with your permission—" He headed for the door.

"If I can't yell at my own staff, whom can I yell at?"

"By your leave, Sire—" They filed past him, bowing, and walked out the door. Some of them were actually grinning. His pages and servants came in and started to undress him.

"Oh, get the hell out of here, I'm sick of being treated like a child." He struck at Corso's hands. "Go on, leave me. Go away."

Corso backed away, drawing the other pages with him; the servants, Cypriots unused to his moods, raced off, ashen. Corso said, "Will there be anything else, Sire?"

Frederick scrubbed his face with his palm. The stubble of his beard rasped his hand. "No. Good night."

"Good night," Corso said. The other pages trotted out; Corso paused to make sure the water pitcher was filled. "Sleep well, Sire."

"Sure."

The boy left. Frederick prowled around the room, not tired, wishing he were back in Sicily. The old man, with his tissue-thin arrogance,—I can do nothing. He betrayed his King and I can do nothing. He washed his face in the water from the pitcher.

"Are you throwing things yet?" Theophano said.

"What?" He spun around. She was standing in the doorway into his dressing chamber, wrapped in a fur rug; she grinned at him. He straightened up, his hands dripping.

"I heard you yelling—I was asleep and it woke me up. I just wondered if you'd gotten to the throwing-things stage yet." She came slowly into the room, yawned, and hitched the fur rug up over her shoulder. "I'm told you had a difficult evening."

"Oh, Christ." He dried his hands and face on a towel and threw it down.

"You looked wonderful, all dressed up. Like something from a play. Why don't you come into the bedroom and let me rub your back?" She removed one arm lanquidly from within the fur and stretched it out. "Come along."

"You're amazing." He went over to her and put his arm around her waist. "How did you know I love being mothered?" Looking down at her face, into her huge dark eyes, he couldn't help grinning.

"That's easy. Why else would you act like a child so often?" She squeezed him. They went through the dressing chamber and into the bedroom. "Some women brought me the most wonderful clothes. Did you see that green silk dress I had on in the great hall?"

"Yes. It's beautiful." She met his eyes as if she had no reason to look away, ever; the last irritation left him. He put his hand on her hair. "You can go to Syria with me, can't you?"

"If you want me to." She tugged at the laces of his shirt. "You look tired. I'll put you to bed." She shrugged off the rug and kicked it away—she wore nothing else, and while she stood casually taking his clothes off for him he wished he weren't so tired. Wait until the morning.

"Do you eat hashish?"

"When I can get it." She looked up sharply at him, frowning, and drew his shirt up around his chest. Holding his arms out, he bent so she could pull it off over his head. "Why?" she said cautiously.

"I have some. In my cherry-wood chest."

"Sometimes you amaze me. Do you want some now?" She led him toward the bed.

"No. I'm too tired, I have to sleep. Later. In the morning." She was going to Syria; she would eat hashish with him. He felt absurdly happy and much less alone. Sprawled on the bed, he watched her trim down the lamps, walking naked around the room, and a soft glow of gratitude filled him.

John d'Ibelin was not in Nicosia when Frederick finally got there; he'd gone to Dieu d'Amour, his castle on the far side of the island. Tommaso frowned, reporting it.

"He sent all his women and the small children there as soon as he got here. I thought you'd said it was mended."

"It is." Frederick signed papers, not bothering to read them. "He'll talk nicely when we catch up with him. Is there any record of his being appointed bailli?"

"No. The Archbishop is checking the accounts now. What did you drag all the Syrian barons here with us for? They're putting everybody out—complaining about the accommodations." Tommaso walked around the porch, scuffing his shoes on the stone floor. "Not that I blame them. Nicosia is a flaming bore, there's nothing for them to do—"

"I want them to get used to me."

The Grand Master looked up from a letter he'd been reading. "That should take some doing."

"Hermann. That wasn't nice." He dipped the pen in ink and scribbled.

Tommaso sank down onto a bench. "Why? It's taken all of us several years at least." He smiled. "What are you writing?"

"Charters. If he was never appointed I don't have to go through the High Court to have him dismissed. I just have to appoint another."

"That might not be so easy. Do you want to start a civil war?" Tommaso smiled. "You could, just by letting that woman of yours spend more time with the Syrians. They're completely overturned by her—she's marvelous."

Frederick grinned. He'd let Theophano—ordered Theophano—to appear at a small reception the evening before, and half the Syrian baronage had trailed around after her the while. Fulk came out onto the porch, saw them, and walked over.

"When are we going?"

"Going where?" the Grand Master said.

"Dio d'Amore," Fulk said. "Anyplace is better than here. Sire, can Ezzo and I go hunting this afternoon?"

"It's not the season for hawks."

"We're taking some dogs."

"Go right ahead. Leave me here buried in work—"

"Thank you." Fulk marched away.

"And when we reach Dieu d'Amour," the Grand Master said, "what then?"

"I tell him he isn't bailli anymore, and he thanks me for relieving him of the chore."

Silence. He finished signing the papers and rang a little silver bell for a page. Out in the courtyard pigeons strutted around pecking at the ground and each other; grass grew up through the cracks in the flagstones, and little trees sprouted from the wall. Frederick got up and walked around, stretching his legs. He needed another haircut. Theophano had said she'd give him one in the afternoon.

"What a name for a castle," the Grand Master said. "Dieu d'Amour."

"The Greeks call it Didymi," Tommaso said, as if he were reciting a lesson. "It's one of the more difficult places on Cyprus to attack."

Frederick had his back to them both. He hooked his thumbs inside his belt and watched a hawk circling above the low hills to the west.

"And the old King gave it to Lord John some years ago," Tommaso said loudly.

The page came; Frederick sent him for Balian of Sidon.

"According to French law," Tommaso went on, as loudly, "no baron can be evicted from—"

"—a castle given him by a former monarch while the present government is a regency," Frederick said. "I know."

The noon sunlight sparkled on bits of mica in the paving stones; the pigeons cooed and strutted around. On the other side of the wall, someone shouted in Cypriot Greek.

"It would be much better if Cyprus were ruled under Sicilian law," Frederick said.

"I think you'll have trouble arranging that," Tommaso said.

"Probably. We can try later. It's a very untidy government."

The Grand Master said, "People rarely like an abrupt change in the nature of rule. It makes them nervous. Sire, why don't you go hunting with Fulk and Ezzo?"

"I have work to do." He flipped his hair out of his eyes. "We're leaving for Dieu d'Amour in two days. Sooner, if Berardo gets done checking the finances."

Balian of Sidon came around the corner, followed by two of his brothers; he saw Frederick and waved cheerfully. Over his shoulder he said something to his brothers, who left through the side gate. Balian sauntered up, smiling, and bowed.

"Good morning. How do you like Nicosia?"

Frederick wrinkled up his nose, and Balian laughed.

"No, neither do we. May I help you?"

"Yes, if you don't mind?" He liked Balian, he couldn't help it—he was as light and sunny as the air. "You're John d'Ibelin's cousin, aren't you?"

"I'm everybody's cousin."

"So am I, but that doesn't help. Can you mediate between us? He's angry, or he wouldn't have run off to that castle."

"Oh." Balian scratched his nose. He wore a ruby ring on one finger that caught the sun and flashed red light across his brown hand. "He's not angry. He's worried, probably—John gets ruffled when people try to force him into things, Sire."

"Do you think he'll agree to terms?"

"I hope so. I think he will. I mean, it's obvious that you can't fight him, but on the other hand you can make trouble for him." Balian smiled. "He can make trouble for you, though, Sire."

"I know. Good. I can count on you, then. We'll leave for Dieu d'Amour as soon as possible—my fleet is meeting me near there to take us to Syria."

Balian's smile disappeared. He looked beyond Frederick to Tommaso, shook his head slightly, and said, "You aren't going to like Acre. Well. With your leave, I have to go."

"Of course."

Balian bowed, backed up three easy strides, and went off. Tommaso said, "What did that mean?"

Frederick shook his head. "I don't know. Maybe he doesn't like Acre and he's judging it by that." But he thought he understood; he frowned, looking out into the dusty sunlight of the courtyard.

"If I were King of Cyprus, I'd tear that castle down." Frederick slung one leg across the pommel of his saddle and scowled at Dieu d'Amour.

King Henri said, "Why?"

"It's too defensible. My God. It's an eyrie." He twisted to look down the slope toward the green plain, where the clusters of tents stood like huge silken flowers. Horses drifted over the grass beyond the tents, and he could see the servants carrying buckets and big panniers from one area of the camp to another. If you can't give them a real war, try a fake one; the Syrians were enjoying this almost as much as fighting a Crusade—a kind of pretty imitation of a siege. Over his head, sprouting from the naked rock of the height of the pass, the tower fluttered with pennants. He could see goats on the lower slopes of the two peaks that gave the castle its Greek name.

"Tell us another riddle," Theophano said.

"I still haven't figured out the last one." The King moved a little closer to her, shy and adoring. "Have you?"

"Ummm—the monk's name was Each."

The King's brow furrowed. Abruptly he grinned. "Oh. I get it."

"Tell us another riddle, Red," she called.

The Saracens laughed out loud, and Frederick turned and glared at them. "I have to get back, we're having a general council."

"Tell us a riddle on the way, then." The King stretched out one hand. "An easy one, this time."

"All right. If we start now I'll have thought of one by the time we get to camp." Frederick swung his leg down and turned his horse. His Saracens and the King's attendants with the picnic baskets banded around them, chattering to each other—the King had insisted that Frederick bring all four Saracens, he said that they made him think of Syria and romantic stories. The picnic itself had been Theophano's idea. They trotted down the steep, rocky slope, within range of Dieu d'Amour's crenelated walls. Theophano rode up next to Frederick and smiled at him.

"Are you angry with me? For calling you Red."

"No." He tapped his horse with his heel, moving in closer to her, and reached for her hand. "You can call me Red any time you want."

"I'm flattered."

Simultaneously they leaned toward each other; Frederick put one hand on her saddle and kissed her. Among the attendants of the young King someone gasped, horrified. Frederick settled back into his saddle and glanced around.

"The name of the castle is Dieu d'Amour, isn't it?"

Henri was watching them longingly. He'd developed a crush on Theophano at the banquet in Nicosia. Frederick grinned at him, and Henri took it as an invitation to ride beside them, next to Theophano.

"Have you thought of a riddle yet?"

Frederick said, "Well, there's one—" Suddenly he saw something in the camp—John d'Ibelin's banner. "Jesus."

"What's wrong?"

"I have to get down there. Here's the riddle. If you fill a cup half-full of wine and another cup half-full of water, and if you—" Balian's banner was there, too, flying from the peak of the red tent in the middle. He stood in his stirrups and looked for Hasan. "If you pour a spoonful of the wine into the cup of water, and then pour an equal spoonful of the mixture into the cup of wine, is there more wine in the water cup or more water in the wine cup?" He grinned at Theophano. "I hope it ties your mind in knots."

Her lips moved; Henri was staring into space, looking blank. Frederick kicked his horse into a gallop. His Saracens thundered after him, racing. In the pretty little camp men pointed at them and shouted. Hasan veered over to ride just ahead of Frederick, showing off his horse's superior speed, and Frederick immediately reined down to a canter. Ayub shouted, "One to you, Hasan."

Frederick turned and made a fig at him. They slowed to a trot through the edge of the camp, where the laundresses had spread acres of linen out to dry, glaring white in the noonday sun, with small boys set around to keep the goats and birds away.

The Grand Master came out on foot to meet him, three tents down from the red one. "We were just about to send for you when we saw you come down from the pass. They've only now arrived; everything looks pleasant." He bawled for a groom to hold Frederick's horse.

"He's been told of the outcome of the investigation?"

"Yes. Naturally, he wasn't surprised. He's feeling vindicated and very up on his dignity."

Frederick dismounted and walked toward the tent, with the Grand Master beside him. "You'd better send for his sons."

"Yes, Sire."

The tent door opened; Tommaso, the Archbishop and Bohemund of Antioch came out. As always, Bohemund's hands fidgeted constantly. Frederick went over to them and they bowed.

"Did you enjoy your picnic?" the Archbishop said. "He's agreed to the terms, and it's time for the kiss of peace."

Bohemund said, "Umm—Your Majesty, when do we,

unh, take ship for Syria?"

"As soon as possible, my Lord, just take it easy."

"Well, I really, unh, have to get back—pressing business in my, unh, councils—"

"Yes. I know. You've been telling me—" Frederick brushed past him into the tent, gritting his teeth. In the dim light he saw nothing for a moment, but he heard the rustle of clothes and the creak of chairs: everybody had stood up to greet him. He made a gesture. "Sit, please." His eyes cleared and he saw John d'Ibelin standing in front of a torch standard.

"Your Majesty," John said coldly.

Frederick eyed him, looked around and saw Balian. Through the door behind him came Guy Embriaco and a pack of his followers. The tent was filling up. Frederick nodded to John and went over to one side of the tent; his people were gathering there. The Archbishop and Tommaso simultaneously reached for the same chair for Frederick.

"Never mind, I'll stand." His hands were dirty and he rubbed them absently together.

Amalric Barlais rushed in, blinking to clear his eyes, and John drew himself up and glared. Frederick glanced around; Bohemund was in one corner, keeping neutral and drinking wine, and a Templar sent along as the observer of the order stood square in the middle of John's section. The rumble of conversation filled the tent. Most of the men had come straight from lounging around the camp, so everything looked too casual and a little sloppy. Frederick shrugged out of his light cloak and let it drop. A page hustled over to take it away.

Balian stepped out into the middle of the tent. "Is everybody here who should be?"

"Yes," Guy Embriaco said. "Let's get on with this."

Frederick said, "My lord the Grand Master has gone to bring Lord John's sons. We'd better wait for him." He picked up a cup from a bright red table in front of him; it was empty. Half a cup of wine and half a cup of water—He held the cup out to one side, not bothering to look, and someone poured him wine. Ezzo and Fulk came in, filthy from hunting.

Suddenly Bohemund rushed out of his quiet corner into the middle of John's supporters. Guy Embriaco, behind Frederick, murmured, "You fool, Prince." Somebody else laughed—over on John's side of the tent. Well over two-thirds of the people massed under the swaying silk walls stood near John. Frederick glumly sipped his wine. He'd spent too much time already on Cyprus, quibbling over this small thing. Through the door John's two sons walked, smiling, went straight to their father, and knelt. John put one hand on each bent head; Frederick rolled his eyes toward the ceiling. The next tableau would be mother and child surrounded by cherubs. Taking off his cloak, the Grand Master moved up beside him.

Balian said, "We'll start now, I think. You all know what has led to this—the accusations against John d'Ibelin, Lord of Beirut, formerly bailli of Cyprus—"

Immediately they were all murmuring, craning to look at John and at Frederick; John's sons stood up, their faces tight. Bohemund crept toward the periphery of John's circle. Frederick looked smiling into his wine cup. It all winds up the same in the end. Balian cleared his throat.

"In Limassol, Lord John gave hostages to His Majesty Frederick, Emperor of the West, in token of his good faith until the charges could be investigated. In Nicosia, the Archbishop Berardo of Palermo investigated the records and found them to be in order. So the hostages are to be returned, and the charges dropped. In addition, King Henri of Cyprus will formally renew his pledge of fealty to the Emperor, and with him all of Cyprus will swear its loyalty. Queen Alice remains the Regent during the King's minority."

Bohemund was inching steadily toward Frederick's

side of the tent.

"The Emperor," Balian said, "will appoint a new bailli, and Lord John will appear before the High Court of Jerusalem as soon as practical to defend his right to the fief of Beirut."

"How did you get him to accept that?" Tommaso whispered.

"We promised him he'll keep it," Frederick said. "But I wanted to make sure he comes to Syria with us."

Smiling, Balian held out his hands, one to John, one to Frederick, and they both advanced. John looked sour. With his right hand in Balian's, Frederick said, "Come, come, cousin. It's all for the best."

John's brow lowered over his nose. "You are arrogant, for such a young man."

"Ssssh." Balian put their hands together. "Greet each other as friends; your dispute has ended."

Stiffly, staring over one another's shoulder, they shook hands. Everybody in the packed tent was watching, rapt. With his hands on John's shoulders, Frederick leaned forward and pressed his cheek to the old man's—this was stupid, nothing was over. He could not believe anyone would think it was. They stepped apart; John's angry face still stared beyond him, shutting him out. Frederick looked curiously at him, wondering what he was thinking—if he was thinking at all, or just feeling. Balian called the others to witness and they answered with the formula phrases. Normally a priest would have said something over them but with Frederick excommunicated they'd dispensed with it, although John had some priests with him. Frederick backed up until he stood on his side of the tent again. What if he regrets it too? How do we really settle it?

"We will sail from Famagusta as soon as we can get there. Most of you, I know, are coming to Acre. It won't be necessary for anyone who has sworn an oath of fealty to King Henri to renew it in person to me; the King's pledge binds you. Thank you."

They all bowed, and started out. Now that it was over, he knew that he'd let his first uncertainty in a place full of enemies stampede him into the mistake at Limassol; he'd have to watch out for that in Syria. Cyprus was only a foretaste. Bohemund was shifting around near the door, making sure Frederick saw him among his party.

"Prince Bohemund," Frederick said, loudly enough for everybody to hear him, and smiling went up to Bohemund and put one hand on his shoulder. "You've never sworn fealty to me for Antioch, have you?"

Bohemund's face turned to wax. His mouth opened slightly, shut again, and he swallowed. Frederick's smile widened into a grin, and with a laugh he went outside.

Sicilian chatelains in all the castles, Amalric Barlais as bailli, the King sworn personally into your service —you'll scare them to death," the Archbishop said. "It all worked out fairly well, but for God's sake don't panic them."

"I'm trying not to."

"Oh, sure," Tommaso said. "Telling Bohemund in front of everybody to swear Antioch over to you. Not scaring them a bit." He leaned back and glared out the porthole into the streaming rain.

"It was a joke. He was making me nervous."

The Archbishop laughed. He swung his feet up onto a stool and beckoned to Corso to serve Frederick again. The rain drummed on the hull of the ship; through the open portholes came the gurgle of the sea in their wake. Frederick spread honey onto the last of the corn cakes.

"Most people don't have your sense of humor," Tommaso said. "They took it as a sign of unlimited ambition. The Empire has never controlled Antioch."

"Bohemund the First was a tenant of the King of Sicily. There's a precedent." He took a cup from Corso and ate the honey cake, washing it down with sips of light wine.

"Precedent," Tommaso said. "You're known to interpret precedent in an original fashion. Bohemund the First was enfeoffed of Taranto; he held Antioch of nobody. God, this voyage is driving me crazy."

"I know." They were packed into the galleys like cattle, and everybody was whining. Bohemund had excused himself from the Crusade for pressing medical reasons, and his people had spread the rumor around Famagusta that he'd suffered a complete collapse. Tommaso was probably right about his comment to Bohemund alarming the other barons.

"They're upset enough about the excommunication,"

Tommaso said. "As for taking a Saracen bodyguard to the Holy Land—"

Frederick put his knife down. "Tommaso, if you don't stop complaining I'm going to put you on another ship. Now, shut up."

Tommaso flushed and looked away, and the Archbishop immediately became fascinated by the far wall. Corso had fallen asleep in his corner—this voyage, he hadn't gotten seasick at all, but the rain made him morose. Just the other side of this partition Theophano would be in bed, sleeping or combing her hair, and Frederick thought of going in there and splitting the rest of the hashish with her.

"What's the age of majority on Cyprus?"

"Fifteen," Tommaso said.

"And Henri is eight?"

Rain blew in the porthole, and Tommaso swung the window closed. "Yes. In Jerusalem the age is twenty-five."

"How difficult would it be to apply that in Cyprus?"

"Not terribly. Henri is too mild to protest, and while his mother is Regent, you'd have no trouble from that direction. Besides, you've just made yourself the actual ruler of the kingdom."

"I was just wondering how long I'd have to work with it."

"Seventeen years. Long enough."

"No," Frederick said. He picked up his knife and another corn cake.

The Archbishop said, "It took you much less than that in Sicily. And you started with chaos."

"That was why it took less time. Everybody was fighting everybody else and the whole structure had broken down. Besides, I had Norman laws. In Cyprus we'd have to break everything down first, get rid of the French law, work through the King—" He put the cake down again. "No chance."

"You'd have less of a chance in Jerusalem. And at least Cyprus would be useful to you," Tommaso said.

"So would Milan. I've been working on Milan for years and gotten absolutely nowhere."

The Archbishop laughed and folded himself more comfortably into his chair. "The Milanese don't believe in laws."

"All the Milanese are natural rebels."

But Cyprus would be . . . good to have. He began to think of ways to circumvent the barons. Having his own men in as chatelains in the castles started it, but the machinery necessary to rule through a regency slowed everything down. Try it, at least. They hated him, though. Maybe for the rest of the Crusade he'd soothe them. The rain clattered on the porthole; in two days they would be in Acre.

Theophano in the next cabin . . . He shut his eyes. They could lie there all day long, dreaming, entwined in each other's arms and legs. Sitting here waiting was sending him wild. Theophano—her long, tilted eyes. What if she doesn't want me as much as I want her? The Archbishop and Tommaso sat with their knees nearly touching, cramped in the tiny cabin, trying to give him enough room to stretch out. They are like my hands, they do as I will. Sometimes. Remember in Capua when we spent three days working out the wording of that one law? Nobody thought it would work, but of course it did, it was the only way. To rule everybody, not only the nobles but everyone in Sicily. Theophano: "That riddle is impossible. Why are your riddles always geometry in disguise?" Most people never realize that. I wish there was no one else on board—I could play sailor. He stood up, and Tommaso and the Archbishop stumbled all over each other, rising.

"I'm going back to bed. Make sure I'm up for dinner, will you?"

* * *

The rain drizzled down over Acre, turning everything gray. Frederick turned toward the Grand Master. "I thought it never rained out here."

"It doesn't," the old man said stiffly. "This is unusual."

The horses splashed through puddles in the streets, past the blank walls of stone buildings. No crowds, no cheering welcome; messengers from the Pope had arrived weeks before and preached in all the churches. *This Emperor is Antichrist.* Take your choice of legends, because one will surely fit. The Grand Master was upset about the lack of a reception, but Frederick was not. He twisted to look back at the train following him and saw the litter that carried Theophano, dripping and bedraggled, the tassle bleeding red dye all over the light blue sides. Hasan moved his mare a little closer to keep the umbrella over Frederick's head.

"It's so empty," Ayub said in Arabic.

"Be quiet," Hasan said.

Ahead of them knights in even rows rode with their lances at salute, just as if there were cheering crowds on either side, and behind them the barons wore their showy cloaks and hoods. Nobody spoke. The hollow clopping of the horses' hoofs boomed off the stone walls all around them. Behind the shutters, probably, the people were watching, all madly excited. *Is this any way to enter a town, like a defeated man sneaking back to the safety of home?* They passed under an archway; pigeons cooed in the dark above his head. Most of the barons had gone quickly off to their town houses when they realized there would be no thrilling ceremony.

They rode slowly through an empty bazaar, the stalls closed up against the rain and the Emperor. Bits of garbage covered the wide square, and in the middle a low circular well overflowed into a rushing gutter. When they turned down a side street, most of the people behind him went off somewhere else. No one left in the train now except his servants and personal friends and bodyguard. Under a round of stone projecting from a shuttered church a boy crouched, ragged, his black hair hanging in his eyes; he watched them go by with a shrewd, old look on his face. Beggar. Living in the streets turns them old fast. I should know. Me, like that, once, long ago: Markwald was entering—triumphal entry into Palermo—and I sneaked out to watch. They say Jerusalem is full of beggars. I wonder what Theophano is thinking.

Brindisi and Barletta after the Children's Crusade had swarmed with children younger than that, but their faces hadn't been shrewd and old. Lost. The sea was supposed to open up and let us pass to Jerusalem. Dry shod, and we were to redeem the world. All the little children, going to redeem the world and rescue Jerusalem. The boy was gone; they rode past houses trimmed with carvings and boxes of flowers, red and purple blotches against the dank, streaming stone. I hate Crusades.

"Here, Sire."

They rode in through an iron gate, and from the house inside the wall people spilled, laughing, waving their arms. Frederick sucked in his breath. These were all Germans, servants of the Teutonic Order, knights and lay brothers. They laughed and crowded around them, handing them fistfuls of flowers, embracing the knights. The Grand Master dismounted and held Frederick's horse; a cluster of knights and monks, all smiling, stood just behind him, looking from the Grand Master to Frederick and back.

"Sire—"

When he turned from the horse, they all knelt, and a cheer rose in German. Tommaso was smiling, the Archbishop was laughing out loud. Frederick spread his arms. "Not here, not in the wet. Let's go inside."

The knights rose and shouted, "Long live the Emperor." Inside, lights showed, and they pushed toward the door. Hands touched him, shyly, and when he looked around they hid themselves behind other men, all grinning. He laughed and reached out to squeeze the Grand Master's shoulder. All around him the patter of German voices drowned the rain. They flooded into a huge room, steaming warm and stinking of wet wool. The smell of meat cooking, of fresh bread and—he sniffed hard. "Beer." The Grand Master turned and grinned, nodding.

Frederick flung off his cloak. Conrad of Hohenlohe, who had come with him but always on another ship, rushed up with a knight in tow: "Sire, do you remember my cousin Richard?" Behind him the others pushed and shoved, trying to get near him. Their voices rose sharply.

"Sire." The Grand Master handed him a tankard of beer. "You didn't expect a small chip of Swabia out here, did you? Come over here and sit and we'll try to make these children observe some kind of order." He turned to bellow at a cook. Hasan and Ayub were standing at Frederick's elbows, looking nervous, and some of the knights were staring openmouthed at them. Frederick kept peering over shoulders and around heads and sniffing the air—everything reminded him of a German castle kitchen, even the wooden benches, the neat arrangement of iron forks and spoons on the wall. He let the Grand Master take him to a chair and sat down. Theophano came into the room.

She paused a moment, looking around, smiling, and in that moment all the knights saw her and stopped talking and looked. There probably hadn't been a woman in this building since . . . Frederick stood up. She saw him and walked through the pack of staring men as if she had always lived there, pulled a stool up to the side of his chair, and sat down at his feet, grinning up at him. The Saracens rushed up to range themselves against the wall behind him.

The room twitched back to life. Frederick drank his beer and gave the tankard to someone to fill up again. Bending, he pulled Theophano's hair and whispered, "Remind me someday to make you an empress."

She laughed. "Why?"

They were bringing out food, and everybody was drinking. Two knights came up and knelt, their eyes bright. "Your Majesty, do you remember us?"

"You were in Aachen," Frederick said. "During the coronation."

They beamed; one put out his hand impulsively, and Frederick shook it. Around their necks they wore gold crosses on chains. Yes—brothers. He said something, and they blushed, pleased that he'd remembered them, that he'd spoken to them. The tankard came back, brimming with beer, and he sipped it. Theophano laid her hand surreptitiously on his knee. Servants brought them wooden plates of meat and bread.

Frederick was the only man sitting down—the rest of them stood, talked, roamed around, laughed, and gestured, plates in their hands, spilling beer all over the stone floor. Conrad of Hohenlohe was greeting everybody with bearhugs and kisses—many of his friends were here, and they hadn't met for years. In the corner a minnesinger tuned his lute.

The Archbishop came up. "God, I'm drunk already. You're staying in the house next door, do you know that, Sire?"

"Yes. Where are you and Tommaso?"

"Across the city, in Tommaso's house near Saint Anthony's Gate. It's smaller than yours."

Ezzo was talking to the minnesinger. "Is that the one Conrad brought with him?" Frederick said, nudging the Archbishop.

"Him? I think so. He's called the Freidank."

"Good. I'm lonely for music." God, what a collection: an excommunicate, a freethinker, a Greek dancing girl, and seventy Teutonic knights. He stroked Theophano's hair. Ezzo came toward him, grinning, and behind him the Freidank rose—lean, his blond hair braided like a girl's with red flowers. The knights hushed expectantly.

"What is the language they speak?" Theophano said.

"German. My father's native tongue." When I'm with Germans my father comes out in me. He sprawled in the chair and flung one leg over the arm.

"Sire," the Freidank called in his clear deep voice. "My Lady." With a bow. "Gentlemen of the Teutonic Order and gentlemen not of the Teutonic Order."

Two Cistercians had come in through a side door; they stood with their hands in their sleeves, murmuring. Fulk came up to Ezzo, took him by the arm, and whispered into his ear. His dark smiled flashed.

The Freidank said, "Legend has it that when an emperor enters Jerusalem, the Golden Age will begin and everybody will be happy again, as they were in the old days."

The Cistercians and some of the others laughed.

"And who could doubt that our Emperor could not tomorrow enter Jerusalem if he so wished?"

"I can," Frederick murmured, but nobody heard.

"So we will sing of the new age."

The man struck a chord and began to sing. Fulk had knelt beside Frederick to ask him something, but he waited, listening. The song was simple enough, and the Freidank played the lute well, but from his first words everybody listened for what he said. "No more dying in the time to come—"

"He's a heretic," Fulk whispered.

"Shut up."

The Freidank walked around, his eyes on the ceiling, singing, and the knights moved quietly out of his way to let him pass, their eyes following him. No more dying, no more wars, and everyone would get his due— "The nobleman now lives at ease, his people slaving on their knees." No more in the time to come. People always think that. I suppose we couldn't live if we didn't. We're all dying to reach heaven. He turned to Fulk.

"May Ezzo and I go out later?"

In the middle of the Freidank's song he caught a passing vision of taverns, of whores and dicing and brawls. No, damn it, if I can't go—

"Yes. Of course."

"Every man will know his way, no one shall be lost again in the golden time to come."

How incredibly boring. But we go on trying to impose order on the world, when we'd go mad if we ever did. He caught Tommaso's eye and mouthed at him to pay the Freidank.

The song ended and everybody applauded; the Freidank went on with a short but pointed piece about the Pope—one of those, apparently, who had lost his way in the time that was. Theophano picked over her plate and fed scraps to a cat that had come in from the rain. The knights punctuated the song with bursts of laughter and shouts. They were drinking without pause, and Frederick knew he was getting drunk. When the Freidank stopped, Tommaso went to him and handed him a purse.

The singer whirled and bowed to Frederick. "The fabled munificence of the Emperor."

Frederick smiled. "If I didn't pay you, Freidank, how long would I be Emperor?"

Some of the knights laughed, and someone shouted. "Forever."

"If you get minnesingers angry, they'll call you all the names there are, and in the end people believe them. It was the minnesingers who brought Otto the Welf down." Lashed to ribbons on the stone floor of a cathedral.

The Freidank came nearer. "The minnesingers and a fairy-tale prince from the south?"

"And the Pope. Intending wickedness and performing

good. Sing me a love song."

The Freidank glanced at Theophano and grinned. "I'm not so good at love songs, Sire."

"Oh? Well—" He hitched himself up and looked around. "Let's try an experiment. Yusuf?"

Yusuf stepped forward, his white robes swirling around him. The knights murmured again; they weren't used to friendly Saracens. Frederick took the lute from the Freidank and handed it up to Yusuf. "Play me something," he said in Arabic.

Hasan said quietly, "Lord, they don't like us here."

"Play anyway."

Yusuf took the lute, glanced warily around, and tuned it. The Freidank said, "This will be interesting."

"Sit down and listen."

The tall man grinned and collapsed crosslegged at Frederick's feet. Yusuf got the lute balanced in his arms. "Lord, you know I'm not used to this kind of—"

The Cistercians came farther into the room, putting their hoods back. Still muttering, the knights nudged each other and frowned. Tommaso and the Archbishop looked distraught. Yusuf began to play a song from the Sicilian hills. In this room, with the smell of beer in the air, with the golden-haired knights and the monks, the rhythms and broken chords of the Arabic music sounded strange and . . . Frederick closed his eyes and saw Sicily. His throat clogged up. Even the muttering stopped, even the soft sound of clothes rustling. Infinitely more complex than the Freidank's songs, the Arab music pulsed with melancholy. When it stopped, the last notes hung quivering in the air.

"You can sing about a golden age until your throat's raw," Frederick said to the Freidank. "Is that beautiful?"

"Yes." The Freidank looked up and nodded. "I couldn't play it, but it is."

"Until everybody else agrees with you, there's no gold."

The Freidank's eyes widened suddenly. Yusuf handed him the lute and went back to the wall, and the knights cleared their throats and talked of something else. Theophano reached for the lute.

"Let me."

The Freidank said, "If you think that way, Sire, you can't be on crusade."

Frederick thought of Fulk and Ezzo cavorting in the local dens of iniquity and didn't answer.

Theophano said, "Tell them it's Greek music if they ask."

She began to play, and the crowd around them shifted back and forth, amazed. Her song sounded completely different from either of the others; Frederick had to make an effort of will to adjust to it. Choppy, rhythmic, the song raced through jangling chords and spills of loose notes. The Freidank laughed and began to clap his hands, and all the knights picked it up. Theophano laughed, swaying back and forth.

"Is she Sicilian?" a Cistercian called.

"Greek," Frederick said.

The Freidank leaped up and danced. Clapping their hands, the knights grinned and watched him, shouting comments back and forth. Frederick turned and looked at Hasan and winked.

"Well," Theophano said, putting the lute down. "Was that beautiful?"

Her eyes were snapping, brilliant black. He stretched his arms over his head. "Magnificent."

"Play another," the Freidank said, and Frederick translated.

"Oh, no. Tell him I'm much too tired." She put her head down quickly on Frederick's knee and straightened up again. While he spoke to the Freidank he saw the envy on the faces of the other men. His body tingled with pride, and he spread his arms out, stretching, to contain himself.

* * *

"They are so charming, these knights," Theophano said. "They're very direct."

"If one of them very directly propositioned you, I'll very directly have him hung." He was writing down his agenda for the next day—he had to organize the Syrian army under its new command, which would be a delicate business. In the golden mirror on the wall next to the table he could see her maids undressing her.

"Naturally not. They're all monks. Besides, they're shy." She stepped out of her gown and walked naked across the room. "Don't, Maria, I won't need it."

The maid with the nightgown stepped back, and the rest of them gathered up her clothes from the floor. Frederick wrote beneath the list of people he'd have to see, "Map of the city." With Tommaso and the Archbishop scattered all over town, he'd have to be able to find his way around. The maids left, whispering their good nights.

"Were you angry?" she said. "Because nobody met us at the harbor?"

"Um-humm. But it wouldn't do any good to yell. I didn't know you played the lute." He scattered sand on the paper to dry the ink.

"I don't—not well. But you'd been so pompous about the Arab music—" She turned, laughing. "It wasn't magnificent, you know, it was sloppy." She sat down on the bed.

"Theophano—" I love you. But never say it. "Get in bed and pull the curtains."

She grinned and rolled in under the covers. The heavy brocade drapes swept closed, and Frederick stood up and pulled on the bellrope near the door. Corso and Giancarlo came in from the next room and started to take off his clothes, and after them, carrying his dressing gown and slippers, the Grand Master and Balian of Sidon walked, arguing softly.

"When do you wish to wake up tomorrow, Sire?" Balian said.

"After dawn. I'm tired."

Strange pages, donated by his host, went around putting out the lamps, and Giancarlo called, "Leave one lit, now, you." His stern, childish voice made Frederick grin. Balian went to the door at the sound of a knock, looked out, and let in Guy Embriaco.

"Sire, may I wish you good night."

"Thank you." Frederick tossed his hair back with both hands. "Corso, tomorrow I'm taking a bath if I have to stand in the rain."

"I'll see to that," Balian said. He glanced toward the bed and frowned at one of the strange pages. "Turn down His Majesty's bed, knave."

Frederick yelped; Corso spun around. "Don't touch that bed, boy. My Lord Balian, please allow us to follow our own routine."

"Excuse me." Balian shrugged, looking puzzled, suddenly understood, and turned bright red. "Excuse me."

"Never mind." Frederick turned his back on Corso so that the boy could put on the dressing gown. "Will you and the Lord Guy attend me tomorrow at noon?"

"We'd be very honored to, Sire." Guy brought over the slippers, and Frederick stuck his feet into them. Giancarlo was hunting for a fresh pen to put beside the bed; he bent down to look under the table, and Frederick couldn't resist smacking him on the rump. Giancarlo muffled a yell, and the men all laughed.

"Good night, Sire," Balian said, and headed for the door. Guy followed him out.

"Good night. Hermann, you'll be at lunch tomorrow too, won't you?"

"Of course." The Grand Master smiled. "Have a good night's sleep, Sire."

"Thank you. Good night." He started toward the bed.

The pages were collecting his dirty clothes and straightening up the room, and one by one they left, chattering softly. The door shut behind Corso, and Frederick threw off the dressing gown.

Softly the door opened again. "Good night, Sire."

"Good night, Corso. Sleep well."

"Tommaso, let me in."

Behind the servant at the door Tommaso whirled and stared. "My God. Leone, let him in. Hurry."

The servant stepped back, still scowling, and Frederick barged through the door. Tommaso knelt briefly. "Sire. What are you—"

Leone gasped and fell to his knees. Frederick nudged him with his toe. "You've got a suspicious doorman. I'm glad you decided to come by—he wasn't going to let me in."

"Leone, go to the kitchens." With a glance outside, Tommaso himself shut the door. "You came alone? No wonder— We have to be suspicious; Acre is full of burglars. Sire, what the devil are you doing all the way out here?"

"What's wrong? Can't I go for a walk?" Frederick went on through the antechamber into the next room. The lamps weren't lit yet and it was nearly dark. "I wanted to talk to you."

"You should have sent for me." Tommaso pulled a bellrope. "I wouldn't advise walking around Acre, Sire—"

"Nobody knows who I am. It was fun. I came through the bazaar." He stripped off his cloak, enjoying Tommaso's flustered efforts to pull himself together. "Everything's gone wrong today."

"Nobody knew you. Trailing a Saracen and talking with a Sicilian accent, nobody knew you." Servants rushed in, and he turned to order them around, to light lamps, to bring something to drink. Frederick sat down and studied the mosaic on the floor. "What went wrong today?"

"Oh—two Franciscans and the Patriarch showed up at noon before we'd done anything at all about the command situation and spent the afternoon telling me I don't belong here." The restless, uneasy depression came back to him. I feel wrong. "In very clear terms."

"Why didn't you kick them out?"

"The Patriarch and a pair of envoys from the Pope?"

"You're already excommunicated—he can't do anything more to you." Tommaso headed for a chair, remembered he hadn't been given permission to sit, and looked over. Frederick nodded.

"You're always telling me I have to be nice to them."

"Not that nice. What have you decided about the command? Anything?"

"Oh. Hermann and I mulled it over this morning. I think I'll arrange it so that the orders all come from the Grand Master or you or a council of all the commanders. Where is al-Kamil?"

"At Nablus. With an immense army. But he isn't doing anything. I'd wager he'll make a foray sometime soon, just to test you. Whom are you sending to him?"

"One of Piero's bright young men. Just to conduct messages."

"Ummm." Tommaso rubbed his finger along his cheek. "Do you like Acre?"

"I like the bazaar. This one up the street with all the arches over it." He kicked his shoes off. "The rest of the city makes me nervous. Is it always this closed up and empty?"

"It's not empty, make no mistake. There are tens of thousands of people in Acre, and every last one of them is looking out for himself—that's all."

"Maybe it's just the way the buildings are." The high walls, without windows, the towers and the guarded gates. Beyond one wall he'd heard the sound of children playing, but the only children he'd seen in his long walk through Acre had been a few beggars and children of the poor.

"Nobody in Acre talks to anybody unless he knows exactly whose party he belongs to," Tommaso said. "They conspire over their morning bread and they plot at night while they're making love."

"It sounds like Milan."

"It sounds like any city that isn't sure it will still be here tomorrow."

"What about en-Nasr?"

Tommaso shrugged. "He's in Damascus."

"Suppose we send greetings to him and to al-Ashraf. Just as a matter of courtesy."

Tommaso frowned, rubbing his hand absently over the arm of his chair. "Whatever for?"

"Courtesy, as I said. And it might be useful. There's no sense in ignoring them."

"If you wish, Sire, of course."

"I wish. Al-Kamil doesn't have en-Nasr tightly invested, does he?"

"No. Just pinned down. En-Nasr would be a fool to leave Damascus."

Frederick flicked a lock of hair out of his eyes. "I'll send an embassy to him, then."

"Why?" Tommaso looked aggravated.

"It might be useful. I left Hasan out in your garden— will he be all right?"

"Certainly, if he doesn't mind the dark. Why didn't you bring him in?"

"Your doorman was fussing enough over me."

Tommaso reached for the bellpull again. "Concerning the army, I should think any arrangement whereby they wouldn't be taking orders from an excommunicate would be sufficient. After all, you aren't planning to use the local army, are you?"

"No." Frederick took a cup of sherbet from a slave and drank. He remembered the towers and the pale brown stone of the walls again. Like a city shut up against him—turn their eyes away when I walk by. Yes, they knew who I was, remember in the bazaar—?

"Not like Palermo, is it?" Tommaso said.

"No." He finished the sherbet. "It . . . makes me jumpy, this town."

"Then, be careful. Abu, give His Majesty more sherbet."

Abu turned with the ewer and Frederick held out his cup. "They're preaching a sermon against me tomorrow in every church in Acre. They told me that to my face."

Leone came in again. Tommaso said, "Are you going to Mass? Leone, let the Saracen in the garden inside, please."

"Have I gone to Mass since you've known me?"

"No."

"I can't now, anyhow."

"Then why bother with them?"

Frederick coiled himself up and burst out of the chair. "Tommaso, damn it, I like people to like me."

"So do I, but not everybody does. Calm down, Sire."

"I'm trying."

"Are you hungry? Have some dinner."

"No. I'm supposed to eat with Guy Embriaco. I'd better get back."

"Let me give you some horses." Tommaso rose.

"No, I'll walk."

"If you wish. Let me send some of my men with you, at least."

"No, that's all right." He looked around at the room; its furniture and the tapestries and the bits of statuary and glass on the shelves and tables all reminded him of Tommaso. "This is a nice house."

"It's pleasant enough. You'll have to come for dinner sometime. My cook is Sicilian." Tommaso smiled. He walked beside Frederick into the antechamber where Hasan stood ignoring Leone, his hands folded over his chest, his dagger gleaming in his sash. When Frederick appeared he whirled and reached for the door.

"We have a meeting tomorrow with the Templars and the Hospitallers," Frederick said. "Which should be a joy equal only to the meeting with the Franciscans. You'd better be there. I've got a draft of the letter to al-Kamil for you to read too."

"Good." Tommaso bowed. "Be careful."

"Yes. I will. Come along, Hasan."

Tommaso called, "Oh, by the way, I'm going to introduce you to a Jew here who's fond of mathematics."

Frederick turned and grinned. "Give me something to do? Good. I'll see you tomorrow."

He walked out into the garden, Hasan behind him. The sweet odors of the Syrian flowers reached him. I'm not used to it, that's all, that's why I feel so . . . In Palermo, in Barletta and Brindisi and Capua he could walk alone into the worst quarters and never worry. He stood while Hasan unhooked the gate and swung it open.

"The evenings are warm here, at least," Hasan said.

"Now that it's stopped raining."

They went down the dark street, walking close to the wall. In the buildings opposite, lights showed, but most people would be in bed now that it was dark. He looked up at the sky, at the wash of stars.

"Maybe Dawud will be with al-Kamil when we meet him."

Hasan nodded. "It would be good to see the Lord Fakhr-ad-Din again."

Why do I get along better with Saracens than anybody else? He and Fakhr-ad-Din had spent hours talking about nothing, laughing and solving the problems of the world and comparing notes on astrology and philosophy and medicine in their different countries. Up ahead a street lamp shone, marking the cross street. His feet slipped on the uneven cobblestones and he shortened stride.

"They never come out into the street here." Hasan said.

They certainly don't. He had that feeling again, that they were all watching from behind their shutters. Turning the corner, he tried to relax. None of the street lights on this street were burning.

"Lord—"

"I see." He stopped. Two men had appeared halfway down the street. They'd been standing in a doorway, but now they started up toward him. "What's behind us?"

Hasan's robes shuffled together. "Two more." He sounded calm. "Do you have a knife?"

"Yes."

It wasn't likely these were thieves. He shifted his feet apart and let his arms hang loosely by his sides, watching the two men coming toward him. They separated, one sliding in close to the wall on Frederick's left hand, the other out in the middle of the street. Hasan whispered a prayer in Arabic.

"Stand still," Frederick called. "Who are you?"

The man next to the wall plunged forward. Just behind Frederick, Hasan leaped violently to meet the other two, and somebody yelped. The fourth man, who looked fat, was charging in from the middle of the street. Frederick drew his dagger and rushed to meet the man near the wall. In the man's hands a long knife flashed blue. He drew his arm back and ran straight for Frederick, and Frederick slashed with his dagger, caught that long blade, and struck it aside. The man ran into him so hard they both left their feet.

Falling, he twisted, hitting the cobblestones with his hip and shoulder instead of his head, and brought his dagger back up. The other one, the fat one, was racing in. Arms clutched him, pinning him down. He wrenched his arm free and grabbed the dagger out of his other hand

and stabbed, and the tip skidded off metal. They were wearing mail. He looked up and saw the fat one with a sword drawn back, his teeth bared, right over him.

The man hanging onto him lunged, throwing Frederick hard against the wall; he kicked out, and the man grunted. The fat one with the sword was dancing around, trying to find a clear angle. Frederick dropped his dagger and grabbed the wrist of the man beside him and kicked again. A fist crashed into his side and the heavy body twisted. The sword slashed down—he flung himself to one side, and sparks flew from the wall. Hasan—

Something sharp glided over his hand; he clutched. It was the long knife. He got to his knees, punching and clawing at the other man, who slugged and clawed back —in the dark they couldn't see to hit anything. The fat one was yelling and dancing around again, hunting an opening. Frederick's side hurt with each breath. He lifted the long knife and ran it into the face of the man he was fighting. The blade rasped over bone and sank abruptly deep, deep into flesh. With a screech the man shrank back, and the knife locked in bone and flew out of Frederick's hand. He dove sideways just before the sword clanged on the stone where he had been.

Leaping up, he put the wall to his back and stared around. Two of them—Hasan was down, a white puddle on the street, and another dead man out there near him. The man he'd knifed screamed again. The two men facing him started in, cautious, their knives and swords held low.

His muscles gathered, and his breath hissed through his teeth. Sliding his feet, he took a step down the wall. Immediately they attacked him, both at once. He thrust out his hands and a dagger ripped along his forearm, but he got a grip on the man nearer him and flung him sideways into the other. Old tricks boiled up into his memory. These weren't street fighters—he could tell that by the way they fought. He scurried a little farther down the wall before they got sorted out and raced in again.

Remember— He kicked out, crouched over, and charged at the thin man. When he shifted to meet him, the knife bright in his hand, Frederick whirled and got his hands on his arm and wrenched him hard over his hip into the wall. The fat one closed in on him, and he feinted to draw him off, and dodged the other's knife and knocked him flat with his fist. The first grappled with him and Frederick brought his knee up into the man's crotch. With a scream like a woman's he fell backward.

The fat one was getting to his feet, his sword still in his hand. Frederick glanced around for a knife, a sword, a dagger; there was nothing in sight but a man clutching himself and moaning and another staggering to his feet. He ran over and jumped on the thin man far down the wall. The fat one lifted his sword and waded in.

The sword was easy to dodge, but Frederick's breath came in rasps and his forearm was turning numb. He ducked under a wild swing of the sword and ran down the street. Footsteps pelted after him—more than one set. I thought they'd all— He slipped and fell, rolling over and scraping his face and hands on the stones. They're coming, they're coming, get up. Just lie here and— He forced himself to his hands and knees. A kick caught him in the ribs and knocked him rolling again. They had him, they were going to— He bounced up and ran, headed for the corner, for Tommaso's house. Suddenly one of the men behind him shouted a warning, and the footsteps stopped. Frederick turned his head to look back and saw them running away and before he could stop himself ran headlong into a horse.

"What's going on here?"

He hung onto the horse's mane, keeping himself on his feet and fighting to get his breath. They spoke Syrian French, whoever they were—the watch, probably. His body started to tremble, and he pressed his face to the horse's neck and shuddered. The horse moved, dragging him. They were yelling somewhere.

"There's a dead Arab here."

He swallowed.

Somebody grabbed him by the shoulders, and he kicked out, trying to get his feet under him, and let go with one hand and flung them off.

"Hold him—knock him out if you have to—"

"You touch me, I'll kill you," he roared. "God damn you—"

"Oh, Christ," the man in the saddle said. "Another of those fucking Italians. Who are the rest of them?"

Frederick slapped futilely at the hands dragging him away, pinioning him. Farther away a voice said, "Oh, God, I think this one's a Templar."

Frederick stopped fighting.

"Where's that torch?" the rider bawled.

"Let me go."

"You aren't going anywhere. You're under arrest."

Light showed, a glimmer, but the torch rolled and the fire spread around the head, bright yellow. Frederick took a deep breath and stood up, easing his weight off the arms holding him. One of them twisted his hand up between his shoulders. "You make a move and I'll gut you."

Three big men in half-armor stood around him, and another sat on the horse; two more were looking over the bodies of the dead. The captain, on the horse, stared at Frederick and frowned.

"I wouldn't like to be you if you've killed a Templar."

Frederick said, "I wouldn't like to be the Templars if that's a Templar. Let me go or I'll hang you all."

The man holding him wrenched his arm, and Frederick yelped. The captain suddenly leaped off his horse. "Let him go, Raymond, for the love of—" The captain went to his knees. "It's the Emperor."

Raymond's breathing stopped. He jerked his hands away from Frederick and stepped back. Wobbling, tasting blood in his mouth, Frederick looked all around—

four men knelt around him, and the two inspecting the bodies were turning to stare. He limped over toward the dead man they had called a Templar. His legs throbbed and ached all over. The two men among the bodies knelt when he approached.

"Bring me a torch."

In the silence he heard the horse sigh; one of the men rushed up with the torch, and he looked down at the corpse in front of him. He'd never seen this man before; he wore plain brown wool. "Is that a Templar?"

The young man kneeling in the street shook his head.

"You said it was before."

"I was mistaken, my—Your Majesty."

"Find out."

He took the torch and went on to Hasan's body. He was dead; his white robes were soggy with blood. Beyond him lay another dead Frank. Were there four or five? He couldn't remember. The man he'd stabbed in the face was gone—and the man he'd jumped on. Probably five. He limped back toward the silent watch.

"Give me your horse. I'm late for dinner."

The captain held out the reins. Frederick leaned on the saddle, trying to get his strength up. Hot rage bubbled up through him, and he turned to the captain. "If you see any more Templars tonight, tell them if they think they paid for the one they killed, they didn't." He dragged himself into the saddle and fumbled with his foot for the stirrup. "But I'll see that they do."

"They weren't Templars," the captain said. "We were—"

Frederick spun the horse and whipped it with the end of the rein into a dead run. His arm burned from the elbow to the wrist, and he could barely close his fingers over the rein. I'll flay them, I'll fry them. He swiped the tears out of his eyes and galloped through the middle of Acre toward his house.

* * *

The Templars' audience was at Sext the next day; the Grand Master brought the news of their arrival up to Frederick, who was sitting on the balcony, looking out toward the sea. Blazing on the water, bouncing back from the dun rocks of the shore, the sunlight cooked the slash on his forearm and made it hurt, and when the Grand Master appeared he didn't turn his head at all.

"The Grand Master of the Order of the Temple of Jerusalem—"

Frederick glared at the distant water.

"Sire," the Grand Master said. "Shall I tell them you're too busy?"

"Oh, no. I shall be most, most pleased to see him. Them. Is the Hospitaller with him?"

"Yes."

"I don't suppose there's any proof those were Templars."

"No." The Grand Master moved around in front of him. "Where are the Saracens?"

"Burying Hasan. I have guards in the next room."

I should kill them all now. Lock the gates, trap them inside, and pitch them one by one into a cauldron full of boiling oil. Hasan was with me so much, I can't get used to his not being here, and he is dead now. I should kill them all.

"Send them up."

"Sire." The Grand Master knelt and looked earnestly up at him. "If you don't feel up to it, tell me. I'll send them away. Why should you treat them like—like allies when they—"

"Send them up, Hermann. I'm perfectly capable of dealing with them." He smiled. "Which they know now."

The Grand Master got up and went out. Frederick touched the scabs on his face—Theophano had said he looked terrible. Guy Embriaco had nearly fallen over when he walked in for dinner. Tucking his hand into his sleeve, he watched the little boats sculling around the busy harbor, carrying goods and people from galley to galley. Jaffa . . .

"Sire."

He lifted one hand and let it drop, acknowledging them, and the three Grand Masters and their attendants came out onto the balcony. The two Frenchmen looked pudgy from good Eastern living, younger and less sol-dierlike than Hermann. The herald was prating. For a moment, while they shuffled around and got themselves arranged in order, Frederick could not move or think or speak—they tried to kill me, they killed Hasan— Abruptly the stiffness in his body eased, and he smiled and acknowledged their bows with a gesture.

"Gentlemen. This will be brief because I know that you have no wish to endanger your immortal souls through overmuch contact with me." And here, name of a name, came the Patriarch of Jerusalem, panting from a long run up the stairs. Frederick bowed to him. "Good father."

"Sire—"

"Please. Sit." He sat. "Hermann, send pages for refreshments, if you will. Gentlemen, may I compliment you on the wealth and splendor of your city."

The Grand Master of the Templars, heavy-jowled and pig-eyed, sank onto a couch. "Your Majesty does us honor. We all wish to offer our apologies on behalf of the city for the outrage Your Majesty suffered—"

"Oh." Another gesture, which made his forearm hurt. "A minor detail. Not every city is Palermo."

He smiled, and the knights all smiled back, uneasy. The sun made them squint. They were facing it, and he had his back to it; the Patriarch lifted one hand to shield his face.

"Gentlemen, we have discussed before the military

problems at hand. Clearly, if I were to assume command myself, nobody would be happy." He smiled again, amazed that it was so easy. "I am taking steps to arrange the command so that no one will be forced to take the orders of an outcast of the Church. In addition, I will rely on your judgment in the selection of a liaison staff."

The Templar frowned and leaned forward. "Sire, we were—" The pages came, their slippers muffled on the carpets over the balcony stone, and the voice died. Frederick watched them grab for the honey cakes, for the sweet Sicilian wine, the gooey candy from Damascus and Cairo. That was how they'd gotten their high color. Chastity, poverty, and obedience. When the pages brought over the golden trays he took a cup of sherbet and waved away the cakes.

"Rich food disagrees with me." He watched the Grand Master start. "So. If you would assume the responsibilities of liaison and organization of the local armies—and the Patriarch, of course, for the local clergy—I would be most grateful. And of course this would ease the burden on me and my staff considerably."

He looked around, eyebrows cocked, nodding, and one by one the startled faces in front of him began nodding too, as if he'd started a wind that set them all in motion. They'd come here with demands, he was sure of it, and now he was ending the audience before it had quite begun. The Hospitaller opened his mouth.

"So." Frederick leaped up. "I thank you for your cooperation."

They all had to rise, naturally, and he went on, "I will leave you to discuss the details with Sir Hermann, rather than endanger you any more by my presence. Thank you again for your forbearance. Feel free to sample the arts of my kitchens. My friends' kitchens." He smiled and walked off the balcony into the cool of the inside room.

"Sire," the Patriarch called, but the Grand Master's

voice started up at once, drowning him out. Corso and two knights were in the dim room he'd entered, and without a word they rose and followed him through the next room, where he began to laugh. Muffled, the laughter came out like choking.

"Sire—"

"Corso, did you talk to What's-his-name—Lothair— about the guards at night?"

"Yes, Sire." Corso rushed up to open the next door for him. "Marino sent me to tell you that there's a . . . messenger in your room."

"A messenger." He turned, frowning, halfway through the little sunlit room. "From whom?"

Hands locked behind his back, his face straight, Corso only shrugged.

"Christian or Moslem?"

Corso said, "I didn't see him, Sire."

"Oho." Frederick headed for the far door. "Go down and see if Theophano wants anything."

"Sire." Corso raced away.

Marino would never let a messenger into Frederick's chambers unless he was far more important than the Templars; it might be the man from al-Kamil. He passed a herd of serving girls, who prostrated themselves neatly out of his path, and cut through his pages' quarters, still trailing the knights. But al-Kamil wouldn't have heard that he was in Acre yet. Unless he had spies, which he did, of course. Three pages nearly leaped out of their untidy hose at the sight of him; he plunged on. The first of his rooms was empty, and in the second two secretaries copied madly.

"Where's Marino?"

The secretaries leaped up and knelt beside their desks. "Inside, Sire."

He headed for the nearest door, and one of the knights raced around to open it for him. The silks rustled; a sudden reek of jasmine reached him like a wave. Before him

the wide, tiled room, filled with sunlight, stretched on
empty for yards, except— "Sire."

Marino came forward, and behind him, standing quietly behind a chair, stood a Moslem in a gray cloak, like a
habit in Holy Orders. Frederick brushed off Marino's
quick explanations. "Thank you, I know." He jabbed a
thumb at the door. "The knights too."

The lean man in the gray cloak came around his chair,
smiling in his dark beard. Around his waist was a red sash,
and in it, half-hidden, a red-hilted yataghan. Frederick
said in Arabic, "My respects to your master, and God
grant him long life."

The man bowed. "Sultan, he begs God the same
wishes for yourself. I am come with these words from
the Sheikh of the Mountain, the Lord of Alamut and
Master of the Hashishiyyun. God be with the Sultan
from the West in his endeavors, and the Sheikh most
humbly begs to be counted among the friends of the Sultan, close as those dwelling in his house."

Frederick drew a deep breath. Against those bloated
men up on the balcony he could use this man's master
and the rest of their order like an ax. He clapped his
hands and a page bolted in.

"Sherbet," Frederick said. "Rosewater for the messenger of the Hashishiyyun."

The lean man jerked a smile onto his face; Frederick
sat down.

"I am most impressed by your order, Emir."

"Sultan, you do me honor. I am only one of the lowest
of us."

Pages came in with more gold trays, this time bearing
sherbet and rosewater and light almond-paste cookies.
Frederick washed his hands and dried them on a cloth
one page held out. "It is I who am honored that your
master would send to me in token of his friendship an
initiate into the mysteries. And is not the lowest of the
Hashishiyyun an emir among ordinary men?"

The lean man smiled. His hands moved lightly over the cookies. "Am I among ordinary men? My master says that I must say to you, Sultan, that of all the lords of the earth, you alone so stir his imagination that he would ask to be taken under your protection."

"So be it," Frederick said mildly. "You might inform him that I have so little attachment to these who mouth the pieties of my religion while bearing swords in the land where Christ walked that I would place him and his above even those who strut so confidently around the streets of this city."

Frederick smiled; the Assassin smiled. For a moment, sipping sherbet, they sat in silence, while Frederick tried to think of suitable presents and phrases. But the Assassin put down his cup and said, "My master wishes you to know that it is not his habit to extend tokens of friendship in place of friendship itself. My business is concluded, except for one detail, and I shall take leave. Acre is not open to me and mine." He stood up, and Frederick stood up, surprised.

"If your master is so superior to tokens, any I gave him would be an insult. Let him know that in Palestine and Syria I will serve him as a friend should."

"Excellent." The Assassin headed for the door. "As for the detail, Sultan, it is this: The Templars, as you know, covet your life."

"I'm glad to know that." He grimaced.

"And the Hashishiyyun offer to do all in our considerable power to see that you are forewarned of the attempts of the swine against you and to protect you against them."

Some of his amazement must have shown on his face; the Assassin smiled, bowed, and left without a word. Frederick sat down. His heart beat excitedly, unevenly. That could mean anything—to a Christian, nothing, without sworn oaths or an exchange of gifts or hostages. But the Assassins had built themselves a reputation in

Syria precisely because they kept their word, however lightly it seemed to be given, and a messenger had come so far, so quickly, when Acre was not safe for Assassins. Al-Kamil didn't like Assassins. Oh, well, one couldn't really expect to please everyone. Pages rushed in and neatened up, chattering softly to themselves, ignoring him. A pair of soft boy's hands reached out, took his cup, and replaced it, full. I love pear sherbet. Outside, in one of the other rooms, men spoke, but he couldn't hear the words. I am the protector of the Assassins, who in return protect me. It would be interesting to see how they went about it. He couldn't calm the frothy excitement in his mind; the whole thing was so enchanting.

"Sire—"

"Yes, Corso."

"Sir Hermann wishes—"

"Send him in." It was a pity he couldn't share this excitement with the Grand Master, who would— "Hermann. How are our piggy friends upstairs?"

The Grand Master, smiling, headed for a chair and settled himself into it. "They don't understand how you managed to give them what they'd thought they already had, thank them for accepting it, and leave without hearing what they came to discuss. No, thank you," to a page, who took off the cups and sherbet and cookies.

"They're French, not Sicilian. What's the news?"

The Grand Master sighed heavily and fiddled with the embroidery on his sleeves. "Not good. Last night several bands of al-Kamil's men raided Christian settlements, burned, looted, and got off completely without pursuit. All the local lords are squabbling over who's responsible for what."

"Naturally." Frederick took a mouthful of pear sherbet and let it lie on his tongue a moment before swallowing it. The warmth of his mouth released all the subtle flavor. "Do you think it would be worth the effort necessary to coordinate their defenses?"

The Grand Master made a face and looked off. Around his gnarled hands the lace curled limply, soaked from the heat. Finally he said, "I'm sure you already have an opinion."

"I do. Want to hear it?"

"Of course."

"The only reason the Moslems have never managed to wipe out all of Outremer's defenses—except Acre, which is reasonably defensible, and Beirut and Tripoli and Antioch—is because all Outremer's defenses are never in the same place, and the Moslems can't find them. Sufficient?"

"Sufficient. You've only been here two days, though, don't—"

"I've been reading before bed. In short, Hermann, my son's little kingdom is mythically defended."

"Did you expect more, Sire?"

"No. The whole construction is against nature. I suppose I could stir up a little amusement bringing them to book over it—"

"Sire—"

"But I tried that on Cyprus and got my imperial rump burned for it. I don't want to stay in Acre."

"Beirut and Antioch are out of the question."

"Actually I was thinking of Jaffa."

"Good God." The Grand Master leaped up. "Jaffa is in ruins."

"Quite. Fotunately we have lots of able-bodied men sitting around here doing nothing except get in trouble. I did find out, you know, why the watch called me 'another fucking Italian.' Jaffa has an excellent harbor and is much closer to Jerusalem than any of the major centers of Outremer. Also, it's not in the hands of a baron. We are going to refortify it." He sipped sherbet.

The Grand Master actually smiled; he enjoyed strategic work. "When shall we start?"

"As soon as I hear from al-Kamil. Incidentally, there

was a message in from Brindisi. Rinaldo has messed things up and the Pope is preparing to invade Sicily. How does that strike you?"

The old man's face tightened. "Invade Sicily."

Frederick nodded, unblinking.

"Surely the reports are wrong."

"On the contrary, if anything, they've underestimated the extent of the operation."

The Grand Master sat down again, his elbows on his wide-spread knees. For a moment he looked nowhere, his eyes moving blindly. "The Holy See has always sworn to protect the holdings of Crusaders against any kind of attack."

"Come now, Hermann. This Crusader is excommunicate."

"By custom you are relieved of your sins when you go on crusade."

"Well, yes, but custom and this particular Pope—"

"There must have been provocation."

"Rinaldo invaded the March of Ancona, which belongs to me anyway and was stolen. Of course there was provocation. I am the provocation. He hates me and he will do anything he can to eliminate me, root and branch. They are moving my children from Andria to Palermo."

"He was misled."

Frederick sighed. "All right. He was misled." He could almost feel the misery of the old man, radiating in the hot, still air. Suddenly he regretted having brought the whole thing up. "Hermann. I'm sorry. It's true, but there was provocation, and after all he's only a man, like me. I'd have done the same thing. Suppose you—"

"He's the Holy Father, he isn't supposed to—"

"Don't interrupt me. Go down and draw up plans for transporting everything to Jaffa. You'd better get hold of Enrico somehow—I don't relish being pinned up against that coast without some way to get off. And we'll probably need supplies while we're there." He stood up and started to take off his coat. "For ten days at least, until we get some kind of commissary set up."

"Yes, Sire." The Grand Master was on his feet, solid and thick-boned, like a knight in some German legend. "As you wish, Sire."

"I'm sorry."

The Grand Master bowed, turned and left. Frederick fought down a surge of irritation. The old man just wouldn't learn, wouldn't realize—throwing off his coat, he yelled for pages to bring him fresh clothes.

All the next week he heard reports from the north, the south, and the east. On Saturday Balian of Sidon came back from Antioch with pages of reports on defenses, attitudes, strategic postures and spies' findings about Damascus; in the afternoon, after lunch with local dignitaries all wanting something, he saw ambassadors from Beirut, confirming things Balian had already said, assuring him of the faith and good fellowship of John d'Ibelin. All evening long he worked on a letter to al-Kamil.

"Being Emperor is hard work," he said to Theophano. She laughed.

"It is. And the trouble is that I have to be Emperor all the time."

"Shall I stroke your brow and whisper soft reassurances?"

"I'd prefer you to stroke a little lower."

Afterward, lying in the moonlight under the round window, he remembered the Assassins' promise. It would be fun to go in disguise into the slums of Acre. Fulk and Ezzo could go with him, and they could dice and drink and make rude remarks about everything and everybody and shock the natives. Theophano, lying half across his shoulder, murmured in her sleep, and her dark hair shifted on the tumbled silk of the bed. He pulled the cover up over her waist. In Palermo . . .

He slept and dreamed of being a little boy in Palermo, stealing oranges from the street vendors, chasing half-wild chickens into the alleys full of trash. Strange music wound itself into the dream, wild, rhythmic music, unlike the Moslem or the Christian; in the dream the music stirred him inutterably, as if he heard it throughout his body. Struggling up toward the surface of consciousness, he heard the music sink down to an ordinary lute's ordinary tunes, and a sense of loss nearly made him weep. When he opened his eyes he saw Theophano sitting naked on a stool under the window, playing a lute.

"What's that?"

"It's Arabic, I think."

Part French, part Syrian, a hybrid, strange . . . "Did you play something else?"

She shook her head, unsmiling. Her eyes watched him through the shadows. The moonlight turned her skin colorless and cold, pale, like an ice statue. Fascinated and vaguely frightened, he watched her until the music and his heavy eyes let him doze off again, and in his sleep he searched everywhere for the strange, heavy music he had heard before.

"Did you sleep well?"

"No."

"I know. You had bad dreams—you woke me up once. You were trying to say something, and your eyes were open, but you were asleep."

"Oh."

"I knew you were asleep, but your eyes were open. I didn't want to wake you up, I was afraid."

"I'm sorry."

"What did you dream of?"

"I . . . don't remember."

Of a forest full of thorny trees, in the middle of which he was a prisoner, in a cage of thorns, while unnatural beasts circled and circled, watching him, hungry.

"They say you're going to Jaffa."

"Yes. Do you want to come?"

"If you want me to."

"Come."

She hugged him, and he pressed his face against her smooth shoulder. The indistinct horror of the dream was fading; he heard pages in the other room, waiting to come in and start his official day. Spreading honey on a biscuit, he slid it into Theophano's mouth and yelled for Corso. She pulled the covers over her and winked at him. He laughed. It was easier with her there, everything was easier. Do I love her? I must. This is the way— Corso came in, with the other pages, and in between bites of biscuit and honey and sips of milk he let them dress him and went out into the antechamber.

A crowd of petitioners surged around him, and his Saracens jumped to hold them back. Good God—the animal faces of the dream came back to him; for a moment he paused on the marble threshold, unsure. But Fulk came forward with a handful of documents, and three secretaries were standing with letters to be signed. Come, come, Sire. Emperors don't . . . He reached for the papers in Fulk's hand and listened to petitions while he read. The first two petitions, by custom, he granted—a pension, a reinstatement at court—and the rest of them he sent off home, to come back in the morning. With them gone, the room seemed bigger.

"Ezzo, how are the stores?"

"Running out, Sire." Ezzo slouched against a wall. "Do I recite?"

"God, no." He gestured to the light screens blocking the windows and a page trotted over to remove them. Another ran by with an armload of fresh flowers for the other rooms. "Find out where Enrico is, he's supposed to be supplying us."

Fulk said quietly, "We've questioned all the watch

again, and none of them will admit—"

"Forget that. I have proof. Unsuitable for a court, but proof. Conrad."

Conrad of Hohenlohe rushed up, glowing. "When do we go to Jaffa?"

"Soon enough. What are you doing back?"

"My tour's over, Sire."

"Oh. Ezzo, it's your turn. Take some troops and ride around the countryside. No trouble, do you hear me?"

"Sire." Ezzo slid away from the wall and left.

Fulk said, "I hope you aren't intending any more forays alone at night."

Ayub had shut the door after Ezzo; he came back, frowning at Fulk's remark. Frederick said. "Why?"

"Well." Fulk crossed his arms over his chest. "There have been four men killed in Acre, at night, by unknown assailants, since the—since you were nearly murdered. Three of them had red hair."

Conrad looked over. "Coincidence."

Fulk didn't even bother to look at him. Along the walls the three Saracens scowled. Fulk said. "Red hair isn't common in Acre. Three out of four is . . . not probable."

Frederick bit his lip. "Well, damn them. That's sheer waste."

Surprised, Fulk laughed, and one by one the Saracens grinned. Frederick said, "No, I won't go drifting around alone at night. Yes, Marino."

Marino came through the door two steps, bowed, and said, "Sire, there are several envoys here. Do you want me to arrange audiences?"

"Are they important?"

"No, Sire. Probably petitioners of a more exalted sort."

"Schedule them for the day after tomorrow. Maybe I won't be here. Conrad, you go with Fulk and try to find out who's killing red-headed men. Marino, send those charters for Cyprus down to me in the garden."

"Sire."

They all bowed, and he went back in to Theophano to change out of his gown into a short coat and hose.

The garden reminded him so much of Sicily that sometimes he couldn't stand even being there. With a secretary shuffling along behind him reading, he walked up and down the tiny pebble paths, staring at flowers. They are killing men because they look like me. His hair swung in his eyes and he studied it. The sunlight turned it bright red. The peach trees were ripe and he picked a peach and ate it, told the secretary to bend over and used his back for a desk to sign a charter giving himself the right to tax the entire population of Cyprus in King Henri's name.

"Lord."

Ayub came down a side path; the pebbles crunched under his boots. Seeing him doing what Hasan had done still jarred Frederick. He thrust the pen at the secretary. "Yes?"

"There is a man here—" Ayub smiled. "Come see."

Frederick took three steps after him, bewildered, and caught sight of the visitor under an apricot tree, sitting on a bench. He stopped dead and stared. The man rose, brushing little curled leaves off his lap, and started forward, smiling.

"Dawud," Frederick yelled. He ran past Ayub, who bounded to one side. The other man ducked swiftly out from under the apricot tree.

"Sultan, I thought perhaps to find you—"

Frederick grabbed him by the arms and swung him around. "Al-Kamil sent you? I never thought he'd—I expected—"

Fakhr-ad-Din flung his head back and roared with laughter. "I insisted. Ah. You look healthy. You should stay in Syria." His arms locked around Frederick in a strong hug. "What happened to your face?"

"I fell down the stairs. You remember Ayub."

"Of course. But where is Hasan?"

Ayub murmured, "Emir." Frederick turned to look at him.

"As long as you remember rank, why don't you send for some of those infidel pages and get us some . . . Dawud." Frederick swung around. "I thought he'd send one of his damned doctors with the . . ."

Fakhr-ad-Din laughed again. "I assured him that I would talk philosophy and mathematics at you until your head turned inside out. I'm supposed to delay you."

"That's not nice." Frederick waved away Ayub and the secretary. "So he hasn't made up his mind, after all those promises."

"God's most holy name," Fakhr-ad-Din said mildly. "If he simply handed you what you asked for, Islam would howl for his head. To be serious, I'm also to prepare you in case he can offer you nothing at all."

"Oh, really." Frederick sank down on his heels next to the bench under the apricot tree. "Go on, sit down, I know you've got weak knees. Don't try to fool me, Dawud. I'm as aware of his situation as he is of mine. Incidentally, is he aware of mine?"

"Of course. If there is— Oh." Fakhr-ad-Din inhaled strongly, so that his nostrils flared. He wore his beard bristly, like a desert Arab, and above it his sharp features always reminded Frederick of an old Jewish philosopher he'd known in his childhood. "I take it you're wondering if your envoy has been granted an audience."

"I assume he's been granted one." Frederick glanced around for Ayub, but he wasn't in sight.

"Yes. Well, one. If I were you, Sultan, I would replace the . . . unfortunate gentleman now with my Lord with Tommaso d'Aquino and Berardo the Archbishop, if he's here. The Sultan doesn't like the one he got."

"Oh. I forgot, Tommaso plays good chess."

"And this business of going to Jaffa, Frederick, now really."

Frederick cocked his eyebrows at him. "Don't brag. You do have excellent spies, I already know that. I—"

Fakhr-ad-Din looked past him and beamed. "Corso. I should have taken it for granted."

Corso knelt, holding out a tray, and made a pleasant face at both of them. "I heard that the most excellent Emir was here and naturally I had to come say that one Sicilian at least is overjoyed that you've come back."

"But you speak Italian," Fakhr-ad-Din said. "I didn't forget your language, but you forgot mine."

Corso blushed. "I didn't get much practice. Shall I leave the tray, Sire?"

"Yes." Frederick kicked at him. "You've disgraced me."

"Sire." Corso made another face and fled.

"Well. I see you didn't budge without the comforts of Sicily." Fakhr-ad-Din scooped up a fruit. "But our peaches are better than yours."

"I'm taking some slips from your trees back with me. Provided I ever go back. I might have to stay here and become a learned professor at a madrassah. You know I can't go back without Jerusalem."

"How wonderful it would be to have you with us forever. Speaking of learned professors, you recall the teacher of mathematics I had with me in Sicily?"

"No."

"That's because you didn't like him. He was caught stealing other people's proofs in solid geometry and sold on the block. Brought very little."

Frederick howled. "My, you're rough. How good are your spies, really? I have to go to Jaffa."

"Simply because it's closer to—"

"Because everybody here wants me dead."

Fakhr-ad-Din's face altered slightly; his eyes searched Frederick's face. "And they pushed you down the stairs?"

"No, I was joking. They ambushed me in the street.

Hasan is dead. They killed him."

"Who?"

"The Templars."

Fakhr-ad-Din's lips drew back from his teeth. "How ugly of them. No. Our spies didn't report that."

"They will. It's all over Acre."

Fakhr-ad-Din jerked his smile back into place. "Jaffa will be a superb place for your retirement. I'm told the ground is lovely for gardens."

"Yes. And how is Khwaresm behaving these days?"

"Khwaresm?" Both shaggy eyebrows arched up. "My dear fellow, how nasty of you. Your spies must be as good as ours."

"Quite."

"Khwaresm loves us like a brother."

"I understand this new Shah is just as ambitious as his father, and he doesn't seem to have learned from his father's unfortunate experience with a certain other tribe of which we really ought to talk. They tell me this Shah definitely wants Syria. He does control Baghdad, after all, and Baghdad without—"

"Sufficient. Yes. Jelal-ad-Din is an irritation to my lord al-Kamil, and al-Mu'azzam at one point acknowledged the sovereignty of Khwaresm over Damascus, which only proves one need not be Christian to be a damned fool."

Peach juice dribbled down Frederick's chin and he swiped at it with the back of his hand. The sun cast his shadow over Fakhr-ad-Din's white-robed knees. "Yes. Now tell me what's behind Khwaresm."

"The Mongols."

"Yes."

Fakhr-ad-Din tossed a peach pit into the bushes. "If you ever saw them you'd think they were beasts, not men at all. They're little, heavy-set, crooked, and intolerably ugly. We had two of their khans to court a few years ago. The damnable thing is that they are men, and they're intelligent. They learn fast. Ten years ago, when we first encountered them, they didn't know how to siege cities, but now . . . it's a crime, when brutes can be clever."

"Shrewd cows and short horns. How is your book?"

"Oh." Fakhr-ad-Din made an embarrassed gesture. "I read it and burned it all."

"That's too bad. Why?"

"Because it wasn't any good. I'm decent at conversation, but writing just isn't my sort of thing. Actually, nothing's my thing, except pleasant talk; if I hadn't been born the son of a sheikh I'd be a slave."

Frederick laughed. "I doubt it. How is al-Kamil?"

"In his element. He loves negotiations. He's dickering with en-Nasr, playing games with al-Ashraf, bargaining with you, and up to his armpits in the business of everybody else within reach. He adores it. Whines all day long that he has no peace and quiet. You know him."

"I don't, really. But we've exchanged some fine letters."

"Ah, yes." Fakhr-ad-Din looked down at him, grinning. "He was most impressed by the letter this Uberto brought with him. He wondered where you'd gotten so gifted an Arabic scribe. I told him you'd probably written it yourself."

"Naturally. Does he think I'd let a scribe handle correspondence that important?"

"Yes. Well, he says your Arabic is ungodly good."

"Of course it is. Come over to the other side of the garden—I want you to meet my new girl."

Once they had passed Caesarea the Jaffa road ran along the coast, past a sea so blue Frederick caught Theophano staring at it for hours and understood. Shortly after they'd left Acre, another Saracen had joined his bodyguard, a man named Feisal, quiet and unobtrusive. After Frederick made sure he was an Assassin, he kept him apart from Fakhr-ad-Din and told Ayub to see that the two never met.

The sea rolled white as cream in to the beach, turned to a pale, fiery blue just beyond the surf, so clear that from the hillside above it Frederick could see submerged rocks, and deepened gradually to a deep, rich blue that ran on to the horizon, and beyond the horizon was Sicily. He dreamed of it at night, sleeping in Theophano's litter with her arms around him—the macchia, sere and barren after the long summer, the marsh and Crane Bay with its cattails.

They were short of supplies, and nobody knew where the fleet was. Sometimes, reining up on top of a crest in the road, he turned and looked back and saw the train of people following him, stretching back along the pale dust of the road between the darker brown of the low scrub grass: thousands of people, because the German pilgrims in Acre had come too, hoping he would take them to Jerusalem. It depressed him. They had no reason to have such faith in him—nobody should ever trust any other man so much. After a while he decided that he felt that way because he was afraid he would fail. Fakhr-ad-Din had said that al-Kamil might not be able to give him anything.

Pay for it. He nudged his horse forward again; they had to move slowly because so many people had to walk. Ahead, Theophano's litter swayed heavily down a hillside, the colors already faded by the sun to the color of the dust in the road. Pay for it, and he needs peace, so give him peace. You told him that already. I will promise you no more Crusades if you will give me Jerusalem. No more Crusades . . . The Christians were tired of that game anyway, now they sent their children out for their salvation, or they sacked Constantinople. It was never a good idea.

He saw the Freidank, far ahead, singing to a group of knights. If you believe that, why are you on Crusade? Because . . . because because. The heat and the sunlight made him thirsty but there was no water, not for another hour. Or more. Beside him the Assassin rode, silent as ever, his dark eyes on the sea. I wish I could go to Alamut and see the Sheikh.

Fulk rode up alongside him. "The Emir is coming."

"Oh. Thank you." He twisted in his saddle and looked back. A faint plume of dust off to one side showed where Fakhr-ad-Din was trotting his horse to catch up. Frederick looked at the Assassin.

"Ride up by that litter, Feisal."

The Assassin without a word kicked his horse into a jog and swung out of line. Fulk was riding beside Frederick, wiping the dust from his face with a scarf. He caught Frederick looking at him and grinned.

"Did you ever wonder what the hell we're doing here?" Frederick said.

"No. I leave that wondering to you, Sire."

Wondering's bad for the mind. I have to stop thinking so much, I tie myself in knots and get nowhere. But the depression dragged at him, drawing him down. Waiting for Fakhr-ad-Din to catch up and start talking, he looked toward the sea and wished he could go home.

"What are you thinking about?"

"Sicily."

She touched his arm. On the other side of the fire, Fakhr-ad-Din looked up from his book and smiled. Frederick put his chin back in his hands.

"Do you want me to find the Freidank for you?" Theophano said.

"No, I'm tired of his music. Leave me alone, I'll be all right."

She left him alone, rare for a woman. He thought of Adelaide, who always brought him presents and insisted on talking to him when he felt like this. Have I ever felt like this before? Certainly. And in a while I'll get angry and start yelling at people. How predictable I am. Oh, Christ. Will you stop thinking.

Theophano was talking to Fakhr-ad-Din in her slow, accented Arabic. She treats everybody as kindly as she treats me. Is that good or bad? He wondered if Fakhr-ad-Din got the same jolt when she looked at him, if Fakhr-ad-Din hunted for things to say that would make her stop and think and say, "That's right. I didn't consider that." Now he was telling her about a Cordovan poet. Damn her, she should talk to me.

He stood up, and both of them looked at him, surprised. Without a word he walked out of the firelight, headed for the cliff over the sea. Immediately his Saracens grouped themselves around him. I'm never alone, I'm not permitted to be alone. They passed the fires of the knights, the pilgrims; nobody noticed him. All across the hillside the campfires glowed. All the way back to the road, hundreds of them. He turned his back on them and sat down cross-legged on the edge of the little cliff and listened to the boom and hiss of the surf beneath his feet. The Saracens moved off, leaving him by himself.

What if I can't take Jerusalem? He made himself think about that. Go home anyway? He'd have to, probably. And fight it out with the Pope for a little bit of a kingdom, everything else lost—the Pope would dictate to him and hedge him in—you failed. Or stay here and live with Theophano on a cliff over the sea and be forgotten. That would be better. Let them make Heinrich the Emperor. Let Heinrich find out for himself what everybody whispered distorted and warped into his ears. My son. Stupid, conniving little—

He could smell the shore and the wind, full of dust. They had enough supplies for two more days. After that we go through the usual: send some men out to steal food and when they come back get all indignant and make them pay for it. With my money. No, with Guy Embriaco's money. If I don't take Jerusalem and I can't go home I can't repay him. Sorry, Guy, old fellow, you lost.

Something moved right behind him, and he spun around. Theophano sat down beside him. "It's only me, Red."

"Oh." She'd come looking for him; he felt inordinately pleased. Her hands touched his shoulders, and shifting herself onto her knees, she began to rub his back. With a sigh he relaxed and shut his eyes, and after a moment she reached around in front of him, unlaced his coat and shirt and pulled them off, and her fingers worked on his bare back.

"Down a little. A little more. To the right. Oooooooh." He put his head back; her fingertips dug into the sore muscles and soothed and loosened them, and he sighed in rhythm to the strokes of her hands. Forget Sicily, forget Jerusalem, right now it's all . . . He arched his back and shivered. "Keep going."

She laughed softly. Behind her the Saracens would be standing in a semicircle, guarding him. He opened his eyes and looked out to sea, quivering under the touch of her hands, feeling much better.

W hat a mess," Fulk said.

"Well, it certainly isn't a garden of delights, is it?" Frederick stepped across a gap in the boards and shaded his eyes with his hands, looking out over Jaffa. The brilliant sunlight flashed off the tumbled stones of the city, off the rippling water in the harbor; all around them lay ruined buildings, without roofs, missing walls, filled with dust. In some of the houses people still lived, and huts crowded the sloping hillside behind the city. There was no wall. It reminded Frederick of an unmade bed, the way it sprawled cluttered and filthy around the crescent of the harbor. But they had discovered that most of the wells still ran full of sweet water, and there was certainly a huge supply of building stone.

"Where do we start?" Fulk said, and shrugged.

"I need a place to live. Everybody needs a place to live." Frederick walked around the top of the Angel Tower, where they stood, looking down through the gaps in the boards that covered it. The top three stories of the tower had collapsed, leaving a trunk like a tree that had been chopped down too high. In the dark down there, he saw heaps of stone, iron rods, dust and rats. "Over there."

Fulk raised his head to look where he was pointing. A huge rambling ruin of a building lay in what had probably been the next street; signs remained of its gateways and balconies and terraces, and the whole first floor stood nearly intact. "That?" Fulk said, uncertainly.

"Yes. I want to be able to see everything." He went to the edge of the tower and jumped down, practically on top of his Saracens. "Let's get back to the camp and start making plans."

Riding back through the city, he saw the knights and the pilgrims scrambling around the wreckage, probably hunting shelter. That had to stop. If they once got comfortable they'd never get to work on improving anything. He kicked his horse into a jog, watching for holes and obstacles in the street. Some of these roads looked like old Roman work, and he decided to dig one of them up to find out if it really was. The Romans had built magnificent roads. He reined in at a place where debris narrowed the street and let Yusuf and the Assassin precede him.

First they had to clean out the wreck of a building he'd decided would be his palace. Once they'd all started working, everything would go along more smoothly. The Grand Master would simply have to pry his men off their rumps and get them out there with hods and shovels, set an example for the pilgrims. The Cistercians with the army would probably leap to work with small shrill cries of joy: they loved manual labor. Or they were supposed to. If I do some work they'll all have to do some work. Shame them into it. He remembered how pulling the oar in the galley had skinned his hands, and made a face. They reached the edge of the city, where remnants of the wall thrust up through coarse grass and dusty plants, and he lifted his horse into a canter toward the camp.

Fakhr-ad-Din, Balian of Sidon, Conrad of Hohenlohe and the Grand Master were waiting outside his tent; when he rode up they dismounted. Yusuf and the Assassin trotted hastily away with the horses, but Frederick caught Fakhr-ad-Din staring thoughtfully after them. He pulled off his filthy cloak and threw it through the door of the tent.

"Gentlemen." He clapped his hands together and grinned. "We are going to have fun."

Fulk muttered under his breath. Fakhr-ad-Din smiled, but the others, more used to Frederick's idea of fun, began to twitch. Frederick paced around in a small circle, rubbing his hands together.

"Hermann. Get all your knights together and give them bags to carry dirt in. Conrad, you arrange for a train of carts to carry away the trash. Balian, you deal with the pilgrims, get them organized and equipped. Fulk—"

"Excuse me, Sire," the Grand Master said. "What are we going to do?"

"Well, first we're going to clean up my palace, and second we're going to rebuild the Angel Tower, and after that we'll work on the wall, and perhaps fourth we'll rebuild the system of quays around the harbor—"

Balian's mouth hung open. Conrad said, "Sire, surely the local peasantry would be—"

"Idle hands," Frederick said, beaming. "Devil's playground. Everybody up, let's get working."

Fakhr-ad-Din laughed. "As an ambassador I feel privileged to observe this."

Frederick gave him a look through the corner of his eye, beamed at the others, and ducked into his tent. In the midst of her native maids, Theophano looked up, and her eyes widened. "Where have you been? You're filthy."

"Inspecting." He yelled for Corso and kicked off his shoes. "You'd better send them into the back while I change my clothes."

The maids rose and quietly left. Theophano said, "The rumor's all around the camp that there's no more food. People are starting to hoard."

"I'll get some food. At least there's plenty of water." Corso got him into fresh hose and a clean shirt. If they were hoarding they'd lost faith in him. Gather them together and feed them loaves and fishes. What do they think I am? Two pages trotted around tidying up after the women, who'd been sewing; they'd left bits of thread and cloth all over everything. Theophano did not sew, she watched. He went over to her and knelt and kissed her.

"I'll be back for dinner."

Her arms slid around his neck. "All dirty again?" With her face so close, he could see nothing else, and when she smiled it filled his vision. "Go play, Red."

He kissed her again and went outside.

Stripped to their underwear, the knights stooped under the broiling sun, shoveling dirt and chunks of stone into baskets the natives had given them, while mules dragged sledges back and forth from the palace to a place near the main gate where Frederick had ordered the debris dumped. They'd set up casks of fresh water all around the building, so that no one went thirsty. Up on the wall, Frederick could feel the heat draining the sweat from his body. He looked up at the pulleys, shading his eyes.

"Well, try it. But I think we'll have to brace up that arm." He jumped down to the ground. His shirt was black with sweat and dirt and he peeled it off, watching the men rig up the ropes and lower the net to the ground. Three other men started heaving a block of fallen stone toward the net. He paced back and forth, his eyes shifting from the pulleys to the knights. A mule with a sledge moved toward them, and he trotted over to direct it.

The stone rolled onto the net, and the men who had pushed it bent to hook the net's corners to the pulley rope. On the wall three more men took hold of the end of the rope. Frederick climbed back onto the wall and looked over the other side. "We can get a mule in there to draw the rope. Why waste men?"

From the top of the wall he could see into the rooms behind them, already swept clean to their tile floors, and on ahead, to the rooms still to be cleaned out. It reminded him of the Augean stables, and he laughed. They'd swayed the chunk of stone up onto the sledge with the pulley, and the mule was drawing it away, out through a door into the street. He went over to supervise the bracing of the crane arm.

I'm glad I have this to do so I haven't got time to worry about . . . Hurriedly he made himself study the angle between the brace and the arm. One of the men went for water and brought him back a cupful, and he drank it. The sun was burning his back, even through what was left of the tan he'd gotten during the sail to Cyprus. I could put a little pressure on him—raid somewhere. While knights cleared away the rubble around the door into the next room, he thought about that. The trouble was that al-Kamil had a gigantic army at Nablus and if he decided to take a raid seriously, refortifying Jaffa wouldn't make any difference at all. Just a friendly raid?

Behind him someone screamed, "Sail—there's a sail in the harbor—" He spun around, all his muscles clenching in surprise, heard what the man had said, and relaxed, grinning. He couldn't see the ship yet, but the others could; they turned and shouted, waving their arms. "There's two—three—it's the fleet!"

Frederick did a little dance on the top of the wall. That meant one less thing to sweat over. He heard the captains of the work crews shouting to their men not to leave the work—"You'll all get a good meal tonight, when we've got this dirt out of here." And now even Frederick could see the galleys moving up toward the shore, the front ranks already lowering their sails and putting out oars. He jumped down from the wall and started through the maze of roofless rooms into the street.

His Saracens fell in around him, joking about the knights working at such menial labor: "After all, they're swine, they belong in dirt." Frederick turned and glared at Ayub, who straightened his face and elbowed the Assassin beside him. Hasan would never have done that; Hasan would have remembered that most of these knights spoke Arabic. Hasan would have used Italian. He grinned and crossed the street and went down another, already cleared and even partially mended. All around them crews lugged baskets of dirt and rocks out into the street, and mule-drawn sledges bumped along picking them up. At this rate the whole section around the palace would be clear by sundown. He took his shirt from Yusuf and draped it around his shoulders, smiling.

Ahead of them an old arch crossed the street, and beyond it he could see the blue of the sea. The stink of wet mortar reached his nose. The arch looked Roman —he couldn't remember whether Jaffa had existed in Roman times. Undoubtedly—some of the architecture looked older than the fancy ruins in Rome. Walking into the shadow of the arch was like stepping into a fall of cold water. He stopped to put his shirt on and wandered over to the wall to look at the way the stones fitted together.

Just the other side of the arch a work crew was sweeping up the street. A man among them straightened up and stared at Frederick—a pilgrim, yellow-haired. Frederick glanced at him and ran one hand over the wall, admiring the closeness of the stone. Suddenly Ayub snapped, "Where do you think—" and he turned and saw the Assassin running straight for the pilgrim ahead of them.

Frederick opened his mouth to yell, the pilgrim whirled and ran, and the other three Saracens charged after him. With a curse Frederick moved out into the sunlight, peering after them. He couldn't figure out what the Assassin was doing—maybe he'd eaten too much hashish. The pilgrim tripped over a line of rubble and the Assassin left the ground completely in a long dive and landed squarely on top of him. The rest of the work crew was shouting and staring from Frederick to the Saracens and back again. Frederick ran down the street toward the fight.

The Assassin had both arms around the pilgrim; they

were rolling around in the dirt, arms and legs thrashing awkwardly, while the other Saracens circled them, unsure what to do. Ayub looked up, saw Frederick coming and bellowed an order. Yusuf jumped in and grabbed the pilgrim, who was nearly out, and Ayub and Masuf wrestled the Assassin up onto his feet and held him.

"He's a Templar," the Assassin screamed. "He's a Templar, don't let him go."

Frederick skidded to a stop. Twisting around, he saw the mob of men behind him—the rest of the work crew and a few others within earshot. Christians on pilgrimage —he jerked around again and shouted, "Ayub, knock him out and drop him," and hoped none of the men behind him spoke Italian. He glanced back and saw that they'd stopped, but their eyes looked angry, and they spoke to each other in quick, harsh voices, their eyes on the Saracens. He ran up and knelt beside the pilgrim, lying in the street.

"Are you sure?" he said softly to the Assassin.

"I know all the Templars in Syria," the Assassin murmured. "That's why I'm here."

Frederick looked down at the face of the pilgrim. He was stirring, and his eyes opened, looked into the bright sun, and shut again. Frederick put his hand out to shade the man's face.

"Are you all right?" he asked, in German. "Can you get up?"

"Yes. Just—groggy." The pilgrim rolled onto his side, lifted his head up and shook it. Frederick shifted his weight and got one foot under him. The pilgrim's head swayed; he reached down to help the man rise.

Lurching up and toward him, his lips curled, the pilgrim jerked out a dagger. Frederick leaped back, both hands on the pilgrim's shoulders, dragged him forward, and smashed his knee into the man's face. The pilgrim gave a choked yelp and fell into the dirt, blood spurting from his nose and mouth. Frederick walked away a little and turned to look at him again.

"Complete idiots. A good street fighter can beat them every time." He jabbed a thumb at Ayub. "Take him someplace. I want to talk to him later." He looked at the pack of spectators, whose mouths hung open, whose eyes bulged—one called, "What happened?"

"Nothing," Frederick said. "The poor soul must have gotten too much sun. Go back to work, you'll have a banquet tonight." He walked down toward the harbor; the Assassin and Yusuf followed him, while the others took the Templar to a prison. Suddenly he remembered why the Templar had been here, why the Assassin was here, and his mouth dried up. They want to kill me. He looked over at the Assassin.

"Thank you, Feisal."

"My Lord." Feisal smiled; he brushed at the dirt on his robes.

"He killed himself," Frederick said. "They put him in chains and he wrapped the chains around his neck and choked himself to death." He stared at the wall and tried to imagine doing that. How could anybody do that?

"He wouldn't have told you anyway," Fakhr-ad-Din said. "Or at least, nothing you don't already know—for instance, what your pet Assassin told you."

Frederick leaned back and watched Theophano cut him slices of meat. Enrico had sent three ships to Acre to buy furniture for his new palace, which they would roof tomorrow. "How did you find out about that?"

"That he's an Assassin?"

"Are you angry?" He studied Fakhr-ad-Din's face.

"Not particularly angry." Fakhr-ad-Din frowned, chewed thoughtfully on a piece of bread, and wiped his hands on a napkin. "Not angry at all, in fact. I knew what he was when I saw his face, he's well known, a sort of local hero to most of the small towns in Syria. It's just that Assassins make me . . . uneasy. How would you feel if you suddenly detected a Milanese in my retinue?"

"I guess I know. Keeping you two separate was a chore anyhow, like that man with the wolf and the cabbage and the goat. I'm glad—"

"The what?"

"The wolf, the cabbage, and the goat. It's a riddle from the time of Carolus Magnus. Haven't you ever heard it?"

"No. Tell me," Theophano said. She handed him some slices of meat. To Fakhr-ad-Din she said. "His riddles keep me awake at night."

Frederick grinned. "That's not called a riddle, sweetheart."

Fakhr-ad-Din laughed, choked it off abruptly, embarrassed, and cleared his throat. "Tell us the riddle, Frederick."

"Well. It seems a man came to a river that he could cross only by a small boat. He had with him a wolf, a cabbage, and a goat. The boat was so small he could transport only one object to the far bank at a time. The problem is; How does he get everything to the far side, when if he leaves the wolf alone with the goat, the wolf will eat the goat, and if he leaves the goat alone with the cabbage—"

"I see," Fakhr-ad-Din said. "Strange travelers you have in your country. What the devil did he want a wolf for?"

"You have to take the goat first, obviously," Theophano said. "If you take the goat over and go back and . . . no, that won't work."

"Of course it will, child," Fakhr-ad-Din said. "You take the goat across, leave it on the far bank, and go back and pick up the cabbage. When you get to the far bank you deposit the cabbage and pick up the goat again. On the near bank you leave off the goat and pick up the wolf, who proceeds to devour you in midstream."

"Oh. Why didn't I think of that?" She slapped her fist on the table. "And you leave the wolf on the far bank, go back, take the goat across—"

"And wind up wolf-bitten with a moldy cabbage and a seasick goat." Fakhr-ad-Din clapped his hands. "It is solved."

Frederick laughed.

Fakhr-ad-Din said, "We have something similar in Cairo, dealing with three newly married couples who arrive at a similar river under similar circumstances and none of the husbands will leave their wives alone with the other men."

"That's slightly more difficult." Frederick ate a bite of meat. The air smelled faintly of dust, and the torches wavered in the light breeze. "Do I have to go through the whole thing or can I give you the number of trips necessary?"

"Make him do the whole thing," Theophano said, "or he'll cheat and figure it out mathematically."

Fakhr-ad-Din, laughing, patted her hand. "Eleven," Frederick said.

"Good. Now, east of Khwaresm but south of the Mongols are a tribe very well versed in algebra and geometry. They have a holy city called Benares, in which is a temple, in which are three diamond needles, around one of which God at the Creation, for reasons best known to Himself, placed sixty-four gold disks graduated in size, with the largest on the bottom and the smallest on the top, arranged so that no disk rests on one smaller than itself."

"You sound like a book I read when I was a child."

"I'm a natural pedagogue. The priests in Benares spend all day transferring the disks from one needle to another, one disk at a time, so that no disk ever rests on one smaller than itself. When the priests have succeeded in moving all sixty-four gold disks from the original diamond needle to another, the world will end."

"How hard do they work at it?" Theophano said.

"We've got a long time to wait," Frederick said. "Don't worry. A million million million years or something on that order."

"Slightly more."

"Where do you learn these things?" Theophano said. "I seem to have missed a whole level of my education."

"We both think too much," Fakhr-ad-Din said, leaning back against a chest covered with a carpet. "Mathematics gives one something to think about that isn't injurious."

"It's a good way to think too," Frederick said. "Everything is reducible to mathematical terms, and if you cut out all the prejudices and personality in figuring something out—" That's why when I make a mistake it's a big one and has to do with personality and prejudice.

"Well," Fakhr-ad-Din said, "when people say you're cold-blooded, that's what they mean."

"Me? Who says I'm cold-blooded?" He started upright.

Theophano grinned. "Very nearly everybody. Guy Embriaco told his wife, whose maids told my maids, who told me that you have serpent's eyes."

"Guy Embriaco has eyes like mud puddles."

"Not everything is reducible to mathematical terms," Fakhr-ad-Din said. "Statecraft is, of course, which is why you're so successful at it, but—"

"The only thing that can't be considered in mathematical terms is God, and I suspect that's simply because we haven't got enough information about God."

Theophano looked up at the sky. "God or Allah?" She used the Greek word for God.

Fakhr-ad-Din laughed and reached for the tray of cookies. "Child, don't start us off on that. We spent weeks in Sicily debating the nature of the perception of God by different tribes."

"When you know the name of something, you control

it," Frederick said, "which is the whole point of witch-craft; isn't it? So we quarrel over the name of God." He stretched out his legs; the comfort of the room, the easy flow of talk soothed and calmed him, and he half shut his eyes.

Theophano's fingers grazed his. "Tell me about state-craft and mathematics."

Fakhr-ad-Din said, "Let me. After all, we shouldn't want to offend his modesty."

Frederick laughed. "Absolutely elemental. If Moham-med refuses to go to the mountain, the mountain, eventu-ally, will be brought to Mohammed."

"That's what I mean. Modesty is not one of the virtues of singularly successful men, I imagine." Fakhr-ad-Din's teeth crunched on a cookie. "When no solution to a problem presents itself, Theo, one can sometimes work the problem backward—start with a solution and recon-struct the problem to fit the answer. In a case of com-plete anarchy and a king without power, one simply states that the king has all the power in the kingdom, and no one else has any at all, which is of course the desirable solution. One then proceeds to rule as if that were in fact so, although it's true only in theory."

"How?"

"Well," Frederick said, "it's geometrical, you see. If I have all the legal power, and nobody else has any, not even the nobility, everybody else is legally equal. So I apply the same laws to everybody. That makes it true that I have all the power. Since the Normans set up the laws in Sicily and the Normans were wild for law, any law I might need already exists in the charters, so obvi-ously I had the power all the time. I never passed a new law in the first three years I ruled in Sicily after I came back from Germany."

"And everybody simply falls into line?" she said slowly.

"Well, they have to, you see. Because if one baron

doesn't, all the others will help me punish him for breaking the law." He looked over at her, grinning. "It's quite simple."

"I still don't see why they didn't all band together and—"

"Oh. Oh, well. That's easy—why do you break the law?"

"So I can do what I want."

"Quite. But most of the things barons want to do that are against the law infringe on the other barons—you see? As for the people who weren't barons, they were so surprised that I intended to take responsibility for them at all, they had no time to complain."

She shook her head. "It's too simple."

"Possibly. It only works in cases where the law is completely unworkable, so that nobody can really obey it— if you obey one law you break another. In a case like Cyprus, where everybody is actually obeying the law, I couldn't do much. I'm going to try, but I doubt I'll get anywhere."

"Try to do what?" Fakhr-ad-Din said.

"Make it orderly. It's a mess, it's impossible to get anything done."

"All Frankish law is like that. I've come to the conclusion after some study of the problem that Frankish law is designed to keep anybody from doing anything efficiently."

"That's because it's all customary law. Made for barons by barons." He reached for Theophano's hand, and their fingers intertwined. "They've gotten along perfectly well with it, though—it's a nice balance between terror and boredom."

Fakhr-ad-Din's brows arched. Pages came in to take away the dishes and bring them sherbet and wine. "This is a new theory; I haven't heard this one, have I?"

"I figured it out on the trip to Acre from Cyprus." Frederick grinned and sat up straight. "It's one of my best, I'm really fond of it. Can I tell it?"

"In Sicily he had some other mad theory about people's motives," Fakhr-ad-Din said to Theophano. "He
develops them like cloud castles, and the wind blows
them away."

"It's a game. This one is nice, though. Life is terrible,
after all; you have nothing to look forward to except
dying, and you can die at any time, it's all uncertain. Or
you can be thrown into prison by a tyrant—"

"Like you," Theophano said.

"I'm a good tyrant. Yes. Or you can starve or thirst—
everything is unsure, and that's terrifying. On the other
hand, what's sure and safe is boring, and people will do
anything to escape boredom. Absolutely anything."

"It was a boring trip, from Cyprus to Acre," Fakhr-ad-
Din told Theophano.

"It was. He was soaring on hashish for most of it."

"Anyhow, all the things we do are an attempt either to
alleviate the pressure of terror or to escape boredom."

"Well. A sweeping generalization of that cosmic order
deserves contemplation." Fakhr-ad-Din drank sherbet.
"Examples?"

"The Crusades. Consider a distant relation of mine—
Fulk Nerra, the Comte d'Anjou. He went on crusade
three times to expiate his sins. In Anjou he was a walking
terror, he fought incessantly. Or Pope Urban's Crusade,
in which others of my relatives figured so prominently.
The Truce of God wasn't working, and the knights
were devastating the countryside, fighting wars to escape
the boredom of home, so he redirected their fighting into
an area where if it did no good it could at least do no
harm."

"What are you doing here?" Theophano said.

"I don't know."

In the little silence that followed, the words sounded
strange, like something heard under hashish.

"Your theories always constitute a direct attack on the

concept of morality," Fakhr-ad-Din said. "Who's your court philosopher these days?"

"I am." He grinned. Come on, Dawud, argue.

"You don't believe that people do certain things out of a sense of altruistic devotion? Out of consideration of a higher ideal?"

"Sometimes. Not often. After all, to consider a high ideal, which isn't something essential to survival, one has to be relatively free of distractions, like terror and boredom."

"Of course. But a man like me is in such a position. To me the pursuit of a generally acceptable ideal is valuable in itself, as an affirmation, as a set of known and tested and functioning hypotheses about life, or simply as a way of life in which friction and discomfort are reduced to a minimum and my personal freedom is practically assured. Yet we're in similar situations, and you consistently deny the value of a general morality."

"That's because I don't believe anybody can learn and progress from one idea to the next and on unless he refuses to accept a minimum of friction and discomfort and a practical assurance of personal freedom. Now, look, Dawud. You develop a skill only as much as you need for the purpose at hand, don't you?"

"What do you mean?" Fakhr-ad-Din snapped his fingers for a page and sent him after more cookies.

"Birds, then. A bird that flies well doesn't learn how to walk well, he doesn't need to. A bird that lives in the water loses the ability to live on land because he doesn't have to live on land. People are the same way. You have to force yourself into uncomfortable situations to develop your intellectual skills."

Theophano clapped her hands together. "Yes. That's right."

"Affirmation from a most excellent source," Fakhr-ad-Din said, and bowed to her. "Frederick, consider that in her travels and her attempts to make a better life for herself, alone, a woman alone, she has certainly encountered more difficulty and seen more levels of life than either of us."

Maybe. He reached for a ewer full of sherbet, resting in a bowl of snow. Is that why I think this way? Because I remember how it was when I was little and alone and had to . . . "Dawud?"

"Thank you." Fakhr-ad-Din held out his cup. "You made an interesting point before—or rather, you skirted it. The direction of warlike men into the Crusade. Don't you think that many of the terrors and most of the boredom you mentioned exist only within people's imaginations, and most often they'll try to focus their emotions on an outward and independent object? Like Jerusalem. It's blindingly clear that a trip to the earthly Jerusalem will save no one who has not already found Jerusalem in his own soul."

"Naturally. The True Cross, relics, saints—it's all magic, it's witchcraft. Your dervishes are another example. Or Francesco—you remember I told you about him."

"The man who received the wounds of Christ. Yes."

"Wounds in his hands, feet, and side. In his hands, that's the especially interesting point. Have you ever seen anyone crucified?"

Fakhr-ad-Din grimaced. "No. I have no wish to."

"You cannot crucify someone by nailing his hands to the wood. His weight will pull his hands right off the nails." He drew a deep breath. The long war with the Saracens in the mountains of Sicily. Everybody had gotten bloodthirsty—me too. Kicked that emir with my spur. But he'd made me angry.

"So if Francesco had received the wounds of God from God Himself," Fakhr-ad-Din said, "he'd have gotten holes—where?"

"In his wrists."

"You can't be sure," Theophano said. "How can you

say something like that? It's of no importance."

"But it is," Frederick said. "Because if it's all so, Francesco was not given the wounds by God, he received them through his own devotion. Which makes the entire outward structure of the Church a lie, and an unnecessary one at that."

"Most people are incapable of that devotion."

"True. It requires a certain amount of faith that I, for one, am unwilling to give."

They sat still, listening to the wind blowing over the roofless building. Tomorrow . . . maybe a message will come from al-Kamil. But I don't think so. Not being sure, not knowing: terror. What am I doing here?

"Well, with your permission, Frederick, I'm going to bed." Fakhr-ad-Din rose. "I expect by tomorrow to see an entire city flourishing on this spot, furnished completely and flowering with gardens. Good night."

With his attendants and torchbearers around him, he walked out the side door. Frederick watched his gold-stitched robes wink in the uneven light. When I wake up, will I be in Sicily again? Everything felt unreal—the whole journey. It seemed that everything had happened so fast he couldn't keep hold of it. What am I doing here? If he knew, he wouldn't be doing it. That makes as much sense as anything else I've said tonight.

"Do you want me to stay, Red? I'm tired."

"No—go on. I'll be in in a moment."

She rose and left, and another pack of servants detached themselves from the shadows and surrounded her. Something Fakhr-ad-Din had said—she knew more about life, she'd done more—as if she'd told him things she'd never told Frederick. Theophano, the juggler's assistant. Justinian's Empress had been a whore—why not? Because polity will eventually provide me with another wife, and I can't afford to waste that kind of currency. Bed-bargains are the best. Maybe al-Kamil has an unmarried daughter. He thought of how that would shock the

Christians and grinned. Why not? King Richard knighted Salah-ad-Din. I can find a precedent for anything, lawyer that I am.

En-Nasr had taken advantage of Frederick's move to Jaffa to raid out of Damascus, cutting down toward Nablus to break al-Kamil's supply lines. I have my allies in strange quarters. It was wise to send him an embassy. I didn't know why at the time, but it was a good thing. More pressure on al-Kamil to end the standoff. And just that afternoon Frederick had sent a messenger to Tommaso in the Sultan's court at Nablus, telling him that Frederick was willing to leave the Haramu'sh-Sharif in Jerusalem under Moslem control if al-Kamil gave him the rest of the city. It was cheaper to bargain with somebody else's goods—the Haramu'sh-Sharif contained the Dome of the Rock and Solomon's Temple, sacred to Islam. Tommaso had said the talks were moving along, but the Archbishop in an independent message had been less optimistic. Which do I believe?

Tomorrow . . . They had the slaves from some of the ships, and they'd found one block of buildings close to the palace that remained almost intact, and they had to start working on the wall. Someday al-Kamil has to tell me, one way or the other. A surge of desperation rushed through him. Please, God—Even if it doesn't please God. He grinned at that, and the amusement took the edge off his nerves. When he stood up, the third group of attendants moved in the shadows, and when he left they followed, lighting his way to Theophano's bed.

"Are you sure we ought to take her?" Fulk whispered. "This is mad. We're bound to get caught."

"Oh, shut up. What if we get caught, so what?" Frederick bent down and crawled out the hole in the wall. They could easily have left through the front gate of the palace, but the whole idea was to escape. Outside in the dark street he moved to the side and let the others through. "We haven't ever gotten caught before, have we?"

"He's mad," Ezzo said. He crept out the hole and reached inside to help Theophano. "This isn't Sicily. What if there's a Templar down there?"

"That's part of the fun." He looked around—the street was lit with torches at regular intervals. Empty and walled off, it reminded him of that street in Acre, and the hair on the back of his neck stood up. Theophano stood beside him, shoving her hair back under her cap.

Fulk said, "You're right, this isn't Sicily, in Sicily we could get horses." He started off down the street, and Frederick followed, his arm around Theophano. Ezzo, muttering, trailed along behind them.

Theophano laughed, and against his side and arm she moved gently, pressing herself close to him. "What if people recognize you and see you fondling your page?"

"Give them something to talk about." Fulk was wearing a sword; so was Ezzo, and they both looked and sounded nervous. He said to Theophano, "We do this all the time in Sicily, it's fun."

At the corner they turned right onto the main street. The breeze from the harbor smelled of salt and rotting seaweed. Frederick lengthened his stride, pulling Theophano along with him. Hooded and cloaked, paying them no attention, a pair of knights passed them, headed for the new barracks. Most of these buildings, squat and flat-roofed, had been repaired, and he supposed pilgrims were living in them, but they all belonged to Frederick. A monk stood outside one, trying futilely to light a lamp that had gone out—some of the German pilgrims had even strung greenery over their doors. The road sloped down to the harbor, and Fulk slipped and swore and walked short on the smooth cobblestones.

In the dark the city looked finished, old and well worn. They walked beneath the arch where the Assassin had seen the Templar, and in the shadows a girl giggled and a man spoke softly and gently. When we came here Jaffa was dead, only a few hundred people lived here, but now . . . and it's only been a couple of weeks. Ahead, down the hill, he could see the white of sea foam and the rocking lights of the galleys anchored along the quays. He hugged Theophano.

Structures. He watched two young men trot up toward them and jog past, shouting to each other in German. He wondered how many people there had to be in a group before it could reconstruct its own way of life in a foreign place. One person wouldn't do it; he'd just blend in, do what the natives did. Through his mind ran a quick image of a man cased in an invisible structure of his habits. Maybe you have to have other people around who understand what the things that you do mean. Up ahead, Fulk turned into an alley.

"No trash," Theophano said.

"Right."

The one mark of how new this part of Jaffa was. But we have whorehouses and taverns and criminals already. He pushed at the thought; there had to be some order, some revelation in it that would be useful in ruling. The alley was warmer than the street. Outside a door they stopped and looked at each other and Fulk knocked.

"Ezzo. Do you remember when we brought all the Saracens in from the island to Lucera?"

Ezzo nodded. "Ten thousand of them. It was amazing."

"How long did it take them to settle down?"

"What did you do that for?" Theophano said.

"Not very long," Ezzo said. "A year."

"Less than that. I'll ask Ayub."

The door opened and they went into a room blazing with lights, packed with tables and sailors and whores and thieves. It stank of wine. Frederick took a quick look around, saw nobody he recognized, and plowed after

Fulk through the mob to a table. Heavy voices jarred in his ears; somebody took a step backward and crashed into him, and without thinking he shoved back. Theophano clutched at his coat with both hands so she wouldn't get separated from him. At the table, Fulk whipped out his sword and slammed it down on the wood, and several people standing nearby spun around. Fulk glared at them, warning them away, and stripped off his coat.

"This is—" Ezzo said, quit, and sank down. "At least we can get drunk."

Pulling chairs around, Frederick made Theophano sit with her back to the wall, and sat down next to her. A boy with a black eye trotted through the mob toward them.

"Do you have wine or beer?" Fulk shouted over the din. Frederick laughed at him, and he blushed. He'd spoken Greek; they'd been using Greek because Theophano spoke no Italian. The boy looked blank.

"Bring us some wine," Frederick said in German. He took out his purse and dropped it on the table.

The boy repeated, "Wine," and ran off again. In front of the table, practically on top of Ezzo, a big sailor threw his arms wide, roaring, and spilled a wooden cup full of beer. Some of the beer splashed on Ezzo, who leapt up, turning, and grabbed the sailor by the shirt.

Fulk groaned and slouched back in his chair. Ezzo was screaming in Italian into the sailor's face, and the sailor and his friends were screaming back in lingua franca. Arms waved. Theophano leaned over and whispered, "Are you going to let him get in a fight?"

Frederick laughed. "That's the whole idea." He stood up and yelled, "Do you need any help, Ezzo?"

Ezzo didn't even look around. He was pounding his fist on the sailor's chest; his face turned bright red with anger. It was so hot the sweat poured down the sailor's face, cutting channels through the dirt. Frederick pulled off his coat and threw it across his chair.

One of the sailor's friends grabbed Ezzo by the sleeve

and cocked his fist back. Before he could throw the punch, before Ezzo could move to meet him, a gigantic black man wearing nothing but a loincloth burst in between them. Theophano murmured something to Fulk. The black thrust Ezzo and the sailor's friend apart, looking down from an immense height at each of them, his face expressionless. Ezzo looked up and his eyes bulged. The black stood head and shoulders taller than he did. With a jerky little bow Ezzo turned and sat down again.

"Who is that?"

The black looked down at Ezzo, glared around once at the sailor and his friends, and turned to Frederick. "Sit down," he said, in the lingua franca. "No trouble. If you give me any trouble, you leave." His jaw muscles clenched momentarily, and with a snort he turned and plunged back through the crowd. Frederick sank down, delighted.

"Fulk. Who is that?"

"He runs this block of taverns. His name is Mutu and he's from Africa somewhere and he can take your head like this"—Fulk spread his hand around the back of Theophano's head—"and crunch. And he doesn't like trouble. I thought it would be safer here."

"Well," Frederick said. "We'll have to give Mutu some trouble."

"He'll kill you," Theophano said. "Don't."

The boy with the black eye brought them their wine, and Fulk paid him and sent him back for a ewer. Theophano made sure her hair was still stuffed under the cap.

"Where's he from?" Ezzo said. "I've never seen him before."

"He came down from Acre, I think," Theophano said. "Mutu is famous. He was in Constantinople once when I was there, and somebody told me al-Mu'azzam ran him out of Damascus for selling opium."

"Opium," Frederick said. He started to grin, and Fulk shut his eyes.

The sailor and his friends had moved off, but now the

man who had nearly hit Ezzo came back, glowering. "You and I have a—"

"Any time," Ezzo said, and stood up and hit him. His fist caught the sailor right in the mouth, and blood spurted in gouts across the man's chest—he fell back into a table with a crash of wood. The crowd screamed. Like a school of fish they churned around, looking for Mutu, making room for the fallen sailor. He sat up and spat out two teeth. Ezzo reached for his wine cup and drained it and started to stand up again.

"Here comes Mutu," Frederick said. He glanced at Theophano.

Ezzo sank back into his chair and fell into deep conversation with Fulk. The sailor gathered himself, flexing his hands, and charged for Ezzo. From behind him a gigantic black arm reached out, took him by the hair, and lifted him completely off the ground. The crowd roared, surging back and forth in the narrow space. Mutu towed off the sailor screaming across and through the packed bodies of the mob and never glanced at Ezzo.

Frederick leaped up on the table to watch. "Jesus. He's incredible. What else can he do?"

Theophano said, "Let me out a moment. I see someone I know." She got up and slithered into the mob. Frederick jumped up and down on the table top.

"Here he comes again." Frederick got down from the table. Mutu had seen him and was plowing through the crowd, which gave him all the room they could. Ezzo shifted his chair closer to the wall. Mutu strode up and cocked his head, looking at Frederick, his hands on his hips.

"I saw you standing on the table. Why did you do that? I don't like people standing on the tables."

Standing up, Frederick had to put his head all the way back to look into Mutu's eyes. He said, "I was curious."

"Haven't I seen you someplace before?" Mutu's eyes narrowed.

Frederick put his hands on his hips. "Maybe."

Theophano was coming back, looking even less like a page than before: the men were staring at her. Mutu said, "Don't give me any shit, you." He poked Frederick in the chest with one finger. "Just don't—" He saw Theophano and his eyes widened. "Theo." His hand reached out for her, and Frederick knocked it down.

"She's with me, Mutu."

Mutu reared back. "She's an old friend of mine, she's a new friend of yours."

Frederick reached out, grabbed Theophano by the arm, and hauled her around behind him, knocking over a chair. "I said she's with me, Mutu."

"Can't I even talk to—" Mutu took him by the arm to pull him away, and Frederick locked his fingers around Mutu's wrist to take his hand off him. The size of the black's arm astonished him; the muscle was hard as bone. Mutu frowned, and his other hand came up.

Fulk smashed his sword down on the table top again. Mutu looked around and saw him and Ezzo on their feet, crouched. His eyes widened. Jerking his head around toward Theophano, he said, "What is this?"

Theophano said, "Don't hurt him and let him do what he wants, or you'll get killed. Red, let him sit with us, I want to talk to him."

Frederick and Mutu let go of each other, and while Mutu brought over a stool Frederick sat down. The ends of his fingers still felt how strong Mutu was. Fulk and Ezzo relaxed.

"Do you usually get into fights?" Theophano said. She leaned her arms on the table. Mutu sat down on Frederick's other side.

"He's one of the Italians," he said to Theophano.

"Yes. I thought you were in Antioch."

"I was, but Bohemund's people started getting nervous." Mutu glanced at Frederick. "I heard a rumor you were with the Emperor. What happened?"

Theophano shrugged one shoulder. "Things like that never last. You don't have any hashish, do you?"

"Not here. I could get some, though—Acre is floating in it, all the Templars and Hospitallers use it."

"Where do they get it?" Frederick said.

Mutu moved his big hands, palms up. "From Damascus, I think. Or Cairo. They're very tight with the Moslems."

Frederick's eyes narrowed. Diplomatic channels . . . The balance and flexibility of the Franks in Syria amazed him, that they could adjust everything so delicately without changing the outward appearance at all. He began to wonder how much an agreement between him and al-Kamil would disturb it—on the other hand, if a detente was already functioning, a legitimate truce should be easier to arrange.

"Mutu, do you know anything about the Saracen spies in Jaffa?"

"Not a thing. They don't circulate around here." Mutu took Ezzo's empty cup, filled it, and threw the wine in a torrent down his throat. "They hang around in the Old Quarter—where the people lived before the Emperor came. Mutaq is the one you want, if you've got something to sell."

Oh, really? "Not right now. Later, maybe. Could you . . . put me in touch with him if I wanted it?"

Mutu shrugged. "I can do anything."

Frederick threw his head back and laughed. Beside him, Theophano whispered, "Mutu, get me some hashish."

"Sure. How much?"

"A jug."

Off across the room somebody shouted and Mutu leaped up. "They're fighting again—I'll be back." He strode through the mob toward the corner near the door, from which came shouts and the meaty thunk of fists on bone. Frederick watched him go and drank some wine.

"Interesting. You never told me you had friends like that."

Theophano grinned. Ezzo said, "Shall we go find Mutaq for you?"

"No. As long as I know where, who, and what, we may as well let them alone." He mulled it over in his mind, working out ways to control the information the spies fed to al-Kamil. "Sometime we ought to go have a talk with him, though."

Mutu was carting out two squirming, shrieking men, one in each hand. Theophano said, "He isn't stupid, you know. The only reason he didn't guess who you were is because he can't imagine anybody like you coming here. Be careful."

"I will." Frederick leaned back and under the table slid his hand through the opening in her coat. "I will."

"I was afraid you'd pick a fight with him, before."

"Who, me?" He looked at her, startled. "Not with him, he'd kill me."

"Then why did you—"

She bit the last word off and looked away, her forehead creased. Under his fingers the smooth skin of her belly grew tight. Mutaq, he thought. Tomorrow . . .

Ezzo said, "Is this all they do, stand around and drink?"

"What do you want?" Theophano said. "You can probably dice upstairs, and there are girls there."

Fulk said, "Next door."

"I mean—let's have a little excitement," Ezzo said.

"Can't." Frederick held the wine ewer over his cup, but nothing came out. "How can anybody start a fight when Mutu's here?" He handed the ewer to Fulk. "Get us some more."

Fulk stood up to look for the boy. Three men arguing were leaning on the table, and Frederick picked up both feet, set them on the rump of the nearest, and shoved. With a wail the man stumbled into the crowd, dragging one of the others with him. The man remaining swung around, but Ezzo picked up his sword, and the man turned hastily to help the other stand. Mutu came back through the mob and sat down again at their table.

"So you might have some reason to go to Mutaq," he said, looking at Frederick. The boy came with the wine, and when Fulk tried to pay, Mutu waved the boy off. "What kind of reason?"

Frederick slid his hands up and down on the table top. Fulk was watching Mutu through eyes closed to slits. "I didn't think you knew anything about that," Frederick said.

"I don't, but I'm curious. What's the matter, aren't you happy with the way the Crusade is going?"

Ezzo obviously didn't know what was happening. Frederick stared at him, ready to shut him up if he spoke. "Let's say I think things could be better."

"Need money?"

Ezzo's head jerked up, and Frederick scowled at him. Beyond Theophano, Fulk was half smiling.

"I might."

"What's your rank?"

Frederick looked calmly from Ezzo to Mutu, who was leaning forward intently. "I'm highly placed. Ask her."

Mutu straightened up, his eyes flickering to the others. With a coil of shoulder muscle he turned his head to look back. "I may know somebody who would . . . be interested in talking to you. If you need money and you . . . agree with him on some things, he might be able to use your help."

Frederick smiled at him. "I don't work for other people. Be more specific."

"No. I don't mix in that kind of thing, I just carry information." Mutu's white teeth gleamed. "I don't work for other people either."

"How would you like to work for me?"

Ezzo got up and walked out. Frederick looked after

him and back to Mutu, who was shaking his head.

"I don't understand."

"You say you carry information. Obviously you get paid well. I'll pay you double if you pass everything on to me as well as the intended ears."

The corners of Mutu's mouth drew down. "Theo—"

"Don't ask her. Will you?"

"I could lose a lot of friends and get myself killed doing that."

"On the other hand, you could get yourself hung for not doing it." Frederick took hold of Theophano's wrist to keep her from saying anything.

In Mutu's steady eyes the faint bewilderment gave way to cold, even anger. "I stepped right into that, didn't I?"

"With both bare feet, yes." Frederick stood up, pulling Theophano up out of her chair. "Somebody will come here tomorrow. If you're still around, I'll take it that you're working for me. We can arrange the details later."

Mutu said nothing; his eyes stared past Frederick's shoulder. Ezzo stood in the side doorway, his sword half hidden under his cloak. Hanging onto Theophano, Frederick headed for the door, almost running.

"Let's go," Ezzo said when they were all outside in the dark. "Let's get out of here."

Fulk said, "That's a good idea. He might try to kill you."

Frederick wrenched his arm out of Ezzo's grasp. "Now, come on, don't get overexcited. I came down here to get drunk and I'm not drunk yet."

"Exactly," Theophano said. "But sober you managed to insult Mutu, and God knows what you'll do when you're drunk."

"I intend to find out." He swung away from them and started down the street. With a rush they caught up with him and grabbed hold of him.

"Are you trying to get yourself—"

"Let go of me," Frederick said.

Ezzo and Fulk stepped back, but Theophano did not, she looked up at him and said, "Let's go back. You can't—"

"I can do whatever I want, and I'm going to, damn you."

"If you talk to me like that again, I'll leave you."

He had already begun to push by her, but he stopped, amazed, and looked down at her face. Her level eyes, the hard set of her mouth—she meant it. He licked his lips. "What do you mean?"

"What I said."

She looked at him a moment longer, lowered her eyes, and started walking away, up the street. Ezzo and Fulk stood on either side, their eyes on him. Waiting for him. He looked after Theophano, who was nearly to the corner. I can let her go and stay down here; in the morning she'll change her mind. A moment after he'd thought it he didn't believe it. If he didn't go with her she wouldn't go back to the palace. Stay anyway. She can't—

Theophano turned the corner out of sight and he broke into a hard run after her. The walls of the buildings on either side threw back the echoes of his and Fulk's and Ezzo's footsteps. Up at the corner a cart drawn by a mule appeared, coming from the harbor—the driver reined in and stared while they ran past.

As soon as he could see her, up ahead, he slowed down to a jog. She had no reason to . . . Stupid, silly, like all women. She heard them coming and stopped and waited, near the arch over the street. Two strides from her, he slowed to a walk; she fell in beside him when he passed her.

"You can't go home alone."

"It isn't that long a distance. You could have sent Fulk with me."

His shoulders quivered. She meant to make him angry,

she had to, or she wouldn't be doing this. He stared straight ahead at the top of the street, where he could see the torches of the watch coming toward them.

"I'm sorry," she said. "I shouldn't have said that."

"You shouldn't have said any of it."

Three more strides, ringing on the cobblestones. The watch came trotting past them on his big horse, the muffled bell tied to the cantle of his saddle clanking with every step.

"I said I was sorry," she said stiffly.

"You can't help it, you're a woman, all women do things like that. I'm going to start in on young boys."

"Oh? How have you managed to overlook them for so long?"

He glared at her. Fulk and Ezzo had dropped back several strides. "Keep on talking like that," Frederick said, snarling.

She stopped dead, her eyes huge with rage. "I intend to. Until I'm dead. And if you don't like it—"

"I don't." He kept on walking. She ran after him, caught up, and clutched his arm to make him stop.

"I said I was sorry. Damn you, will you stand still?"

"All right." He stood still. She threw off her cap—her hair was hanging in her eyes—and with both hands flung her hair back over her shoulders.

"I said I was sorry. That's all I'm saying. I'm not going one step farther until you apologize to me."

For a moment he was so angry he couldn't get the words out straight. He raised both hands, got himself back together, and shouted, "For what?"

Her mouth fell open. "Why—for talking to me like that."

"Like what? I still don't know why the hell you're acting like this, except I wanted to go get drunk and you—"

"Forget it," she said, and smiled. Abruptly her whole face was soft again, the hard lines gone, and her eyes bright. "I'm sorry." She hugged him, and he put his arms around her, completely bewildered.

"Theophano—"

"Let's go home."

I'm lying here in this bed and in a while I'll call the pages and have breakfast and get dressed, and there will be no message from al-Kamil. I'll go through the whole day waiting for the message from al-Kamil and there will be none; I'll keep wishing the night would come so I could sleep and get rid of the time until morning, when a message might come, but in the morning a message will not have come. . . .

"What's wrong?" Theophano said.

"Nothing."

"Shall I call the pages in?"

"If you want to."

He thought of the work he had to do—the organization of a local government for Jaffa, the daily work of the Crusade, the decisions for Sicily—and shut his eyes. Too much. I'll never do it, I don't know where to start. How am I going to get from here to there? Everything overwhelmed him in a tide and he rolled over and put his head in his arms.

"Red."

She put her arms around him, pressing herself against his back, and curled her legs around his. Warm and moist, her breath came and went against his neck. He sighed; the cradle of her arms and legs made him feel better, but he didn't know why. I love you. Something always held him back from saying it. She would . . . withdraw from him. He didn't know how he knew it. She would start talking about other things and he'd lose the moment, and he wanted to hang onto it.

"Call the pages," she murmured.

"All right."

Sitting up, he shook his hair back out of his eyes. One

thing at a time, bit by bit, put it all together like a puzzle and make it look good. He yelled for Corso and slid out of the bed.

When he was dressed and had eaten and dealt with a handful of early-morning petitioners and sent Marino off to find some old charters, he went out onto the balcony of the palace and leaned on the rail. From here to the harbor the city was clean and filled with people and donkeys and carts—they even had a bazaar set up at the far end of this street. He looked toward the wall, squinting against the sun; the Grand Master was supervising the rebuilding of it. Swarms of men covered it, lugging stone around, filling the gaps with mortar and mud, and a train of mules ran off into the hazy distance. Dull as lead, his mood pressed down around his heart and lungs, and for a moment he concentrated on staying alive.

"Your Majesty."

"Yes, Marino."

"Excuse me, Sire, for disturbing you, but this is urgent." Marino came out onto the balcony, his feet scuffing the new carpet—a present from Balian of Sidon. In his hand was a thick packet of paper. Frederick turned and took it from him. On the seal was Piero's special mark, and the whole outside of the packet was scribbled with instructions and cryptic notations.

"Shall I wait, Sire?"

"No." He read the note in Piero's handwriting—"Most express and secret." His skin grew cold. Taking the dagger from his belt, he slit the packet open and unfolded it.

"From Palermo, this seventh day of December in the year of our Lord 1228—"

"Palermo," Frederick said. He glanced around—Marino had gone; through the open doors he saw people moving around inside, but no one had heard him. He swallowed and flipped to the important part of the letter, marked in red ink.

"The mercenaries of the Pope under the command of John of Brienne have seized control of all of mainland Sicily. Lucera holds out but is steadily besieged. We have moved the apparatus of government to Palermo and continue to rule from here, in Your Majesty's name."

The letter blurred. Frederick stood still, aware of the heat of the sun and the noise from the street, of the harsh rustle of the papers in his hands. His hands were trembling. He dropped the letter on the floor and wrapped his arms around himself. Gradually his sight cleared—everything looked extraordinarily sharp and real. So even if I win here, everything there will be lost. He thought of Sicily—of the macchia, the wide, empty horizon, and the marshes. He has it. He took it. And I can't go back and . . .

"Frederick."

"Good morning, Dawud." He stared blindly into the distance.

Fakhr-ad-Din came slowly over to the railing and turned to face him. "I'm sorry. I have nothing to give you except the dubious benefits of my conversation."

Frederick jerked his gaze around toward him. "Do you know about this?"

Fakhr-ad-Din nodded. "We've known of it for some time. You see, one of our best spies is the Pope himself, who tells us what he thinks will keep us from helping you."

Within Frederick's chest something leaped violently. He dropped his arms to his sides. "Tell al-Kamil that he might find it less troublesome to give me Jerusalem and let me go home than to have me here as King of Jaffa."

"We've considered that."

"If I have to, I'll start all over again, Dawud. Here in Jaffa. And he'll have more to worry about than en-Nasr and al-Ashraf and the Khwaresmians, even if I'm king of nothing but lizards."

Fakhr-ad-Din smiled. "Of this there's no need to

convince me. The rebuilding of Jaffa and the depths to which you're already involved in the affairs of Syria are sufficient evidence. Corso told me that you ate very little at breakfast—will you have something with me?"

The other man's direct eyes and his smile loosened something in Frederick's mind. He looked toward the wall again, and toward the Angel Tower, half rebuilt; they were swaying up a net full of iron rods to the top level.

"Yes. Fine."

Fakhr-ad-Din clapped his hands and through the doors came files of pages with small tables and chairs and trays of jellied meats and fruit and bread cut into stars and circles, soaked in butter and toasted brown. Frederick's mouth watered. While the pages set up their tables and spread out the food he and Fakhr-ad-Din sat down and washed their hands in little golden bowls of scented water. Fakhr-ad-Din lifted the top from a pot of couscous and sniffed.

"Ummm. Marvelous." He put the top back. "Your commander in Sicily doesn't seem to be entirely adequate."

"He's brash." Frederick dried his hands and sent a page after the letter, which had blown into a corner. "And the Pope has the money to buy the best generals in Europe." He took the letter and flipped through it.

"Well, you know, if you'd left your barons in possession of their castles, Sicily would be in better condition to face something like this."

"Un-hunh." Piero had written a brief summary of the campaign—the Pope had met no resistance except at Lucera and a few other fortified towns that they'd managed to garrison. "I hate wars."

Fakhr-ad-Din directed a page to serve him couscous and fruit. "So do I, of course. How extensive do you think the damage is?"

"I don't know. I won't be able to figure that out until

I've had a chance to read this through." He folded the papers and thrust them inside his coat. "Corso, ask Yusuf to come here and play for us." He watched his hands moving with the spoon and fork. How can I do this? I ought to be screaming and banging my head against the wall. More structure. If I keep going through the motions, everything will be all right. Maybe.

"The Angel Tower is coming along very well," Fakhr-ad-Din said. "Somebody told me that they're rebuilding it to your design."

"The old one was too tall for its width. It's nicely placed; I want to use it as a watch tower."

"I suppose you can see the harbor and the hillside behind the town from the summit? Excellent. This peach jam is wonderful, very fresh."

"What's Nablus like?"

Fakhr-ad-Din made a face. "It's a typical oasis city, dusty and unentertaining and full of human debris. Al-Kamil hates it. He says if it weren't the perfect position from which to watch you, his brother, and his nephew, he'd never be there. You'd like Cairo." Fakhr-ad-Din grinned around a mouthful of bread and peach jam. "Cairo has everything you love—music, philosophy, cutthroats, and sin. Lots and lots of sin in Cairo."

Yusuf, sitting on a stool to one side, started to laugh and played a Sicilian mountain song. Frederick thought of Palermo and ate a bite of couscous.

"Nothing compares with Palermo. Not just in sin. You can buy anything, you can sell anything, and you can talk any language and be understood."

"I know, I've been there." Fakhr-ad-Din's face screwed up pleasantly. "One of the great surprises of my trip was having a street boy with a Greek face and Norman coloring tell me in very nice Arabic what I could do with myself. And the paintings on the carts, I liked them too."

"In Germany they paint scenes from the Bible onto

the fronts of their houses, and when you get someone's address it's liable to be something like 'Jacob's story, third house down in the High Street.' What's al-Kamil's court like?"

"Yours, a lot. He makes sure he's surrounded by learned men, but if they can't talk to him about the pleasures of women, he won't keep them on. He's liable to walk out of a good party for no reason and send his slaves back to tell everybody to go home. But I think that's part of his concern for the way other people think of him—he hates to be predictable. If you want to read that letter, go ahead, please."

"Thank you." He took the packet from his coat and opened it again. His hands moved jerkily, as if they weren't entirely under control.

Only half the letter was written in Piero's handwriting; the rest was in a scribe's and reported the facts of the invasion. As always, Piero had marked in red and blue ink the sections to be read first. Frederick had trouble reading it—he didn't want to, and there was so much to be understood, he had to stop every once in a while and think and absorb it.

The Pope's armies had met little resistance, but because of it, almost everything was intact. Princess Yolande and the young King of Jerusalem were safe in La Favara Palace. The entire government had moved in a clump from Troia, where it had been seated, to Palermo. Most of the town governments remained in place. Piero had closed Brindisi's port and the Sicilian fleet was using Palermo and Messina instead, and the Pope had no control over the seas. The peasants had brought in the harvests as usual; in the areas still under control Piero's agents were collecting taxes, and the Cistercians were serving as a liaison between the conquered towns and estates and the free government. But the Pope's soldiers had imposed a curfew and were busy lining up their supporters. Piero thought they'd have sufficient local help by the end of the spring to start removing Frederick's podestàs.

"It doesn't sound too bad," he said to Fakhr-ad-Din. "Being in possession of land is infinitely different from ruling the people who live on it."

"Well, Sicilians have always been conservative."

Fakhr-ad-Din laughed. The clink of dishes and dinner-ware and the low voices of the pages mingled with the erratic chords and arpeggios of Yusuf's guitarra. Piero had written, "We are working to create tension between the people and the Pope's garrisons—to keep them hostile as much as possible. This I have undertaken as we dis-cussed the problem, before Your Majesty's departure. Until further notice we shall continue along the lines your general instructions indicated."

"One thing al-Kamil doesn't have," Frederick said. He looked around for something to drink and took a cup of sherbet. "Piero della Vigne."

"Your colorless little secretary. Yes. My master's servants are more dramatic and considerably less effec-tive. I told him he should send some boys to your schools to be trained."

"Tell him to hurry up, I keep thinking of closing down the university." The strategy against the Pope's soldiers they had worked out in the autumn before last while he'd been lying on a bed in Pozzuoli, incapable of moving his head on the pillow, waiting out the malaria. They say I may still get spells of that. Haven't yet. Re-membering it frightened him, as if he could feel the fever coming on.

"Frederick?"

"What?"

Fakhr-ad-Din was staring at him, smiling, his eye-brows lowered slightly. "I've just asked you the same question five times."

"Oh. I'm . . . thinking—in Italian—and you know I wouldn't hear Arabic."

Fakhr-ad-Din shrugged, but the frown remained on his face. "Would you rather I leave?"

"No, of course—" It occurred to him suddenly that he did want it; he had to think. "Would you?"

"Yes." Smiling Fakhr-ad-Din stood up, beckoning to his attendants. "I'll see you at dinner. Have a good day." With another laugh he walked, surrounded by his retainers, in through the nearest door.

Frederick hunched down in his chair and braced his feet on the table. They'd borrowed the plan for maintaining the kingdom against invaders from the Saracens of the Sicilian mountains. In each town and on each estate in Sicily they'd found one man whom they could trust to aggravate the enemy armies into mistreating the Sicilians, who would therefore hate the newcomers and want Frederick back, their lovable King. Piero had been all for secret societies with a whole series of detailed strategems, passwords, and disguises, but the Sicilians would have grown bored with the rigor. Straight in with the knife under the ribs, hit them over the head with a hammer; he'd been handling them like that for years. They loved the spontaneity of it, and if either Piero or the Pope got up a schedule, the Sicilians would hate it. I'm Sicilian and I need enemies.

Just indoors, workmen were painting the walls of the chambers, filling in the sketches the artists had made. The scent of paint reached him. Lifting his head, he looked toward the wall again, the sun so bright he could barely make out the men climbing across it. The leaden uncertainty was pressing against his heart again. Keep it off with work, hold it back, and soon it will be night and I can sleep, and maybe, in the morning, a message from al-Kamil—

Mutu said, "The Pope has sent a message to al-Kamil telling him on no condition to give Jerusalem to the Emperor. A man whose name I don't know went recently to Damascus from Antioch and I am to tell the agent of the Hospitallers that what he carried got there safely. John d'Ibelin of Beirut is in close touch with John of Brienne, the new Eastern Emperor, and this Emperor's father-in-law, who is commanding the armies of the Pope in Sicily."

Paying out coins, Fulk turned his head and looked at Frederick, sitting to one side wrapped in a cloak. Frederick cocked his eyebrows.

"Three of the night watchmen in the Old Quarter will take bribes to overlook robbery and murder. There is a man in the harbor district selling wheat stolen from the granaries of the Emperor."

Mutu's voice ground on, even and unemphasized; Frederick began to wonder at his memory. Twice now they'd come and sat in this room and Mutu had recited an incredible list of facts ranging from small details about Jaffa to enormities about the world at large, and everything Frederick had been able to verify had been true. He'd always known that information circulated widely through a network of criminals and spies and whores and drunks and beggars—he'd learned that in Palermo and he'd made use of it in Sicily—but Mutu was the perfect contact. He knew about everything. Watching the gold coins clink down onto the rug between Mutu's feet, Frederick decided that everybody thought that, and probably everybody else believed, the way you believed you'd never die, that Mutu was keeping faith with him alone. By now everybody with a penny to pay for it knew that the Emperor was cutting in on the game. Which might well serve its own purposes. He licked a last taste of hashish out of his mouth and swallowed, grinning.

He'd given the Assassin a chunk of hashish the size of his fist, and the Assassin's eyes had glowed like carbuncles. "Lord." The warm fuzziness spread through him, and his skin tingled pleasantly. I am in a wonderfully good mood and I will think about al-Kamil tomorrow.

"Is that all?" Fulk said.

"All?" Mutu snorted. "I spilled my brains, didn't I?" Scooping up the money into a leather bag, he looked toward Frederick. "Suppose we do some business in my direction now. This must be expensive for you."

"It's not my money."

"Well, then." Mutu yanked the strings tight on the bag. "What if your master found out you've been eating hashish?"

Frederick twitched, startled; he'd almost forgotten the role he played with Mutu, and yet he'd been acting it only a moment before. The hashish made it hard to think and he got scared he'd botch the whole thing, so he said nothing.

"Wouldn't like that, would he?" Mutu said gently. "He might even decide to find out where you got it."

"He knows I traffic with you," Frederick said. "I'm His Majesty's agent to you."

"But he might think you're paying for it with certain things he wouldn't like me to know. And that wouldn't incline him to like you, would it?"

Mutu, Frederick thought. How unkind of you. He glanced at Fulk, who was sitting back on his heels, his face as secretive as a cat's.

"Wait for me outside, Fulk."

Fulk got up and went silently out the door, and the curtain swung closed behind him. Frederick fought against the tendency of the hashish to pull him off course.

"Do you trust him?" Mutu jabbed his thumb at the door. "Fulk."

"Yes. Make it worth my while to tell you what I know."

"What do you know?"

"Something worth half that gold."

"How do I know? Tell me, and I'll see what it's worth."

Frederick shook his head, grinning. Balancing the sack in his hand, Mutu made it clink, his eyes speculative. Finally he opened the sack and dumped out part of the coins into a little shimmering mound on the rug.

"Tell me. If it's worth more than that I'll give it to you."

Frederick shrugged. "The Emperor has an embassy in Damascus."

"Everybody knows that."

"Very few people know he sent special instructions to the envoy just before en-Nasr led his army down to raid al-Kamil's supply lines around Nablus, and that the envoy went with en-Nasr and is negotiating with him for an alliance."

Mutu's nostrils flared. "No. Very few people know that. Is it true?" His voice was pitched higher than before, for all he tried to sound bored.

Frederick nodded. "The Emperor wants Jerusalem. He doesn't much care whom he gets it from." His heart beat raggedly, excited; nobody would be able to prove that either way, and it might . . . If it got to al-Kamil, that might make up his mind for him. He stared at Mutu until his eyes began to burn.

"Take it." Mutu threw the sack into Frederick's lap. "And hurry, before I decide you're lying." He gathered up the coins on the rug. Frederick laughed and thrust the sack into his belt.

"I'm not lying. It's not worth it to me." He ducked out the curtain into the dark street. Fulk was waiting at the corner, leaning against the wall of a building with one foot drawn up. When Frederick came toward him in the darkness, Fulk straightened casually and fell in beside him.

"What happened?"

"Teased him a little bit."

"Maybe you'd better stop coming down here. If he ever finds out who you are, he'll figure out a way to make a fortune on it, and that might not be safe for you."

Frederick nodded. "I'm not coming again." They turned the corner and started up toward the arch. "Ezzo can come with you, I just wanted to see what happened this time. Remember what he said about the watchmen and the stolen grain, will you?"

"Yes. I'll take care of it tomorrow."

The moonlight turned the street nearly as bright as day, and up under the arch the whores were parading back and forth. This street was becoming as familiar to him as the streets of Barletta or Troia or Castellamare; already he had trouble remembering what in the beginning had been most striking to him about it. Maybe it was the hashish. The good mood was fading, and now he was merely numb. In the morning he had to wake up and go through the whole thing again. But what else was there to do? He'd never done anything else, his whole life went on and on, backward and forward, days full of the same thing. He hunched his shoulders, morose.

Theophano was watching the pages put away his new coats; the tailors had sent in eighteen of them at noon. She shook her head. "How can you possibly wear so many clothes?"

"I don't." He straightened the one he had on and nodded to Corso to bring the mirror over. "I like this one, don't you? I like the sleeves." He walked back and forth in front of the mirror, grinning at his image, making the short skirt swing out. It was weighted down with gold thread and swung dramatically.

She giggled at him. "I've seen women less vain than you."

"I'm not vain." He took off the belt and picked up another from the couch. "I'm only trying to look the way people expect me to. I need another haircut." He put on the belt and settled it on his hips, watching himself in the mirror.

Corso said, "He isn't vain, my Lady—you should have seen the way he went around on shipboard. Sire, you can't wear that belt with that coat. Giancarlo, bring me the Byzantine belt."

"I like this belt with this coat." He pulled down the cuffs of the sleeves. "Somebody tell them to make the sleeves longer on the next one."

Giancarlo trotted up to him with what Corso called the Byzantine belt, made of gold filigree, and Corso deftly unbuckled the one already around his waist.

"Do you miss Sicily, Corso?" Theophano said, practicing her Italian.

"Oh, no," Corso said. "I love Jaffa—this is fun."

"I'm glad you like it," Frederick said. "We may be here a while." He scowled into the mirror.

Giancarlo murmured a protest, but Corso smacked him across the back with his open hand. "Shut up, Gian, how can you be a poet if you've never been in exile?"

Giancarlo blushed dark red. Frederick took the new belt and put it on. "Giancarlo. Are you writing poetry these days?"

Backing off, Giancarlo glared at Corso. "You promised you wouldn't tell anybody."

The other pages were watching, their faces intent, fascinated. Frederick looked at himself in the mirror. While he turned slowly around, contemplating the belt, Corso said, "Well, you ought to have somebody read them and find out if they're any good. Just because I think they're awful—"

Theophano said, "Oh, Corso, be quiet. Gian, please get me something to drink, I'm thirsty."

Giancarlo ran off, beet-colored. Corso said, "That belt looks much better, Sire."

"I still like the other one. This one won't sit right." He

unhooked the belt, moved it around, and hooked it again on the same hook. "What's Giancarlo's poetry about?"

"Girls—whom he doesn't know anything about." Corso went behind him to straighten the coat under the belt. "It's in Latin too."

"Tell him I'll read it if he wants me to." The glistening white of the coat somehow managed to clash with the Byzantine belt. He took it off. "What's wrong with Latin poetry?"

"Giancarlo is terrible at Latin," Corso said. "Besides, you don't write in Latin, Sire."

"Quid libet, licet. I didn't know you were a Latin scholar, Corso." He turned his back to the mirror and looked into it over his shoulder, frowning at the lines of the coat. "I don't need a belt."

"If you wish, Sire." Corso's voice was perfectly non-committal.

"Do you write poetry?" Theophano said.

"I used to. I don't anymore." He nodded to Corso, who started to take off the coat. Giancarlo came back with a tray of cups and a ewer, and he poured Theophano wine.

"Why not?" she said drinking.

"I haven't got the time. And anyhow I had it on good authority that I'm no poet." He shrugged back into his old coat. "On better authority than Corso della Messina." He grinned.

"I liked your poetry," Corso said, taking away the new coat.

Giancarlo said softly, "So did I, Sire." And blushed again.

"You'll have to show me some," Theophano said.

"It's in Italian, and you don't read Italian. Not yet." She could hardly speak it, although she understood most of what she heard. He took a cup from Giancarlo, sniffed it, and sent him out for sherbet.

"What was your poetry about?" she said in Greek.

Frederick grinned. "Girls. Like Giancarlo's." He pulled a stool over and sat next to her. "I'll translate some for you later if you'd like."

Corso called, "Sire, Marino is here."

"Let him in."

"Write me something in Greek," Theophano said, smiling. "Something I can keep."

"You can keep me, you don't need a poem. Hello, Dawud. What's it like out?"

"Beautiful, as ever," Fakhr-ad-Din said. He began to smile. "May I speak with you alone a moment?"

"Naturally." Frederick stood up. Theophano and the pages left, and he looked around. Giancarlo had put the sherbet on a little table. Working to stay calm, he went over and poured some. "Are you thirsty?"

"No, but I'll have some anyway. I've been noticing that of late you seem to be sinking into boredom, Frederick. Have you considered a hunting trip, perhaps? A few days spent in the desert, with the hawks and horses, should freshen your appetite for . . ." He made gestures, vague in the air, and smiled even wider.

"An expedition of sorts?" Frederick handed him a cup of sherbet. "I could be interested." But he had trouble keeping his voice even, and Fakhr-ad-Din took one look at his face and laughed.

"Tomorrow, perhaps?"

"I could leave tomorrow. Where?"

"I'll go along to see you don't get lost. I'd suggest you bring your entire retinue, bar of course the Assassin, and a small guard of knights. One never knows what one might encounter in the desert."

"Of course not." He laughed out loud. "What constitutes a small guard of knights?"

"A hundred men or so." Fakhr-ad-Din sat down. "And be prepared to bargain."

Frederick whooped. Stretching his arms over his head, he jumped so high his knuckles grazed the ceiling, whirled, and ran into the room Theophano had gone into. She was sitting on their bed, with her women around her sewing and mixing perfume and face cream. Frederick dodged through the pots, leapt onto the bed, and wrapped both arms around her waist. All the women screamed except Theophano.

"What's happened?" she said.

"Nothing. Not yet." He kissed her. "I'll be gone for a little while, starting tomorrow. Can you live without me?"

Her eyes blazed. "It came."

"Well, an invitation to it."

She flung her arms around him. "I knew it would— today felt lucky."

They rolled around on the bed a while, kissing and nuzzling each other. Frederick began to take off her clothes.

"Can I tell anybody?"

"No," he said. "The way it came, I'm supposed to keep it secret." He undid a bow and pulled her bodice away from her breast. It would be best to let out the news immediately—it would get them scared, up in Acre and Cyprus and in Rome. Mutu was going to be useful again. He pressed his mouth to her breast, chewing and sucking on her nipple. Her hand tangled itself in his hair.

"Shouldn't you be praying or something?"

"I am. Thank God." He glanced around; her maids had left, and he kicked his way awkwardly out of his clothes. Theophano stroked her thighs against him. He rolled over, pulling her on top of him, and shut his eyes. Love me—love me back. It was all over, all the waiting— he gulped and tightened his arms around her. "Oh, yes, oh, yes." Heat poured through him in gigantic waves, and he hid his contorted face in her hair.

*　*　*

"We are within a day's ride of Ramleh to the southeast," Fakhr-ad-Din said. "That's where King Baldwin beat an enormous army with a handful of knights. To make sure no one thought it luck, he repeated it a few years later. King Baldwin the First, that was. Nablus is to the northeast. Beyond Ramleh is Hebron."

"In the summer this must be hell." Frederick slewed around in his saddle to look back toward the wall, where his men were setting up tents. The gray-brown desert stretched out toward the horizon, pocked with dusty bushes. On his tongue he tasted the metallic harshness of the well water. "I assume we aren't going to ride together, he and I, horse to horse."

"The Sultan is a short way away. He has caused a tent to be erected where you may meet. But that's tomorrow."

"What decided him, do you know?"

Fakhr-ad-Din squinted into the sun. On his hands jeweled rings flashed. "I'm not sure. Perhaps he's reluctant to leave Nablus with this unfinished, and the need to leave Nablus grows great. Perhaps he simply got tired of listening to his council tell him how treacherous you are." He touched his beard with his fingertips, and his eyes moved to regard Frederick solemnly. "Possibly he realized that unless he made a firm ally of you, your restless spirit, of which I and others have spoken, might induce you to adventures dangerous to him. Now, Frederick, you haven't been talking to en-Nasr behind our backs, have you?"

"I? Never."

Fakhr-ad-Din blinked once slowly. "Yet an ally who believes himself lightly considered might chafe and become a bad enemy. We should go back—standing around in the hot sun isn't good for one's health."

"I should send messengers to him—to arrange for the minor details." Frederick turned his horse. The Saracens and Fakhr-ad-Din's few attendants wheeled to follow.

"I assure you, Frederick, he's seen to that. All that's

necessary is that you arrive at the appointed place on the appointed morning." Fakhr-ad-Din smiled, pulling his headcloth straight.

"Splendid. How large is the tent, where do we sit, how many scribes and pages do we bring, do we bring soldiers with us, and if so, how many, how do we enter the tent—?"

Fakhr-ad-Din frowned at him. "Frederick, you're not a Moslem. These things ought not to concern you."

"I'm a Christian, and they do." He watched a vulture circling, far above them and down the sky. "Who takes precedence in entering the tent?"

"Obviously, since al-Kamil is the Sultan of Egypt and Syria, and you are a visitor—"

"I'm Emperor. There is no other Emperor besides me, except the one in Constantinople, and he's a forgery. Clearly, therefore, I take precedence over a Sultan when everybody knows that there are at least three Sultans and probably—"

"What if the Sultan were to be seated in the tent when you entered?"

"Out of the question."

They rode into the camp, and grooms ran alongside, ready to take their horses. The Grand Master had seen to setting up the camp; everything looked neat and in place and working. Frederick took a quick glance around and dismounted.

"He has what you want," Fakhr-ad-Din said. "To be blunt." He swung his leg across the cantle of his saddle and stepped down; grooms led the horses out from between them. "Obviously, you have to give him precedence." He was grinning.

"Well, I must have something he wants, or he wouldn't give me what I want." Frederick carefully took precedence over Fakhr-ad-Din entering the tent. Corso came up to take his cloak. "And since he asked me to come here, I ought to take precedence over him." He took a gulp of the odd-tasting water and sat down. "By the way, are you authorized to discuss this kind of thing?"

"Naturally," Fakhr-ad-Din said. "Why change horses so close to the end of the race? What about separate entrances, and both of you entering on a prescribed signal?"

"Fine. But they have to be within sight of each other or he'll try to sneak in ahead of me."

"Or you ahead of him." Fakhr-ad-Din laced his fingers together. "I can see this will be delicate. Corso, don't you have anything but water?"

"I'll bring you some sherbet," Corso said. He left. Frederick took paper and a brush and ink from a chest on the table and in Arabic wrote: "Two entrances, within sight of each other."

"How do we sit?"

"Side by side," Fakhr-ad-Din said.

"No. Then we have the quibble about left hand or right hand. What do we sit on? Camel saddles? Stone thrones?"

Fakhr-ad-Din pursed his lips and thought. Frederick said, "Rugs with cushions?"

"Suitable."

"Two rugs each and three cushions? That ought to keep us comfortable."

"Make it six cushions. My master sometimes likes to stretch out."

"Fine." He wrote that beneath the first specification.

"Attendants," Fakhr-ad-Din said. "On this he is adamant. Two scribes for each, and the discussion is to be in Arabic without translators."

Frederick threw the brush down. "Oh, no."

"He speaks no Italian, and the only member of his staff who does is I myself. I am a bad translator. He insists. You and most of your staff speak Arabic."

"I have no Arabic-writing scribes."

"We will provide you with one."

"I'll provide mine with a translator. With two translators. Tommaso d'Aquino and Sir Hermann von Salza."

Fakhr-ad-Din made a face. "That's . . . difficult."

"I'd be glad to provide him with translators if he wishes them."

"That won't be necessary, I'll be in his retinue. Tommaso d'Aquino may come as a translator, but Sir Hermann will have to be reckoned one of your staff."

"All right." Make the minor concession generously. "How many in the staff of each of us?"

"Five. None to rank beneath the rank of emir."

"Tommaso for a translator. Balian of Sidon."

"Very good."

"Sir Hermann."

"Yes."

"The Archbishop."

"Yes."

"Ricardo Filangieri."

"Is no emir. No."

"Guy Embriaco."

"Satisfactory but not quite excellent."

"Conrad of Hohenlohe."

"Yes."

"And how many others can I take with me but not into the tent?"

"Not above twenty knights and ten attendants."

"Fifty and thirty."

"There isn't enough water in the well to keep them from thirst."

"We'll bring our own water."

"Forty knights and ten attendants."

"Ten knights and forty attendants."

Fakhr-ad-Din was staring into space, all his attention focused on the problem. Frederick scribbled down the names of his staff.

"Twenty knights and thirty attendants."

"Good. Fifty's a nice number. Banners?"

"Inside the tent, your personal banner and the banner of the King of Jerusalem. Al-Kamil will bring his personal banner."

"My imperial banner, Dawud. Give me some rank."

"My dear fellow, doesn't your personal banner denote your rank?" Fakhr-ad-Din gave him an owl-eyed stare.

"Yes. As Duke of Swabia. What about outside the tent?"

"That's up to the personal taste and abilities of you both." Fakhr-ad-Din bowed.

"Um-hmm." Frederick wrote. If Fakhr-ad-Din and al-Kamil thought because he wasn't in Sicily he couldn't devise a display worth a Sultan's, they were both piteously deluded. "Who will be with him?"

"Ah. But you probably won't recognize the names."

"Try me."

"Myself, although I'm the least, of course." Fakhr-ad-Din ticked the names off on his fingers. "As-Salih Ayub."

"His eldest son. And al-Adil abu Bakr?"

Fakhr-ad-Din nodded, beaming. "Charming young men, you'll like them. Az-Zahir, King of Aleppo."

"He does seem to be fencing himself around with relatives." Az-Zahir was al-Kamil's cousin, the son of his uncle Salah-ad-Din. Since that side of the family had always quarreled with al-Kamil's, they were clearly showing off their unity against Christians.

"And his younger son, al-Musud," Fakhr-ad-Din said. "He's learned. So, of course, is my master."

"I know." Frederick wrote down the names on another piece of paper. "What about eating and drinking and other details?"

"You may bring five pages. We will provide the refreshments."

Frederick nodded. "The rugs ought to be on opposite sides of the tent, but not so far away we have to shout. I'm willing to face Jerusalem if he's willing to face Mecca."

"Excellent."

Frederick stared at the paper, trying to think of what he'd forgotten. He still couldn't believe that this was happening finally, that tomorrow he would see al-Kamil and they would talk. That tomorrow he might have Jerusalem. He said, "Dawud, tell him that I would never push him so hard if I didn't have to have it."

"I think he knows. He's looking forward to seeing you."

"Yes." Frederick grinned. "I'm sending a mule train of presents over there, do you want to send a message with it?"

"I'll use my own means, if you don't mind. I should have an answer by sundown." Fakhr-ad-Din stretched, sighing. "This is all starting to fit together and I'm glad."

"So am I." He had to talk to Marino, to Tommaso, who had come into camp with the Archbishop that morning, to the Grand Master and Balian and Corso—millions of details to work out. He took another sip of the harsh water, got out another piece of paper, and started writing out instructions; his hands were so unsteady with excitement that he could barely hold the brush.

With his answer al-Kamil sent presents in a vast train, piles of silk and cotton cloth, mounds of jewels and gold, pepper and sugar and camels and ivory, a chess set carved from some precious stone—green and white—that Frederick didn't even recognize, and perfume, attar gûl and myrrh, books on arithmetic and medicine and geography, and a map of the world engraved on a silver disk, imitating Idrisi's.

"He cleaned out all the closets in Nablus," Frederick said, delighted. "I miss the six Sudanese slaves with red roses in their hair."

Tommaso said, "I trust you were as generous, Sire. You know how the Moslems fret about appearances."

"Don't worry, he'll have to build a new palace to hold it all." They were to meet at noon. Tommaso was already dressed, standing stiffly gorgeous in acres of red and white satin. Frederick tried on rings. "Wait until you see my new coat. How bad would it be if we got there before al-Kamil?"

"Tragic," Tommaso said. "We have to arrive at the same time or a little after, or else it will look as if we're waiting for him. Or worse, as if we're cheering him when he arrives."

"I thought so. Ayub?"

Ayub came out of the back of the tent, his headcloth in his hand.

"Send someone out ahead of us to watch the meeting place, and when al-Kamil and his train come in sight, let us know. We're leaving in a little while, once those damned pages get ready."

"Lord." Ayub grinned. "They'll never be ready, they keep changing one another's clothes."

"Well, get in there and tell them if they aren't out here by the time I've got my coat, they aren't going."

Ayub beamed and went out the side door toward the tent full of pages. Tommaso walked in a little circle. His silver-encrusted coat, draped artistically into dozens of deep folds, swept the carpets and brushed with a clatter against the furniture. Frederick drifted to the door and looked out into the camp. Men ran in all directions through it, carrying packages, leading horses and mules, shouting orders, and the constant babble of their voices rang in the dusty air. Across the way, eighteen Teutonic knights, their armor glistening, paced nervously back and forth in front of the Grand Master's tent, their banner fluttering overhead.

"Sire."

He turned—the three pages assigned to attend him while his regular pages got dressed were waiting with his coat. Grimacing, Tommaso stared at it.

"I knew it. We're all gotten up like Popes, we can't move for all the clothes, and you're going as if it were a hunting trip." He turned his back.

Frederick stood still while the pages put stools around him, climbed up onto them, and put on the coat over his head. "I'm doing the talking, you're just translating. I have to be comfortable." One arm got stuck in a sleeve and he fought with it, nearly tearing the soft cloth. The pages adjusted the coat; one of them was crying.

"What's the matter with you?"

"I wanted to go," the page wailed. "I wanted to go and Giancarlo got to go and I didn't." He snuffled tremendously and went for a brush to buff the hem of the coat.

The Archbishop burst in, blazing with the rubies sewn onto his robes, and knocked over a chair with his sleeve. "Oh, Christ." He tried to bend and pick it up, nearly fell over, and straightened with an audible click. "We should be leaving, Sire."

"I'm coming." He took the diamond chain from the page who was crying and hung it around his neck. Leaping up onto a stool, a page combed his hair. Through the side door came Ayub, Yusuf and the five pages going with them; Corso snapped his cuffs and shook his wrists to fluff out the lace.

Frederick howled. "Corso. You're as bad as I am." He started forward and a page yipped. "Oh. I forgot." While the page put on his spurs, he studied himself in the mirror. "How do I look?"

"Comfortable," the Archbishop said. "Which is better than the rest of us." He nodded to Corso, who brought over the crown on a satin cushion. Outside, horses snorted and stamped.

The ride to the meeting place was a short gallop, but of course they'd have to keep the horses to a walk. Frederick went out into the steaming sunlight. Before his tent the horses stood thick as a wall, covered with embossed leather worked with gold. The Grand Master in his silk cloak strode forward, leading Frederick's horse. He spoke, but so many people were shouting, Frederick could hear nothing. He bent his knee and the Grand Master gave him a leg up into the saddle.

As if he stood on a watch tower, suddenly he saw everything—beyond the wall of horses and knights, those who weren't going stood packed in a circle, their eyes on him, and when they saw him they cheered, waving their arms. The Saracens galloped up, making their horses curvet and kick out. Almost in unison, the Teutonic knights mounted, and their raised lances swung up like masts into the sky. There was another cheer. Frederick's horse shied sideways, crushing his leg against the Archbishop's mule, and threw its head up and neighed. The Grand Master, mounted up, leaned over to talk to his standard-bearer, and the gonfalon dipped and swirled and dipped again.

Half the knights in a double file trotted quickly out of the swarm of people and horses. Frederick looked around, his heart beating irregularly. Out of the churning disorder, order came as easily as if they were chess pieces. Tommaso raised the imperial standard, looking down to talk to the man easing the butt of the staff into his stirrup, and beside him the Archbishop held the box with the crown and the cushion on his thighs and stared around, squinting into the brilliant sun. They started off after the knights, and Frederick nudged his horse to follow. The Saracens made a triangle around him, Ayub in front carrying the standard of the King of Jerusalem.

His attendants—the pages, the officers of his court, Fulk and Ezzo and Guy Embriaco, Balian and Conrad—fell into the line in ranks of four, wearing their fortunes on their backs. Those not going ran along beside the little cavalcade, cheering and shouting. Frederick's horse took a violent dislike to Yusuf's, just behind and to one side, and kept swinging its rump around to kick, and Frederick jabbed it in the mouth with the bit. Whoever had gotten him this horse was going to answer for it—the horse lowered its head, took hold of the bit, and shied, grunting. They left the camp and the crowd of screaming people behind.

"Yusuf, do you have a stick?"

Yusuf reined his horse up next to Frederick's and reached out to hand him his leather-bound riding whip. Frederick grabbed it; while he was off balance the horse darted swiftly to the other side, nearly dumping him. Up ahead, the Archbishop twisted his neck awkwardly to look. Because of all the trappings and harness, finding a place to whip the horse turned out to be almost as much trouble as staying with its mad leaps from side to side, and finally Frederick slashed it hard across the neck. The horse bucked. He brought the stick down as hard as he could, jabbed his spurs in, and yanked the horse in the mouth, all at the same time. God, if I have to change horses, I'll kill this brute. But the horse subsided, sulking.

They moved elegantly across the barren sand; the fluttering banners cast their shadows over the ground and the riders, and the sunlight bounced off the armor and all that gold. Frederick began to consider a charge of Templars tearing them to pieces. This is all very pretty, but it does have its drawbacks. He handed the stick back to Yusuf, who at a signal from Ayub jogged out of the line and galloped up ahead to see if al-Kamil had reached the meeting place yet. All along the line heads turned to watch him pass, his white robes streaming around him.

Theophano . . . He'd missed her last night; he'd crawled into a camp bed alone and tossed around, thinking about the meeting, unable to get comfortable. If she'd been there I could have gone to sleep. I could have made love until I was so tired I had to sleep. Something she'd said came back to him—"Write me a poem in Greek, something I can keep." She's going to leave me. His heart clenched. I won't let her. I'll take her back with me even if she doesn't want to go. But if she doesn't want to go? What if she doesn't want me anymore? He closed his eyes. I won't take it. I won't let her—The horse sensed that he wasn't paying attention and coiled up into a terrific buck, and he hauled on the bit and slashed with his spurs, and the horse bounded sideways out of the line, its head thrown back and its nose up, kicking out.

Up near the horizon the tops of trees appeared, and Yusuf was coming back, like a white bird with his robes flying around him, waving his arms. The knights called out to him. Frederick forced his horse back into the line, and Ayub screamed in Arabic, "Is he there yet?"

Yusuf reined in hard. "He's coming into the camp. The tent's bright green, it's beautiful—wait until you see it."

Ayub looked back, and Frederick nodded. The unhappy yearning for Theophano tugged at his mind and he crushed it back. No, let's do this right. He raised his arm, and the Grand Master circled back to ride beside him.

"We'll go in now," Frederick said. "Do you remember the order?"

The Grand Master nodded. Bright and dark, his eyes fixed on Frederick's face. "Sire," he said, "you are about to recover Jerusalem." Abruptly his face split into a tremendous smile, and he took Frederick's hand in his mailed glove and kissed it. With his head back, he cantered up to the head of the line and yelled to his standard-bearer, and the gonfalon swung in an arc across the sky.

Jerusalem. Of course; he'd almost forgotten. The blazing happiness in the old man's face struck him again through his memory. But that isn't really why I'm here —it's because of Sicily, not Jerusalem, to save Sicily. They don't know that. I am their instrument for something else. He felt suddenly deserted, as if he'd taken one fork of the road and they'd gone happily off down the other, not noticing.

The Teutonic knights swung out of line and formed up in four ranks, wide apart, their lances at salute. Balian of Sidon trotted up, calling out to the others, who broke up their triple file and milled around; Balian, Conrad of Hohenlohe, Tommaso and the Archbishop gathered in a tight rank in front of Frederick, with the Saracens on either side and behind him, and the rest of his retinue organized themselves into a square around them all. Tommaso looked up at the banner to make sure it hadn't gotten fouled on the staff, and Ayub rode hastily up to give the standard of Jerusalem to Balian. For a moment, while they got the heavy staff settled in Balian's stirrup, the tasseled silk draped itself over them. Frederick's horse shied tentatively.

They rode over the low rise and down the slope toward the camp called Saint Paul's Well by the Crusaders and the Well of the Hawk by the Moslems. Shaking in the slight breeze, the huge green tent sprawled across the dun-colored ground. Al-Kamil was just entering the camp from the far side, his retinue got up in ostrich plumes and cloth of gold in spite of the heat of the noon sun. Before the well, in among the dusty date palms, white camels lay, each with a Moslem soldier standing at its head. Frederick stood in his stirrups, looking for al-Kamil. After all those letters, my my. The knights rode down and stopped in a crescent, facing the Moslems, the Grand Master in the midst of them.

In al-Kamil's train, drums started up; on Frederick's side, the flute players and the trumpeters with their dog-headed horns began to play, and Frederick's horse quit being good. It tried to spin and bolt, but Frederick wrestled it savagely back on course. The horse bucked, reared, and on its hind legs leaped down the slope almost into the palms. A camel bawled. Frederick lost both stirrups. He wondered what al-Kamil would say if the horse pitched him. The drums boomed merrily on, and the horse neighed. Foam splattered across its neck from its mouth, blood-flecked. Somebody yelled somewhere, and the flutes and horns sang out. Frederick set one hand and hauled as hard as he could on the other rein, and the horse shuddered to a braced halt, in between the knights and al-Kamil's wide-eyed retinue. The drums gave one last boom, and all the horns blasted. The horse quivered violently.

"Ayub," Frederick roared, "come get this pig of a horse before I kill it."

Ayub, Yusuf and Masuf raced down to him, flung themselves off their horses, and grabbed Frederick's reins. Masuf held up a napkin. All around them al-Kamil's and his own retinues were staring, openmouthed. Frederick swiped at the sweat on his face with the napkin, threw it down, and grabbed the reins of Masuf's white mare. His horse half reared, fighting the hands on its bridle; Frederick kicked it sideways until it was parallel to the mare and scrambled into the other saddle. Grooms from al-Kamil's side were running up to help, and Frederick backed the white mare neatly away from the frothing, squealing horse, wheeled her, and cantered back up to his place in the line.

In Arabic and Latin, heralds were proclaiming who everybody was. Frederick mopped his face and surreptitiously scratched his back where the sweat was trickling down his spine. He decided al-Kamil was the bearded man laughing in the middle of a flock of sober younger men.

"Now, what?" Tommaso said.

"What do you mean?"

"How do we get from here to there?"

"We ride." Frederick pressed his leg against the white mare's side, and mercifully, she obeyed, moving out of line and around the end of the knights. The others followed, and from the ranks around them came a cheer. Al-Kamil and his five witnesses were advancing, straight-faced. Passing Fulk, Frederick glanced at him out of the corner of his eye; Fulk was chatting to Ezzo, looking as if he spent the noons of all his days like this, in the middle of the desert dressed like a prince. Frederick grinned.

Moving at precisely the same speed, he and al-Kamil approached the tent, their banners flapping overhead. Al-Kamil caught Frederick's eye and smiled, and Frederick grinned. He'd expected an older man—but al-Kamil was older than he, he just looked young. He couldn't keep from staring into the man's face: it was a continual shock to remember that he was actually al-Kamil. In front of the tent he dismounted, and al-Kamil an instant later stepped down and came forward.

"Sultan," Frederick said. "I'm not sure I know how to speak to you, when we've done all our talking with letters." He saw Fakhr-ad-Din in the midst of al-Kamil's sons and cousins and lifted one hand to him, and Fakhr-ad-Din bowed.

Al-Kamil laughed. "I think we'll learn how. Shall we go inside?"

He nodded to the door, which had been widened, and a stake set in the middle, to make two entranceways. Solemnly, with their men around them, they walked together into the tent, where it was much cooler. Frederick's pages scurried past him, bowed to the two rugs set up for them, and arranged themselves around a table loaded with fruit and jugs set in snow. Balian and Tommaso set their standards into the ground, called over pages to hold them, and stood behind Frederick. Opening the box, the Archbishop got out the crown, and gave it to Frederick to put on his own head. The cool edge of the gold made him sigh. Al-Kamil's eldest son, Ayub, took the Sultan's banner around behind the rug and stood with it, and for a moment they all stood there, looking at each other across six feet of Bokhara carpeting.

"Well," al-Kamil said. "One, two, three, sit."

Frederick laughed. He let al-Kamil sit down before he

did; it seemed the best way to pay him back. Immediately his pages and al-Kamil's slaves, who seemed to wear nothing but jewels, trotted around with cups and bowls of peaches.

"Well," al-Kamil said. "Have you enjoyed your stay in Syria, Sultan?"

"It's been interesting. I've done lots of things I never did before. And the weather's certainly better."

"Sometime perhaps I could visit Sicily." Al-Kamil didn't sound enthusiastic. "I understand you've been having difficulties with those of your own faith."

"Nothing I can't deal with, either here or in my own kingdom." Frederick sipped sherbet and licked his upper lip. "If you came to Sicily, Sultan, we'd show the rest of the world how to entertain kings."

"Even lizard kings?"

Frederick laughed, and Fakhr-ad-Din turned and whispered to al-Adil abu Bakr, who gave Frederick a curious stare and bent to whisper to as-Salih Ayub. Al-Kamil drank milk and wiped his mouth with a napkin.

"The problem of Jerusalem," he said, "is one more troublesome than many believe. The city is the holy place of the Christians, of course, but it's also the holy place of the Jews and the third most holy city of Islam. In a sense it is not mine to give up, nor yours to receive, and before we agree on such a transfer of responsibility, perhaps we should discuss the smaller details."

Frederick nodded. Tommaso was translating swiftly into the ear of the scribe sitting on his left, and the whisper of the brush on paper blended with his voice. Frederick said, "Jerusalem above all cities ought never to be fought over, and yet it's fought over more than any other. If the question in your mind, Sultan, concerns the liberty of the people living there who are not Christian, and the rights of prayer of pilgrims coming to Jerusalem who are not Christian, I can assure you they shall be safeguarded as diligently as if they followed the Cross."

Al-Kamil steepled his fingers; behind him his relatives murmured and raised their eyebrows and looked at one another. Fakhr-ad-Din leaned forward and spoke in a low voice to al-Kamil, who turned his head slightly and nodded. Through it all ran the sound of the scribes' brushes and Tommaso's voice. Frederick looked up at the peak of the tent, where the silk glowed bright green under the sun.

"The walls of Jerusalem are in disrepair," al-Kamil said. "The city lacks the fortifications necessary to defend herself. Would you desire, if you held her, to rebuild these walls, Sultan?"

Frederick glanced at the Grand Master, who was frowning. In his mind he pulled together all the elements of his argument, taking a moment to organize the words. Looking back across the carpet, he met al-Kamil's eyes.

"If it were my choice alone, Sultan, I would tear down the walls entirely. The City of God needs no fortifications. Yet such a decision is beyond even my power to make. Jerusalem is a great city. Ought she to remain in disarray? Yes, I would rebuild the walls."

The Moslems behind al-Kamil whispered among themselves.

"However," Frederick said, without raising his voice, "I would request of you, Sultan, as I have made clear in my letters, no more territory than the city itself and a strip of land from the coast to Jerusalem, over which pilgrims may travel. I require no more land than that, and without the territory surrounding Jerusalem, she cannot be defended against a serious attack. Therefore, Sultan, you may see that my interests are peaceful, and that I mean to insure the rights of all pilgrims and residents of Jerusalem, for without the means to defend the city, who would risk incurring the wrath of Islam against her?"

Al-Kamil nodded. "This you have indeed made clear, and I am satisfied that you intend what you say. Yet if the Christians cannot defend the city, they might be seduced into wars of conquest in order to be able to protect her."

"Sultan, I will not question your clear-sighted knowledge of the affairs of Syria. However, I would like to point out to you that the Franks have no power to conquer. And while the truce between us lasts I can assure you that there will be no Crusade."

"So." Al-Kamil looked toward the Grand Master. "What does this knight think of such an arrangement?"

The Grand Master said in his halting Arabic, "The recovery of Jerusalem is my only wish."

"Even if the city lay at the mercy of any Moslem attack?" al-Kamil said. "Even if the only assurances against attack were good faith? Even if, at any time, Jerusalem might fall again into the hands of the people you call unbelieving?"

The Grand Master looked over at Frederick and said in German, "Do you wish me to answer?"

Frederick snapped, "Tommaso, translate this for them. Say what you want, Hermann. Say what you think."

Tommaso translated it loudly into Arabic. The Grand Master frowned, while all the Moslems watched him, their faces carefully inexpressive. Finally he said, "I would have grave reservations about any treaty in which Jerusalem was not fully under the control of Christendom. If the city cannot be defended it isn't ours, really. A few years ago the Syrian Franks rejected a treaty that would offer them Jerusalem under much the same terms, and for the reasons I have just mentioned."

Frederick thought, I doubt we have a right to Jerusalem at all, anyway. He watched al-Kamil mull that over, what the Grand Master had said. If I am Sicilian, how can I own a city in Syria?

"He is your own man," al-Kamil said gently. "Yet even he can't support what you suggest. Can you imagine, Sultan, what your enemies will say?"

Frederick turned and beckoned to Corso, who went back to the refreshment table. "Sultan, what my enemies say is of no use to me. My enemies in Sicily are telling my people that I am dead. Am I to lie down and die for them?"

Corso brought him a cup of sherbet to replace the empty one he held. Behind him Balian cleared his throat —Balian, who held land in Syria, who had to live here when Frederick had gone back home. Al-Kamil's eyes shifted toward him and back to Frederick.

"The Haramu'sh-Sharif, you have written, might be left in the hands of Moslems, with Christians allowed to pray there."

"That I promise you."

The Grand Master said, "The Templars won't like that."

Tommaso began to translate. Frederick said, "Good for them. I won't help the Templars recover anything, not if I could give them all they want by lifting my right hand." He bit down on the last word.

"Moslems may pray in other areas of the city?" al-Kamil said. "For instance, the Mosque of 'Umar?"

Frederick nodded. "That's to be taken for granted."

"Between us, Sultan." Al-Kamil's teeth showed in a grin. "Between the average Christian and the average Moslem, no. We should discuss the length of the truce."

Tommaso said quietly, "We mentioned ten years once, I believe." He spoke Arabic.

"I'd prefer a truce for twenty-five years," Frederick said.

Al-Kamil sipped milk. Al-Adil abu Bakr leaned forward and spoke to him, one hand gesturing. Under the crown Frederick's forehead started to itch, and he was getting a headache. He looked around for the Archbishop and made a gesture, and the Archbishop came over, took the crown, and put it gently on the cushion beside him. Frederick ran both hands through his hair and shook his head, relieved.

"Sultan, you are a young man still, but I am not." With a gesture al-Kamil sent a slave for fruit. "In twenty-five years I expect to be dead. In twenty-five years you might well be dead. The agreement is fragile enough without depending upon the like minds of our heirs."

"In twenty-five years maybe people will have gotten used to the arrangement. In ten, they won't—they'll see an end to it."

The slave held out a tray to al-Kamil, who took a peach and sent the tray across to Frederick. "You think in terms of changing things for good. I doubt you see the difficulties I do. Sultan, I cannot agree to a twenty-five-year truce."

Besides, in ten years maybe you'll want everything back. Frederick studied the ripe, flawless fruit, took an apple, and sent the tray away.

"It has never been my purpose to disrupt the balance of Syria. It's occurred to me more than once that what I do here could have repercussions none of us could predict, not only among the Christians and between Christian and Moslem but in Islam as well. If ten years is suitable to you, I can only agree to it."

"Your sentiments are certainly admirable and well taken, Sultan. And, before we go into the details other than Jerusalem itself, I have another point to make, which what you have just said leads into very well. If we conclude a treaty, I must ask you to consider it exclusive, in that you might not negotiate with any other Moslem ruler while this treaty holds."

Frederick nearly choked. Into his mind leaped the memory of him, Mutu, and a heap of gold, and his own voice saying coolly, "The Emperor is negotiating with en-Nasr . . ." He paused long enough to control his laughter and said decorously, "Sultan, if you believe that I would commit such a crime against our friendship, you must believe me so treacherous you would conclude no treaty at all."

Al-Kamil's steady black eyes burned with amusement. "I am struck with shame that I mentioned it at all, Sultan."

"I assure you I need no other alliance in the East than yours, Sultan."

"Let it be so."

"There is the question of Nazareth."

"Nazareth is yours. Provided, of course, the possession of it is merely for the purposes of prayer."

Sublime. Frederick contemplated that. Al-Kamil went on, "I will grant you as well control of the strip of land from Jaffa to Jerusalem that we discussed in our letters."

"The wisdom of this, Sultan, is yours as well as mine."

Fakhr-ad-Din's eyes widened; Frederick decided he was wondering what Frederick meant. Al-Kamil put his fingertips against the rug and traced the design. "In addition, Sultan, you mentioned certain areas you wished ceded to you. This, of course, is of little moment to me, since I do not now control Jaffa, Sidon, Acre or Caesarea."

Balian moved abruptly behind Frederick. Tommaso turned to look back at him. Shifting his weight more comfortably on his crossed legs, Frederick said, "Yet once they were Syrian cities, and the rights of the Franks over them are the rights of conquest. For the duration of the truce I require the measure of control your words can give me over them."

Tommaso went back to translating, and al-Kamil gave him time to catch up. Smiling, he looked around at his relations, who all smiled back at him. Clearly they didn't realize what was so amusing. Al-Kamil rocked gently on his cushions.

"You are no longer King of Jerusalem, are you, Sultan."

"My son Conrad is King. I am Regent only."

"Then let me hasten to help you establish your control over the Franks of Syria. Jaffa, Sidon, Caesarea, and Acre are yours. For ten years."

Frederick bowed, and al-Kamil bowed. Al-Kamil went on, "I wish no hostages. This treaty has been drawn up through the free will and request of both of us, and we shouldn't place constraints upon each other in any way. Shall we leave the scribes and the diplomats to draw up the formal agreements? It is my custom at this time of the day to relax. If you will join me, Sultan?"

"I would be most happy to."

Now they had the problem of who was going to rise first. Frederick looked across the carpet into al-Kamil's eyes, grinned and counted inaudibly to three. Al-Kamil smiled. In unison they stood up, and the others scrambled to their feet.

"Very pleasant," Fakhr-ad-Din said. "Now if only the scribes can get organized, everything ought to work out beautifully." He put one hand on Frederick's sleeve and turned toward al-Kamil.

"Sire," Balian said. "May I have my city back?"

Frederick swung around to face him. "Naturally. It's a point of law, that's all."

"It's a point of scaring every Frank in the East," the Archbishop said. "Excuse me, Sire." He bowed and went over to where Tommaso and the scribes from both sides and al-Adil abu Bakr were talking. Al-Kamil came over to Frederick, smiling.

"Let's hope the rest of the ten years are as harmonious. We have a saying in the East—Trust in God, but tie your camel. I doubt too many people are going to like this treaty."

"Too many camels roaming around loose?" Frederick took a plate from one of his pages; a slave was waiting with one for al-Kamil. "They needn't like it, as long as they abide by it."

Al-Kamil nodded, chewing. "The lamb is excellent. Try some. This business with Jaffa and Acre, now. I thought perhaps you meant to try to rule here the way you do in Sicily."

"I'm just trying to keep them from ruling me." He ate some of the lamb and nodded. "This is good. You have another saying—A thief is a king until he's caught. There are too many kings among the Franks. It doesn't suit my sense of order." He looked around for Corso and sent him after milk.

"I have nothing against Franks singly, but as a group they're impossible."

Frederick laughed. Their retainers were standing around them in clumps, eating and watching them covertly. He gave the plate to Corso to hold and drank his milk.

"When are you coming to Jerusalem?" al-Kamil said. "We'll have to have a banquet."

"As soon as the treaty is drawn up and signed and sealed. I have to get back home before the Pope divides my kingdom from the rest of Italy and lets it float out to sea." With Corso holding the plate for him, he cut meat. "You've got things of your own to do, haven't you?"

Al-Kamil made a face. "Quite. I've been held up too long at Nablus. Which is not an amusing city either. This treaty will put some pressure on my nephew in Damascus. I just hope he doesn't decide that his best chance lies with Khwaresm. You said something about repercussions —I liked that, it was nicely put, and very true."

Fakhr-ad-Din came up beside Frederick. "You are coming to Jerusalem, though."

"I have to. Would I come all this way and never go to Jerusalem? I plan on being crowned in the Church of Saint Sepulcher." Frederick shooed Corso away with the plate and washed his hands in a bowl Giancarlo brought. Giancarlo stared at al-Kamil, his jaw hanging open, and al-Kamil smiled at him. Giancarlo's eyes widened and he swallowed.

"You can stay with me, then," Fakhr-ad-Din said. "At

the Qadi's. Shamsu'd-Din."

"Crowned as what?" al-Kamil asked. "If I'm not being too inquisitive."

"I'll think of something." Frederick eyed Fakhr-ad-Din. "You just want Theophano near you again."

Fakhr-ad-Din mimed astonishment. "I? Let me assure you, Frederick, my only interest is your comfort."

Frederick laughed and drank from a cup Corso held out. "I'm sure I'll be comfortable at the Qadi's." He turned to look at the scribes.

They had finished comparing notes; Tommaso was reading a sheet of paper, tapping his fingers idly against his chin. When he saw Frederick looking at him, he nodded and came forward. Al-Kamil swung away from al-Adil abu Bakr.

"Sultan, I shall see you in Jerusalem, then." He bowed slightly. "Until then."

"Sultan." Frederick bobbed his head. "Until then."

Al-Kamil with his retainers left the tent, and outside, people cheered in Arabic. Tommaso said quietly, "Their scribes will make up the first draft and send it to us for corrections and changes. It shouldn't take long."

"He was certainly agreeable," the Archbishop said. "We had our doubts when we left Nablus."

Frederick looked around—all the Moslems were gone, and he sat down on the cushions behind him. "What do you mean?"

The Archbishop shrugged. "He had said he would surrender control of Jerusalem, but nothing else, and that he had his reservations about that. I don't think he'd really made up his mind. What you said reassured him. He was afraid Jerusalem would turn into an armed camp of Christians."

Tommaso looked quickly over his shoulder and said softly, "What Sir Hermann said ought to have unreassured him. He's right—the Sultan, I mean. Acre and Rome are not going to like this treaty."

Frederick drew up one knee and rested his forearms on it. "Tommaso, when I hold Jerusalem it will make no difference what they like. How long do you think this drafting will take?"

"A few weeks. No more."

"Hunh." He stared at the trembling green silk of the far wall. He'd thought he'd be jubilant, now that it was all but ended, but he was not—the leaden depression nudged at the edge of his mind again, like the beginning of a headache. Quickly, almost frightened, he stood up and headed for the door.

Why don't you have him arrested?" Theophano said.

"Because . . . it would be too much trouble." Frederick took a deep breath and leaned on the railing, looking down into the street. At least the crowd was quiet, although there were nearly a hundred people down there, listening to the Franciscan monk shout. From this distance he could hear only a little—every fourth or fifth word.

"Antichrist," the monk bellowed, and jabbed his arm at Frederick. "Antichrist—" And bawled something about defiling holy places. The crowd slewed around to look up at the balcony. Frederick bit down hard on his lower lip.

"Then, why listen?" Theophano said.

"I'm a flagellant." Even to him his voice sounded harsh and overloaded, and he cleared his throat. The Franciscan jumped off his perch on the wall and ran through the crowd and the stream of passers-by to confront him.

"You are damned," the monk shouted. "Will you damn all these people as well? Use Jerusalem as a lure to entice them into sin?" He flung out his arms. "Do not go to Jerusalem, Antichrist."

He was a young man, barefoot and ragged in his brown cassock, and his face burned with ardor. Frederick looked down at him and said nothing. That morning they'd sent back the final draft of the treaty for al-Kamil to approve and sign, and in less than a week the treaty would come back to Jaffa for him to sign, and immediately after they were leaving for Jerusalem. But the Franciscans had been here for three weeks now, and he couldn't ride down the street without them shouting at him. They kept vigil on his palace and swarmed in the bazaar and preached against him in the churches. He clenched his teeth and stared down at the monk.

"Even you might be saved," the monk was saying. "Repent and rejoice in God, and in His mercy find salvation."

The crowd was drifting off, bored. Theophano came over to the railing to look, and the monk saw her and shouted, "Harlot."

Frederick jerked. Theophano looked over at him and quietly moved back where the monk couldn't see her. "Red, come inside, it's too hot out here."

The monk, glancing around, saw that he'd lost his audience. He backed up into the middle of the street and knelt and began to pray. The people moving along the street passed by, glancing curiously at him or simply ignoring him—Franciscans had been praying in the streets around the palace ever since they'd heard about the treaty. Something—the way the young man knelt there, the way the constant traffic eddied around him—Frederick shook himself.

"Red."

"I'm coming."

What if I'm wrong? He backed away from the railing; the sun flashed off the sea and dazzled him, and he put his hands to his eyes. If I go to Jerusalem . . . He backed into a chair.

"Ouch."

"Are you all right?"

"Yes." He hobbled through the door, gasping and yelping at the pain in his shin. "Oh, Jesus. How did I do that? Ouch." He sat down and held onto his leg with both hands.

"You were feeling guilty or something. Very dramatic." She sent her maids away and called for a page to bring in her lute. Frederick turned to look out the door, but naturally he couldn't see the monk.

She ran off a scale. "Why do you let them stay if they upset you so much?"

"Because if I make any trouble with them they'll look

more right than they do now. Simple diplomacy." He
got up and walked around, testing his leg, and sat down
on a couch. She began to play softly.

"Am I going to Jerusalem with you?"

"Yes."

The Patriarch had forbidden anybody to follow him
to Jerusalem, on pain of excommunication; Mutu had
said that in Acre nobody talked about anything but the
treaty and how it betrayed Christ because there had been
no fighting. Fulk had said even he'd laughed at that. The
Patriarch was threatening to excommunicate the entire
city of Jerusalem if Frederick went anywhere near it. He
contemplated the idea that the most holy places in Christendom were about to fall under the ban of the Church.

"There's art to it," he said. "There's a certain genius to
it."

"Are you bragging again?"

"This I had nothing to do with, it's all the Pope. And
the Patriarch. And I was so looking forward to having
him crown me."

She laughed. Her long fingers trailed over the strings.
For a moment Frederick felt buoyant again, even happy,
but the same old gloomy feeling nudged him, and he got
up and walked around, trying to find something to do to
keep himself busy. If they are right . . .

"Tell me about your children," Theophano said.

"My God. Why?"

She shrugged—since she'd been with him she'd been
practising the lute, and the notes ran lightly, accurately
from her fingertips. "I'm a woman, I'm curious." She
gave him a sly look. "Do you want me to rub your
back?"

"Later."

"Tell me about your children."

He stood in front of a chest and picked up a little jar of
perfume. "Well. There's Heinrich, who's King of the
Romans—he's eighteen. And a prize. He doesn't think I

know what he's doing, but I do." Unscrewing the top, he sniffed. "This is the stuff you wore yesterday. I like this."

"What's Heinrich planning to do?"

"Let's say he's under the influence of evil counselors. I don't like him anyway—he's colossally stupid. He takes after his mother." He put the top back onto the jar and opened another.

"What's this?"

She looked. "Cream for my skin. Don't leave the tops off, will you? They'll dry up."

"I won't. Conrad is only eight months old, so he's no problem yet, but I imagine he will be. Yolande is three." He couldn't really remember if she was three or four; he screwed his face up, trying to think. "She takes after her mother too. And Enzio, he's my bastard. None of them takes after me. Enzio's fun, he does nothing but play and the court spoils him silly. Are you pregnant?"

"Why do you ask?"

"Why did you ask about my children?"

"Not that I know of, no. I just wanted you to think about something other than Jerusalem and monks and excommunications."

I want a son like me, who thinks like me and who . . . likes me. He rubbed some of the cream into the back of his hand. Theophano's son. Heinrich, whom he hadn't seen in nearly ten years, was plotting to overthrow him, depose him as Emperor and take his place and be a blessing to Mother Church. Soft and cool, the cream vanished into his skin. The monk praying in the street was probably only a little older than Heinrich.

"Heinrich and I—"

"I'm sorry I ever brought it up," she said.

"Well, you did." He put the top on the jar of cream and went back to the couch. "Heinrich is a typical Hohenstaufen. My father must have been like him, except that my father was clever and knew how to govern and

Heinrich doesn't."

"Is he in Italy?"

"No. He's in Germany, I left him there when I came back."

She drew one foot up beneath her. "What?"

"Oh. I went to Germany to be crowned Emperor, had Heinrich crowned King of the Romans—my heir—and went back to Sicily." He made a mixing gesture with one hand. "It's all complicated—I spent a lot of time in Germany figuring it all out. I had an idea in my head for ruling, and I knew it wouldn't work in Germany, but before I went home I had to fix everything so the Germans wouldn't rebel against me and get me involved in something outside Sicily. So I gave them Heinrich and told them to rule themselves."

She was nodding, looking solemn, but her eyes sparkled. "I see. Very logical."

"That's what I like about you, you understand what I say. That was nearly ten years ago, and I haven't seen Heinrich since. So he doesn't really know anything, because I never taught him anything except not to bother me when I was working."

She cocked her head. "When is your birthday?"

"The day after Christmas. I forgot it this year; I didn't go to Christmas Mass because I'm excommunicate. I'm under Capricorn. Anyway, Heinrich has nothing to teach him except his blood."

"Does he dislike you?"

"Yes. I dislike him too."

"By letter, I take it. Why?"

"He hates me because I'm a heretic and I hate him because he's a German. Will you let me make my point?"

"Certainly." Solemn again. "Go on."

"The Germans make everything dark. It's amazing. Their cathedrals are dark, their castles are dark, their legends are full of dark stories, everything is gloomy and frightened. They hunt heresy in themselves like the signs of physical disease. They are afraid of God and the devil and themselves—what are you smiling about?"

"Nothing. Poor Heinrich." She put the lute down and came over to sit next to him on the couch.

"Naturally. He's part German, and he was raised in Germany, and that brought it all out in him—" He raised his hands, palms up. "They're afraid of sin in Germany, so they find sin in everything."

"You're part German too. More German than he is." She reached out and took a hank of hair in her hand. "But I've never noticed you to find sin in anything."

She put her arms around his neck and kissed him. With his arms around her waist, he pulled her close to him, inhaling the fragrance of her hair and her skin. "Well," he said, his mouth close to her ear, "I'm Sicilian really." He thought of the monk in the street, but that seemed unimportant. He laid his head on her shoulder and shut his eyes.

"Jerusalem," the Grand Master whispered. "Jerusalem."

Frederick looked down at him, amazed. The old man stood in the road, tears streaming down his face, staring at the city waiting for them there, and abruptly he knelt. With a crash of armor all the Teutonic knights went to their knees as well. Frederick looked back at the hordes of pilgrims following them; many of them weren't close enough yet to see the Holy City, and they were hurrying up, but those in the front ranks were kneeling too, and they were weeping like the Grand Master. He turned his head to look at the city. The road wound across the rumpled, sandy slope toward the Gate of King David; he could see David's Tower from here, half in ruins, and something that looked like Tancred's Tower, and a rise that could be the Mount of Olives beyond the gray stone of the crumbling walls.

His skin crawled. The Mount of Olives, the Holy Sepulcher, Gethsemane and the Vale of Kedron and the Via Dolorosa. This was real, this had stood when Christ came here to be murdered. He heard the pilgrims stumbling along the slope to places where they could see and pray, but his sight was blurring and there was a lump in his throat. He dismounted and threw his horse's reins blindly to Ayub and knelt down.

The Grand Master's ragged voice reached his ears, specific in the general mumble of the crowd. He thought of praying but did not; he only stared at the city out there across the dusty desert bushes. And the emotion was fading away—he snatched at it, wanting it back, but it drained out of him, and he sat back on his heels. Well, it was good while it lasted. That rush of joy and awe: he could remember what it had been like, but the feeling itself he couldn't recreate. He caught himself comparing it to the overwhelming, blinding burst of sensuality he got from eating hashish, and his face turned hot with shame. But a moment later he decided that it was just to compare them, they were nearly the same thing. He looked around curiously at the pilgrims.

They covered the slope, all of them in tears, crossing themselves and rocking back and forth in a kind of ecstasy. His Saracens had dismounted and stood beside their horses, and just beyond them, next to her horse, Theophano knelt among her maids, looking over at him. He caught her eye and smiled, and her wide mouth curled into a grin.

The stony ground hurt his knees, and the sun lay like a weight on his head and shoulders. The air smelled rank with the dust and the oily scent of the low shrubs that covered the ground. Inside the walls there was food and something to drink and good company. He stood up. Wide-eyed, the men around him looked at him, still half submerged in their emotions. Ayub came around to help him mount, and he waved him away.

"I'll walk."

Ayub nodded and led off his horse. With a rustle like leaves, the mob on the slope got to its feet. Frederick started down the road, his Saracens moving up on foot to bracket him, leading their horses.

Behind him a clear voice started singing the Te Deum laudamus, and immediately other voices took it and bellowed it out. Frederick glanced back and saw the Freidank near him, walking with some of the Teutonic knights, singing. The Grand Master, Tommaso, the Archbishop, and Fulk and Ezzo had gotten inside the ring of the Saracens, and even they were singing. The Assassin, walking to Frederick's left, kept shooting looks at them from the corner of his eye; he was chewing like a cow working a cud, and Frederick nearly laughed. A high, ringing pleasure filled him.

David's Gate stood open, and while he watched, a file of Moslems rode out. The welcoming party. He wondered what they thought of this—a mass of Christians stumbling over their rocky ground, singing at the top of their lungs and weeping. His chest swelled with joy, although he didn't understand why, and he couldn't stop smiling. Fulk, beside him, was swearing in a desperate, quiet voice that sounded like prayer.

Theophano was walking along a little beyond the Assassin, leading her horse with one hand and holding up her skirts bunched in the other fist. Her long hair had gone loose from its net and swung around her shoulders. She passed through a patch of lavender windflowers and bent and picked one, and holding it in the same hand that held her skirts, trotted a few steps to catch up. When she was nearly even again with Frederick, she stopped a moment and thrust the flower into her hair behind one ear, and her horse lowered its head and took a mouthful of the harsh desert grass. The pause left her behind again, and she ran two strides—the horse jogged beside her, and the purple flower bounced against her shining black hair.

The thundering voices of the pilgrims sang on. They were near enough that Frederick could see Fakhr-ad-Din among the Moslems waiting for them. His feet hurt from walking on the rough ground. Up on the walls clusters of heads appeared: the Moslems who lived there come to see the Christians who for some reason now owned the city. The last time we took it, we killed everybody. This time . . .

He walked into the shadow under the great gate, looked up into the crumbling stone of the arch, and went over to the waiting Moslems. Fakhr-ad-Din and an un-smiling man with pouches under his eyes stepped forward.

"Your Majesty," Fakhr-ad-Din said, "may I present the Qadi Shamsu'd-Din."

The Qadi bowed stiffly. "I am at the service of the Emperor." He didn't sound as if he meant it, and his eyes turned toward the mass of pilgrims. Frederick swung around—the pilgrims were clogging up the gate and the road to it, packed together and shoving. The singing died away. The Qadi said, "We were not expecting so many."

Frederick called to the Grand Master, and while the old man was fighting his way through the mob toward him, said, "Well, we'd better get them inside before they decide they've been cheated. Dawud, do you have guides in there?"

"Yes. But not enough." Fakhr-ad-Din's mouth tightened. The crowd was muttering, and in their voices was a note of rising excitement—they thought they were being kept out of the city deliberately. If they panicked—if they began to struggle—The Grand Master came up, his face stained from crying.

"Break them up into groups," Frederick said. "Small groups. And get them in there and put away safely before they . . ."

Fulk came up. "Sire, I've seen the plan of the city, I

can probably reach the Hospital."

"Good." Frederick nodded.

A shrill German voice from the middle of the crowd yelled, "Let us in. Why is the gate closed?" And somewhere else a man shouted angrily.

Frederick raised his arm to Ayub. Fulk plunged off into the crowd, shoving his way through toward the gate. The Teutonic knights were blocking it—they had the sense not to go in alone, but the crowd was pushing at them. Frederick whirled and saw Ezzo and grabbed him by the sleeve.

"Find Theophano and get her out of that crowd."

Ezzo plunged away. Ayub was there with Frederick's horse, and he grabbed the reins and the high pommel of the saddle and mounted. From that height he could see the pilgrims spread out under the walls, packed forward, pushed from behind, and a man screamed, "Let us in." On the walls the Moslems were moving around nervously. A stone flew out of the crowd, aimed at them, but it rebounded harmlessly off the high wall.

Frederick kicked his horse forward. The crowd was milling, and their excitement radiated from them like a fever. Up at the gate the guides were finally leading off the knights, but the pilgrims crushed into the space around the gate faster than they could organize them and take them away. He saw Fulk herd a group of at least sixty off into the Street of King David, and he saw people going in alone, unguided; he kicked the horse straight into the crowd.

"Watch out—watch out—"

Hands caught at him and at the horse, trying to hold him off. He clenched his fists on the reins, frightened of trampling them, frightened of not getting to the gate before too many wandered into the city alone. Suddenly someone called, "The Emperor—it's the Emperor—" and they turned to look at him. The crowd had been brown and gray before, the color of their clothes, but now it was a mass of pale, upturned faces. They cheered, holding up their hands to him.

"Calm down," he shouted. "Just wait, be patient— they didn't know there would be so many of us. You'll need guides—you'll never find your way around alone. Just wait a little, you'll all get in."

Immediately he knew they hadn't all heard him, because like a wave they surged toward him, pushed on by the ones in back who hadn't heard and were shouting, "What did he say? Is it closed to us?" Their arms waved, and in the mob of faces their mouths opened and shut grotesquely. He looked toward the gate and saw Tommaso leading off another pack. Fakhr-ad-Din was scrambling through the crowd near the wall to the gate. The Qadi looked dour and did not move.

The Freidank pushed up to Frederick's stirrup, grinned cheerfully at him, and started to sing the Te Deum again. The song spread through the mob, and they slackened off, they stopped pushing, and spaces opened up among them. Frederick's shoulders slumped. He twisted in his saddle and saw Theophano standing with Ezzo, near the Qadi, who was staring at her and scowling. Fulk had come back with a horse, and the Moslem guides were shouting in bad Latin, waving their arms.

Gradually the crowd thinned out, moving into the city—they took the song with them, and disjointed verses spilled back through the gate and clashed with the version sung outside. Frederick's horse walked with the crowd up to the gate, and he had to rein it down to keep it from carrying him into the city. He thought, I should have known something like this would happen. The faces of the people swarming past him filled him with uneasiness—they looked so happy, and yet only a little while before they'd been working themselves up to storm the city barehanded. Crowds. Christ, I hate crowds. He glanced at Theophano again and saw her talking calmly to Ezzo, the blue flower still in her long black hair.

His horse slacked its weight off one hip and lowered its head, and he let the reins slide. The pilgrims walked past him in a thinning stream. His throat was coated with dust, and he couldn't swallow. His suite was gathering, over near Theophano; the pages sat on the ground and looked up at the wall and chattered happily, he could hear their voices even above the shuffling of the pilgrims' feet. Fakhr-ad-Din came out the gate, pushing through the space between the pilgrims and the wall, and stopped beside him.

"That was a tense moment."

Frederick nodded. "We could have planned it better."

Fakhr-ad-Din said, "We heard about the ban and we didn't think so many would come. It was my fault." He looked up, smiling; his face was filmed with dust. "It's a fine tribute to you."

"One I could endure without." The last of the pilgrims, two old men and a boy on crutches, went off with a chattering Armenian. Their quavering voices took the Te Deum with them. Frederick stared after them into the city—the Street of King David stretched out straight from the gate, narrow between the two rows of stone buildings; two other streets ran off to the left and right, black with shadow from the late-afternoon sun.

"Come along," Fakhr-ad-Din said gently, "you must be thirsty. The Qadi's house is prepared for you, let me lead the way."

"What do you think of Jerusalem, Sultan?" the Qadi said.

"It's very pleasant."

"I'm pleased you think so, since you are now the ruler of it." The Qadi beckoned to a slave to fill up Frederick's plate again and stared out across the room. Since their meeting he hadn't smiled, and in everything he said sounded the same bitter note, sometimes more muted than now. Frederick ate lamb and rice and drank a little wine.

"There's a minaret across the square from my window, but I didn't hear the muezzin call."

For a moment the Qadi's stony profile didn't alter. The clatter of the other people around them filled Frederick's ears. Suddenly the Qadi turned to look at him, his black eyes wider than before. "I asked him not to. I thought not to offend you, Sultan."

"If you were in my city of Palermo, Qadi, you would hear the muezzins five times a day. It would offend me not to hear him tomorrow at dawn."

Beyond the Qadi, Fakhr-ad-Din leaned forward to look at the older man's face. The Qadi shut his eyes and bowed his head. "I accede to your will, Sultan. It shall be done."

"Your Majesty," Fakhr-ad-Din said. "How long will you remain in Jerusalem?"

"Not long enough. I have to get back to Sicily." Frederick tapped his cup, and Corso came up to fill it. "I'm being crowned the day after tomorrow."

"The Sultan al-Kamil has sent his regrets that he'll be unable to attend," the Qadi said. "He has to go to Damascus."

"Oh?" Frederick grinned.

"Well," Fakhr-ad-Din said. "Near Damascus. But we're having a banquet tomorrow, and I'll take you around to all the sights during the day."

"Good." Frederick looked at the Qadi. "Have I your permission to enter the Haramu'sh-Sharif?"

The Qadi's mouth twitched toward a smile. "Naturally." He turned his head toward Fakhr-ad-Din, and when he faced Frederick again he was almost grinning. "If I might attend you. The Emir is, perhaps, less acquainted with the city than I."

"I'd be very pleased if you would. Does Abu Musa Nizam al Tawli still live in Jerusalem?"

The Qadi's eyes opened twice as wide as Frederick had ever seen them before. "How do you know Nizam?"

"He and I corresponded awhile on the subject of quadratic equations."

The Qadi was speechless. Fakhr-ad-Din leaned forward again. "He's gone to Cairo, Frederick—al-Kamil wanted him for his court."

"Are you a mathematician, Your Majesty?" the Qadi said.

"Not really. I pretend a lot."

Fakhr-ad-Din snorted. Frederick grinned at him and looked over toward the table where his staff was eating; Tommaso caught his eye and cocked his eyebrows and looked pointedly at the Qadi. When his gaze returned to him, Frederick nodded slightly. Tommaso smiled, and leaning back, began to talk to the Grand Master. Frederick lifted his cup.

The Latin chapel in St. Sepulcher was small and dark. After the Dome of the Rock, covered with brilliant glazed tiles and the inscriptions of Salah-ad-Din and carpeted with the prayer rugs of the Moslems, the little church seemed cold and damp, like a tomb. It was a tomb. Frederick walked alone up the aisle, past the ranks of the Teutonic knights and the men who had come with him from Sicily. In the nave overhead sparrows twittered and swooped—they kept them out with grates in the Dome of the Rock.

No one spoke. Except for the swallows and the soft padding of his own feet, there was no sound. He kept his eyes on the altar ahead of them; beyond it, shielded in marble, one end of the sepulcher itself was visible, worn slick with kisses and the tears of pilgrims. A stone, like the Kaaba, a mere stone. Against it the chipped gilt of the altar looked tawdry.

There was no priest here to crown him, to say Mass

and to preach some dutiful sermon. On the low altar they had put a crown, resting on a cushion. Tall candles flanked it, but they weren't lit—this wasn't really a service. To me this is the only service. He stopped before the altar and looked to either side. The mass of armored men behind him did not move and said nothing, and the swallows' chirping seemed weak and far away. He looked up into the dome above the sepulcher. The plaster was flaking. In the dim light he could see the outlines of painted figures, and in the gaps in the plaster, older faces: Christ, the Apostles, the Day of Judgment. Their Byzantine eyes reminded him of the paintings in the old churches in Sicily.

I need no priest. He felt taut and strong and charged with purpose, as if all his will and energy were gathered up and focused on this single moment, this crown and this act. Lowering his eyes, he stared over the altar toward the sepulcher, reached out, and lifted the crown from its cushion. Heavy in his hands, solid and cool and real: I need no priest, this I do by myself and to myself, this is my stigmata. He lifted the crown and set it on his head.

Behind him, with a thunderous clash of armor, they all knelt. He shut his eyes, trembling with exaltation. Oh God, he thought, now I am Emperor. The crown on his head weighed less than the air; the hatred of his enemies seemed less important than the twittering of the sparrows in the nave.

"And after we go to the Jordan?"

"Back to Acre," he said, and put another date into his mouth. "From there, home." Through the open windows he could see the whole Arab Quarter, filled with the luminous twilight, brilliant blue. Beyond the Dome of the Rock and Mount of Olives rose, low and shaggy with trees. The white walls of the houses shone in the deepening blue light. At the end of this street someone was hawking mulberries in a shrill voice.

"Have you done something scandalous again?" Theophano said. She came over to look out the window. "They tell me you nearly killed a priest."

"God, that was long ago." Yesterday. He leaned against the wall, still looking out the window. "He was begging in the Haramu'sh-Sharif. And I didn't nearly kill him, I only threatened to."

She was watching him, her arms folded over her breasts; one curl of her hair lay against her throat. Being reminded of the priest had nettled him. He reached out and took the tress of hair between his fingers and pulled it gently.

"Tired?"

"Yes. I want to go home." He draped the tress carefully against her throat again and smiled.

"Red—" She looked out the window. "When are you going to ask me if I'm going to Sicily with you?"

Not now. His chest constricted. "How do you know I will?"

"I know you." Her hand moved along her upper arm. "You'd better ask now, putting it off won't help."

He rested his head against the wall and shut his eyes. In the next room they were setting out the dinnerware; the rumble of voices reached in through the lattice screen across the door. A lump came into his throat.

"That's enough of an answer, isn't it?"

"Yes," she said wearily. "I guess it is."

He opened his eyes onto the beautiful, luminous blue of the air. She was running one finger over the carved stone of the window sill, her eyes downcast.

"Theophano. I love you."

"I know. You nearly said it once."

Her voice was thick. If she's unhappy, why—

"Do you love me? At all?"

Her head bobbed up and down once. "But I won't go

to Sicily with you."

"Why not?" He clenched his fists. "Why not?"

"No."

"Why?"

"Because . . . this is where I belong. I wouldn't be happy somewhere else."

"How do you know? How can you possibly—"

"And because in Sicily you won't be lonely, you won't have enemies all around, and you won't love me anymore."

Her voice had hardened and sharpened, like a knife. He drew a deep breath. "How do you know?"

"Because I know you. Do we have to do this?"

"You brought it up."

"I did." She glanced at him and quickly turned away. "I'm sorry."

"If you don't like it there, I'll let you go. You can come back here."

She shook her head. "I have a son in Antioch. That's where I live. He's there with my mother."

"You can bring him. And her." But he didn't want that, and his voice showed it. "Theophano."

She shook her head. Confused, he hunted desperately for the arguments, for the right words, but nothing came into his mind. All he could think of was being without her. He thought, I'll marry her, and his mind flinched away from it, and he understood finally; it jarred him as if he'd been struck. He turned slightly to put his back to the wall and stared across the room. Gradually his mind quieted, everything settling down again.

"I'm sorry," he said. "That's how I am, I can't change it now."

"Nobody wants you to."

He looked over and saw her smiling, her face calm and her eyes bright. "Will you go with me to Acre?"

"I'm going that way. If you want me with you, I will."

"I do."

For a moment they looked into each other's eyes, silent. She moved a little, and he straightened up away from the wall.

"You were going to write me a poem once," she said. "Will you now?"

"Now? Here?" He looked around, startled.

"Yes. Now." She pulled him over toward the table. "Giancarlo, come light the lamps, please." Dragging over a stool, she sat down next to the chair at the table and grinned up at him. Giancarlo jogged in with a taper, and the lamps glowed and filled the room with clear yellow light. Frederick sat down at the table and got out paper and ink.

"It usually takes me a while. Shall I do it in Italian or Arabic?"

"Arabic. So I can read it. Do you usually write in Arabic?"

He shook his head. "This is . . . not an inspiring moment." Elusive images filled his mind, floating just beyond the reach of words. "You can't laugh."

"I won't." She craned her neck to watch the pen he held over the paper. "Go on."

"Don't rush me." He wrote: *Love bird, fly to me.* . . . "Can you read Arabic?"

"A little. You'll tell me what the words mean and I'll remember."

"Oh, marvelous." He glanced at Giancarlo, who was loitering in a corner. "Get out."

Giancarlo left, humming to himself. In the next room dishes rang together.

Love bird, fly to me, come and nest in my love tree. He hunted around for another verse.

"What will you do? In Antioch."

"Live," she said. "What I usually do."

Love bird, sing your song, sing in my window all night long. She won't go. Will you think of me sometimes? "This one will be short."

"So long as it's good."

"I'm not really a poet."

The Arabic script decorated the page in a strange design. He wanted to change the structure; he knew what he wanted to say, but the words for it refused to come. Scraps of metaphor came into his mind, and even before he wrote them down in the margin, he knew they were no good. For a moment he fretted, trying to fit darkness, the moon, the wind and the love bird all into one verse, and suddenly the right way came to him, including none of them.

> *My heart is a thorn thicket to the white doe*
> *My heart is a parched desert to the lioness*
> *For you my heart is a flowering tree*
> *Full of the wind's music*

Beneath that he wrote the first two verses again, and sat back, mildly amazed. It was one of his better efforts, at least in Arabic. When he read it over, the lines gave him back the precision and softness he'd felt in thinking of them; even in Arabic the first and last parts sounded like Italian, which he liked.

"Is it finished?"

He nodded, shy about reading it.

"Tell it to me."

He did, his eyes on the page. A moment after he'd finished he looked up at her over the top of the paper. Her eyes wide, she was watching him.

"Red. That's beautiful."

"Do you like it?"

"Yes." She took the paper and looked down at it, her lips moving silently. In the next room people laughed.

"It's very like you," she said. "It's very sensual."

"Do you really like it?"

Now her eyes were amused. "Yes. Very much. Thank you." Tucking the paper into her blouse, she leaned forward and kissed him. "Thank you."

Immoderately pleased, he grinned at her, took hold of her hair, and pulled her toward him again. In the middle of the kiss Marino called them in to dinner, and holding her by the hand, he got up and headed for the door. She would go with him, he knew it—she had to. Smiling, he led her around the lattice screen into the gaudy light of the next room.

Turtledoves brawled and cooed in the peak of the arched gate he rode through into Acre, his Saracens and his knights around him like a moving fortress. Their shadows coiling and uncoiling over the neck of his horse, his banners flapped in the hot spring wind. People crowded the walls, but there were no cheers. He kept his eyes straight ahead. I brought you back Jerusalem and you won't even call to me in the street.

Riding along the Wall Street, they passed the English Tower, the Accursed Tower, the Tower of Saint Nicholas, riding in and out of the stripes of shade they threw across the bright dust. Up on the rampart the people of Acre stood and watched in silence, and in the houses on the inside of the street, windows opened, heads thrust out. At one corner, just after the street turned the angle under the Accursed Tower, a Franciscan stood; he shouted, "Traitor," in a voice like the clank of iron. But no one picked up the shout, and it died in the hot afternoon wind. Frederick's hair swung in his eyes, and he flipped it back over his shoulders. For a while a black dog trotted along beside them, a little bell on its collar jingling softly.

"Heretic," someone whispered up on the wall.

He looked up; the people were moving along the rampart, keeping even with him, their faces thrust toward him, pale and fierce, like masks, their lips drawn back from their teeth. He made a face and looked straight again. It would have made him angry once, even afraid, but now he was tired of it. They turned through the gate into the compound of the Teutonic knights.

Grooms came out quietly to take their horses; in the ranks around him voices started up, relieved. The big gates swung closed. Frederick dismounted and turned to find Tommaso at his side.

"That's a beautiful horse," Tommaso said.

Frederick glanced around. "Yes. She's nice to ride too —very easy gaits."

"Where did you get her?"

Tommaso knew that. Frederick stared at him, bewildered. "The Qadi gave her to me when I left Jerusalem. Weren't you there?"

"I was." Tommaso looked away. "I was there, too, when he met you at the gate when you entered, and he didn't like you then. I was there at dinner afterward when you charmed him into liking you." His eyes rose to Frederick's and he cocked his head. "Why can't you do that with the people of Acre?"

Frederick went around him toward the door, exasperated. Tommaso stuck to him. "They aren't worth it," Frederick said.

Tommaso strode around to open the door for him. His face was perfectly expressionless. "If you say so, Sire."

"Hunh." Frederick went inside, into the knights' front hall—there was a passage off it into his house next door. Rapidly the room filled up with his retinue and knights, still subdued from the icy reception they'd gotten. Corso and Giancarlo ran up to take Frederick's cloak.

"Giancarlo. I thought you were going to show me some of your poetry."

The boy looked up, startled, and smiled. "I will, Sire." He ran off, his arms full of the light cloak. Frederick looked around—someone offered him a tankard of beer, but he turned it down. The Grand Master and the Archbishop were conferring near the doorway to the passage.

Beyond them, leaning up against the wall, Enrico da Malta was drinking beer; Frederick grinned. When Enrico lowered his mug, he beckoned to him, and Enrico, smiling, came quickly through the crowd toward him.

"Sire." Enrico knelt briefly. "Congratulations."

"Mixed, I'm sure. Do you have my ships here?"

"Forty-eight galleys, ready to be loaded. When do we set sail?"

"Within the week, I hope. I have a lot to do before then." Frederick headed for the passageway. "I'll know for certain by the day after tomorrow. What's the news from Sicily?"

"Everybody thinks you're dead."

"Other than that." His staff was following him; his pages ran up to open the door. Ayub ducked into the corridor ahead of Frederick, the Assassin close behind.

"Not bad, actually," Enrico said. He held back so that Frederick could precede him. "The Pope's armies hold the mainland, but it's gone sour on them—you know Sicily. Papal soldiers keep winding up in ditches with their throats cut. That sort of thing."

Frederick grinned. The corridor smelled foul, and the walls dripped steadily, but it was short; ahead, light showed through the open door. The pages ran through, with Corso shouting orders. He ducked his head to keep from knocking it on the lintel and stepped out into a bright, fresh room.

"They'll run," Enrico said. "Della Vigne said that I should tell you that. As soon as you step foot in Sicily, the Pope's whole army will turn and run—the Pope's been telling even them that you're dead, or else they'd never stay."

The Grand Master said, "Sire, are you going to call a council?"

"Yes. I want to get some kind of statement out about the treaty." He went across the room for a cup of wine and caught a glimpse of Theophano and her maids in the next room. "As soon as possible," he said, watching her. Theophano turned her head and smiled at him, and he waved and went back toward the little knot of his officers. "And we have appointments to make. Baillis and constables and the like. Tommaso, draw me up a list of candidates. Berardo, will you go to the Patriarch and ask him to reconsider the interdict?"

The Archbishop snorted. "It can't possibly stand. How could anybody declare Jerusalem excommunicate?"

Frederick laughed. "Well, make the point to him." The Bishop of Caesarea had arrived in Jerusalem, all fulminations and wild looks, on the day they'd left, and he'd mentioned the Church of St. Sepulcher specifically in the ban. It was a nice point of canon law whether anybody could call down anathema on the tomb of Christ. He went over to a table to put his cup down. "Hermann, who's constable of Acre?"

"Garnier the German, I think. He's an old friend of John of Brienne's."

"Oh, well, then, you'd better keep watch on the city. I didn't like the . . . mood of the people when we came in."

The Grand Master rubbed his jaw. "Neither did I. Garnier is an intelligent man—don't judge him by his friends, Sire. I think Enrico had some messages for you."

Frederick swung around; Enrico was coming in from the passageway, a packet of letters under his arm. "Oh. Good." He stretched out one hand to take them, and Enrico lengthened his stride toward him.

Falk and Ezzo came in, armed with wine cups. Fulk looked around, stared out the window, and said glumly, "Here we are again, back in jolly old Acre."

"Well," Frederick said, "we'll be going home before you can get into any trouble." He grinned, looking through the thick stack of letters. "You have my leave, all of you."

"Mutu has come up from Jaffa," Theophano said. "One of my maids saw him in the street."

Frederick looked up. She was sitting on the couch, combing her hair. "Oh." He studied her, the grace of the long lines of her body, her eyes and her hair. "Have I ever told you you're beautiful?"

"No," she said, and smiled, looking at him out of the corners of her eyes. "Not in words."

He leaned back. He'd been drawing up the list of appointments, and it had to be done before tomorrow, but to look at her pleased him so much he couldn't look away. She knew he was watching, and she moved under his eyes, stretching, showing off. He laughed and went back to the list.

"You are."

Balian of Sidon he meant to name one of the baillis of the Kingdom of Jerusalem, but the other was still open, and he didn't like any of the choices. While he thought it over he filled in several of the smaller offices, rewarding the men who had stayed with him from the beginning of the Crusade. Theophano came softly across the carpet toward him.

"You weren't listening to me."

"If you come much closer I'll do more than listen." Garnier the German was on Tommaso's list; if he'd been friends with John of Brienne, he probably hated Frederick, but the Grand Master liked him, and a German might be . . . Anyhow, it would be a nice gesture. "What do you mean, I wasn't listening?"

"When I said that Mutu is here."

"I heard that." He wrote in Garnier's name next to Balian's.

"Well," she said, "he says there's going to be trouble."

"One needn't be big and black to know that. The question is when." He needed five baillis for Cyprus.

"Tonight."

The brush left a smear across the paper. "God damn." He stood up, his mind racing. "Was he sure?"

"Yes," she said, and looked up at him curiously. "What are you going to do?"

"I don't know." His hands on his hips, he wandered

around the room, considering whether he should act on Mutu's information. If he did, he might only create the situation he was trying to protect himself against. Trouble in a city usually meant mobs and mobs made him nervous, he didn't understand them. He pulled a bellrope and Giancarlo came in.

"Sire."

"Send for Sir Hermann, Fulk of Ancerra, Ezzo d'Iste and Ricardo Filangieri."

Giancarlo bowed and ran. Theophano said, "Do you think . . . What do you think they'll try to do?"

"I don't know. I wish I did." I wish I knew what was going on out there. "Did Mutu say who was stirring it up?"

"No. Just that everybody in the harbor district was getting ready for a riot. Red, they can't hurt us here. Why not let them run it off?"

"Oh, well. I like to dabble in civic affairs." He stared at the far wall; on it was painted the Flight into Egypt in broad splashes of color.

"Sire," the Grand Master said. Coming into the room, he bent his knee slightly and bowed to Theophano.

"Hermann. Unh—come next door." He glanced at Theophano. "I'll be back in a little while."

She smiled. "Don't be rash, Red."

"Why not? It's fun." He led the Grand Master out of the room and into the larger one across the antechamber. Fulk and Ezzo met them in the middle.

"Fulk," Frederick said. "I hope you and Ezzo are properly bored by now?"

"God. This city drives me wild." Fulk thrust his hands into his belt. "Is there something amusing we can do?" Grinning.

"Yes, in fact. Take horses and go out and ride around. I want to know if trouble starts anywhere, and who's there when it does. If it does. Go down through the harbor and up past the Templars' Quarter. Stay together; I wouldn't like it at all if you got killed."

"Sire." Fulk bowed and started for the door.

"Fulk."

"Sire?"

"Don't start anything. If you do, I'll be very, very angry."

Fulk blinked. "Sire. Would we do such a thing?" He bowed and went out, with Ezzo at his heels. Just beyond the door they both laughed.

Frederick made a fig at the door. "They'll get me in trouble someday."

"When you want them to." The Grand Master pulled a drapery closed over one of the windows to keep out the draft. "Are you expecting some trouble, Sire?"

"Yes. But don't tell anybody. My sources aren't beyond reproach. Where's— Rico, come in. Both Ricos."

Ricardo Filangieri and Enrico da Malta bowed and advanced. Filangieri had his cap in his hands, and he wore boots; he'd been out or going out. Frederick lifted his eyebrows. "Did I interfere with some errand?"

"An unimportant one." Filangieri put his cap on the table.

"Enrico, where are the ships in the harbor?"

"At anchor," Enrico said. "Why, do you want them brought in to the quays?"

"No. Leave them out. Rico, I want you and Hermann to take two companies of knights and have them ready. If there's any trouble in Acre tonight—any sign of large crowds gathering, any unusual noise or fighting—you" —pointing to Filangieri—"seal off the city, and you"— to the Grand Master—"seal off the Templars' Quarter. No one leaves or enters. Is that clear?"

"Are you sure, Sire, that—"

"Yes. I am." Frederick smiled. "Do as I say, now, I have my reasons. Enrico, you're in charge of the harbor. I don't want those ships in any danger."

Enrico, who wore slippers and a loose gown, shrugged

and started for the door. The Grand Master said, "Sire, what of your personal safety?"

"Leave me some of the knights and my Saracens. The compound walls are strong enough. Leave me ten knights."

Filangieri picked up his cap. "Sir Hermann, we should start now."

"Don't do anything that might cause trouble," Frederick said. "Don't act as if it's inevitable. Just in case, hunh? Be careful."

Corso came in and made a fuss about drawing the draperies and lighting the lamps and ordering Giancarlo around. Filangieri and the Grand Master left, and Frederick stood in the middle of the room, imagining a map of the city and working out the possible trouble centers, while the two pages trotted around him. Frederick thought of the city's garrison, over which he had no control. We'll see what they do when the time comes.

"Corso, bring me a light supper in my room."

"Sire, is there something going on?"

Frederick, headed for his room, turned and grinned. "Little boys don't ask questions like that." He went back across the antechamber and into the unlit quiet of his bedroom.

"Sire?"

He lifted his head, surprised—it was full dark and he'd been sleeping. Theophano, in his arms, still had her arms around him, and when he moved, she sighed and shifted around, tangled in her long black hair. Corso was standing just inside the door.

"What is it?"

"Fulk and Balian of Sidon are here."

"I'll be right out."

Corso came farther into the room and went around lighting the lamps. Frederick lay still, propped up on one elbow, waiting for the rest of him to wake up. With one forefinger he touched Theophano's cheekbone. She opened her eyes and smiled and immediately went back to sleep again, and he grinned. Outside, in the antechamber, he heard a growing murmur of voices. Getting up, he pulled himself back into his clothes, drank half the watery wine on the tray beside the bed, and went out into the antechamber.

Fulk was sitting beside the window; he jumped up. Beside him and Balian half a dozen other men were there, Tommaso and the Archbishop among them. Balian's face was taut, and he kept tugging at his belt. He bowed and said, "Your Majesty, there's trouble all over the city, and somebody said you'd taken measures—"

"What kind of trouble?" Frederick was still buckling his belt. He went over to the window beside Fulk and looked out, but all he could see was the knights' compound and the outer wall.

"Mobs, rioting, looting, and they're setting fires," Fulk said. "Milling around and throwing rocks and breaking into houses."

"Where?"

"Over by the Genoese Quarter, near Saint Anthony's Gate, and up around the Templars' Quarter." Balian glanced around. "Have you taken measures?"

"Some." Frederick leaned out the window and looked up at the roof. It was flat, and if he could get up there— He turned back into the room.

Abruptly in the city behind him a muffled boom thudded in the air and he jumped, startled. Fulk swore. "That was a granary, I hope."

"Where's Ezzo?"

"Down with Filangieri and his men."

"Come on." He started for the door and Balian jumped to open it.

Outside, the Saracens were talking together, and when he came out they stepped apart, watching him. "Ayub, come with me. All of you." He walked through this room into the next, stopped, and looked around, uncertain where to go. Ayub brushed past him to a window and looked out. Somebody brought in a torch; the black smoke curled thickly, caught the faint breeze, and streamed away. Corso tugged at his sleeve and held out a cloak.

"Not now. Later. Ayub?"

Ayub turned and waved to him. When Frederick went to the window he could hear the sound of shouting far away. His skin prickled up.

Ezzo and Conrad of Hohenlohe burst into the room, and Ezzo came straight over to him, his face red and one eye swollen nearly shut. "They're starting fires now, see?"

"I see it." Beyond the wall of the compound light flickered and grew stronger. He couldn't tell where it was, he was completely disoriented. His heart beat painfully fast. Stripping off his burnoose, Ayub crowded past him into the window, climbed up on the ledge, and leaned out, his hands over his head.

Conrad said, "Sire, do you want the gates guarded?"

"I told Hermann to do that this afternoon."

Ayub's body slid quietly off the window ledge and vanished upward. The Assassin and Masuf leaned out the window to shout at him. Corso began to dance up and down.

"Sire, wait for ladders, please."

"God, no." He thrust his head and shoulders out the window. "Ayub. Can you see anything?"

"Fires," Ayub shouted in Arabic. "And there are a lot of people in the streets. Coming toward us."

"Aha." Frederick ducked back into the room. "Rico, put a guard on this palace. Corso, when the ladders come, bring us some chairs and something to eat and drink." Circus Maximus, he thought. In the ancient honorable tradition of Nero. When he looked out the window again, Ayub was leaning down to help him climb up. The roof was only a few feet above the top of the window, but if he fell he'd die. Beyond the walls he could hear high, wild voices shouting. He climbed up on the ledge.

"Sire," Conrad bawled. Frederick stood up on the ledge outside the window, holding on with one hand, and stretched the other arm up to Ayub. In the courtyard below him a man shouted in German. Ayub's fingers closed over his wrist, and he let go with the other hand and scrabbled along the wall for a handhold. Ayub was drawing him up—he kicked his feet against the wall, pushing himself along, and fell across the eave onto the flat cold stone. Ayub bellowed to Yusuf and turned.

"There. See?" He pointed.

Frederick stood up, wiping his hands on his thighs. From here he could see nearly the whole city. A building only three blocks away was burning, entirely wrapped in flames; the light played over the houses around it, and in the street beside it people ran, waving their arms, carrying torches. He sucked in his breath. The mob moving toward the compound was spilling along the Wall Street, screaming. While he watched, the courtyard below filled up with knights, armed and in mail. Five of them ran along the inner rampart of the compound wall and jumped down to the lower wall around his house.

"They were looting all through that area over there," Fulk said, coming up beside him. "Where that house is burning."

Frederick walked up and down the roof, his arms folded over his chest. It was chilly and he wished he'd brought the cloak. The mob had almost reached his house. A torch sailed over the wall, turning end over end, and fell into the courtyard, and a soldier ran over to put it out.

The burning house fell in on itself with a crash that made Fulk swear. Frederick walked quickly over to the other side of the roof. He could just see the harbor from here, around the dome of the Patriarchate; the streets along the waterfront swarmed, and something down there was burning too, the glow lighting the square tower of the church of St. Andrew. He was too far from the Templars' Quarter to see what was going on there.

The mob had reached his house. Their shouts rang out —"Traitor . . . Heretic—" He kept his back to them and wished Corso would bring him the cloak. Ayub came over to him.

"Lord, Balian of Sidon wishes to talk to you."

"I'll be right there." He squinted, trying to make out the ships in the harbor. Enrico would make sure nothing happened to them. He began to shudder uncontrollably with cold. What if they burned and he had to wait here while they built new ones? He turned and went back to the other side of the roof.

"Sire," Balian called. He was riding his horse around the courtyard. "May we attack them?"

Something flew over the wall and splashed on the courtyard stones. Frederick looked at Ayub. "What are they throwing?"

Azub shrugged. "Rocks. Torches. Entrails. And shit."

"Well, it's an interesting variation on stoning." His face burned with embarrassment. Leaning over the edge of the roof, he called, "Balian, are they dangerous?"

A volley of rocks and softer missiles pelted down around Balian, whose horse shied violently, snorting. "They can't get in. It depends on what you mean by dangerous."

"Don't hurt them unless you have to to keep them out." He hunkered at the roof's edge. The knights along the ramparts were shouting back at the mob, and the noise clogged up his ears. Balian swung his horse and rode around calling out orders.

Fulk said, "One charge and they'd all go home—the ones who could still move to get there."

Frederick nodded. He looked down at the roof top and ran his fingers over the coarse stone. It would do no good, it would make them think they were important, and they'd only riot again at the first opportunity. And there was no sense training people in street fighting. He wasn't embarrassed anymore, just bored and cold. Looking up, he saw that the mob had set the house opposite his on fire.

"They'll burn the city down if we let them, Sire," Fulk said.

"That's not my problem. The barons and the priests all say I have no control over the local operation, anyhow." He grinned; it was the barons' property that burned. Let them take care of their own. "Come on, let's go back inside."

The Patriarch said, "This is obscene."

Frederick put his hands on the arms of his chair, stared at the old man's gaunt, bad-tempered face, and looked over at the Grand Master of the Hospitallers. "Did you have something to say?"

"The treaty itself is illegal," the Hospitaller said. "As Regent of Jerusalem you had no right to make a truce with the infidels without the consent of the High Court and the Council."

The men behind him murmured and shuffled their feet. Frederick leaned his head back against the chair. This crowd packed the little room; it stank of sweat and dirt and their steaming breath, and they'd tracked in mud on the carpet. On either side of him, standing against the wall, his Saracens held their lances at salute and stared coldly at the knights staring at them.

"Lord John," Frederick said. "Perhaps you have a complaint to make as well?"

"Only to repeat what all these others have said," John d'Ibelin boomed in his orator's voice. "The treaty is illegal, and to block off the Templars' Quarter and the gates of the city with your troops is the foulest kind of insult. How can you expect—"

The Grand Master came into the room, flanked by Tommaso and Filangieri, carrying Frederick's cherrywood chest. He set it on the table and withdrew to one side, looking nowhere but at Frederick.

"Your complaints are well taken," Frederick said. They'd made him angry in the beginning, but now they only bored him, and he had to work to keep from showing it. "You are perfectly right, of course, from your viewpoint. However, you might bear in mind that the arrangement of a treaty for Jerusalem is an issue concerning all Christendom, not merely a collection of petty barons on the fringe of the Christian world—"

John d'Ibelin said, "If you continue to insult—"

"—and therefore ought to be the work of the only temporal office in Christendom with the power to speak for the entire community, which is mine, Lord John, and not yours. I did not sign that treaty as Regent of Jerusalem—"

"You had yourself crowned when you are not the King—"

"—but as the legate of Christendom. You don't know what I crowned myself in Jerusalem, Lord John, you only know that I crowned myself, and while you're not in possession of all the facts you had best keep your mouth shut." He clenched his jaws, fighting down a rush of anger. John looked around at the others and snapped his gaze back to Frederick.

"If you gentlemen will not keep the interests of the entire community in mind, someone must, and I find myself in a position to. You object because Jerusalem cannot be adequately defended against the Moslems. If you have to fight for Jerusalem to feel that she is yours, I contend you are not Christian. As for the actions I took to contain the Templars during last night's interesting little display of civic order . . ."

He looked at the Templars' Grand Master, who stood near the window breathing heavily through his nose, and opened the cherry-wood chest. "I think, if you can discard your personal hatred for me for a moment, you'll find this justification enough." He took the top two papers off the heap in the chest and laid them on the table, turned so that the men in front of him could read them. No one moved forward; the Patriarch craned his neck to see, but he was too far away to make them out.

"This," Frederick said, tapping the first page, "is a note from the Templars to the Sultan al-Kamil, advising him that my trip to the Jordan River, to the place where Christ was baptized, was the perfect moment to have me seized and killed."

The Hospitaller's head flew up and the Patriarch jerked his hands. Frederick looked around at them— none of them looked at the Templar in their midst, only at him, the blood draining from their faces, their lips tight. Oh, well, he thought, that's interesting; so most of you knew about it already. He indicated the other paper. "That's a note from al-Kamil to me, full of amusing little remarks, that he sent along with the Templars' letter."

The Templar said, "This is a lie. Those are forgeries."

"Oh, my. How guileless I am, to let al-Kamil dupe me so. To turn me against my own kind. I would like to point out to you, Sir Roger, that you are still alive, something which even I find surprising at times. There's a lesson in that, which I hope you'll learn. I hope all of you will learn it."

"You came here excommunicate," the Patriarch said, and Frederick shut his eyes for a moment. "We are Christians, we hate and fear sin, and we hate and fear you as we fear sin. Against this crime you have committed, to pollute the holiest ground of our faith, no soft words of yours may prevail. You are damned, and it endangers our souls to stand in the same room with you, to breathe the air you breathe. You are an enemy worse than the Sultan, you are the hammer of the Church, you are Antichrist."

"As I said, you are entitled to your own viewpoint."

Lord John stepped forward. "You mock us, you think we're so much less than you, but even while you sit there mocking us, His Holiness has won your kingdom from you. 'Ephriam is like a dove, silly and without sense; they call to Egypt, they go to Syria.' If you'd stayed where you belonged, you might still have Sicily as a refuge, heretic. What now? When you leave Acre, where can you go?"

"To Sicily." Frederick leaned back, smiling. "And I'm leaving tomorrow. There's more to Hosea than doves and Ephriam, Lord John. 'Yea, though they have hired among the nations, now will I gather them, and they shall sorrow a little for the burden of the king of princes.' And if you think I'm blaspheming, gentlemen, wait until you hear what the Pope has to say about it. Get out of here, you're making me angry."

They started, nervous as birds, and the men at the back of the room turned for the door. The Patriarch said, "I won't leave until I hear what you mean to do about our demands."

"Nothing," Frederick said, and stood up. "As I said, you have your viewpoint, gentlemen. But I have mine, and I prefer mine, and I'm in a position to enforce mine." He looked at them a moment, watching them grow uncertain. "What's the matter, fellow Christians? You stole it all in the first place, why can't you realize that now I've stolen it from you? You have my leave."

The Hospitaller stepped forward. "Your Majesty—"

"You have my leave."

The Patriarch set himself, although the others were leaving as fast as they could reach the door. Frederick looked into the old man's dark, furious eyes, smiled, and said, "Ayub."

Ayub started around the long oak table. The Patriarch backed up two steps, stammering with amazement, and John d'Ibelin barged between them; the other Saracens moved up. They used their lances to shove the other men out of their way. John's face was gray with shock—the Patriarch whirled and clawed his way toward the door.

"Now you see why my guards are Saracens," Frederick said, and left the room.

"We'll have to leave at daybreak," Enrico said. "When the tides are ebbing. Do you want to go on board tonight, Sire?"

Frederick shook his head. Corso and Giancarlo were taking off his heavy state robe, and he bent so that they could unhook the collar. "I'll come down in the morning. Make sure everybody else is on board by then—I won't wait for them." With the robe off, he went to the side door and looked into the next room. The Grand Master came in behind him.

"Sire—"

"Wait a moment." He went back into the middle of the room—Corso helped him into his coat, standing behind him. Softly he said, "Where is Theophano?"

Corso whispered, "She's gone—she left while you were talking to the nobles."

"Oh."

For an instant everything froze; he could hear his voice, the sound hanging in the air. Abruptly his arms thrust into the sleeves of the coat and he swung around, and the room filled up with motion again—pages running back and forth, Enrico and the Grand Master talking. She didn't wait to tell me good-by.

"With your leave, Sire," Enrico said, "I should—"

"Yes."

Enrico went to the door, bowed, and left. The Grand

Master came over to him. "Would you care for wine, Sire?"

"Yes. Please."

Corso put a belt around his waist; he watched the old man pour the wine from the big gold ewer on the table. He felt as if everything he did he had to force himself to do—as if breathing were an act of will.

"How upset were they? The barons."

"More scared than upset," the Grand Master said. He brought over a cup and Frederick took it in his numb fingers. "And impressed. They're considerably less sure now than they were before you spoke to them."

"Naturally." He raised the cup and sipped at it. All this while he'd never really thought she'd go.

"What impressed them most, I think, was when you called yourself the legate of Christendom. They believe you, and that in itself frightened them. They saw you differently than they had before. It was interesting, the way they reacted to your sending Ayub to chase out the Patriarch—in the anteroom they were calling it his fault, that he should never have defied you."

"They should have realized . . . that I had no reason to be good to them anymore."

His eyes burned, and he turned his back on the Grand Master, ashamed that the old man might see him cry. She's gone, she left me. He even knew where she had gone; she would have found Mutu, she would go to Antioch with Mutu or through Mutu's arrangements.

"When we return, do you think we'll need an army to meet the Pope's, Sire?"

"No. Only the soldiers on the galleys." His throat tightened up, and he shut his eyes against the stinging tears. "Piero . . . Piero said the people are so much against him that all I have to do is come home." She didn't even wait to see me before she left.

The Grand Master stopped talking; Frederick could feel his eyes on him and even sense that the old man was puzzled and startled. He couldn't speak, and there was nothing to say in any case. The pages darted around the room, and Corso shouted to someone to bring in fresh flowers, and in the midst of it Frederick turned his head away and wept.

No lights showed on the shore; in the darkness the only sound was the slap and suck of the water against the side of the galley. Frederick leaned on the railing and stared toward Brindisi. The moist heat made his shirt cling, sodden, to his back. Looking around the sky, he found the Dog Star, burning hot and red low in the sky. A pirate taught me about that star. It was impossible not to think of Theophano—whenever he was alone with nothing to do, he thought of her—and he sank his head down between his shoulders and remembered her eyes and the sheen of her skin. Everything worth knowing I've learned from outlaws.

"We could sail to Monopoli if Brindisi isn't friendly to us," Enrico said, coming up behind him.

"If Brindisi isn't open, we may as well go back to Jaffa." The Pope would have use of the Pisan fleet, and as soon as they knew he was in Sicily, the swift galleys of the Pisans would be rowing up and down the coast. There is Sicily, right there, so close I can smell the shore. What does it mean that they've chained off the inner harbor? He strained his eyes, trying to see what he'd stared at all afternoon—the logs, half submerged, that held up the chain over the mouth of the canal, rolling sluggishly like the backs of sea dragons in the wash of the tide. "Can they know we're coming?"

"We made the fastest run here from Acre I've ever heard of," Enrico said. "We outsailed our own fleet. They can't know we're here."

"But they know we're coming. They would have sent word when I came into Acre from Jerusalem."

And they would know he'd try first for Brindisi. His throat tightened. In his mind's eye Theophano's face dissolved—this at least was a problem he could attack, with enemies, with tactics and necessary points to cover. Abruptly he gave a choked cry—down where he knew the chain to be, a light bobbed.

"Yes," Enrico said, and turned and bellowed for the Captain. "Can you see? They're taking up the chain."

Frederick couldn't see, not clearly; the light danced on the water, moving gradually from the left to right, and his body grew stiff with eagerness. He'd know in a few moments—they could be enticing him inside, where they could capture him at their leisure, trapped in the narrow bay. The Captain of the galley ran up, and Enrico gave him quiet orders. Other feet pounded on the decking—Fulk and Ezzo and the Saracens came running, pulling on their clothes. Frederick caught his breath.

"Enrico—"

"I'm taking her in, Sire, restrain your impatience."

Frederick banged his fist on the railing. Enrico had the nicest ways of telling him to shut up. He leaned forward, straining to see—the light was almost halfway to the other side of the canal. With a harsh rattle, the sailors began to turn the capstan, drawing up the anchor, and all over the ship small noises grew steadily toward an uproar —the slaves talking on their benches, the oars running out.

"Anchor up."

They would have taken down the chain even if they were enemies, to lure him inside. Take the risk. He was dizzy with excitement, with anticipation—in a little while he'd know for sure, he'd know at last. All the long voyage, thinking of Theophano: she had left him, she had found something lacking in him. The galley glided forward, the oars grating and splashing down, and his heart lifted. They'd reached Brindisi at sunset, and now it must be past midnight—all that waiting. I've always been bad at waiting. He found himself pushing against the railing, as if by that he could make the ship go faster.

The bouncing light grew more distinct—now he could see the men in the boat, resting at their oars, the chain looped over the stern so that the bow thrust awkwardly into the air. The even rhythm of the oars filled him. They glided through the opening in the chain, into the inner harbor of Brindisi. Only a few other ships lay in the harbor, and the town was dark—he could see the campanile of the cathedral. The galley skimmed through the water, swerving around toward the wharf below the castle, and no ships moved out to meet them, no lights showed anywhere. The feeling grew swiftly in him that he was safe, that he'd beaten them, at least for the moment. He leaned forward, forcing his eyes to see the wharf beneath the dark bulk of the castle—the raging excitement shortened his breath and brought him close to giggling. Alarmed, he made himself calm down.

The wharf came steadily nearer. Now he could see men waiting, with horses and a banner. God, he thought wildly, I'm my own banner, how many redheads are there in Brindisi? Enrico was speaking to the Captain, who bellowed orders into the waist. All Frederick could hear was a roar in his ears. He thought, I have to calm down or I'll never be able to—never be able to— The galley rasped against the wharf and rattled down its length, grinding wood on wood, and a lanky man on the dock ran to catch the rope.

"Sire—"

There were horses waiting in the dark, and a mob of people standing around them, their faces turned up to the ship. Frederick moved down to the ladder, and suddenly a cheer rose, muffled and full of relief. He climbed awkwardly down, groping with his feet for the rungs of the ladder, and descended into a sea of arms, all reaching to touch him, hands gliding over him, as if he had climbed down into a warm sea. When he turned, the eyes of the men around him aimed at his face, and with a rustle they all knelt.

"Your Majesty—"

Hurry, he thought. Hurry. He walked through them toward the horses. All the furious eagerness died down into a cold implacable purpose. But nothing seemed real, it seemed to him as if he'd brought it to life from his own mind. When he took hold of the reins of the nearest horse it surprised him to find them solid, stiff leather in his hands. He mounted, and above them, sitting in the saddle, he looked across a sea of swaying bodies, all their eyes fixed on him. Now others were mounting—Fulk and Ezzo, Enrico, his Saracens. He looked around, and what he had to do fell into place with a click.

"Ezzo. Go to Lucera and tell the Qadi that I'm back. Bring them all to Troia—I'll meet them at Troia. Fulk, go to San Martino and call up all the knights loyal to me in the area and bring them to Troia. Enrico, you'd better sail to Palermo."

"My Lord," a man said softly at his stirrup. "There are many men loyal to you in Brindisi—hundreds."

"Raise them. I'll be at the castle for as long as it takes me to get fresh horses and eat something."

"Where are you going?" another voice said.

"To Troia." He turned the horse into the mob, and they divided to give him a path through. The horse's hoofs boomed on the wharf, and the others, mounted, followed him, raising a clatter. When he reached the solid ground the sound of the horses muted, and his mount stretched out, more confident. He headed up through the groves of olive trees toward the dark castle.

Enrico cantered up beside him. "They say that the castle was garrisoned with the Pope's troops, but that they've fled now that they know you've come back."

"The cowards."

Enrico laughed. The branches of the trees stirred in the wind; at the end of the road Frederick saw the gate of the castle, standing open, and a mass of people before it. Kicking his horse into a gallop, he rode into their midst. Their voices rose around him, soft and full of his name.

"Sire." A man pushed up to catch hold of his stirrup.

"Sire, let me welcome you back from your glorious and wonderful—"

"Are there any troops of the Pope here?" Frederick half dragged him through the gate—the courtyard was empty, all the doors standing open. In the darkness the wind rustled through the trees along the inside of the wall and around the arch into the inner ward.

"There is no one here but loves the Emperor," the man at his stirrup said.

"Get me something to eat—and to drink, I'm thirsty. Get me fresh horses. I can't wait, I'm going to Troia." He looked around for Fulk and Ezzo, but they were gone.

The castle servants rushed off, scattering. Through the gate behind, more men pressed, mounted and leading horses and on foot, until the courtyard was packed. Lights shone in the towers over his head. He thought, I have to hurry—catch them before they can . . . A plate of hot meat was thrust into his hands and he took a fork and began to stuff food into his mouth. Someone else held up a tankard of beer.

"There are thirty knights here already," someone told him in a confidential tone. "If you wait until daybreak, we can raise a hundred men or more."

"I can't wait." He looked around—a troop of knights was gathering in the court, most of them in armor and carrying lances. Some of them even had their squires with them. Looking down, Frederick gave the plate and the cup to the first hands he saw. "Who is the captain of those knights?"

"Asclettin," someone told him, and he nodded and swung his horse, pressing it with difficulty through the crowd struggling around him, to touch him, to see him, their eyes and hands raised. I have to catch an enemy somewhere, they can't all run. Some of them will stand and face me. After all the honeyed words, the juggling, the careful pressure on the minds of the men he needed, he wanted to fight outright. I will teach them to . . . He rode out into the open ground, the cool wind and wide road north, and the knights behind him let out a harsh cheer. Give me some clean action with an obvious victory at the end. The moon was rising, dead and old, faintly orange; he started down the road at a lope, headed for the next fortress on the road to Troia.

"They've gone," Asclettin said, expressionless. "They heard you had landed and they have all gone north."

Frederick bit his lip. Above them the castle thrust out from a cliff's rock face, and the winding road to it looked like a thread drawn on the sheer stone. No banners flew from the tower and the gate stood wide open. "Is there anyone there?"

"A few servants," Asclettin said. "Twenty men and women."

"No horses."

"They took them all. They . . . stripped the castle bare, in fact. I have men bringing in more from the countryside."

"Jesus in heaven. Am I to ride a plow horse into Troia?" He looked around. The road was clogged with his men—more than five hundred now, and more joined him every day, knights coming all the way from the southern tip of Apulia, some even from Calabria, and still they hadn't fought, not one battle, not even an ambush. He felt cheated and humiliated.

"Sire, they have food for us, if we go up there." Asclettin was watching him, almost imploring.

Frederick nodded. He hated the time spent on eating, on drinking and sleep and finding fresh horses, because surely the garrison could not have left too long before he reached this castle, the news couldn't have traveled so fast. . . . Yet villages they had traveled through were filled with people who cheered and called his name and the word *Jerusalem*, and who said they had known for days that he was back. He nudged his horse into a jog up the road toward the castle.

They hung back when he rode in—he'd noticed that before, that the people would not come near him but stayed in the background, hid behind one another; their children with their bright eyes would run laughing in front of his horse, but the older people seemed afraid to come near him. He looked around the courtyard—in the middle stood a well covered with climbing roses, all in bloom, turning the gray stone pink. He thought, I have to sleep. But the urgency riding him struggled to keep him going, because once he held Troia he held Apulia and the pass into the west, and the Pope could no longer resist him. They weren't resisting him now. They were running, every troop, every soldier of the papal army, giving him nothing to fight. If I fight no one, how will I know it has ended? He dismounted, and when his feet hit the ground, nearly fell.

"Are you hungry? Are you thirsty? Sire, we have—"

He couldn't remember how long he'd been back, how many days—he'd stopped at four castles, never for more than a few hours, sleeping in the saddle or in a strange bed and waking up with the sun glaring through a strange window. This was bad, this was base, to want to catch them and kill them before they could flee. They only did what they were told was right. But this far from Brindisi they'd had time, before they fled, to loot, and all that day he'd seen the vineyards stripped and burned, the fields trampled under hoof, and the villages full of sullen faces: Is it over? Are you back forever now, and no one will come to steal and destroy what is ours, because of you? I'm tired, that's why I'm thinking this way. He stumbled on the stair but thrust away the men who tried to help him. It was like a nightmare, in the faces of the servants he saw the same accusation: You delivered us up to save yourself. It wasn't there. In the moments when his lack of sleep wasn't riding him like a weight on his shoulders he knew that it wasn't so, but he remembered Theophano's face and that meant the same thing to him, that for all his justifying what he had done, all the elegant abstractions, it had been to save himself. He had loved her to save himself. The bedchamber they took him to was empty, a perfect square. They had stolen all the furniture. Men spread straw on the floor and blankets on the straw and threadbare linen, borrowed from the villagers, on the blankets. Even if they don't know, I know. His fingers pulled ineffectually at his shirt, but other hands were there, they undressed him, and he lay down on the straw and put his head down, asleep although his mind went on thinking, longing for an enemy to fight.

"The town is in the hands of the Lancias," Asclettin said, impassive. "The garrison has fled."

Frederick lifted his fist with the reins and let it fall again to his saddle pommel. "God. Have they no courage at all?" But the name tugged him off course. "The Lancias? Manfredo?"

"The men I spoke to wore his livery, Sire. I don't know who— Here comes someone to welcome you."

Frederick looked around him down the road. The music of flutes and tambourines reached him, jangling in the hot, windless noon. Behind him the knights sighed and murmured, and his horse took a step to the side and lowered its head, relaxing. Amazed, Frederick saw a parade moving down the road toward him—silk ribbons floated from the manes of white horses, and canopies of red and green, sewn with the insignia of the Lancias, swayed above the musicians. Frederick made a small noise in his throat. Baskets of flowers on their arms, pages ran alongside the horses. The sunlight flashed on gold and jewels, on the broad banners spread over the arched necks of the horses: the Lancia pennon, the banner of Jerusalem, and his own, above them both, not the imperial standard but the red and gold of the Hohenstaufens. He looked once more at the city on its spur of rock, from which this pretty cavalcade had come, and watched the rider under the center canopy approach.

Veering off, the musicians and the pages with their flowers lined up on either side of the road, and down the middle of them, flanked by Saracens, rode Bianca Lancia, her face grave and her eyes on Frederick's. He thought, I hope they have prisoners—the ritual wants a blood sacrifice. But he couldn't help laughing, delighted.

"Your Majesty," Bianca said. "We bring the welcome of Troia for the triumphant Crusader."

He grinned—he could think of nothing to say. In her heart-shaped face her blue eyes were steady, and older than he remembered, full of secrets. She smiled, and that drove him to laugh again. "Did you chase out the Pope for me, Lady?"

"You chased the Pope out, Your Majesty, when you entered Jerusalem." Her eyes shone, fixed on his face. Lifting his reins, Frederick nudged his horse on down the road, and when she tried to ride behind him, he caught her rein.

"No. Stay here, with me." All around them the flutes and tambourines started up again; he glanced around at them and turned back to her. "Tell me what went on while I was gone."

Cecelia Holland

Cecelia Holland was born in Nevada on New Year's Eve, 1943. Raised in Metuchen, New Jersey, she now divides her time between New York City and California. A graduate of Connecticut College, she is the author of four earlier novels, *The Firedrake* (1966), dealing with the Norman invasion of England, *Rakóssy* (1967), a novel of the Turk-Magyar wars of the early sixteenth century, *The Kings in Winter* (1968), the scene of which is Ireland in the early part of the eleventh century, and *Until the Sun Falls* (1969), about the Mongol invasion of Russia and Europe in the thirteenth century. She is also the author of a book for children, *Ghost on the Steppe* (1969).